The Still Life of Hannah Morgan
A novel by
Lora Deeprose

This is a work of fiction. All characters and events in this book are products of the author's imagination or are used fictitiously.

THE STILL LIFE OF HANNAH MORGAN

Edited by Loretta Sylvestre
Cover art, design, and layout by Ilsie

Remastered and Published in Print January 2016

ISBN: 978-1-9405102-8-6

Marion Margaret Press
Business Office:
PO Box 245
Hebron, NE 68370

email: publisher@marionmargaretpress.com
        www.marionmargaretpress.com

A sister is a gift to the heart, a friend to the spirit, a golden thread to the meaning of life.
—Isadora James

To my sisters,
Cari, Amy, Lisa, and Tanya
with gratitude and love.

Thank you to the following circle of amazing women: Loretta Sylvestre, Sharon Partington, Diana Cacy Hawkins, and Deena Mauldin.

I am profoundly grateful for their talent, creativity, and support without which this book would not exist.

Goddess Magazine
   We are all women
   Everywhere

September Issue

Health and Beauty

Q: What will give you an instant face-lift, give your overall look a feeling of polished perfection, can be done in less than thirty minutes, and cost less than twenty dollars?

A: An eyebrow shaping. Brows that are shaped to complement your face will open up the area around the eye, making your face look brighter and more refreshed. However, before you take up your tweezers with enthusiasm at the prospect of creating a new you, remember to heed the following words and proceed with caution: a botched brow shaping can make you look worse than before you tweezed.

   I strongly suggest everyone get their brows done professionally at least once. Then you can maintain the shape with a minimal amount of tweezing on your part. A professional shaping would include determining the best shape and size of brow for the client, a waxing to remove the majority of unwanted hair, and a detailed tweezing to ensure the proper shape.

Chapter One

Oh my God! What did I do? I stared down at the waxing strip in my hand.

Just take another look. Maybe it's just a trick of the light. I tried not to panic.

I stole a quick glance at my client's face, at her eyebrows in particular, and confirmed my worst fears. It was not an illusion caused by bad lighting. I had removed Mrs. Weatherbee's entire left eyebrow.

I held the strip up to my face, squinting at it just to be sure. There, embedded in the wax, was her missing eyebrow.

"Why have you stopped?" Mrs. Weatherbee opened her eyes and looked up at me from the treatment table. "Is there a problem?"

Was there a problem? Well that depended on whether or not she thought walking around with one eyebrow was a bad thing. Maybe she could start a new fashion trend.

"Uhm." I quickly threw the offending wax strip in the garbage. Maybe if I just drew the missing eyebrow back on she wouldn't notice.

"Hand me a mirror." Mrs. Weatherbee heaved her considerable bulk up from the treatment table.

I obeyed, passing her a small silver mirror. I looked down at my hands while she examined her face. Perspiration beaded my forehead and trickled down my neck.

Terence was going to kill me.

"You stupid girl, what have you done?" Mrs. Weatherbee shouted, fingering her forehead where her eyebrow used to be. "I have a charity event to host tomorrow. I can't go out looking like this!"

"I'm really sorry, Mrs. Weatherbee, it was an accident."

"An accident? Do you realize what you have done to me? I want to speak to Terence!"

I couldn't move.

"Now!" she screamed, her voice reaching an even higher pitch of hysteria. She looked down at my nametag, "Hannah!"

Startled into action by the sound of my name, I nodded and hastily retreated from the room.

Maybe, if I just kept on walking and headed out the front doors, no one would notice. But, then what would I do? Where would I go? I could join the circus and work as a trapeze artist, or maybe I could be a spy for the Canadian Government. Do we even have spies in Canada?

Instead of running for freedom, I headed down the hall, through the Great Room, where several robe-clad guests were relaxing between services, and around the corner to Terence's office. I stood there for a moment staring at the brass nameplate on his door. Taking a deep breath, I knocked softly. Maybe he wasn't in today. Maybe he'd won the lottery and quit his job. Even better, maybe he contracted scarlet fever and wouldn't be in for months.

"Enter," Terence's voice commanded.

I opened the door and stepped in. Terence was sitting behind his desk typing madly on his computer, his long spider-like fingers scuttling furiously across the keyboard. His thick black frames were perched at the end of his pinched nose while his eyes, so dark they looked like tiny chunks of coal, remained glued to the computer screen.

I looked over his shoulder at the large Carrico print, entitled *The Unknowable*, hanging on the wall behind him. I loved the precise lines and balance of the white geometric shapes floating against the slate blue background. But I cringed inside because I knew that Terence chose the picture, not for its beauty or purity of form, but because it matched the cool blues and silvery grey tones of the minimalist decor in his office.

"Sorry to bother you but—" I said.

"Make it quick, I'm in the middle of something."

"It's about Mrs. Weatherbee."

Terence's fingers stopped in mid-air. He looked up and pinned me with his beady eyes, his normally baby smooth forehead furrowed with wrinkles. "What have you done now?"

"Nothing, really. I was doing an eyebrow wax on her, and I seem to have accidentally removed too much. And... she wants to see you."

Terence stood up and moved towards the door with lightning speed.

"Mrs. Weatherbee is one of our Gold Card Members. If you did anything to jeopardize the reputation of this spa, I will have your head on a platter."

"But I didn't mean to do it!"

"Be quiet and follow me," he barked, heading out the door. Terence sped down the corridor to the waxing area with me following behind.

"What room is she in?" he asked over his shoulder.

"One," I replied, finally catching up to him.

Terence knocked on the door, called out Mrs. Weatherbee's name, and walked in without waiting for her to reply. Mrs. Weatherbee sat on the edge of the treatment table where I'd left her, still holding the mirror in front of her face.

"Mrs. Weatherbee," Terence's voice softened and filled with concern. "What seems to be the problem?"

She slowly lowered the mirror onto her lap.

"Oh my!" Terence took an involuntary step backwards bumping into me. I stumbled into the wall but managed to stop myself from falling. He turned to me, his eyes narrowed and his nostrils flared like an angry bull. "Wait outside."

I scrambled out of the room barely making it over the threshold before Terence shut the door. I stood out in the dimly lit hallway awaiting my fate. After a few moments, when Terence hadn't come out, I closed my eyes and listened to the music floating down from the speakers hidden in the ceiling. I tried to let the gentle surf sound and Celtic harp music calm me. I listened to the hushed voices of people talking in the Great Room and wished I could be anywhere but at work. I wished I could start this horrible day over and make the outcome different.

Earlier, I thought my day couldn't get any worse. Now I was going to be canned. All because of one little eyebrow. It wasn't like I scarred her for life or cut off a limb.

Maybe I'd get off with a slap on the wrist. I had worked at the Serenity Day Spa for almost three years, and this was the first time I had done anything really bad. I mean, calling in sick because of a hangover or forgetting a client in a mud wrap and going home didn't really count. I clung to that thought.

Fifteen minutes later, the door opened and Terence stepped out. At five foot nine, Terence wasn't much taller than I was, but as he walked towards me, his anger transformed him into a towering menace.

"You," he whispered, jabbing his finger in my face, "will report down to the laundry room for the rest of your shift. I'm moving your clients over to the other girls. I've done what I can to smooth things over with Mrs. Weatherbee. You can consider yourself lucky that I didn't fire you on the spot."

I relaxed a bit.

"Well, what are you standing around for? Go! Go! Go!" Terence waved his hands in my face, shooing me away.

I turned to leave, but Terence stopped me before I could even take a step.

"And Hannah, you will report to my office tomorrow at eight-thirty a.m. sharp. Understood?"

"Understood."

I should have expected this. I had gotten off way too easily. I knew Terence wanted to prolong my punishment and state of panic as long as he could. He got off on seeing other people squirm.

I straightened my shoulders and headed through the spa, past the Great Room, and down the small corridor that led to the basement stairs. As I passed some of my coworkers in the hallway, the heat rose in my face and I struggled not to cry. They looked at me curiously, but no one had the nerve to say anything. One of the strictly enforced rules at Serenity was no unnecessary talking or socializing amongst the staff while on the floor. Besides, the whole spa would know what happened by the end of the day.

The thing about working with a bunch of women was that gossip was more popular than the chocolate body scrub on Valentine's Day and spread through the spa in less time than it took to remove an eyebrow. I admit that I enjoyed my fair share of whispering in the halls and passing on juicy tidbits about the love lives of my co-workers or which client had recently had plastic surgery. But now I was about to be the subject of conversation. I could already imagine the hushed giggles that would stop abruptly to be replaced by that uncomfortable silence that lets you know you've just walked in on a conversation about you. Somehow, gossiping didn't seem like such a harmless pastime when I was going to be the topic.

I heaved open the heavy, metal door that led down to the basement. As it swung closed behind me, hot, angry tears spilled down my cheeks.

Excerpt from Serenity Day Spa promotional brochure:

Let your cares melt away in our Zen inspired surroundings at the Serenity Day Spa. Relax and be pampered by our professional team trained in the latest body and skin treatments. Choose from an extensive menu of exclusive spa services. Come Restore and Revitalize your body, mind, and spirit. All conveniently located in downtown Calgary's historical Devonshire Building.

Book your appointment today
And ask about our Gold Card Membership

Chapter Two

  I walked down the concrete stairs to the basement and impatiently scrubbed away my tears with the back of my hand. Because of the age of the building and the limited space available, the designers of the spa had no choice but to locate the spa's laundry services, the staff lockers, and the break room in the same basement room. There were bound to be a few staff members in the break room, and Ruth, the head of laundry services, would definitely be washing the loads of linens we sent down. I hated crying in front of people.

  As I made my way down the narrow, musty corridor, the florescent lights above me flickered, casting eerie shadows on the hospital green walls. The flickering gave me a headache. On the left side of the hall, I pushed open a gunmetal grey door with the words "Employees Only" painted on it in large red letters. Inside, the comforting smell of laundry greeted me. That clean soapy smell mingled with the unmistakable, astringent odor of bleach. The air was warm and damp because the exhaust from the industrial sized dryers didn't vent properly.

I walked through the break room, which was the first area off the hallway. The room was empty. So far, so good. The break room was half the size of the laundry area and furnished in secondhand pieces including a sofa that had seen better days, a beaten up futon couch, and a couple of painfully uncomfortable wooden chairs that probably started their lives in a classroom. Along one wall ran a bank of lockers for the estheticians. There was a small counter with a sink at the back of the room. A bar fridge was tucked under the counter and a small, white microwave sat on top, dominating the shallow space. The few upper cabinets stored coffee mugs, a few mismatched plates, and a mountain of plastic containers that people brought their lunches in, but for some strange reason never took home.

The most dominant thing in the staff room was the white board. It took up most of the wall that it hung on. Before I worked at Serenity, I didn't think they even made them that big. It had to be eight feet tall and ten feet wide, at least. The white board was Terence's idea, and he was the only one allowed to write on it. Once a hapless esthetician had the nerve to scribble a joke on the board. When Terence found out, he fired her.

Terence used the board to post our monthly sales quotas, the spa promotions for the month, notices for upcoming staff meetings, or reminders of the many rules we had to follow. I firmly believed that Terence stayed up late at night concocting these inane rules for the sole purpose of sucking out all the fun of working at the spa.

I ignored the board and crossed into the laundry area. Thankfully, Ruth was the only one there. She stood with her back towards me unloading one of the dryers. The fabric of her white uniform pulled tight against her ample hips as she bent down to pull the clean linens out of the dryer.

The laundry room was twice the size of the staff room and housed three industrial sized washers and an equal amount of dryers. In the centre of the room stood a waist-high worktable that was wide enough to fold the large, white, cotton sheets used for draping massage tables. Several large, plastic laundry bins, each one clearly labeled for soiled and clean laundry, lined the wall opposite the washers and dryers.

"Hi, Ruth." I tried to sound cheerful.

At the sound of my voice, Ruth looked up from folding the sheets and smiled. Her teeth looked brilliantly white against her ebony skin. I gave her a weak smile in return.

"What are you doing down here? It's not break time." She put down the sheet she was folding on the worktable and came over to me. "What's up? Are you not feeling well?"

"No, I'm fine. Terence sent me down to help you out for the rest of the day."

Ruth arched her brows but didn't probe further. "That's mighty kind of you. I can always use an extra pair of hands, especially since Becky called in sick this morning, and I sure do enjoy the company."

"What would you like me to do?"

"Why don't you head over to that pile of clean towels and start folding. You can put them in there when you're done." She pointed to one of the large industrial linen carts.

We worked in companionable silence, me folding towels, Ruth loading the washers and dryers. As the hours ticked by, I felt less like crying and more like throwing up. I tried to focus on the job at hand, to think of nothing but folding the warm, clean towels, but my mind kept going back to earlier in the day and the incident that started all my problems.

* * * *

The night before, I was supposed to go to a movie with my boyfriend, Mason Connor. He had called at the last minute and cancelled because he had come down with a nasty stomach flu. I offered to come by his place and take care of him, but he put me off, saying he wasn't very good company and all he needed was some rest.

My shift today didn't start until one in the afternoon, so after putting together a care package containing chicken soup, soda crackers, a bottle of ginger ale, and my special blend of essential oils I called Flu-Be-Gone, I headed out on the bus to Mason's apartment.

The bus ride from my apartment on the southeast side of the city to his Kensington apartment took about an hour and a half. It started to rain half way through the trip. It was a cold, hard, fall rain. If the temperature outside had been just a few degrees lower, it would have resulted in snow instead of raindrops. By the time I got off the bus and lugged the paper bag full of remedies the six blocks to Mason's building, I was cold and soaked to the bone. I should've grabbed an umbrella.

I used the key Mason gave me last month and let myself into the lobby. I shook the rain from my hair and headed up the stairs. I was out of breath by the time I reached the third floor. I balanced the soggy paper bag on my hip and jiggled the key in the lock of his apartment door.

"How's my sick boy doing?" I called out as I opened the door. Just as I stepped inside, the bottom of the bag gave way and the contents spilled to the floor.

Shit.

I had chicken noodle soup all over my shoes and the glass vile containing my flu-be-gone elixir had smashed on the floor. The apartment smelled like a chicken with a head cold. I bent down to retrieve the plastic soup container, brushing wet noodles off my pant leg. When I stood up, Mason's head appeared from behind the back of the sofa, followed by another, blonder, prettier head. Mason was obviously feeling just fine.

"Hannah, what are you doing here? Fuck—what's that God awful smell." Mason crinkled his nose.

His little playmate put her hand over her mouth and giggled, her bare shoulders shaking slightly.

I stood there with my mouth hanging open, looking back and forth between my boyfriend and his little tart. Then I turned around and ran. I flew down the three flights of stairs, banging my elbow as I pushed my way out of the lobby, and back into the pelting rain.

When I arrived home, I was frozen and my toes were numb. I stripped off my soggy clothes and jumped into my tiny, metal shower stall, turning the hot on full. But, with the iffy plumbing in my building, all I got was a lukewarm drizzle. I fumed while I prayed that by some miracle the water would transform into something approaching hot.

That stupid jerk. How could he? I'd been dating Mason for six months, and I thought the relationship was actually going somewhere. He'd given me the key to his apartment, for God's sakes! By the time I'd dried off and dressed in my work uniform, the clock on the microwave told me I only had five minutes to catch the bus. I rushed out the door, forgetting the dinner I had packed for the day in the fridge. I caught the bus just as it was pulling away from the curb. On the ride into work, I alternated from wanting to throttle Mason's skinny little, two-timing neck, and feeling like the world's biggest loser.

That's why poor Mrs. Weatherbee now looked like a sideshow freak and I was folding towels in the basement, praying that I still had a job. All because of a lousy guy.

* * * *

Ruth finished loading the machines, singing softly to herself, and walked over to the folding table to help me. The washers made a rhythmic swooshing sound, the dryers quietly humming. The mechanical music calmed my frazzled nerves. I started to feel better.

"Hey, Hannah, I hear Terence's knickers are in a twist and you're the cause of it. Way to go!" Jas burst into the room.

Jasmine Blue. Yes, that's her real name; it says so on her driver's license. She looked like a pixie. A pixie with attitude and a killer fashion sense. Even wearing the stilettos she favoured, she stood a mere five foot three. Her delicate frame belied her physical strength, which I experienced the first time she gave me a friendly hug. Today she wore bright red gloss on her Cupid's bow lips and rimmed her hazel eyes in kohl. Her flaxen hair fell like a cascade down to her shoulders. She'd been blonde for three months—the longest she'd kept her hair one colour since I'd known her.

Jas is the top hair stylist at The Edge salon and my best friend. The salon was located in the same building as the spa and when it was too cold for us to meet outside for our breaks, she frequently came down to the break room to hang out with me. To her credit, Terence had never caught her down here, nor had anyone ever ratted on her. Not that she cared. People like Terence never intimidated her.

"How do you know what happened? You don't even work here. God, did someone broadcast my mistake over the radio?" I furiously folded another towel.

"I have my sources." She walked over to me on her four-inch heels, her hips swaying in her black and white leather mini. The stack of silver bracelets at her wrist jangled musically as she moved. She gave me a bone-crushing hug and stepped back to look at me.

"Are you doing okay?"

I opened my mouth to say something and burst into tears instead. "I think I might get fired."

"Oh, chickie poo, cheer up. Terence is not going to fire you over a botched eyebrow job. The spa is short-staffed. He couldn't afford to let you go, especially not with that big corporate function coming up."

"Do you really think so?" I sniffed.

Ruth handed me a tissue and returned to folding towels.

"Ruth, can Hannah take a five minute break?" She asked over her shoulder, leading me by the hand to the break area.

"Of course, I think I'll join you after I run these upstairs." Ruth wheeled the now full linen cart out of the room and down the hall to the service elevator.

"You, sit." Jas pushed me down onto the sagging, threadbare sofa and headed over to plug in the kettle in the makeshift kitchenette.

She was just pouring three mugs of Chamomile Soother when Ruth returned with the empty cart. Jas handed out the steaming tea and settled on the couch next to me. Ruth took a seat on the futon and put her feet up on an upturned plastic milk crate. She picked up a dog-eared copy of *People* magazine that lay nearby and thumbed through it.

"So, what's really going on?" Jas tucked her curtain of blond hair behind her ears and leaned forward, her eyes searched my face intently for a clue.

"How do you know there's more?"

"Because, sweetie pie, I've known you for three years. If your best friend can't figure out there's something you haven't told yet, then she's not a very good friend. Now spill."

I didn't want to tell her. From the first time I introduced Mason to Jas, she had taken an instant dislike to him. In our years of friendship, he was the only thing we'd ever disagreed on. Turns out, she was right about him. My stomach twisted. I needed to share my pain with someone who understood me, even though telling her would be admitting she was right. I finally caved and told her what happened that morning, and how Mason wasn't even ashamed about being caught.

"Mason's a prick. I hate to remind you, but I did tell you you were going to get hurt if you hooked up with him. I mean, come on, the man had a velvet Elvis painting hanging in his living room. Enough said. Besides, you're too good for him. Honestly, I don't know what you saw in him anyway."

I was too mortified to tell her the truth. Mason was the first man to notice me since I moved to Calgary. I knew being lonely wasn't the greatest criteria for hooking up with someone, but it seemed logical at the time.

Jas sipped her tea. "Now, I need to know, did you really take off the old bat's eyebrow?"

"Yes, but I didn't mean to. I wasn't paying attention to what I was doing. I was still so upset from this morning."

"How funny did she look?"

"Pretty funny." I stared into my mug trying not to smile as I pictured the damage I had done to the society matron's face.

"Serves her right. She doesn't tip and she's always late for appointments and expects us to bump our other clients for her. And to top it off, she's always complaining about the service she gets, even though we bend over backwards for her. I'm sure she's the same way here at the spa. What happened was divine retribution, and you were just the instrument that carried it out."

She finished her tea, rinsed her mug in the sink, and left it on the drain board to dry. "Look, I have to get back upstairs to the salon. I left a client processing and it's time to rinse out her highlights. Why don't we go for drinks at the Bear and Dingo after work, my treat? Okay?"

"Yeah, that sounds great." She was almost to the door when I called out after her. "Jas—"

"Yeah?"

"Thanks."

She beamed me one of her thousand watt smiles before letting the heavy door shut behind her.

I quickly swallowed the rest of my now cold tea, rinsed out my mug, and set it on the drain board next to Jas's.

Ruth, who sat quietly drinking her tea and reading her magazine, finally spoke up, "Shall we get back to it?"

Reluctantly, I nodded and headed back into the laundry room to finish my shift.

Chapter Three

The incessant beeping of my alarm clock startled me awake. I groaned burrowing deeper under the covers. Last night at the pub, I'd had too many gin and tonics with Jas and didn't get to bed until after two in the morning. I hoped that I had accidentally set the alarm for the wrong time and really had a couple more hours of much needed rest.

I rolled over onto my stomach and eyed the clock. The glowing green numbers dashed my hopes of more sleep. I desperately wanted to hit the snooze button and give myself fifteen more minutes of blissful escape. Fifteen more minutes of not having to face what the day might bring at the hands of Terence. My heart sank when I realized if I wanted to be on time for my eight thirty meeting, I had to get up.

Last night, Jas kept reassuring me that I wasn't going to be fired. I believed her then. Now, sitting alone on my bed, tired but sober, my belief rapidly dissolved. I reluctantly headed to the bathroom to have yet another lukewarm shower. I dressed in record time, grabbed my purse and my lunch, and headed out the door with ten minutes to spare. I wasn't going to be late today.

Jas was already waiting for me at the bus stop. She'd offered to come in with me for moral support, even though she didn't have to leave for work for another hour.

She gave me a wave and a sassy wiggle of her hips. She was dressed for early October in her version of fall outerwear. She wore an electric blue, fake fur coat that came down to her knees and chunky heeled, high black boots that just touched the hem of her coat. Her hair was piled high on her head in a complicated explosion of spikes interspersed with blue feathers. They moved softly in the chilly breeze and looked more like blue fur. They would have looked absolutely ridiculous on anyone else; on her they looked right, cutting edge cool. The sun had just begun to peek over the horizon, and, even though the sky still held on to a band of deep purple, she wore sunglasses—big, black, oversized 'Jackie O' sunglasses. With those on, I wasn't sure how she could've even made out that it was me walking down the street.

I was thankful that I had on my long, black wool coat so that no one could see what I was wearing. Working as an esthetician, the spa supplied us with three pairs of pants and four shirts. Estheticians at the Serenity are meant to blend into the surroundings so we don't interfere with the client's experience of relaxation. So lucky me, I had to wear the ugliest pair of black polyester pants ever created; they even had a permanent crease sewn down the front. These beauties were topped with a beige polo shirt with the Serenity logo embroidered on the breast pocket. My work shoes, which I stuffed into my oversized purse, were the kind you see old ladies with support hose wearing. Think comfort and practicality.

I gave her a big hug and thanked her again for coming with me. I absently ran my hand over my long, black hair that I had scraped back into the regulation ponytail. I tried to ignore how frumpy I felt standing next to her.

When the bus pulled up, we took our regular seats near the back. All the way to work, Jas kept the conversation light, purposely avoiding mentioning my impending meeting with the Spa Nazi.

I never had a best friend before. Growing up on a farm didn't allow many opportunities to meet someone my own age, and at school I kept mostly to myself. I wasn't interested in sports, or cheerleading, or hanging with the popular girls. My grandmother, Noni, had always been my closest friend and confidante. She shared my interest and passion for art. When she died, I had no one.

Jas's friendship helped to fill the void Noni had left. But my friendship with her was more than that. When we first met, we'd instantly shared a connection, a sisterly vibe I'd never experienced with other girls my age.

We met on my first day at the spa. I was struggling to get my card key to work on the back door without any success. With each failed attempt, my panic increased. I swore under my breath and frantically looked around the empty back alley for someone to help me. There was no one around. I jammed the card key into its slot one more time, willing the stupid indicator light to turn green. Nothing happened. I contemplated going into the spa from the front, risking a reprimand on my first day. Terence had specifically instructed all the new employees at orientation that we were never to enter the spa from the front door.

I was just about to give up and head for the front when Jas came up behind me and offered to help. I wasn't quite sure what to make of her. I tried not to stare. Dressed the way she was, I couldn't image she worked at the spa. She looked more like she was going to a costume party dressed as a Go-Go dancer than someone heading into work in the Devonshire. She wore a shocking pink, skintight body suit trimmed in marabou feathers, and white patent platforms.

She gave me a warm smile, took the card from my hand, and flipped it over. She slid it into the slot and the light turned green. The sound of the deadbolt sliding back filled me with relief. She held the heavy door open for me and followed me in.

"You're new to the spa aren't you?"

"Yes, this is my first day. Thanks for the help. If you hadn't come along, I'd have given up in frustration and just gone home," I said as we both stepped into the back corridor.

"I'm Jas. I work down the hall at the Edge." She took off her cat's eye sunglasses studded with rhinestones and tucked a strand of bright orange hair behind her ear.

"I'm Hannah Morgan."

"Well, Hannah Morgan, it's nice to meet you. I usually sneak out back for my break, if the weather's nice, at about eleven most days. Maybe I'll see you out there. Tootles."

With a wave of her hand, she headed down the hall. I didn't see her again until the following week.

"Hey, how's the new job going?" She was leaning up against the brick wall of the building sipping tea in a to-go cup.

I joined her in the alley, taking a swig from my bottle of coke. Her hair was midnight black and she wore a long, dark overcoat that swayed around her small frame when she moved.

"Not so bad. The girls I work with are pretty nice, and I'm starting to get the hang of things." I didn't want to tell her the truth: I felt lost and totally overwhelmed. I changed the subject.

"Jazz. That's an unusual name. Were you named after the music?"

"No, my real name is Jasmine, but everyone just calls me Jas. My mom, Khandi, spelled K-H-A-N-D-I, has a bit of a dramatic side. She named me Jasmine because it sounded exotic and she liked how it sounded with our last name, which is Blue. My mom changed her last name from Petro sky to Blue when she became a famous exotic dancer." She smiled.

25

"Does she still dance?" I asked, trying not to show my shock.

"No, at the height of her career she hooked up with a con man who promised her the world and ended up leaving her when she got pregnant with me. I've never met the sperm donor, and don't care if I ever do. My mom is first-rate, though, and still super cool. She put herself through night school, and now she is a chartered accountant. Most of her clients are the owners of the clubs she used to dance in." Jas crumpled up her cup and threw it into a nearby dumpster, but she missed her mark, and the cup bounced off the bin. She went to retrieve it, throwing it over her shoulder into the bin this time. "What about your parents? With a name like Morgan they sound like pretty upstanding people."

"Yeah they are. Salt of the earth and all that. My parents have a farm about fifty miles southwest of the city. That's where I grew up."

"A real farm with cows, horses, and pigs?"

"Yes to the cows and one horse. We have a few chickens but no pigs. My dad also leases out some land to our neighbors who grow grain crops and raise cattle."

"So how long have you been living in the big, bad city?"

"Only a couple of weeks. I moved into an apartment on Sixth Street a week before I started at the spa. When I was going to beauty school, I lived at home and borrowed my da's truck to save money."

"Your rent must be pretty steep living downtown."

"Yeah, it's pretty pricey, but I don't own a car, and I wanted to be able to walk to work."

"You should look for a place where I live. I share an apartment with two other girls, so I can't offer you a place, but I've noticed a couple of apartments with 'for rent' signs posted. It's out in suburbia, but the rents are dirt-cheap, the buses run regularly to the downtown core, and there's a pub that serves fairly decent hot wings. I'll show you around and help you look for a place if you want."

"That would be great. I would really appreciate it."

"It's a date, then."

We exchanged phone numbers, and when our days off coincided, we went apartment hunting. I found something suitable almost immediately. It was a modestly priced, furnished, bachelor suite just blocks from her apartment. She toured me through the neat, quiet streets, pointing out the small Mom and Pop convenience store and the Bear and Dingo pub. With Jas's help and my da's truck, I moved into my new apartment a few weeks later. We've been good friends ever since.

* * * *

Eventually, Jas and I arrived at our stop and I was one step closer to the dreaded meeting with Terence. We walked the few remaining blocks to work in silence. My stomach flip-flopped and my gloved hands were ice cold from nerves. We stopped at the employee entrance at the back of the building. Jas took out her key card and slipped it into the slot. The staff entrance led to a back hallway that ran the length of the building. There were two stairways: one leading to the basement and the spa staff room, the other to the second floor and the businesses located there. Once inside, she hugged me one last time and headed down the corridor to the salon's back door. I headed in the opposite direction, out the door that led into the spa and towards Terence's office.

I glanced at my watch as I knocked on his door. I was right on time.

"Enter." Terence never said 'come in,' it was always "enter." It made him sound like Captain Jean Luc Picard of the *Enterprise* instead of just a manager of a spa.

I walked into his office, butterflies fluttering furiously in my stomach. I just wanted to get this over with so I could breathe again.

"Take a seat."

I obeyed, perching on the edge of the chair across from Terence. He held a file folder in his lap. I peered over his desk and saw my name typed on the top.

"You know why you are here, so I'll just get right down to it."

"Okay," I whispered.

"Number one: what you did to Mrs. Weatherbee was inexcusable. I have sent a complimentary gift basket to her home, and she will receive free waxing services from now on. You, however, will never be assigned to her again. I really should fire you, but we are stretched a little thin for staffing right now, so you can count your lucky stars that I'm even giving you a second chance."

To me that didn't sound like a punishment. Maybe things would turn out just fine.

"Number two: you will write Mrs. Weatherbee a letter of apology and have it on my desk by the end of the business day." Terence ticked off the points on his fingers. "Number three: you are formally notified that, commencing today, you are on three months probation." Terence looked up from his file folder.

"Probation!"

"It would really be in your best interest not to speak until I'm finished."

My cheeks flushed red with embarrassment.

"The duty roster has been reworked and your privilege of having two consecutive days off has been revoked. If you receive a satisfactory rating on your performance appraisal at the end of the three months, you will be reinstated. However, if you continue as you have been and there isn't a vast improvement, your employment with us will be terminated. Also, you will be monitored closely and you will *not* be assigned any high profile clients." He steepled his fingers under his chin.

I kept my mouth shut this time.

He continued speaking, but I stopped listening. I couldn't believe I wouldn't be getting two days off in a row anymore. Having two consecutive days off in the spa industry was a luxury, especially when the spa was open seven days a week. On top of that, not getting the rich clients meant smaller tips for me. I didn't know why I was surprised by this. I had screwed up Big Time, but it still sucked. I didn't have many options. My skills were limited to being an esthetician, and my current financial situation meant I couldn't just quit, as much as I wanted to. This gig paid better than any minimum wage job I was qualified for.

"And lastly, you will be required to take a refresher course in waxing. You are scheduled to attend class this Sunday with the new girls I've hired."

I resisted the overwhelming urge to take Terence's stupid file folder and ram it down his throat. I was trapped, furious, and embarrassed.

"Now, if there is nothing more, you can start your shift. You've wasted enough of my time, and I have a meeting with Accounting in ten minutes." Terence turned to his computer and started typing.

Clearly, I was dismissed. I quickly got up out of my chair and left before he could think up any more ridiculous punishments to heap on me.

Goddess Magazine
We are all women
Everywhere

October Issue

Health and Beauty

Q: My big toenails look so bad that I am embarrassed to walk around in flip-flops. The nails are thick and yellow. What do you think is wrong with them?

A: You may have one of two problems: you may have a fungal infection, or you've damaged the nail bed. The only way to find out exactly what you have is to see your doctor.

     If your doctor diagnoses your problem as a nail fungus, she can prescribe either a topical cream or an oral medication. Unfortunately, it will take at least six months for your toenail to grow out, regardless of what the problem is. So, it'll be at least that long before you are ready to show your feet off in public. In the meantime, I suggest that you apply a dark, sexy polish to conceal your damaged digits.

Chapter Four

I stomped down the hall to the Prep Room. I needed my job, and I knew I had screwed up, but it didn't mean I had to like what my life was now going to be like.

The Prep Room was situated just before the Women's Change Room. Nothing more than a closet, really, housing treatment supplies and extra linens. A couple of UV sterilization units and several glass containers of blue antifungal and antibacterial solutions sat on the work counter by the sink. The rest of the room was floor to ceiling shelves packed full of sheets, towels, and blankets, along with jars, bottles, and lotions used for every type of service the spa offered.

I shouldered the door open.

"Morning, Hannah."

"Hey, Chris." I grabbed my daily schedule out of my slot trying to sound pleasant. I scanned down the sheet. My whole day was booked with pedicures and nothing else. I groaned.

"Yeah, I know, my day's packed too. I wonder when Terence is going to hire more staff like he keeps promising." Chris pulled down a jar of mud from one of the shelves. "I'm booked for three pedicures, a facial, a couple of waxings, and a mud wrap."

"I think he has already hired some new girls."

"Good, I'm tired of working my ass off." Chris held up the jar of mud. "Gotta go."

"Yah, see you later." The muscles in my back already ached at the thought of doing that many pedicures in a row. I grabbed a set of pedicure tools and headed to the pedicure room to set up.

I slammed down my tools on the workstation, knocking over the nail polish tray. Little jewel-coloured bottles rolled all over the table and a few scattered to the floor. I picked up the fallen bottles and righted them haphazardly on the tray. I snatched a stack of towels from the back counter and plunked them down on my station.

I checked my watch. I'd just enough time before my client to go see Jas. I walked quickly through the spa and out the staff entrance into the back hall. I glanced over my shoulder to make sure Terence wasn't around before making my way in the opposite direction of the basement stairs. I stopped at a door about halfway down the back corridor and knocked. Two quick, three slow. I waited, tapping my rubber soled shoe on the concrete.

"Hey, come on in. Want a coffee?" Jas opened the door wider.

"I'd love one." I took a seat on a rickety old chair in the corner. The salon's back room was a hive of activity. Stylists streamed in to grab their morning coffees, chatting with each other and getting supplies for the day.

"So how did it go?"

I shrugged and sipped my coffee. "You were right. I still have my job, but that's about it.

Telling Jas about all my punishments, I felt the beginning of a headache brewing behind my eyes.

"And it gets worse," I finished, "I have nothing but pedicures for the rest of the day."

"That's rough. You know, you can always quit and find another job."

"Right, and work where? Do you think if I quit Terence would give me a glowing letter of recommendation? Who would touch me?" I snapped at her. "I can't afford to lose this job."

Jas was silent.

I took a deep breath. "Look, I'm sorry. I'm just not in the greatest of moods."

"No biggie. Do you still get this Monday off?"

"Yes, as far as I know." I slurped my coffee.

"Then, why don't you come by the salon on Monday. You are due for a haircut, and I'll throw a colour in for free. You need to treat yourself."

I highly doubted a new shade of hair colour was going to make getting through the next three months any easier, but I was touched by Jas's attempt to make me feel better. I thanked her, and left the salon the way I'd come, taking my coffee with me. Down in the break room, I rummaged through my locker, finding a few wrinkled sheets of paper and a pen. I had written most of the apology letter by the time the rest of the staff started coming in for the morning. I didn't feel like staying in the staff room. Some of the girls had already asked me to recount what happened yesterday. I stuffed the letter into my locker before slamming the door shut. I'd finish the rest of it on my lunch break.

My first client, Monica Stewart, was already dressed in her terry robe and spa sandals when I stepped into the Great Room. She was flipping through a magazine and sipping a glass of orange juice. I introduced myself, escorted her to the pedicure room, and waited while she took a seat in the pedicure chair. The chair looked like a recliner sitting on a raised pedestal with a built-in sink at the base. I filled the foot basin with warm sudsy water and, before placing her feet in to soak, I examined them. I was doing everything by the book, no screw-ups today.

Monica's nails were yellow and woody looking, and the putrid smell turned my stomach. Great, she had nail fungus. If my life was a B horror flick, there would be a crash of thunder, a flash of lightening. As the sound track crescendoed, the camera would zoom in for a close up of my face as I let out a horrified scream. As if my life, pathetic as it was, wasn't a horror flick, I calmly and pleasantly informed my client about the condition of her nail.

"That can't be. You must be wrong. My toenail just grows funny." She looked down her nose at me.

I pulled on a pair of latex gloves and ignored her huff of indignation. After soaking her feet for a few minutes, I pulled out my nail clippers and started trimming the gross one first. Just as I started to ask if she wanted to add a paraffin dip to her service, the nail flew off the blade of the clippers and landed squarely in my mouth. Before I thought about what I was doing, I spat it out, quite forcefully. It went flying at my client and beaned her on the forehead.

"Hey!" she exclaimed and plucked the nail off the front of her robe where it landed.

"If you would excuse me for a moment?" Not waiting for a reply, I jumped up from my stool.

I was out the room in a flash. I ran to the women's change rooms, not caring if I was caught. I thought I was going to hurl and I wasn't sure I would make it all the way to the back of the Spa where the staff washroom was. I ran over to the teak counter brimming with grooming products for the guests to use— deodorant, hair spray, talcum powder, mouthwash, and feminine products. Ignoring the looks from the women in various stages of disrobing for their treatments, I grabbed two of the mini bottles of mouthwash and rinsed my mouth out until my tongue burned. My stomach threatened to bring up the measly breakfast of raisin bran I had eaten earlier. I caught myself in the mirror on my fifth and final rinse with the mouthwash.

Hannah, you are such a loser. And you wonder why your life is such a mess. You are just one screw up after another. I stuck my tongue out at my reflection and headed back to finish the pedicure.

The rest of the day went by without me ingesting any more body parts. My eyes felt grainy and my back ached by the time I finished my last pedicure. I also managed to finish the apology letter on my lunch break as I skipped lunch all together. Surprisingly, after eating a client's toenail, I didn't have much of an appetite. I placed the letter on Terence's empty desk and left for the day.

It was seven o'clock when I stepped on the bus that would take me home. I was so tired I fell asleep as the bus jounced and swayed down Deerfoot Highway. Thank God the bus driver knew my stop and woke me up when he came to it.

Once home, I threw off my coat, said hello to Noni's self-portrait that sat on my nightstand, and put a large pot of water on the stove to boil. I didn't bother to fill her in on my day. There was nothing positive to tell. Still, she smiled her enigmatic smile as always, as if she knew my secrets anyway.

While I waited for the water to boil, I took a quick shower to relax the tension in my back. Miracle of miracles, I actually had hot water for a change. Something good on a day filled with nothing but bad. It was a small thing, but I'd take it, grateful to feel the heat and steam filling the shower stall. My back pain slowly dissolved as the hot water swirled down the drain.

By the time I stepped out of the steamy bathroom and dressed in my comfy grey sweats, I felt restored, physically if not emotionally. The water on the stove had just started to boil. I threw in a handful of spaghetti and made a small green salad while the pasta cooked. When the pasta was ready, I pulled down a medium sized mixing bowl, poured the spaghetti and sauce into the bottom of the bowl, and threw the salad on top.

I took my dinner, grabbed my favorite blanket, and curled up on the couch. When I'd eaten my fill, I grabbed my sketchpad and pencil from the battered pine coffee table that had come with the place. My nerves jangled with unspent anger, and drawing had always been a sure fire way to calm myself. In the past, when I allowed myself the pleasure, I emerged from the creative process and went back to the daily grind of my existence uplifted and recharged.

I flipped the pad to an empty sheet, my pencil poised over the pristine page and waited. Nothing came. I scribbled circles and loops, but I couldn't conjure up a suitable idea. Images of Terence scowling at me, taking my measure, and finding me woefully inadequate filled my thoughts, followed closely by all the demanding, arrogant clients.

I looked down at the pad to find I had covered the paper with angry slashes and scribbles. Disgusted with myself, I flung the sketchpad across the room. It sailed through the air, the pages fluttering, until it bounced off the television and landed on the floor. I grabbed the TV remote from the coffee table and stabbed at the buttons searching for something suitably mind-numbing. I settled for a reality show where the contestants plotted and schemed to get the most annoying player voted off the game. I tucked the blanket under my chin and focused on the flickering images. Eventually I fell asleep in front of the television.

Chapter Five

I breezed through the entrance of the Devonshire Building on my way to my hair appointment. I quickly glanced at my reflection in the beveled glass panes of the door as it swung open. Jas was right; my hair was too long. I hadn't cut it in years. I was tired of looking dowdy. It was time for a change. Once inside the building, I shrugged off my heavy coat.

I dressed up for the occasion, as dressed up as I could get on an esthetician's wages. I wore my favorite black dress pants. They draped over my curves, enhancing my figure, unlike my work pants, which made me look squat and dumpy. I topped the pants with a crisp, white cotton dress shirt and large, silver hoop earrings.

I walked to the salon and past the spa without giving it as much as a backward glance. Today was all about treating myself and I wasn't going to ruin it by thinking about work.

Sunday's waxing class had been excruciating. Terence finally hired three new girls, and part of their training was to be educated in the Serenity way of doing services. Magda, the senior esthetician who'd been with the Serenity since it opened, had run the class. Thank God, she was a kind and compassionate woman. She tried to keep my embarrassment down to a minimum by not calling any extra attention to me. Still, I couldn't ignore the blatant stares from some of the new girls when I walked in, and I was sure the whispering and suppressed giggles were about what I had done to Mrs. Weatherbee. Someone must have told them when they had their orientation tour. It had been the longest day of my life.

Okay, enough. No more work thoughts.

I pushed open the frosted glass doors to the salon, and the throbbing techno-beat instantly engulfed me. I walked over to the reception desk to check in. Jamie, one of the stylists and a mutual friend of Jas and mine, was standing at the stainless steel and frosted glass front counter. He smiled when he saw me and gave me a warm hug. He told the receptionist that he would take me over to the changing room.

"So is it true?"

"Is what true?"

"You know—that you disfigured Mrs. Weatherbee," he said in a theatrical stage whisper.

"No, it wasn't as dramatic as all that. It was more of a de-furring than a maiming."

"And you still have a job?"

"Yes, lucky me." I stepped into the cubicle and drew the curtain, cutting off any more questions.

I removed my shirt and put on a black cotton, knee-length kimono supplied by the salon and went to the waiting area. I joined the rest of the clients, clad in similar kimonos, and took a seat in a vacant, white, Saarinen inspired chair. The chairs were grouped in clusters with small, round, matching end tables snugged between them. I perused the stack of magazine fanned neatly on the table beside me. I passed over the current issues of *In Style, Canadian Elle,* and *Goddess* and picked up the local *Avenue* magazine. I flipped to an article highlighting a local glassblower who was showing her work at the Crossroads Artspace.

I was dazzled by the colours she used. The clear, saturated swirls looked alive and glowing, like each piece was a breathing, living thing. I marveled at the whimsical, organic shapes. I was reading about her background and training when someone walked past me.

I glanced up as a man took a seat across from me, catching the barest whiff of his cologne when he walked by. It wasn't an overpowering smell; it was, well, yummy. I took a deep breath. The scent reminded me of a forest of ancient cedars, of lush green plants, and sunshine.

I stole a quick look at his face. My breath caught in my throat as I looked into a pair of the most gentle brown eyes I had ever seen. Little jolts of electricity shivered up my spine. Without even thinking about it, I smiled at him. The eyes staring back at me crinkled deliciously and he smiled back.

I caught myself staring at his lips. I looked down at the magazine in my lap. I flipped through the glossy pages, but my mind wasn't registering what the images were, much less the actual words.

Oh my God, he looks as delicious as he smells.

I wanted to look at him again, to take him all in, but I was nervous. Nervous and stupid. He just smiled to be polite, and I acted like some giggly schoolgirl. I couldn't help myself; I stole another quick glance at him anyway. He had sandy blond hair, high cheekbones, and an aquiline nose that would have made him look too haughty if it were not for his eyes. A girl could definitely get lost in those eyes.

"Hi," he said.

"Hi," I mumbled back.

"We're ready for you now." The shampoo girl approached from behind me.

Startled, I dropped the magazine on the floor. I stood up feeling like an idiot. Yummy Man reached down and retrieved the magazine from the floor.

"Here you go." He held the magazine out for me to take.

I couldn't think of anything witty to say so I just smiled, took the magazine, and let the shampoo girl lead me over to the sinks. I focused all my energy on looking nonchalant as I walked to the shampoo chair, hoping my legs wouldn't give way before I sat down.

Hannah get a grip, an attractive man smiles and says hello, and you turn into a brainless twit.

I pretended not to notice the sly smile on the shampoo girl's face. Instead, I leaned back and closed my eyes, enjoying the feel of the hot spray on my head.

When the shampoo girl finished washing my hair, she wrapped my head in a towel and helped me to sit up. I moseyed over and took a seat at Jas's station.

"Jas will be right with you. Can I get you something to drink?"

"A coffee would be great, one sugar, two creams. Thanks. Could you take this please? I'm done with it." I handed her the magazine.

Jas appeared moments later bringing me the coffee. She was dressed in a simple black sheath and patent leather boots with needle thin heels. She'd pulled her hair back in a sleek French twist.

"Hello, poopie."

"Hi, thanks again for this treat. I really appreciate you throwing in the colour for free."

"Like I said before, that's what friends do. Besides your hair is in dire need of a change, and I've got some great ideas on how to spruce up your look." She combed out my hair.

"Hey, I'm all yours. The only thing I ask is that I can still put it back in a ponytail for work."

"I kept that in mind when I came up with the style. Now be quiet; the artist will begin." With a flourish, she pulled out her scissors from the black leather tool belt slung on her hips and began cutting.

I kept my eyes closed, relishing the calming effect of her expert hands working on my hair and the soft snicking of her scissors. When she finished cutting, she worked silently, applying the colour, letting me enjoy my coffee and zone out in peace.

In what felt like mere minutes later, I had my colour rinsed and was back in Jas's chair. I glanced at the mirror, checking out my new hair, just as Jas turned on the hair dryer to style it. Even wet, my hair looked amazing. She had taken about four inches off, so my hair sat just below my shoulders, with soft, flattering layers framing my face.

"You like?" She asked over the noise of the blow dryer.

"It's fabulous."

"Just wait 'till you see the colour when it's dry."

Thirty minutes later, I stared at my reflection in the mirror. I looked totally amazing. My raven black hair was still dark, but she did something with the colour so that it looked deeper, shinier. The colour made my eyes appear more violet and my skin looked like I just had a facial. When I moved my head, the light caught strands of glittering gold in amongst the black. Not blonde but gold. I'd never seen anything like it before.

"Now for the finishing touch." She pulled out a straightening iron.

"Seems like a bit of overkill. My hair is already straight."

Jas just rolled her eyes and told me to keep quiet.

She was right. The flat iron made my hair sleeker. It moved like a curtain of water just like hers. I kept moving my head from side to side to make it shimmer. I couldn't stop staring at my reflection.

I thanked Jas, told her I would see her later that night, and went to pay for the cut. I pulled out my credit card and handed it over to the receptionist while I furiously did calculations in my head. I wasn't sure if my card was already maxed out. I had a moment of panic while I waited for the transaction to go through. I was slipping my card back in my wallet when the hairs on the back of my neck stood up.

"It looks great."

Yummy Man leaned up against the counter. His hair had been a little shaggy in the back, but was now neatly cut and styled. A clean-shaven face replaced the traces of beard he had sported earlier. I wanted to touch his cheeks to see if they felt as soft as they looked. He was over six feet tall, with broad shoulders and a muscular build. The expensive looking, charcoal grey suit he was wearing accented his frame in all the right places. It had to have been custom made to drape that way and to fit such a tall man so perfectly.

"Thanks." I didn't know why I was so nervous with him standing so close. All I could think was to get away as fast as I could before I said something dorky and embarrassed myself. When the receptionist handed me my receipt, I stuffed it in my purse and headed out the door.

I walked in no particular direction, waiting for my heart to stop racing. When I calmed down sufficiently, I realized I didn't want to go home right away. I felt great with my new haircut and was still basking in the glow of being noticed by a hunky stranger. It seemed wrong to go home, so I decided to go window-shopping instead.

I proceeded at a more leisurely pace, taking in the merchandise in the window displays. Impulsively, I stepped into a small storefront gallery that I normally avoided. A soft tinkling from the bells that hung over the door announced my entrance. There was no one standing behind the Chippendale desk, and no one came out of the back room to greet me. I walked around the gallery, looking at the few photos that hung on the walls. I assessed each picture, noting the ones that spoke to me.

I turned my attention to a series of photos of street scenes in India mounted on the wall to the left of the entrance. I was drawn to each of the beautiful images, but one in particular made me catch my breath and sent shivers down my arms. The photo showed an old woman standing in a crowded marketplace holding a large, flat basket, piled high with several neatly mounded pyramids of coloured henna powder. Her deeply lined, weathered face was in sharp contrast to the bright orange sari she wore and the intensely vivid pigments of the coloured henna. The photographer had captured a moment when she had turned away from the throngs of market goers, her eyes looking off into some unknown distance. The unguarded sadness in her eyes provoked a visceral reaction in me. The intensity of the emotion radiated off the photo. I stepped closer.

I almost jumped out of my skin when a soft voice behind me asked, "Can I be of any assistance?"

I turned to face the small, round man who had spoken. He only came up to my shoulder and had to crane his neck to look me in the eye. His wispy, grey hair stood out from his head like a halo of steel wool. He had outrageously bushy eyebrows that gave him an owlish appearance.

"No, I was just looking around, thanks."

"It's exquisite, isn't it?" The proprietor pointed a pudgy finger at the photo before us.

"Yes, it's so incredibly sad and so heartbreakingly beautiful."

The bells over the door tinkled.

"Hey, Bernie."

Bernie and I turned around to see who had spoken. A lanky man with hair the colour of dark, rich chocolate entered, holding a square, shallow, cardboard box.

"Aaron, I wasn't expecting you to come by today. Is that the photo for Mrs. Anderson?"

"Yes."

"You didn't have to go through the trouble of dropping it off. I told you I would send my assistant around later to pick it up."

"That's okay, I had to run a few errands, and since I was going to be in the neighborhood anyway, I thought I would bring it by on my way through. Save Kelly the trip."

"I'll just put it in the back, and I'll have Kelly deliver it when she gets in this afternoon." Bernie relieved Aaron of his package and headed to the back room.

"So do you like that one?" Aaron approached me.

"They're all beautiful, but this one really hit an emotional nerve. I can't take my eyes off the woman's face."

"It's my favorite too. I took that one last year on a trip to Calcutta. The woman wasn't even supposed to be the subject of that picture. I was focused on the vendor in the next stall and I just happened to glance in her direction. I had the camera up and took the shot before I was even aware I was going to do it. It was just a brief moment when she let her guard down, that's when her true self emerged."

The intensity of his focus on the image and the pure, charismatic energy he exuded captivated me. I stared at him while he continued to tell the story, his focus still on the photo.

His dark, wavy hair just brushed his shoulders, and unlike Yummy Man, Aaron had a five o'clock shadow that accentuated his strong jaw. He was average height with a long, lean frame. I could tell he definitely didn't spend hours in the gym lifting weights, but he was in no way a wimp, judging by the way that his sweater pulled nicely over the curve of his bicep when he raised his arm to gesture at the photo.

Where were all these good-looking men when I started dating Mason, and why were they all popping out of the woodwork today? Things were definitely starting to look up. Maybe my life and my luck were taking a turn for the better. I felt a giddy impulse to start humming *"It's Raining Men"* when Aaron suddenly turned his gaze on me. His eyes were a very pale blue, almost a silvery colour.

"When we allow those pure moments of being human to come to the surface, to give expression to all that we are feeling, there is a beauty in that, and a common connectedness that really hits you here." He placed his hand over his heart.

We stood silently looking at each other for a few minutes before he broke the spell.

"Sorry, I can go a little over the top sometimes." He glanced down at his shoes then back up at me.

"No need to apologize. I think what you said was exactly what I was feeling."

"I'm Aaron, by the way."

"Hi, I'm Hannah." We shook hands.

"Well, I'd better get going. It was nice meeting you." He tried to leave but seemed to realize we were still holding hands. He let go, looking flustered. Backing up towards the door, he almost tripped over his own feet.

It was adorable.

"Aaron?" Bernie emerged out of the back room.

"Yes." Aaron turned around.

"I'll call you when I have the cheque from the sale."

"Sure, that'd be good." Aaron narrowly missed running into the door as he swung it open to leave.

With Aaron gone, Bernie turned his focus back to me. "So do you collect or are you an artist yourself?"

I didn't know what had possessed me to come in there in the first place, and, with Bernie's question hanging in the air, the harsh reality of my answer filled me with frustration and disappointment.

No, I'm not an artist, at least not anymore. "Neither. Thanks for your time."

I left before the little man could say anything. The bells chimed as I retreated to the safety of the sidewalk. I walked briskly, trying to put as much distance between me and the gallery as I could. I took a deep breath of the crisp autumn air and forced myself to slow down. I was having such a good day and now it was ruined.

Reality bites.

I wanted to recapture that feeling of giddiness and lightness I was feeling earlier. Damned if I was going to let my life get in the way. Just for *one* day, I wanted to feel happy. Determined to enjoy the rest of the day, I continued to window shop. I popped into a few of the clothing stores along the street, thumbing through racks of beautiful and trendy clothes, looking for nothing in particular and trying to forget my earlier stop.

In one small store that sold ethnic clothes, incense, and silver jewelry, I spotted a beautiful bracelet sitting on the display counter. It was a thick, heavy, piece engraved with a flowing Sanskrit symbol on the top. I turned the bracelet around in my hand, enjoying the cool smoothness of the metal. The silver caught the light and revealed another engraving on the inside of the band. Etched in the metal was the word Goddess. Suddenly, I wanted the bracelet. Badly.

I knew I was doing it again, what I called Poor Me spending. When I was having a particularly bad day at work, or when the bills started piling up, or I didn't get as many tips as I had hoped, I would buy stupid things, mostly on credit. Sometimes it was a new face cream or the latest nail polish colour, which was ridiculous because I didn't need any anti-aging cream, and I never painted my nails. Other times I would buy a nice top, or a pair of pants, or a pair of fancy earrings, which were equally ridiculous because I rarely went anywhere that required dressing up. I knew what I was doing and why, but that never stopped me from pulling out my plastic and buying one more thing I didn't need and would have to find room for in my tiny apartment.

I looked at the price tag again. The bracelet was exquisite. Exquisitely out of my reach. Even if I could've justified spending $150 on a bracelet, I didn't have that kind of cash or available credit. Even though my hair colour was free and Jas gave me a discount on the cut, I had officially maxed out my card, and I'd tipped the shampoo girl with my last five dollars. Reluctantly, I put the bracelet down and headed for home.

Chapter Six

It was late afternoon when I returned to my one-room apartment. It had come furnished with bargain basement pieces: a Formica kitchen table and chairs, a futon, a battered wood coffee table, and a double bed with matching nightstand. The warm glow of sunshine bathed the walls, making my dreary space feel comfy and inviting.

"Hey Noni, I'm home." I said to the small painting sitting on my nightstand as I tossed my coat over the back of the couch and toed off my boots.

"Do you like my new haircut?" I turned my head this way and that.

I stripped out of my clothes, carefully hanging them in my tiny closet, while I filled Noni in on my encounters with Yummy Man and the cute photographer. I slipped into a t-shirt and jeans and started to prepare dinner. Jas was coming over for our weekly dinner and a movie. I took out a frozen lasagna and popped it in the oven, and then started on the salad. She arrived just as I was tossing the bottled dressing and greens together. She carried a bottle of wine, a small chocolate cake, and a movie.

"Hi Noni," Jas said to the painting as she put her contributions on the kitchen counter.

The first time Jas came over for dinner, she had asked about the painting. I told her about my grandmother's talent as a painter, her quirky outlook on life, and the gifts that she passed on to me. I shared how lost I felt when Noni passed away. To my surprise, I ended up telling her that since Noni's death, I talked to my dead grandmother's self-portrait. It was then that I knew she truly understood who I was because she didn't skip a beat in her conversation or make an excuse and leave early. From then on, whenever she came over she always said hello to my grandmother.

"Tonight we are celebrating," she announced.

"And what are we celebrating exactly?"

"Several things, dear heart." She retrieved the corkscrew from the cutlery drawer and uncorked the wine. "We are celebrating how fabulous you look." She poured the wine and handed me a glass.

I took a sip. The wine tasted of black cherries with a hint of oak.

"We are celebrating your top marks in your waxing class."

"Ha, ha." I sneered and took another sip of wine.

"And last, but not least, we're celebrating because I'm opening my own salon."

"What?" I slowly put my glass down on the kitchen counter.

Glass raised high, Jas twirled around my kitchen and stopped to face me. "You heard what I said. I found the most perfect location yesterday. It's amazing. It needs a bit of work, but it has so much potential, and the landlord is this totally cool guy. He is charging an amount I can actually afford, and he is going to give me a break on the rent for the first six months."

For as long as I'd known her, she had talked about opening up her own salon. "That's wonderful! Why didn't you tell me this when you saw me today?"

"I wanted it to be a surprise, and I didn't think it would be wise to announce my intention of becoming the Edge's competition when I'm still working there." She gave me a sly grin.

"You're actually going to do this." I hugged her tight while she held her glass above her head to avoid spilling her wine. I stepped back, still holding her by the shoulders. "You have to tell me everything. Where is the place? What needs to be done? When do you get it?"

I topped off our wine glasses and sat with Jas on the couch.

Facing me, she cradled her wine glass by her fingertips. "The building is a little store front, about eight hundred square feet, located on Ninth Avenue in Inglewood. I know what you're thinking, but the area is really improving. There's already an ultra-cool martini bar called Saturn and a couple of clothing stores that cater to the hip crowd. And because the area hasn't quite taken off, the rents are still pretty cheap. Much better than some of the places I looked at. The other fabulous thing is the landlord is so desperate to rent the space out that he offered to kick in some cash for improvements. I haven't signed anything yet because I really want you to take a look at it and tell me what you think."

"Yes, I'd love to see it. When?"

"I'll call the landlord in the morning and see if we can get in after work tomorrow."

"I can't wait to see it! I also can't believe you are actually doing this."

"I know, I can't believe it either. I'm finally getting my own shop. Woo, woo!"

The timer buzzed on the stove. Jas refilled our glasses and put the movie into the DVD player. This week's movie selection was *Sherlock* with Benedict Cumberbatch. We'd both seen the BBC series a dozen times. It was one of our favorites, mostly because of Benedict. Count on Jas to pick the perfect show knowing how watching a romantic comedy would be the last thing I would want to sit through.

We ate sitting on the couch, the movie playing more for background noise than entertainment, while we talked about Jas's plans for the space. The evening went by quickly as we talked about colour schemes and the layout of the salon. The bottle of wine was soon empty, so we switched to drinking coffee with our dessert.

"Has that slime-ball Mason called you?"

Just hearing his name made me blush with embarrassment. "No, not a peep, and I'm not about to call him. I still can't believe he did that to me." Tears formed at the corners of my eyes, but I ignored them. I was not going to give Mason the satisfaction of crying over him.

"Well, thank God he finally showed his true colours before you decided to do something really stupid like move in with him."

I bit my lip and looked away. I never told her that Mason had actually suggested that very thing about a month ago. I told him no. I wasn't ready for such a big change for two reasons: one, if my parents found out I was living with a guy I'd just met, I wouldn't be able to cope with my da's silent disappointment and my mother's full on emotional tirade, and two, I knew that Mason was just filler, a distraction from feeling alone. He definitely wasn't my soul mate. Even though he wasn't a long-term thing, it still hurt like hell to be cheated on.

"Do you mind if we talk about something else?" I cleared my throat and took a sip of my coffee.

"Sure, sorry."

We spent the rest of the evening talking about more pleasant things as Jas dreamed aloud about her new business. It was one in the morning by the time we said good night, and she was still flying high on excitement. With the combination of coffee, wine, and chocolate, I doubted she was going to get much sleep tonight. Before going to bed, I stacked the dirty dishes in the sink, put the leftovers in the fridge, and brushed my teeth. I fell into bed still wearing my sweats.

Alone in the dark, staring up at the ceiling, I tried to be excited for Jas, but there was a small, cold fear in the pit of my stomach. She was going to leave the Edge. For three years we took the bus to work together, and up until I was put on probation, we shared the same days off. At work, we hung out together on our breaks. My daily life was so full of being with her the thought of not having her be a part of it anymore made me anxious. I was being childish, but I couldn't help it. I wanted her to go after her dreams, but I didn't want her to leave me to fend for myself. I tossed and turned before finally falling into a fitful sleep filled with vague, uneasy dreams.

Chapter Seven

Just before six the next evening, Jas and I pulled up in a cab in front of the building she wanted to lease for her salon. It was Jas's idea to splurge on a cab instead of schlepping across town on the bus. For the entire thirty-minute drive, she told me about her plans right down to the name she had picked out, Blue Funk Salon.

With the cab fare paid, we stepped out onto the curb, and I took my first look at the building. The façade was a combination of buff coloured sandstone and Alberta red brick. It probably was a grand building in its time, but now it was definitely showing its age. Soot and city grime clung to the stone, muddying the once light colour, and I couldn't help but notice the air of neglect that hung about its darkened and filthy windows.

The landlord was already waiting for us on the stoop. He stood, rubbing his gloved hands together to keep warm against the evening's chill. He was a heavyset man, but not fat—what people would describe as burly or stocky. He looked to be in his late fifties, and I assumed he was probably bald under the tight, black watch cap he was wearing. He sported a neatly trimmed, salt and pepper beard, and his eyes were sharp and inquisitive. I shook his hand as Jas introduced him as Mac. I was strangely pleased when he took off his gloves before shaking my hand.

With introductions out of the way, Mac unlocked the heavy wooden door inlaid with large panes of leaded glass. The gloom of the early evening's fading light shrouded the place, turning everything into indistinct shapes in shades of grey. Mac flipped a switch and I had to shade my eyes from the sudden glare from several bare bulbs hanging down from the ceiling. It took a moment for my eyes to adjust before I could take my first good look at the space.

The room was mostly empty; a thin film of gritty dust covered a few discarded pieces of furniture. Sagging cobwebs festooned the ceiling, and they moved gently as we passed underneath. The floor was wide-plank pine, and it creaked and snapped as we moved farther into the room.

"The building was used as a haberdashery until the late twenties. Since then it was split into smaller spaces to accommodate more trades. It housed everything from a coffee shop, a pottery store, and, most recently, a second-hand furniture shop," Mac said as we walked the perimeter of the room. "When this area of town was first built, back at the turn of the last century, it must have been something. I know Inglewood had quite the reputation as a haven for drug dealers and prostitutes, but the local business association has done a really good job at turning the neighbourhood around. We already have a few solid businesses relocating here, and I'm sure your salon will do a booming trade too. Trust me; this area is going to be even bigger than Marda Loop."

Jas nodded in agreement. Mac relaxed his shoulders and smiled.

We wandered through the space, picking our way through discarded tables and overturned chairs. All the while, Jas talked with focused animation, gesturing where she envisioned the hair stations, the shampoo sinks, and the reception desk would be. Her enthusiasm painted a vivid picture, and it wasn't long before I caught her excitement. I could clearly see her vision through the cobwebs and dust. When we headed into the small back room, she pointed to a narrow staircase.

"This is another great thing about the space. Come see!" She grabbed my hand and tugged me up the stairs.

I followed her blindly up the dark staircase, hoping she could see where she was going and wouldn't lead me into a wall or stumbling over a piece of long-forgotten furniture. She flipped on the light, and I stared into a small apartment. Our tour around the upstairs revealed two bedrooms and a tiny bathroom with a rusted claw-foot tub and a hole stuffed with a nasty looking rag where a toilet used to be. There was a u-shaped kitchen missing the appliances and a small open area probably once used as a dining area and sitting room.

"The apartment is in better condition than I had hoped. What do you think?" Jas nervously bounced on the balls of her feet.

I struggled to think of something to say. "I think it's got potential. I like the layout of the place, and it has a lot of character. But, I don't understand. Are you planning on renting out the space for added income?"

"Not exactly. I was thinking about living here myself. I wasn't sure how to tell you. I was hoping you would be as excited as I was when you saw the building and you would be happy for me." She touched my arm. "Please don't be upset. If I live here, I save eight hundred dollars a month that I would normally be paying for rent. It makes perfect sense, and I won't be living that far from you. Please, please be happy for me."

What could I say? The small fear that had been with me since yesterday grew into a heavy sinking dread in my belly. Everything around me was shifting. Jas was moving forward and away from me, and I hadn't even seen it coming. I tried to absorb what these changes would mean to me. Not only was she no longer going to work in the same building, she wasn't going to be living in the same part of the city.

I put on the biggest smile I could manage and looked her in the eye. "Of course, I'm happy for you. It's just that it's going to take me a while to get used to the idea of you living here."

"It won't be as bad as you think. We can still do Girl's Night. In fact, I can have it here. You can come over right after work because it's closer than going home, and you can spend the night. We can stay up late and drink all the wine we want, and you don't have to worry about being late for work. The bus from here to the spa is only fifteen minutes. You could even sleep in. You'll see, it'll be great."

"Yah, sure, it does sound great," I said, not convinced at all.

There was nothing more for us to see upstairs, so we went back down; I led the way while Jas shut off the lights.

When we joined Mac downstairs, he was leaning up against an old wooden worktable with a silver cell phone pressed to his ear. Mac finished his call, tucked his cell into the inside pocket of his well-worn leather jacket, and turned to us.

Looking at me, he asked, "So, do we have your seal of approval?"

I glanced at Jas. "Yes, I think it's fabulous."

"It's decided, then. I'll take it!" She clapped her hands in delight.

Jas and Mac arranged to meet at his office the next day to sign the necessary papers. With this out of the way, we headed out and left Mac to lock up. Jas said she was starving, so we decided to have a late dinner at the little Asian restaurant just across the street.

The Jade China Inn was the size of a closet, with only six tables squeezed into the cramped space. I didn't think I was hungry, not with so many emotions twisting through me, but my stomach growled loudly when the smell of food reached my nose.

After taking turns in the ladies room washing off the grime we accumulated from our tour of what was now Jas's new space, we took our seats at a table for two. It was past eight on a weekday and the place was deserted. The only other patrons were an elderly couple sharing a large bowl of wonton soup.

A tiny, dark-haired woman came out of the kitchen and approached our table. She carried two plastic menus tucked under her arm, a teapot in one hand, and in her other hand two cups nestled one on top of the other. She gingerly placed the teapot and cups down on the table and handed us our menus.

"I give you a few minutes to look over, no problem?"

"Yes, thank you," Jas replied, and the woman disappeared through the swinging doors into the kitchen.

I poured us each a cup of steaming tea and took a cautious sip. I don't normally like tea but I love the Jasmine green tea that they serve at Chinese restaurants. If summer sunshine had a taste, it would be this tea. Hot, clean, tasting like the perfume of exotic flowers.

After perusing the menus, we decided on a plate of salt and pepper squid, pork and vegetable dumplings, mixed vegetables, and steamed rice. We placed our order, and Jas told me about the financial aspects of opening up her own business while we waited for our food. She'd written up a business plan, and had finally managed to convince a bank to give her a small business loan to add to the money she had saved. Mac giving her a break on the rent and being able to live rent-free on the property were both things that were really going to make it possible for her to make a go of her dream.

Our dinner arrived, and I was past the point of being hungry; I was ravenous. The food was fragrant and steaming. Silence descended on our table while we dug into our meal with gusto. When we finished stuffing ourselves, we picked up our conversation again, deciding how best to get Jas's shop from a cobweb infested, dust palace to an ultra-amazing salon called Blue Funk. She figured it would take about three months of hard work to get the place shipshape. She had already managed to line up workers from her mom's accounting clients to help with the more complicated work like electrical and plumbing.

Midway through our discussion on what colour the shampoo sinks should be, Jas abruptly put down the chopstick she was fiddling with. "You're sure you're okay with all this? I know it is all happening so fast, but this is what I've wanted forever. I'd understand if you're a little miffed with me for not being straight with you about the apartment. I didn't know until I saw the space whether it would work or not. And I didn't know when the right time to bring it up would be, so I just waited until the last possible minute. Are you pissed? If you are, I would completely understand."

"I was just a bit shocked when you said you were going to live there, but," I held up my hand to stop her from apologizing again, "you need to believe me when I say I am completely behind you on this. You know you're like a sister to me and I want to do whatever I can to help. I'm good at cleaning and painting. I can help move stuff and set up the space. Whatever you need, you can count on me."

"Thank you, that means a lot." She reached over and squeezed my hand affectionately. "There is another way you can help me out. I still need to find a receptionist. I can't pay what the spa does, but I can guarantee you'd have a lot more fun working with me."

"It's a tempting offer, but right now I'm going to have to say no. As much as working at the spa sucks, I need the money."

Our waitress appeared and quietly placed a small tray containing two fortune cookies and the bill between us on the table. Then she cleared away the empty plates and disappeared into the kitchen again.

"You go first," I said as we both broke open our cookies.

She held up the tiny ribbon of paper and broke into a huge smile. "It says, "*You are about to embark on a new and prosperous journey.*" What does yours say?"

I looked at mine and frowned. "'If you risk nothing, you gain nothing.'"

Chapter Eight

A week had passed since Jas took me to look at her new salon. She signed the lease the next day, and I spent my Sunday off helping her cart away all the junk left behind by the previous tenant. I cleaned and scrubbed until my hands were raw and my knees were sore.

I tried hard to be a hundred percent happy for her, and, when I was around her, I put up a good front. But, when I was alone, usually at night as I lay in bed, or like now, sitting in a stupid staff meeting, my secret thoughts came bubbling up, and I was ashamed of myself. A part of me was jealous of her apparent ease at making her dreams come true.

Why couldn't I get my shit together that easily? Other than agreeing to help Jas paint her place, I hadn't done my own kind of painting in way too long. I still worked as an esthetician, a job I detested. I hated my life. What was it about finding success that I couldn't seem to master?

I mulled over these dark thoughts while I scanned the room, saying hi to a few of my coworkers as they slowly filtered in for our monthly 9:00 A.M. meeting. Some of the girls grabbed a coffee or a tea from the back table before finding a seat.

All the estheticians had to attend these meetings. They consisted of going over the logistics of any special after-hours bookings, reviewing new promotions and products, and announcing the sales quotas. They were notoriously boring, and I dreaded the announcement of the sales figures. Terence always had a graph depicting all the estheticians' take for the previous month. It showed who was top in sales and who hadn't made their quota, all done up in bold colours. It was grounds to be fired if you couldn't keep your numbers up. I really had to focus on selling just to make it into the middle of the pack.

Terence entered the room promptly at 8:30, followed by a few stragglers who quickly took their seats. He walked to the front of the room ignoring us as he passed by. The meeting hadn't even started and already I was fidgeting, trying to find a comfortable position on the hard plastic, folding chair.

Terence stepped behind the podium on the carpeted platform, adjusting his glasses and scanning the room. I instinctively shrank down in my chair trying to make myself as small and inconspicuous as possible. Lately, I was getting rather good at avoiding him.

Terence cleared his throat. "The meeting will now begin. Sarah, you can distribute the handouts."

Sarah, one of the girls who worked the front desk, was waiting at the back of the room, her arms weighed down by a stack of papers. She walked down the aisle, handing out several copies to the person at the end of each row. I glanced at the top sheet as I took one and passed it down the line. It outlined the special corporate event the Serenity was hosting tomorrow for Thorpe Industries' staff appreciation night.

I wouldn't mind working for a place that valued their employees enough to give them perks like a visit to a high-end spa. I scanned down the page looking for the company description. The write-up stated that Thorpe Industries was one of the largest companies in Calgary and was involved in a little bit of everything from oil and gas exploration to a coffee roasting plant. We were hosting the staff from the IT Department.

Terence droned on about the event, and I tried to follow what he was saying, but my mind kept drifting. My butt had fallen asleep, and the more I stared at him, the more my eyes wouldn't focus. I doodled on the handouts, drawing a rather accurate caricature of Terence with horns growing out of his slicked back hair and a scaly tail slithering out from under his suit jacket. I scribbled over the image and started to sketch something more attractive.

I started to draw Yummy Man. When I finished the sketch, it looked wrong. The problem wasn't in the proportions, and I'd definitely captured Yummy Man's body, hair, and full mouth. Then it dawned on me. It was the eyes. They were the wrong shape. Yummy Man's eyes were round, dark and warm with lovely character lines around them that deepened when he smiled. The eyes I drew had a slight almond shape to them, a touch exotic, and I left the iris' light with just a few faint lines to indicate colour. I had drawn Aaron's eyes.

How curious.

I had thought about both of them quite a lot since that strange day. They were two very interesting men, two very handsome men in very different ways.

I snapped out of my daydreaming and put my pen down when everyone around me flipped through the handouts. I quickly looked over to the girl on my left to see what page she was on.

"This month," Terence prattled on. "Our promotion is called the Bliss Package. It includes a mud wrap, a facial, and a moisture application for ninety-nine dollars. Your goal is to sell at least ten of these packages each. Now if everyone could turn to the sales figures from last month."

Now came the part I dreaded most. Normally, I just squeaked by on my quotas, but lately I sucked at it. I had too much on my mind to care about the three percent commission. Considering my finances of late, I cared now. I scanned the paper to find the detailed sales graph. I couldn't find my name. I skimmed down further and there it was right at the bottom.

"Congratulations, Natasha, on selling six hundred dollars above your quota. Keep up the good work." Terence gave Natasha a thin smile. "For the most part, I am pleased with everyone's performance. Those of you at the bottom of the graph need to focus more on your selling techniques. I expect each and every one of you to improve on last month's figures."

Was it my imagination or was Terence directing that comment directly at me? I shuffled my handouts hiding my doodles. Terence arched his eyebrow and steeled me with a look before I glanced sheepishly at the floor. Terence signaled Sarah to hand out one more sheet—our sales goals for this month and suggested products to focus on—before ending the meeting.

"That concludes the meeting. And just a reminder, I expect everyone to be ready thirty minutes before their scheduled shift for the corporate event with Thorpe Industries tomorrow evening." Terence snatched up his clipboard and walked briskly towards the door.

As soon as he had his hand on the doorknob, everyone prepared to leave. Before I even had a chance to stand up, Terence turned around and looked at me. "I need to see you in my office before you start work."

Not again. I didn't even have to ask why he wanted to see me. I had the evidence clutched in my hands. I followed him to his office without looking up. This time he didn't invite me to sit down. He just stood next to his desk, his arms folded across his chest.

"Your sales for last month are abysmal. Your commitment to working as a team player is lacking, and if you don't increase your sales figures, your time with us will be short. Need I remind you that you are still on probation?"

I had to resist the urge to stick my tongue out at him.

"Do you understand the seriousness of what I'm saying? You are skating on very thin ice right now."

"Yes, I do. I promise to try harder." I hoped that sounded more sincere than it felt.

"No, Hannah, you will not try harder, you will do better."

I looked over his shoulder at the abstract art on the wall. "May I go now?"

He dismissed me with a wave of his hand.

Because Terrance had kept me after the meeting, I had to hustle to get started on my first treatment of the day. I just made it in time to grab my schedule, check to see who my first client was, and collect her from the Great Room. I glanced at my schedule. I was still down for a lot more pedicures than most of the staff but, to my surprise, my first service was a waxing.

I guess my performance at my refresher course was enough to convince Terence that I wasn't going to remove any hair that I wasn't supposed to; it was either that or we were still crazy overbooked and the receptionist couldn't find any other esthetician to do it. I decided to believe the first reason.

My client, Pepper Dempsey, looked to be in her mid-thirties with strawberry blond hair worn in a chin length bob. Her tastefully done makeup only enhanced her brilliant green eyes. Even sitting in a terry robe you could tell she was the type of person who always looked put together. She had a polished air about her. She gave me a smile as I approached.

"Hello, Ms. Dempsey, I'm Hannah, and I'll be your esthetician today."

"Call me Pepper, everyone does."

I smiled and led Pepper down the hall to the waxing room. I waited outside to give her time to slip off her robe and get on the waxing table. I knocked after a few minutes and asked if she was ready.

"Yes, come on in."

You have to give credit to women who can undergo a full leg and bikini wax. It takes a thorough esthetician an hour to complete the job. That's a lot of ripping out of hair by the roots.

I went to work applying the pre-wax numbing lotion to Pepper's leg when a low buzzing sound started somewhere in the room. I looked around to find the source.

"Sorry," Pepper said sheepishly. "That's my cell. Would you do me a favor and bring it over? It's in the pocket of my robe. I know I'm not supposed to bring it in, but I am expecting a very important call. Do you mind?"

What was I going to say? I went over to her robe hanging on the wall hook, dug out her phone, and handed it to her. I rearranged the waxing strips on the counter and gave the wax another stir while I waited.

"I don't care if the colour looks fine, it's not the colour that was approved on the proof I signed. *And* the font on the header is the wrong size. I expect to have a new set of invitations ready by tomorrow with the correct colour and font size. Is that clear? I'll be by later today to approve the final copy." Pepper ended the conversation and turned off her cell phone.

"Okay that's it. No more interruptions, I promise." Pepper turned off her cell phone and handed it to me to put away. "I don't normally do that, in fact I hate those people who carry their phones around as if they're so important that they must be able to be contacted at all times. Believe me, I'm not one of those people. It's just that I'm on the board of the Friends of the Glenbow, and the printer responsible for the invitations for the gala opening of the Rodin exhibit seems to have ignored everything I requested."

"I've been looking forward to going to that exhibit when it opens to the public," I said before I realized how lame that sounded. Why would she care if I were going to the museum or not?

"Did you happen to catch the exhibit last year on the Bog People? It was absolutely fascinating."

"No, I wanted to but I was too busy with work," I lied. Noni and I had loved exploring the museum. It hurt too much to go back there without her. "I have a membership, and I used to go to the museum quite a bit."

I slathered her leg with wax, applied a linen strip, and ripped it off with one quick motion. Pepper didn't so much as flinch. We discussed which exhibits we enjoyed and which of Rodin's sculptures we were most interested in seeing.

Half way through the service, I noticed I was dropping hot, sticky wax all over the place. More than I normally did. I was never great at multi-tasking. For me, waxing a client and talking about art consisted of two tasks. When I painted, I could only focus on the canvas in front of me. I couldn't even have music playing in the background because I found it too distracting.

I plunged the wooden stick into the wax pot to apply more wax to Pepper's leg, and when I pulled it out, loaded with wax, it slipped from my hands. The stick moved in slow motion. I followed the arc it made in the air, praying that it wasn't going to land on the floor. I made a feeble attempt to grab it, and, instead of hitting the floor, it landed squarely on my chest.

Why does stuff like this keep happening to me?

I pulled the offending stick off my shirt and threw it away. I removed as much of the wax off my chest as I could but it was hopeless. I laughed it off, trying not to look as dumb as I felt, and proceeded with the rest of the waxing.

I finished Pepper's left leg and picked up a small bottle of after-wax lotion. I pushed down on the nozzle. It was slippery from the product and the nozzle flew off the bottle hitting Pepper in the eye.

"Ouch!" Pepper quickly sat up covering her eye with one hand and clutching the modesty sheet to her chest with the other.

"Oh my God. Are you okay?"

"Yes, I'm fine. I was just startled." She lowered her hand and blinked. Her eye was tearing up. I scrambled to get her a tissue.

"I'm so sorry. I don't know what's wrong with me today. I'm normally not this klutzy." I was mortified.

"Really, don't worry about it." Pepper dabbed at her eye, then lay back down on the table.

I apologized again, retrieved the wayward nozzle, and finished applying the lotion to her leg.

Focus, Hannah. Don't screw this up.

I spread a thin layer of wax on Pepper's other leg, totally focused on what I was doing. I walked the two steps to the waxing counter, grabbed a linen strip, and turned back to apply it on her wax-coated leg. When I stepped forward, my right foot remained firmly stuck to the floor. Unfortunately, I had momentum working against me. I was ass over teakettle before I could even put my hands out to stop my fall.

I could only imagine what it looked like from Pepper's viewpoint. One moment I was standing next to her applying wax; the next, I disappeared from view followed by a loud thud as I hit the floor. I lay on the floor trying to catch my breath and waited for the shock of falling flat on my face to dissipate.

"Oh my goodness, are you okay?" Pepper jumped off the table wrapping herself in the modesty sheet. She crouched down next to my sprawled body.

"I'm fine, really, I'm okay." I had no idea if this was true; I just wanted to finish the service before one of us got seriously hurt.

Pepper helped me up. I stood gingerly on my right foot testing my weight. A painful twinge shot through my ankle, but I gritted my teeth and told Pepper again that I was fine. It was only then that I realized I was missing a shoe. I turned around and spotted it stuck to the floor. I yanked it off the floor and tried to scrape as much of the wax off as I could before putting it back on. However, my foot kept sticking to the floor every time I took a step.

Pepper got back on the table. The modesty sheet was stuck to her leg where I had applied the wax. I carefully prised it off before draping her with a clean one. For the rest of the appointment, I did my best not to hobble around or inflict any more damage on Pepper or myself.

I wouldn't blame her for never wanting to have me work on her again. I guess I could kiss another tip goodbye. If she said anything to the receptionists at the front desk, I knew I could kiss my job goodbye too.

To my surprise, by quitting time, I hadn't been called into Terence's office, and the girls up front didn't mention anything to me when I passed by. Maybe my guardian angels were watching out for me today. If it was true, I wondered why they let me fall on my face in the first place. I hobbled down the stairs to the break room.

Jas was there, waiting for me. When she raised a questioning eyebrow at my limp, I told her what I had done. She made me sit down on the couch, pulled up my pant leg, and gently rolled down my sock to look. My ankle was puffy and there was an angry looking bruise already forming.

I had promised her that I would go with her after work to check out the progress on her space. Today the electrician was to begin the wiring. She took one look at my foot and announced that I was to go home and ice it. I didn't want to disappoint her, but I knew she was right. I couldn't call in sick tomorrow because I had to work the corporate event. To top it off, I had agreed to work a double shift because I was desperate for the cash.

Jas wanted to call a cab and pay the fare, but I refused. Instead, she helped me out to the bus stop, and, when we got to my apartment, she supported me while I hobbled up the stairs. I changed out of my uniform while she put together an ice pack and wrapped it in a towel. I settled myself on the couch with the ice thankfully numbing my foot.

She said she was going to stay with me, but I insisted that she go check on the progress at her salon. I finally convinced her I would be fine on my own, and it would be okay for her to go.

"Thanks again for helping me." I seemed to be thanking her a lot lately.

"You're welcome. Call me on your break tomorrow, and I'll give you an update. Are you sure you're going to be okay by yourself?"

"Yeah sure, I'll be fine. Get going." I ordered her out.

I sat on the couch, not even bothering to turn the TV on for distraction.

"Sure, I'll be fine. Right, Noni?" I said to my empty apartment.

The silence was my answer. It grew until the weight of it pressed down on me. I was not fine, not even close. I stared down at the ice pack on my foot and wondered how I ended up with someone else's sorry excuse for a life. This was not where I imagined I would end up. I had big dreams for myself. Why did I let go of them so easily?

Chapter Nine

In the morning, my ankle was still stiff and sore, and the rest of me wasn't fairing any better. My eyes were swollen and puffy from crying, the bruise on my foot had turned a sickening eggplant colour, and I had woken up with stiffness in my arms and back, no doubt from the fall. When had I become such a train wreck? I didn't spend time contemplating the answer; instead, I got ready for work, wrapped my ankle in a tensor bandage, and headed off to catch the bus. It was going to be a long day.

My first shift of the day was uneventful. Blessedly, serenely uneventful. I hadn't injured any of my clients or myself, and I managed to go a whole day without a run-in with Terence. It was a pretty sad state of affairs when I counted a good day as not inflicting pain or swallowing body parts. I had to start my second shift in less than an hour. A little application of the under eye cream I'd snagged from one of the treatment rooms resolved my tear ravaged complexion, and the soreness in my back and arms had almost disappeared. My ankle was the only thing that wasn't doing very well.

The break room was quickly filling up with the employees who were working the event, and everyone was talking about what was taking place upstairs.

The caterers were already setting up in the conference rooms. In all the time I'd worked at the Serenity, I'd never seen such a production as the one that was taking shape above us. Curiosity finally got the better of me, and I snuck upstairs and peeked into the conference rooms before heading back downstairs to have my dinner.

The spa was purposely designed to host large, after-hours events to increase the profits it could bring in. The designers had created two decent-sized conference rooms that had a retractable wall between them, enabling the two rooms to become one big space. Although the spa hosted a steady stream of private events, rarely did it require opening up both rooms. According to the handouts Terence had given us, they would need to open the space up to accommodate the hundred and fifty guests that were expected.

Several large buffet tables, covered in crisp, white tablecloths, lined the back wall. Platters of canapés, crudities, and fruit had been arranged into artistic displays. Eight silver chargers of raw oysters shared space on the table with four huge crystal bowls in which tins of caviar nestled snuggly in crushed ice. The dessert tables groaned under the weight of a confectionary delight of tortes, petite fours, cream puffs, and a large croquembouche, its caramel webbing glistening appetizingly under the lights. Three of the buffet tables were set up for hot food and the servers were just setting up the warming trays to receive the dishes that would be coming later.

The spa had a small kitchen behind the conference rooms that was just adequate to allow caterers to serve their food for the smaller functions. I had never seen such an elaborate set-up before and wondered how they were going to manage to serve dinner from such a small kitchen. The bar looked equally well stocked, complete with two cute bartenders.

Two items in the room made my jaw drop. One was a four foot ice sculpture of the Thorpe Industries logo that was lit from underneath with coloured lights that slowly changed from shades of blue to purple to pink. The other was a large fountain with chocolate cascading down four tiers in velvet ripples.

I finally pulled myself away from watching the set-up just as the florists were placing the centrepieces of white peonies at each table. My mind boggled at how much something like this must cost. Renting the space and paying for the spa treatments alone would be pricey. Whoever this Thorpe guy was, he was definitely rolling in money.

After looking at all that exquisite food, I was hungry. I went downstairs and ate my disappointing dinner of a soggy cheese sandwich and a bag of plain potato chips. I had accidentally sat on my lunch bag on the way to work, and now the chips were mostly just dust. I threw away the remains of my crappy dinner and moved to make room for more of my coworkers as they trickled in.

My job tonight was pretty easy. I was responsible for the hydrotherapy room. For corporate events, Serenity offered the guests abbreviated services, so that they had the opportunity to indulge in at least two treatments.

After dinner, the clients would be invited to make their way into the Great Room where three hostesses would sign them up for services and escort them into the appropriate rooms. Those were the hardest jobs of the night. The hostesses had to manage the scheduling of the treatments, keep track of which treatment rooms were in use, and make sure that all the guests' needs were being taken care of.

Compared to what those girls had to do, my duties were a cakewalk. I was smart enough to realize he had assigned me to the hydro-tub, not as a reward, but because Terence figured it was so easy that even I couldn't mess it up.

All I had to do was fill the hydro-tub and mix in whatever essential oil blend the client wanted, tell the client when it was time to get out, then take the client to the adjoining room, apply a moisturizer, and take the client back to the Great Room. Then I would drain the tub, disinfect it, and fill it for the next person. Simple.

Thirty minutes before the start of the function, the break room was full to bursting. When the heavy door swung open once again and Terence stepped in, the chatter immediately stopped. Terence had decked himself out in a black Armani suit and a pair of Gucci loafers. He clapped his hands to get our attention, which was unnecessary because we all had shut up the instant he entered the room.

"Your attention, everyone." Terence struck a pose like a strutting peacock. "You all know what your duties are tonight and what is expected of you. Remember that you represent Serenity, and I depend on you to live up to our reputation of excellence. I expect no less than perfection in the performance of your duties this evening. Not only are we honored to be hosting this event for one of the biggest companies in the Western provinces, but we are also to be graced with the presence of the CEO of Thorpe Industries himself."

No wonder Terrance assigned me to the back rooms of the spa. The Big Wig himself was going to be here tonight.

"Now I want you to line up single file, and exit one at a time so that I may do a final inspection."

Final inspection? What was this? Boot camp? A few of the girls boldly rolled their eyes at Terence's ridiculous command. I kept my feelings to myself, and tried hard to keep my face neutral.

By the time it was my turn to stand in front of Terence, he had already sent three girls to the staff washrooms to make corrections in their appearance. One to wash off her too garish eye shadow, one to pull her hair back more neatly, and one to polish the scuff marks off her shoes.

I knew I was presentable, but when I stood under Terence's gaze, I began to panic. Was my shirt tucked in properly? Were there any stray hairs escaping my regulation ponytail? Was my make-up discrete enough?

My ankle was still sore, and I bit my lip to keep myself from hobbling as I walked up to him. Pepper Dempsey had obviously kept her waxing experience to herself, and the last thing I needed was Terence grilling me about why I was limping.

Terence held up his hand to stop me. He put his hands on his hips and looked down his long beak. I felt like a deer caught in the headlights. Try as he might, Terence couldn't find anything to reprimand me for. He scrutinized me with his dark little eyes, his Gucci clad foot tapping on the concrete floor. Finally he dismissed me with an imperious wave. As soon as I got away from him, I relaxed and headed upstairs, being careful not to put my full weight on my tender ankle.

The distinct sounds of a string quartet enveloped me as I entered the corridor heading to the Great Room. The music was classical and soothing. I continued towards the Front desk to check out the music. There was an actual string quartet playing in the lobby. Wow, this guy, Thorpe, sure knew how to plan a party. I left the lobby and went to the Hydrotherapy Room. I looked over my station, making sure I had everything I needed for my services, and settled down to wait for my first client.

It proved to be a long wait, but Terrance had told us to stay in our assigned treatment rooms until the guests were done eating and ready for their treatments. He didn't want us loitering about the Great Room. I wished I had figured out a way to sneak a book in with me to pass the time, but I was afraid Terrance might make a final check of all the rooms. He would have a cow if he found me relaxing in the Hydrotherapy Room reading.

Two hours later, the guests, having had their fill at the banquet, slowly made their way into the spa area, many of them carrying glasses of wine or champagne. Their laughter and easy chatter echoed down the hallways. With a relaxed pace that only comes with the consumption of good food and a free bar, the guests began to file into the locker rooms to change into robes and sign up for treatments.

After the sixth hydro tub treatment of the evening, I ran out of towels. I told Jessica, one of the hostesses stationed in the Great Room, where I was going so she wouldn't send a client to my room while I was gone. I headed into the Prep Room and grabbed a bunch of towels. I was tired and didn't want to make a second trip, so I took a few more than I could comfortably manage. I couldn't really see where I was going because the stack of towels obscured my view.

On my way back to the treatment room, I tried to ignore the drumbeat in my foot that was growing more persistent as the evening wore on. I turned the corner too quickly and the stack of towels started to teeter. As I tried to stop them from falling, I ran smack into someone coming around the corner from the other direction. The towels toppled and scattered to the floor. I threw my arms out and braced myself against the wall barely stopping myself from following them.

"Sorry!"

"No reason to apologize," said the robe-clad guest with startling familiar brown eyes.

It was Yummy Man from the salon. I started picking up the towels. My hands shook as I snatched up the towels as fast as I could. Yummy Man bent down to help me and I noticed the tie on his robe had come undone. He was wearing a pair of navy boxers and nothing else. It was hard not to stare at an almost naked man, a very buff almost naked man, crouched only inches away from me. Embarrassed, I looked down at the floor, at his ankles, anywhere but at his exposed body.

"Uhm." I stumbled for the right words. "Your, uhm." I resorted to pointing.

"Oh God," Yummy Man chuckled and retied his robe. "That's one way to impress a girl, or scare her off completely."

I laughed. We stood in the hallway, each of us clutching an armful of rumpled towels.

"You look vaguely familiar. Have we met before?"

"Yeah, at The Edge about a week and a half ago."

"Yes, that's it. I have a good memory for faces. I'm Christian, by the way."

"Hannah," I said, my heart fluttered wildly. We automatically went to shake hands but the towels got in our way. I laughed again. "I'll take those." I held out my arms to take the rest of the towels from him.

"It was nice bumping into you again," Christian said. "See you around."

"See you," I said to his back as he headed down the hall and into a treatment room. I glanced around nervously, afraid that the Dark Lord of the Spa was lurking in the corridor ready to reprimand me for yet another of my blunders.

I shuffled as quickly as I could with my bum ankle and armload of rumpled towels to the Prep Room to fetch another load of clean ones. Holding firmly to a new, smaller stack of towels, I quickly walked back through the Great Room. When I passed Jessica, I tried to avoid making eye contact with her. I told her I'd only be a few minutes. That was twenty minutes ago. She pinned me with a death ray look.

"I'm sorry," I whispered. "I got held up by a guest." I rushed back to my room to run the tub for the next client, feeling strangely giddy.

Chapter Ten

How was it possible to feel that time was standing still and racing forward at break neck speed all at the same time? At work, the days dragged on, each second, each minute, inching along on crippled legs. Hours went on for days. When I worked frantically with Jas to get her shop ready, time sprouted wings and flew. I blinked, and two hours had gone by without me having sensed the passage of time.

Time was definitely not my ally. Personally, I felt trapped in a time warp from which I could not escape. While everyone around me seemed to be moving forward in their lives, I stood still, mired in old decisions and bad choices, too afraid to stop trudging through the same old muck and look at what else was out there. I skimmed over the surface of these worrying thoughts, careful not to dive too deeply in case I bumped up against the truth of why I chose to remain in my comfortable misery. Was it just easier to deal with the drudgery I knew than reaching out into the unknown?

It had been six weeks since Jas signed the lease for the salon, and every day I saw Jas's dream get closer and closer to reality. She was more excited about the risk than frightened or worried. From dust and dreams, she slowly assembled her desire, her salon. Penny by penny she saved her money, met with bank after bank to secure the loan she would need, all the while holding down a steady job. What made her different from me?

I worked hard too. Where did my money go? I had a sneaking suspicion I knew what I had spent it on, but I didn't want to go there. What the hell was I afraid of any way? When was the last time I'd picked up a brush and put paint to canvas?

It wasn't just in my work life that I contracted back into myself. My love life was no better. Mason was not the first bad choice I made in my dating career. Although I found myself fantasizing about Christian since our first meeting, the thought of dating him was so far from reality that I felt safe in my infatuation.

Thankfully, my shift was over and I only had one more thing to do before meeting up with Jas to paint her apartment. I needed to go upstairs to the Accounting office to pick up my cheque. This was the twenty-first century and the spa still didn't have direct deposit for the payroll.

Instead, the spa paid us every two weeks, and we picked up our money from Danielle, the accountant. On paydays, Danielle kept the door to her office open, and people trickled in to get their wages. Near the end of the day, the trickle would inevitably turn into a stampede as everyone rushed to get their money before Danielle left for the day.

As usual, Danielle's door was open. She looked up from her computer screen and gave me a nervous smile when I entered.

"Could you shut the door please?"

For a brief second I panicked. Had I done something wrong and pissed off Danielle? I couldn't think of anything. Lately, I'd been the poster child for toeing the line.

"Here's your cheque." Danielle handed me a white envelope and I signed my name on the clipboard she kept on the corner of her desk. This was part of the normal routine, so why did she ask me to shut the door?

82

"There's one more thing. When you go to cash this, could you deposit it in the bank machine instead of going to the teller?" Danielle nervously plucked at the fabric of her skirt removing imaginary lint.

"Why, what's going on?"

"It's nothing to be concerned about, just a small timing error. It's a cash flow thing, and by next week everything will be fine. If you use a teller, the bank will process the cheque immediately, as opposed to on Monday if you use the bank machine. If you use the teller, I can't guarantee that your cheque won't bounce. The money is coming in, but like I said, it's just a matter of timing, that's all." Danielle's face was flushed, and she wouldn't look me in the eye.

"Sure, no problem. I usually just put it in the bank machine anyway. Do I have any tips for this week?" I needed to get going and just wanted my money.

"Yes, I think you do." Danielle rummaged through the small locked cash box sitting on the corner of her desk. She pulled out a small stack of brown envelopes with my name on them and handed them to me.

When clients pay for their treatments at the front desk, there is a little locked box with empty brown envelopes next to it. The receptionist takes the tips, writes our names on the envelopes, seals them, and drops the envelopes in the box. Danielle gets the box for safekeeping at the end of each day.

I took my envelopes, thanked Danielle, and left. The stack was substantially smaller than the tips I used to get before being on probation. I was still scheduled for more than my share of pedicures and a lot of clients with gift certificates. Clients that come because of a gift certificate usually don't tip.

I stopped at the bank machine around the corner and deposited my cheque before heading out on the bus. On the way over to Jas's shop, I sat at the back of the bus and counted my tips, ripping open the sealed envelopes one by one. Before the Mrs. Weatherbee debacle, I could get up to eighty dollars in tips a day. As I tore open the little brown envelopes, I could tell that I was nowhere near that. The weight of the envelopes gave it away before I even opened them. Most of my tips were loonies and twoonies. Coins weigh more than paper money. I transferred my handful of change into my purse. For the week, I only made thirty dollars in tips. I tried not to be disappointed.

I crumpled the empty envelopes in my hand and rested my head against the window of the bus as it rattled along its route. The window was cool on my skin. It was just approaching seven in the evening, and already the sky had gone fully dark. We had entered the bleak, dark days of winter despite it only being mid-November. Although there was just a skiff of snow on the ground, a mild winter by Calgary standards, the sunlight had disappeared and wouldn't make its return until late May. It was dark when I got up in the morning, and it was dark by the time I got off work. I spent the only daylight hours in rooms with no windows. In the winter, I never felt fully awake.

The bus filled up with people making their way from their downtown office jobs to their families waiting in the suburbs. The air smelled like wet wool and close bodies. I squished myself against the window to make room for an elderly woman carrying two large, overstuffed, plastic bags and a large needlepoint handbag. I kept my gaze focused out the window, but because it was dark outside and the bus was lit from the glowing advertisements above my head, the window acted more like a mirror. I saw the old woman and the people around me reflected back in the glass.

"Excuse me dear, could I ask a favor?" The old woman tapped me lightly on the shoulder.

I turned reluctantly to face her. "Sure."

The old woman scrounged around in one of the bags, trying to balance the other one and her large purse on her knee. "Oh dear, this is just too awkward. Here, take this for a moment."

Before I could protest, the woman plunked the larger of the two bags and her purse onto my lap. I had to juggle my knapsack and my handful of empty envelopes to adjust to the new load. Her purse was surprisingly heavy.

"Here it is," she exclaimed, pulling a big purple scarf out of the depths of her bag. "I've been knitting this for my granddaughter for Christmas, and I'm not sure about this purple. I couldn't help but notice that you have her same colouring. I just want to see if this shade is right for her hair and eyes."

Before I knew what was happening she threw the scarf over my head and wound it several times around my neck. It was very long and very purple. The yarn was soft as a whisper. It felt comforting up against my cheek.

"Now let's take a look." The old woman dug her hand underneath her coat and produced a pair of half lenses attached to a gold chain looped around her neck. She placed her spectacles gingerly on the end of her nose and surveyed her scarf. "Yes, that is darling, isn't it. I was right. It makes your eyes more violet, and your skin warms to this colour."

Satisfied with her assessment, the old woman removed her glasses, returning them to the depths under her overcoat.

"You do have very pretty eyes. Not many people have that colour. They're a true violet, not just dark blue. And such a pretty mouth. Too bad you are ruining your looks with so much worry." She pointed to the area around my eyes and mouth.

I kept silent, but that didn't stop her from giving me more advice.

"The longer you choose to play it safe, the more miserable your life will become. The universe rewards risk my dear; you know what you need to do."

The bus lurched to a stop and the old woman looked up. "I must be going, this is my stop."

She stood up, and I quickly unraveled the scarf, savoring the delicate feel of the yarn, and handed it over.

"Thank you, I would have forgotten that and my granddaughter would have been without a Christmas present." The woman stuffed the scarf in her bag, grabbed up her purse and the other bags that were sitting in my lap. She carefully walked up the aisle and stepped off the bus.

What a strange woman.

I settled back down into the seat and looked out the window again. I avoided my own reflection and the lines of worry that I knew were there. Fifteen minutes later, I got off the bus at the Inglewood stop and walked the few blocks to Jas's salon. On the way, I passed a garbage can and tossed the crumpled envelopes. When I reached the salon, I knocked loudly on the wooden doorframe.

She was working on the main floor. All the windows were covered over with newspaper, but light filtered through the spaces between the paper and every once in a while I saw her shadow flicker across the window. Jas's response to my knock was muffled, but she soon appeared in the doorway.

"Hi." She stepped back to allow me inside. Paint spattered her baggy overalls and t-shirt and even her ponytail. Her face was devoid of makeup except for the large splash of white paint across her forehead. I smiled at her disheveled appearance.

I'd gone with Jas to buy her construction gear at the local thrift shop. Although the overalls were secondhand, they were clean when she bought them. Now they read like a journal of her activities. There were paint splotches in white, cream, and blue; large goopy drips of plaster; and a light coating of sawdust. She'd been a very busy girl of late. So had I, for that matter. Jas looked filthy and tired—and the happiest I had ever seen her.

Our traditional once a week dinner and a movie had evolved into evenings spent painting, cleaning, and working on small construction projects. I didn't mind helping out, but it was more physically demanding than sitting on the couch. A fact my muscles reminded me of daily.

I stepped past her and into the space. It was quickly taking shape, and the feeling of something exciting being created was almost as palpable as the strong smell of paint that hung in the air. When I walked, my feet made crinkly sounds on the builder's kraft paper taped to the floor to protect the hardwood from any further damage during the renovation. Jas planned to fix the loose boards but wanted to keep the rustic look of the floor. Although I witnessed the whole transformation of the space from the beginning, I was still surprised and thrilled by how it looked.

Three large, halogen, construction lights were set up around the room, washing everything in their stark light. A light wheat-coloured paint covered the once grimy, grey walls. The crumbling ceiling tiles had been replaced with four-foot square wood panels installed so that the grain of the wood alternated between the squares. There were electrical wires dangling from holes in the ceiling where the light fixtures would soon be installed. The shampoo sinks were in place, and the reception desk was sitting under a drop cloth for protection. All in all, it looked pretty damn amazing.

She was painting the cornice molding on the ceiling when I arrived and interrupted her work.

"I'd give you a hug, pumpkin, but I'd hate to get paint on your jacket. Let me just finish up down here and then we can get started upstairs. I won't be but a minute. You can change in the washroom in the back. The plumber was by today and it actually has running water." She climbed back up the ladder to finish her painting, and I went to the back of the shop.

On my way to the bathroom, I passed the mirrors for the cutting stations leaning up against the wall still covered in their protective bubble wrap. I opened the washroom door and was delighted to see a gleaming white porcelain sink and matching toilet. Before the renovation, there had been an old toilet, its bowl stained a scary rust colour and its tank hopelessly cracked. Instead of a vanity, there had been a battered plastic utility sink.

I quickly changed out of my Serenity uniform and into an old pair of sweat pants and a t-shirt so worn the cotton was thin and soft. My outfit carried the same paint stains as Jas's. It felt good to get out of my uniform. I crammed the pants and polo shirt carelessly into my knapsack. Before leaving the bathroom, I splashed warm water on my face and blotted it dry with a square of paper towel from the roll sitting on the toilet tank. I felt refreshed and strangely elated.

The old woman's face from the bus popped into my head. I shook my head to dislodge the image of her kindly face and the memory of her strange words. I met up with Jas just as she was coming to get me.

"Well, that's done." She wrapped the paintbrush in cling film to prevent it from drying out. She placed it on a workbench filled with paint cans, caulking guns, brushes, rollers, and painter's tape. "Ready to start upstairs?"

"Lead on, Mac Duff."

I followed her up the narrow wooden stairs. I wasn't worried about stumbling over myself like the first time because now a new light fixture flooded light into the once dark tunnel.

Upstairs, our hard work was also evident. Like the salon below, we had stripped the apartment down to its bare bones. The electrician had upgraded the old wiring and added a few more lights in the ceiling. Now the only things cluttering the apartment were paint cans, a set of rollers and brushes, and drop clothes placed in the middle of the sitting room.

"Wait until you see the colours for up here." Jas knelt in front of the cans and pried open the first one with the flat end of a screwdriver. I had helped her choose the colours for the salon, but she had wanted to pick the colours for the upstairs.

"This one is for the kitchen and sitting room." It was a fresh apple green. The next can revealed a soft periwinkle. "That's for the bedrooms." She pointed with the screwdriver at the blue paint. "And this cream colour is for the trim."

We started in the sitting room. I dipped my roller in the paint tray and watched the paint soak into the fuzzy roller sleeve. The colour reminded me of crisp Granny Smith apples, and of tender blades of spring grass, and the underside of a leaf.

"You're going to drip paint."

"Oops, sorry." I quickly put the roller to the wall and started painting.

I really enjoyed helping Jas with all the painting she needed done. I was continually surprised at how good I felt seeing that first ribbon of paint on the wall. The fresh colour against the tired, old walls spoke of the possibility of new things.

We had been working for about forty-five minutes, getting the first coat on three of the walls, when someone banged on the front door downstairs.

"Food's here!" She announced, putting her paint roller back in its tray and heading downstairs.

I hadn't even thought about dinner and I was starving. She must have ordered food before I got here. I closed up the paint cans, covered the paint trays and rollers with cling wrap, and went downstairs to wash up. Jas was shaking out a drop cloth and placing it on the floor of the sitting room when I returned. The aroma of cheese and pepperoni made my mouth water. She arranged the pizza on an upturned cardboard box, tore off two sheets of paper towel for placemats, and we dug in.

"Would you go into the kitchen and open the cooler that's on the floor."

"Sure."

I did as she asked and found, cradled in the ice, frosty bottles of Bavaria beer. My favorite. I rescued two out of the icy water and joined her on the floor.

Jas produced a bottle opener from the front pocket of her overalls and opened our drinks. She lifted her bottle. "Here's to great friends. I couldn't have done this without your help."

We clinked our bottles and tipped them back. The beer was icy cold and felt wonderful on my parched throat. The pizza was hot and gooey with extra cheese. After eating two more slices of pizza and polishing off another beer, I was so full it hurt. I slipped into a food coma and I knew Jas was feeling the effects of the food and booze too, as we both fell into a comfortable sleepy silence. I leaned against one of the unpainted walls with my legs straight out in front of me and sighed deeply.

She was the first to break the silence. "Are you happy?"

Maybe it was the mellowing effects of the beer I'd consumed or my full stomach, but I stopped myself before saying something flippant.

Was I happy? I searched for the answer. I was grateful to have loving people in my life, my parents (well, my da anyway), Jas, even Ruth. I was thankful that I had a roof over my head and a steady job. But, was I happy?

I was surprised when I replied, "No, I'm not."

I was even more surprised when I started to cry. Big, fat tears rolled down my cheeks. I hid my head on my arms. What had gotten into me lately? She came over and sat next to me. I leaned into her as she put her arm around my shoulders.

"Hannah," she said gently, "why are you doing this to yourself?"

"Doing what?" I pressed the heels of my hands into my eyes.

"Living a life you don't want—that isn't you. When we first met, you said you'd taken the job at the spa to make money to go to art school. What happened? You still have the application form stuck on your fridge, and you're still working at the spa. You can't tell me that this is what you wanted for yourself. Why did you settle?"

A million excuses were on the tip of my tongue: I have bills and rent to pay, I have responsibilities, I didn't have enough money for college, but I let these pathetic reasons die before speaking them.

"Because I'm afraid," I whispered.

She let go of my shoulders and sat back to look at me. "What I'm about to say to you might make you angry, but remember I am only saying this because I love you and, frankly, I'm worried about you."

My heart beat frantically.

"You're not the only one that's scared. I am too. Some nights I wake up in a cold sweat when I think about what I'm doing. I've put everything I have into this venture, and if this flops, I'll have nothing to show for all my hard work except being up to my eyeballs in bank payments and debt. But I don't let that stop me. This is what I want for my life, and if I don't do everything in my power to create my dream then what's the point? If being an esthetician was your passion we wouldn't be having this conversation. But it isn't. If you don't put everything into being who you really are, you'll never feel any better. If you don't take a risk, nothing will change, so risk something."

When I finally spoke, my voice sounded small and far away. "I know, but I feel like my life has overwhelmed me, and I don't know how to stop the flow of it. I don't know how to change direction."

Instead of answering me, she tipped her beer back and, finding it empty, pushed herself off the floor to get another one. She came back, sat back down on the floor next to me, and handed me a fresh bottle.

She slowly sipped her beer before she spoke. "You already know what you need to do. I bet you're feeling lost, but trust me on this: start small, and above all, listen to your heart. Now, I think that's enough soul searching for one night. We'll finish painting later. I think what you need is a good night's rest and some time to think."

I agreed with her because I didn't think I could stand another moment of having to listen to her unsolicited advice. When had Jas morphed into my mother?

She pulled her cell phone from her back pocket and called us a cab. We were just finishing our last beer when the taxi driver honked his horn. We went downstairs, Jas shutting off lights as we went. It was late and my head hurt from so many things pressing inside. We rode in silence all the way home.

Chapter Eleven

Over the next few weeks, Jas's words from that evening of painting stayed with me, echoing over and over in my brain. Had I made any dramatic changes to my life? I wished I could've said I went home that night, reassessed what I needed to do, and then put in place the things that needed to happen. No, I didn't go in the next day and give my notice at the spa or pursue my painting. I still went into work every day. Besides, who was Jas to say that my life, such as it was, wasn't worthwhile, wasn't complete? The more I thought about it the more I felt attacked and put out. A dark and foul mood descended on me.

Jas must have felt my anger because she wasn't her normal bubbly self when we talked, but at least she didn't mention my attitude or try to bring up changing my life again. I started to avoid her and made excuses why I couldn't help her out at the salon.

Work was work. I went in, I did what I was told, and I went home. Each day it became more unbearable to be at the spa. When I was home, the thought of going to work made me want to throw up. The people I worked with were still the same nice people, with the exception of Terence, and even he was behaving within his normal Diva Queen parameters, but I was irritated just being around them. I had to be pleasant and professional with clients, but when I was finished with work, all I wanted to do was run and hide.

As far as my commissions went, I knuckled down and really focused on doing the best job that I could to push product and to get my sales numbers up. I couldn't wait for the next staff meeting and the look on Terence's face when he discovered I wasn't at the bottom of the list.

I thought, maybe, if I just focused on the job and on paying off my debts, that the hollow empty feeling would go away. It didn't, and I still had a stack of unpaid bills sitting on my kitchen counter to show for my efforts.

I had a bad habit of not picking up my mail for weeks at a time. I figured, what's the point of getting it every day when I knew what I'd find there: junk mail and bills. When I did get my mail, I just threw it on the kitchen counter without even opening it. In my mind, if I didn't open them they didn't exist.

Now, because of my backwards logic, I was behind in almost all of my bills. When payday came around, I never had enough to pay the balances. The amounts kept getting bigger because of the late charges and interest. I'd just put down a little on each one, hoping to delay getting my phone cut off or my credit card cancelled. So far, it seemed to be working.

I finished tidying up the treatment room from my last waxing appointment before going home. Now that my shift was over, all I wanted to do was pick up my paycheque and get out of there.

All day, a feeling of dread had been building in me, and I couldn't shake it. While I finished up and shut the door to the treatment room, my level of anxiety increased. I couldn't pin my uneasiness on anything. It had been an uneventful day and I was looking forward to doing a little early Christmas shopping and spending the rest of the night on my couch watching TV. Nothing earth shattering and definitely nothing to be nervous about. If anything, I should be feeling relieved as it was payday, and not just any payday.

My Christmas bonus would be included in this paycheque. Every year, Serenity gave the staff their Christmas bonus at the end of November. It was nice to get it early so I could plan my holiday spending. The bonus was calculated on how well each of us did with our sales and how much money the spa made. It was one of the few perks we received. With my new heads down, work, work, work attitude, I should be getting at least $500 for my bonus. I planned to use the money to buy Christmas presents. I wouldn't be able to get a lot, but at least it was something. Maybe tonight I'd treat myself to a pint of Häagen-Dazs cookie dough ice cream after doing my shopping.

I walked into the Accounting office. Danielle had her head down with her hands fisted in her hair. She looked up when I stepped into her office. She lowered her hands and her hair stayed scrunched up and messy. Her face and neck were red and blotchy. She stared at me, looking bewildered, like she just woke up from a bad dream.

"Hi, I'm here to pick up my cheque." I hoped the sound of my voice would snap her out of her confusion.

"Oh, yes, yes. Here you go." She slid a white envelope across her desk. The envelope looked thicker than normal. She handed me a pen and the clipboard to sign for my pay. I quickly scribbled my signature, took my envelope and my small stack of tips. I was just about to leave when Danielle stopped me.

"I need to ask you to put your cheque into the bank machine again instead of using a teller or if you could...wait until Friday to cash it?"

I stopped dead in my tracks.

"The spa still having cash flow problems?" I turned to face her.

She had to be joking. The spa was exceptionally busy of late, and all the girls had been busting their butts to sell product and gift certificates. Now Danielle was trying to tell me there was still a cash flow problem. How stupid did she think I was? What were the owners doing with the money? Burning it?

A terrible realization came over me. I tore open my envelope. I pulled out my cheque and looked for my bonus. It wasn't there. There was a small piece of thick paper stuck at the bottom of the envelope. I squeezed the edges of the envelope and shook the stubborn bit of paper onto Danielle's desk. I picked it up and read it. It was a free pass for a matinee at one of the big theatre chains.

"What is this?" I picked up the ticket.

"That is your Christmas bonus." Danielle cleared her throat.

"No, this is not my bonus. My bonus is a cheque for five hundred dollars. That's what I earned selling expensive crap to rich women that don't even need the stuff." My voice sounded shrill and white-hot anger thrummed in my temples. "This...is a joke!" I shouted, waving the movie ticket in front of Danielle's face. "I was counting on that money! I need that money!"

I know I sounded hysterical, but I didn't care. What the hell was I going to do now? I stormed out of Danielle's office slamming the door behind me. I was so angry I couldn't see straight. I don't remember walking through the spa or heading out onto the street. I walked three blocks before I noticed that it was snowing heavily. The first real snowstorm of the season.

Big, fat flakes spun lazily down through the endlessly black sky. I stopped on the street and tilted my head back looking into the velvety blackness. I closed my eyes, the snow caressing my face with tiny, cold whispers before melting on my skin.

What was I going to do?

Breathe, Hannah, focus.

Christmas shopping was definitely out of the question, seeing as most stores don't accept free movie passes as legal tender. An image of all the unpaid bills stacked up on my kitchen counter flashed before my eyes. Even if I used all of my cheque and tip money I wouldn't have enough to cover just the balances. I didn't know what to do about those either.

I'd think of something. I just needed to calm down and come up with a plan. My world was disintegrating around me, and I couldn't seem to stop the avalanche. I needed to go somewhere quiet and safe where I could think things through. I couldn't go see Jas. After our last heart-to-heart, I didn't feel up to another lecture and the thought of going home to my empty apartment didn't appeal to me either.

I lowered my head and slowly opened my eyes. I blinked snowflakes off my eyelashes and headed for the bus. Ten minutes later, I pushed open the doors to the Glenbow Museum and stepped out of the swirling snow and into my past.

It was an hour before closing, and the rotunda was deserted except for the docent behind the glassed-in admissions booth. I dug inside my purse and pulled out my membership card from my wallet. I hadn't visited here for a long time, but every year I renewed my membership card. I could have used the money for other things, like bills, but I just couldn't bring myself to cut that thread from my past.

My boots, wet from the snow, squeaked on the marble floor as I headed over to the booth. The docent looked up from the book she was reading. I didn't recognize her. There was a time when not only did I know almost all the volunteers who worked here, but they knew me and would greet me by name when I came in.

The woman put her book down on the counter and waited for me. She was in her mid-fifties and wore her steal grey hair short and tightly curled. I smiled to myself as I remembered what Noni used to call that matronly style of hair: a poodle perm. Whenever we were out together and she saw a woman of a certain age sporting a poodle perm, Noni would say that she would rather stick needles in her eyes than resort to that type of serviceable hairstyle. Noni always had worn her hair in a chic bob even after her hair had turned silver.

I got half way to the booth, my membership card in hand, before I stopped myself. What was I thinking coming here? What was I hoping to get out of coming back to a place so filled with memories of Noni that I could feel a lump of emotion hurting my throat?

I smiled at the docent and put my card back in my wallet. I turned right and headed for the museum's coffee shop, The Lazy Loaf and Kettle. Because of the snowstorm and it being so close to closing, the coffee shop was deserted. I ordered a coffee and sat at the back of the restaurant at a small table facing the rotunda. I liberally dosed the coffee with sugar.

A maintenance worker slowly made his way around the marble floors pushing a large broom in front of him. A security guard approached the admissions booth and chatted with the docent. She giggled at something he said and coyly patted her helmet of curls. In the gift shop, a young girl started counting out the change from the till in anticipation of closing. I read the large banner hanging in the lobby announcing the opening of the Rodin exhibit next month. Noni would have loved to see it.

I was six or seven when Noni brought me here for the first time. It was also my first visit to the big city. I remembered feeling overwhelmed and scared surrounded by the thunder of traffic and the clatter of the C-train as it made its way down Fourth Street. The closed in feeling of the buildings blotting out the sky, and so many people rushing down the sidewalk was too much for me to take in. By the time Noni had parked the car and guided me towards the museum, I was clutching her hand tightly.

When we stepped into the hushed atmosphere of the museum, I felt safe. The docent greeted Noni by her first name and leaned down to shake my hand as if I were a grown-up. The two of us spent the afternoon going from exhibit to exhibit, and afterwards we stopped at the Lazy Loaf for a treat. I had chocolate milk, and Noni and I shared an oversized cinnamon bun grilled and oozing butter.

On the ride home, I curled up in the back seat and dreamed of all the wonders that had been opened to me—a place of colour and texture, of shadow and light, of images that felt more real than the people and places that populated my small world. I didn't understand it all, but I felt the magic and I wanted more. I wanted to be a part of that world.

When I was older, I always looked forward to trips to the museum with Noni. Our time together there wasn't only about the paintings. The other exhibits and Special Collections were just as intriguing. Noni felt that it was important for me to understand about the world and its people, its vast and varied history and culture and our place in it. Most importantly, she taught me that despite the passage of time and the differences in culture and beliefs, the essence of the human experience, our cherished desires and secret dreams, were the same.

"Our emotions are and always will be the common thread that connects us all," she used to say.

Now, I sat in our favorite place alone. Unshed tears burned my eyes. I blinked furiously and stared out into the rotunda, refusing to give my grief a chance to slip out. If I started to cry, I didn't think I would stop.

A man came out of the exhibit hall and headed towards the exit. His hands were shoved in the pockets of his wrinkled chinos, his gaze focused down at the tips of his running shoes that squeaked on the polished marble floors. He was either deep in thought, or judging by the tousled look of his hair, just got up from a nap.

I focused on the measure of his gait; anything to get my mind away from the pain I was feeling. When he neared the exit, I realized it was Aaron. Aaron with the striking blue eyes. I raised my hand and waved, and before I knew what I was doing, I called out his name.

He raised his head and looked around in my direction. He pulled his hands out of his pockets and gave a wave back—that kind of vague half-hearted thing people do when they don't know who the person is that waved first. I expected him to keep walking out of the museum, but instead he headed over in my direction.

As he approached my table, he ran his fingers through his mussed hair, a confused look on his face. "Hey."

I could tell by the look on his face he didn't recognize me. "Hi, I'm Hannah. You probably don't remember me. We met at the Albright gallery a while ago."

"Yeah, yeah, I remember. Can I join you?"

I nodded and he pulled out a chair and sat down.

"So what exhibit did you come to see on such a blustery night?" I asked.

"I'm embarrassed to admit this, but I didn't come here specifically, it was just convenient. I spent all day in my darkroom and I wasn't thrilled with my latest efforts. I just needed to get some fresh air and a new perspective. Walking usually helps clear my head. I forgot my coat and when it started to snow, I ducked in here to get warm. It was closer than trying to make it all the way back to my place. Since I was here, I figured I'd go check out a couple of exhibits until I thawed out enough to head back home."

"So do you frequently go out in the middle of winter without a coat?" I couldn't wait to tell Jas that I wasn't the only adult on the planet that forgets things like coats and hats. Then with a pang of guilt, I remembered that I was avoiding her.

"Yeah, I guess I do. When I'm working on a project, I sometimes get a little too focused on what I'm doing and I don't notice things like if I'm wearing a coat. I once forgot to eat for three days. Drives my girlfriend crazy. Sandy said it's selfish the way I go off into my own world, behaving like no one and nothing else exists. I guess she has a point." He stared at his hands.

I felt a strange prick of disappointment at the mention of his girlfriend. I didn't know what was wrong with me. Yes, he was attractive and yes, the fact that he was a real artist, someone that made a living doing what he loved, was immensely appealing. Here was someone that would have understood my desire to paint. He certainly was charming in a boyish way, but having a girlfriend meant he was off limits.

I don't know why I was even going there with my thoughts. Even if he was single, I had too much to deal with without adding a boyfriend in the mix. I sipped my coffee and Aaron continued to stare at his hands, the silence building between us until I finally couldn't take it anymore.

"So what are you working on right now?"

"Oh." He looked up at me, shaking his head slightly as if waking from a dream. His blue eyes locked onto mine and it felt as if he was looking right into my soul. A pleasant warmth filled my belly.

What am I doing? I chided myself. *No men, no relationships.*

"I'm working on a series of photos depicting the beauty of the female form," he explained. "I'm using black and white film, and instead of shooting the whole body, I'm doing close up studies of individual parts. You know," he said, using his hands to draw shapes in the air, "the elegant shape of a hand, the round sensuous curve of a hip, the powerful tension of an extended leg, the strength and softness of a shoulder."

I could see in my mind's eye exactly what he was talking about, how each photo would look. A rush of excitement washed over me followed by a hollow envy.

He must have seen something in my eyes or sensed the shift in my mood because he abruptly stopped. "Sorry, I'm doing it again."

"Don't be, I was enjoying hearing about your work."

"Thanks, but enough about me. What made you come here on such an awful night? Was there a particular exhibit you came to see?"

"No, actually it's more along the same reason you came in here," I lied. No sense in dumping my current problems on a stranger, no matter how cute he was. "I was going to do some Christmas shopping after work, and when it started to snow, I came in here to warm up. I used to come here quite often, but it's been a while since I've had the time. Work, you know, keeps me busy."

"What kind of work would that be?"

Aaron's hands rested on the table dangerously close to mine. I gripped my coffee cup and took a sip, putting it back down again as far from his hands as I could. I wanted to reach out and touch them, to stroke his long fingers and feel the strength of them.

"It must be something mysterious and top secret."

I didn't want to tell him the truth. It was too depressing.

"You're right, it is very top secret. If I told you what I do for a living I'd have to kill you," I joked back.

"Good evening." The security guard approached our table. "I just wanted to let you two know that the museum is closing in a few minutes."

I started to gather my things, but Aaron spoke up. "Would you pose for me?"

I didn't know what to say. Was he hitting on me or did he really just want to take my picture? What would his girlfriend think?

"No, I don't think that would be a good idea." I stood up to leave.

"That came out wrong. I wasn't trying to pick you up, really I wasn't. I mean, not that any man with two eyes in his head wouldn't want to pick you up." He paused when I glared at him. "I'm making this worse aren't I? What I meant to say was that I would love to hire you as one of my models. I wasn't happy with the last one, she wasn't right. It was serendipitous that we ran into each other tonight. Your look would be perfect for what I'm trying to achieve."

"No, I don't think so, but thanks all the same."

"Well, if you change your mind, here's my card. And I pay a hundred and fifty dollars for the sitting."

"I'll think about it." I tucked his card in my purse. I really could use the money right now, but I had enough complications in my life and this just felt like another one, even if he did say it was just business.

We crossed the lobby together, and Aaron held the door open as we both stepped out into the wintry night. We were going in opposite directions, but before we parted, he tried again.

"Good night, Hannah; if you change your mind about sitting for me, please call me."

"Sure."

He looked like he was going to say something more, but instead he gave me a wave goodbye and turned around to walk home, his hands stuffed back into his pants pockets, his head bowed against the blowing snow.

I gathered my coat tightly around me against the bitter wind and headed for the bus stop. There was a shift in the core of my being as I trudged up the street. Aaron was right about one thing. It was serendipitous that we met again. His passion for his art was contagious. The pang of jealousy made me realize I missed painting, that certain thrill of creating. I wanted it back. I took our meeting as a sign, but not that I was going to pose for him. Instead, I felt it was a push from the universe. It was time to get my life in order. I didn't know how I was going to do it, but I felt a new resolve and quiet sense of peace as I boarded the bus home.

Chapter Twelve

A few days later, I followed through on my new resolve to change the things in my life that were no longer working for me. First, I gave my apartment a good going over. What better way to kick-start my new life than to start with a clean living space? I hadn't cleaned my apartment for months, and to describe my abode's current condition as a chaotic disaster was putting it mildly. After working all day at the spa and the time I put in helping Jas with her salon, I just didn't have the energy to keep up with my own housework.

Whom did I need to impress with a clean apartment and freshly laundered linens? Since Jas decided to open her own shop, she and I spent all of our time at her place, so no need to tidy up for her. And I was still avoiding her anyway. As far as visitors of the male persuasion were concerned, the two men who had been starring in my daydreams didn't care about the dust bunnies under the bed. That was the great thing about imaginary boyfriends; their expectations about housekeeping were rather low.

I pulled out all my cleaning supplies from under the sink, grabbed some clean rags and a bucket, and started in. I scrubbed every corner of my apartment, wiping away the dust and grime that had accumulated during my neglect.

In the bathroom, I pulled open the first drawer under the vanity and yanked out all of my makeup. I threw away half-empty tubes of lotions, eye shadows in colours I would never be caught dead in, and year old mascaras that flaked off the moment I put them on. I lined up all the unused products along the bathroom counter. It made me slightly nauseous when I counted fifteen lipsticks, their shrink-wrapped cellophane packaging still intact. Even with my ten percent staff discount, I was staring at hundreds of dollars of stuff I hadn't even opened. I put all the unopened cosmetics in a grocery bag. If Jas didn't want any of it, maybe some of the girls at the salon might.

I continued on, purging the space under the sink of half-empty bottles of shampoo, conditioner, and other hair products I had barely used. Then I scrubbed the sink, shower stall, and toilet until every surface gleamed. I left my spotless bathroom feeling pleased with the results. I removed the curtains from all the windows, stripped my bed, and headed down to the laundry room.

Back upstairs, I decided to take a break and grab something to eat while my sheets were in the laundry. I opened the fridge and stood staring, disappointed with the contents. It had been a while since I had grocery shopped. The only salvageable things were a couple of stale heels of bread and a small block of cheese with a little mold on the corner. I saved what cheese I could for my sandwich and threw the fuzz encrusted remains in the trash. In the cupboard, I found one, lonely can of tomato soup. I had to be satisfied making it with water because there wasn't any milk.

I sat down at the table with my watery tomato soup and stale toasted cheese sandwich. This was the first time I'd eaten at the table in months. Now that I'd cleaned up the stacks of papers, bills, and empty bags, I had more than enough space to put my bowl and plate on its now polished surface. Before I sat down, I grabbed the towering pile of mail I'd neatly stacked on the bookshelf.

I was on a de-cluttering roll, and I was determined to get my life in order. Nibbling on a corner of my sandwich I opened each envelope, sorted the bills into one pile and the empty envelopes and junk mail in another. I went through each bill noting the amount owing and the due date. I was disturbed to find a couple of final notices, one for my cell phone and the other for my maxed out Visa. That familiar dread started to build in the pit of my stomach and threatened to overwhelm me. I refocused on the bills in my hand.

My appetite disappeared. I pushed my untouched bowl of soup out of the way, splashing the table with the contents. Ignoring the mess, I spread out all my bills before me. I had deposited my paycheque in the bank machine in the morning so I knew exactly how much I had in my account. I figured I could pay my rent, my student loan payment, and part of my phone and Visa bills. That left me with a whopping $24.62 until next payday. Twenty-four dollars and sixty-two cents! How was I supposed to live on that for two weeks? Not to mention Christmas was just around the corner, and I hadn't bought a single present. I fought the urge to fling all the bills papering the table onto the floor and throw a first class fit. Instead, I took a deep breath and exhaled loudly.

Determined, I grabbed my cell phone and called up my banking app. before I could chicken out. I had just entered the last bill and hit pay when my phone rang. I hit answer at the same time I noted the caller id. I winced.

"Hello?"

"Hello, Hannah."

"Hi, mom. What's up?" My stomach dropped. She rarely called and never just to say hi. My mother was the one who called me at the Tack Shop, where I was working at the time, to tell me that Noni had died.

"I've been trying to reach Khandi to organize the final preparations for Christmas dinner but I keep getting her voicemail. I've tried Jasmine, but she hasn't returned my phone calls either," she huffed. "I find it inconsiderate to not promptly return phone calls."

Jas and her mom had shared Christmas dinner with us for three years. We were an odd collection of people but it seemed to work, and my mother actually got along with Khandi, which is something I never would have imagined.

"I think Khandi is on a business trip in Las Vegas; Jas mentioned she'd be back this weekend, and Jas probably hasn't had time to call you because she is busy trying to get her salon ready to open."

"She's opening her own salon?"

"Yes, she signed the lease back in October. She and I have been renovating the space."

"My, that girl's got drive. You could learn a thing or two from her."

I tucked the phone under my chin and picked up my discarded dinner. I threw out what was left of my sandwich and poured the runny soup down the drain. I snatched up the pile of junk mail and stuffed them into the garbage under the sink.

"Are you still there?"

"Yes, mom, I'm here."

"Tell Jasmine to get Khandi to call me as soon as she gets back. No, on second thought, just tell her to call me. I'd like to congratulate her on her good news. And if you are currently seeing someone, you can invite him too but I need to know right away so I know how many to expect for dinner."

"No, I'm not dating anyone right now."

"You still haven't met anyone yet? I don't understand, you're living in the city where there are lots of eligible men. What's wrong with you?"

"Mother, please, not tonight."

"You don't have to get snippy with me, young lady. I'm only concerned about your well-being. You're not getting any younger, and the selection of eligible men just keeps getting smaller as all the good ones get snatched up."

I rolled my eyes. "Mom, I've got to go. I'll let Jas know you called. Say hi to Da for me." I hung up before she could say anything more.

I paced my tiny apartment, trying not to let what my mother said get under my skin. Why did she always find a way to belittle me? I needed to get out of the apartment before I threw something.

I grabbed the laundry basket I'd left by the front door and was going to go down to the laundry to retrieve the curtains I'd put through the wash but before I could leave the apartment, my intercom buzzed.

It was Jas asking to come up. It wasn't movie night and it wasn't like her to just pop by without calling. I buzzed her in without asking her why she was coming by as I didn't want her standing outside on such a cold night. I opened the door a few seconds later to let her in.

"Hi, I'm so glad you're home." She was out of breath, and her nose glowed red from the cold. She carried a picnic basked in her gloved hands and as she stepped past me into the apartment I could smell snow clinging to her coat. "I tried calling earlier to say I was coming over, but it kept going to voicemail. I figured you were talking to your parents, so I took the chance that you would still be at home when I got here."

Of course, she guessed I was talking to my parents. If I'm not on the phone with her, my parents are really the only other people I talk to. And of course, I would be home. I only went out with her, so where else would I be?

Jas put the picnic basket down with a thump and threw her coat, scarf, hat, and gloves in a heap on my sofa. I gathered up her things and hung them neatly in the closet along with my own coat.

"Wow, someone's been busy. Can I hire you to clean my place next? It's an absolute disaster area. My roommates don't seem to care, and I haven't had a moment to spare on anything but getting the salon ready and working my hours at The Edge. Hey, you even cleaned off your table, perfect." She brought the basket closer to the table and started unpacking its contents. She pulled out a bottle of red wine, a lemon meringue pie, and a huge assortment of beauty products and placed this menagerie on the table.

"I need to decide what beauty products and lines to carry in the salon, and I thought what better way to figure it out than by having a spa night with someone who knows products and just happens to be my best friend," Jas explained. "And of course, you can't do this kind of heavy duty research without a little fortification." She pointed to the wine and dessert.

I knew this was her way of apologizing for what she said earlier, and my irritation lessened. Unlike my mother, who said hurtful things all the time and never said sorry, Jas really did care. This was turning out be a great evening after all.

Before I went downstairs to get my laundry, I handed her the bag of unopened spa products from the bathroom. I left her to continue unpacking her basket full of little tubes and jars of every conceivable beauty treatment.

Half a bottle of wine later, we managed to devour almost the whole pie while trying glycolic scrubs, wrinkle erasers, hydrating hand and foot treatments, and under-eye creams. We currently had a refining clay mask slathered on our faces. Jas reclined on the sofa while her mask hardened. She had two cotton pads infused with cucumber extract over her eyes. These pads promised to reduce puffiness and dark circles under the eyes.

I sat on the floor with my back resting against the sofa also with a mask hardening on my face and a recently refilled glass of wine in my hand. I had to purse my lips like a fish every time I took a sip of wine so I didn't crack the mask.

"Hannah," the mask restricted her ability to speak so her words came out sounding like she had a mouth full of cotton, "I'm sorry if I was a bit rough on you the night we painted my apartment. I only want you to be happy, and frankly, you've been spiraling down into a bit of a black hole. I know you've been avoiding me since then, and I don't want this to come between us." She pushed herself up on her elbows and removed her eye treatments so she could look at me.

"It's okay, really." I tried to talk around the clay tightening my face and I sounded as muffled and funny as Jas. "I'm ashamed to admit it, but I have been avoiding you. I was annoyed at first, but I've had some time to think about what you said. It's not you I'm mad at, it's me. I think that's what ticked me off the most. My life is a shambles, and I have no one to blame but myself."

I wanted to tell her about not getting a Christmas bonus and about the bills that needed to be paid. I wanted to share how scared I was, but I couldn't. I didn't want a repeat performance of our last conversation. I didn't want her to know how fucked up I really was.

"Are we still good?" I asked.

"Of course we are. I'm still your friend. Besides, it's a best friend's job to ride her girlfriend's ass when she gets off track, and I expect her to do the same for me."

"So noted." I took another careful sip of wine, grateful that the green clay mask hid the flush of irritation.

Why couldn't she have just said sorry and left it at that? I felt strange and uncomfortable sitting with Jas. It was the first time in our friendship that I was unsure of how to be with her. I wanted the weird feeling to go away.

"I've been meaning to tell you about this really cute guy I keep bumping into," I said, steering the conversation into neutral territory. I was referring to Christian, but I also wanted to tell her about Aaron. Telling her that I was attracted to two men, one who was already spoken for, was just asking for another unwanted advice session. That was the last thing I needed right now.

She sat up straight and perched herself on the edge of the sofa. "A guy? Do tell, and don't hold out on the juicy bits."

In her enthusiasm, she forgot to be careful about her facemask and it cracked in several places, making her look like some ancient mummy. Pieces of her mask flaked off, sprinkling her t-shirt.

I chuckled. "Why don't we wash this gunk off so that I can talk without the risk of my face cracking off? It looks like the masks are dry and you've just lost most of yours any way."

She went into the bathroom to rinse off the clay, and I headed into the kitchen to do the same. I rinsed my face and ran an evaluating finger over my skin. It felt soft and a bit tight. There was a nice tingly sensation on my cheeks.

"I really like the face mask." I walked into the bathroom and stood behind Jas.

She examined her face in the mirror as I looked over her shoulder. Our faces glowed and we both looked like we'd had a good night's rest.

"I think you're right." She lightly touched the delicate skin under her eyes. "The bags under my eyes seem to have disappeared. The eye treatments and the mask are definite keepers.

"Now, on to more important things." She steered me out of the bathroom and back to the couch. "I want details, lots of juicy details."

When we'd settled on the couch, I took a sip of wine.

"Hurry up girl, this is torture." She laughed.

"It's nothing really. I met this guy when I got my haircut. He was in for an appointment too and we said hello. Then I met him again at the Thorpe function at the spa. Actually, I almost knocked him over coming around a corner."

"What does he look like? Tall, dark, and handsome or short, pasty, and homely?"

"I have better taste than that. And don't even think about bringing up Mason. Anyway, he's about six-two, fabulous honey blonde hair; big, brown eyes with long lashes; and a body to die for."

"And how exactly do you know he has a body to die for, Hannah darling. Is there more to the story than you're telling me?"

"Well, when I ran into him, he accidentally exposed himself."

"What? How does somebody accidentally flash you? And does this pervert have a name?"

"It's not what you think, and, yes, his name is Christian."

"And?"

"He's not a pervert. I dropped a stack of towels when I ran into him and he bent down to help me. When he did, his robe came undone. And what's a girl to do in a situation like that? I had to look."

I started to giggle and couldn't stop. My laughing fit was contagious and within minutes, both of us doubled over, laughing hysterically, tears streaming down our faces. We'd found our comfortable rhythm again. The old us was back and it felt good.

Chapter Thirteen

There were only a few empty spots left at the far end of the parking lot when Jamie, Jas, and I arrived at the Karma Kafe. Jamie ignored them and aimed the car closer to the doors of the club.

"Jamie," Jas said as she applied lipstick using the mirrored visor on the passenger side of the car. "You're not going to get any closer. Just park the car already."

"Ha, Rock Star parking," Jamie said triumphantly, edging his apple green VW Beetle into a spot next to the entrance. "I'm telling you, it works every time. You ask your angels for Rock Star parking, and you always find a spot close to the door. And, Honey, in weather like this it pays to work with angelic forces if it means not having to dash across the lot in the freezing cold."

We all piled out of the car. Jas held out her hand to help me crawl out of the tiny back seat.

"Okay, Jamie, if you have a direct connection to divine forces, when you start working at my salon, could you ask them for Rock Star clients?" Jas teased as we headed into the Kafe.

"For you, *Mon Cherie*, anything." Jamie sent air kisses in her direction with the wave of his hand.

Once inside the club, we made our way to the long banquet tables that ran the length of the small space. A large window took up the whole wall behind the old worn leather benches. The view overlooked the bare tree limbs lining the streets of Marda Loop. Jas and I took a seat next to each other on the bench. Jamie pulled out a chair to sit opposite.

After the waitress took our drink orders—Cosmopolitans for Jas and I and a soda and lime for Jamie, Jamie entertained us with a running fashion commentary of the patrons seated around us, pointing out the good, the bad, and, as Jamie put it, "the let's not go there" disasters.

When the drinks arrived, Jamie raised his glass. "To Jas, on her last day of work at the Edge. And too much success at her own salon."

"To Jas," I chimed in.

I sipped my drink as I half listened to Jas and Jamie talk about work. They were going on about an unfortunate dye job that was supposed to be blonde but instead turned the colour of wasabi. I glanced around the room, enjoying the sound of their voices, the warmth of the club, the clatter of dishes coming from the kitchen, and the voices of the other patrons. Just for tonight, it felt good to forget about the dreariness of my current situation.

The little club was quickly filling up, and the noise level steadily increased from a low murmur to a loud din. The brisk business the Kafe was doing mid-week on a bleak winter evening was no doubt due to the homegrown talent that was about to take the stage. That was one of the reasons the three of us decided to face going out in the frigid night to celebrate.

The Karma Kafe was more artsy hangout than a club or restaurant. It was a place to hear great, local musicians and soak up the creative vibes. The club was in a narrow, brick building that wasn't much wider than an alleyway. A small, plywood platform tucked at the end of the long, dark wood bar served as a makeshift stage. Scarred concrete replaced the original flooring, and paintings from Calgary artists hung on the unevenly plastered, ochre-coloured walls. I sipped my drink as my eyes roamed over the canvases. A sharp stab of jealousy pierced my chest.

What would it feel like to have my art hanging here? I squashed the thought and the feeling with a large gulp of my drink.

An hour later, after we had finished a plate of Calamari and polished off several more drinks, the lights dimmed and the night's showcase artist, Amy Miller, stepped onto the stage, guitar in hand. She greeted the audience as she adjusted the microphone down to accommodate her barely five foot stature. The conversation in the room hushed as Amy strummed a few experimental chords. She introduced her first song, and then her smoky and surprisingly powerful voice filled the tiny space, mesmerizing the audience, including myself. Small, delicious shivers raced up my arms as I was swept up by her passion and the emotions of her lyrics. By the time Amy took her first break, the place was packed. It was standing room only. I was glad we had decided to come early.

During Amy's break, we were all ready for another round, but trying to get the attention of anyone to take our drink orders was turning out to be impossible. All the servers were being run off their feet trying to keep up with the orders. The waitresses struggled to make their way through the sea of people and had to hold their drink-laden trays high above their heads to avoid spilling their orders.

Finally, realizing the futility of our efforts, Jamie volunteered to hazard the crush of people to go to the bar and get our drinks himself. Jamie's progress was made considerably slower because he kept stopping along the way to chat to friends. Jamie had made it up to the bar and signaled the harried bartender when a splash of colour drifted past my peripheral vision.

I turned my head to see what had caught my eye. It was a man in a well-cut business suit and a flashy red tie. He stuck out like a sore thumb in the crowd of Boho artists. Definitely slumming it, probably amusing himself with how the other half lived. He made his way through the crowd with a relaxed gate. He didn't have to elbow his way through the press of bodies or shout 'excuse me' to people's backs blocking his path. Instead, the other people magically squashed into each other to make room for him when he passed. It was like he had an electrical field around him that drove back the crush of people, allowing him to walk unmolested through the throng.

I stared, fascinated, as the man headed in our direction. He was almost at our table before I recognized his face in the dim light of the club.

It was Christian. I couldn't believe it. What were the odds of seeing him again and here of all places?

I turned to tell Jas, but she had her back to me talking to a friend of hers at the next table. I tried to tug nonchalantly on her sleeve to get her attention before he closed the gap between us, but, before she could turn around, he was already standing above me. My heart was pounding.

"Hi, Hannah."

Finally, she turned around at the sound of his voice.

"Hey, Christian, what are you doing here?" I said, trying to sound cool.

"I imagine the same thing you are: enjoying the music, relaxing after a long day of work."

"So, do you come here often?" I cringed. I hadn't meant it to sound like some corny pick-up line. What I really wanted to ask was if someone like him really did hang out here.

"No, this is the first time I've been. I was in the neighborhood on business and didn't feel like going home. On the way to my car, I heard the music and decided to check it out. May I join you?"

"Sure."

Jas and I scooted down the bench seat to make room for him.

"Hi, I'm Christian." He held his hand out to Jas before he took his seat.

She took his hand and introduced herself. I felt like such a dork.

"Here comes your hostess with the mostest," sang out Jamie, as he plunked our drinks on the table. "Ladies, I can't believe you." He placed his hands on his hips. "I leave for a mere moment and you've already replaced me."

This time I was on the ball and introduced him to Jamie.

"Charmed." Jamie flashed Christian a big toothy grin.

Jamie passed around our drinks and settled into his chair. Amy was making her way back up to the stage when Christian held up his hand to catch the eye of a waitress. One materialized instantly and took his drink order. I glanced over at Jamie. He raised an eyebrow at Jas, but before I could figure out what it meant, Amy started to sing, and everyone turned their attention to her performance.

As much as I loved listening to Amy's music, I couldn't concentrate on her singing with Christian sitting so close. He looked great and smelled even better. Then he did something that had me gulping for air. Ever so slowly, he moved closer to me, keeping his eyes focused on the stage. When our knees touched, I could feel the heat of him sending jolts of excitement up my leg. My stomach muscles tightened in anticipation.

He continued to sip his drink one handed while he casually slipped his other hand under the table. He slowly placed it on my thigh, his fingers drawing lazy circles across the fabric of my skintight jeans. I almost stopped breathing. I gulped down the rest of my drink and tried to focus the performance.

When the song ended, I clapped, along with everyone else. I nodded my head when Jamie glanced my way as if nothing was going on under the table.

Jas leaned over and whispered something to me, but I couldn't make sense of her words. I just nodded agreement and that seemed to do the trick. When Amy's second set was over and she'd left the stage, Jamie was the first to speak.

"So, tell me about yourself."

Christian put both hands on the table as if he hadn't been doing anything at all and gave me a quick glance before responding to Jamie's question. A crooked smile played over his lips. I couldn't read his expression. Was it amusement or desire?

"What would you like to know?"

"For starters, where did the two of you meet?"

"Actually," I interrupted. "We just keep bumping into each other. This is the third time we've met up by accident."

"And what do you do for a living?" Jamie continued.

"I run a company."

"What kind of company: oil and gas, cattle? Would I have heard of it?"

"I don't know, have you heard of Thorpe Industries?"

"I may be a hair stylist but you would have to be dead not to have heard about the biggest Oil and Gas distributor in Western Canada. So you're what, a manager of one of their departments or a trader?"

"No, I'm the CEO."

"Wow, you don't look old enough to be the head of a corporation. How did you manage that? Marry the boss's daughter?"

I tried to kick Jamie under the table, but all I connected with was air.

"No, I'm the boss's son."

Christian was *the* Christian Thorpe. I tried not to look shocked.

Jas chuckled under her breath.

"Touché," Jamie said, finally backing down.

I didn't know what to think. Christian's leg was still snuggled up close to mine and any coherent thought seemed an impossible challenge.

Christian suggested another round of drinks on him and again magically summoned a waitress out of thin air.

Before Amy came onto the stage for her last set of the evening, he had completely charmed Jamie. It was a good thing that he was straight or I would have had some serious competition where Jamie was concerned.

Jas was a different story. When Christian asked her questions, she would only answer in one-word sentences. I gave her a nudge under to table to ask what was up, but she ignored me and remained uncharacteristically cool with him.

When Amy started to sing again, Christian repeated his performance of fondling my leg under the table, his hand slowly creeping up to the crease in my jeans. Even though I was focused on what was happening under the table, I had enough presence of mind to notice that a guy I didn't recognize had joined our table. He was whispering something to Jas, but I couldn't hear what they were talking about over the music.

Suddenly, Christian's wandering hand had my complete focus. As much as I was enjoying our little under-the-table tryst, he was about to cross the line from a public display of affection to something that should be done behind closed doors. I dropped my hand under the table and placed it on his before he went too far. I stole a quick glance at him. He smiled and curled his fingers around mine.

The last set was over. Amy took her bows, the bartender announced last call, and the house lights came up. I blinked while my eyes tried to adjust to the change of light.

"Christian, it was nice meeting you," Jas said.

It wasn't until then that I noticed the guy who had been sitting next to Jas was gone. Jas put her purse on the table and stood up, a sure sign she wanted to leave.

"It was nice to meet you too. Why don't we have once last round before we call it a night."

"I don't know about you guys, but I have to work in the morning and I need my beauty sleep," Jamie said. "I have a full day tomorrow, and since I'm the designated driver that means the girlies are leaving too."

"Come on, ladies, stay for another drink." Christian looked at me.

"Let's stay for just one more drink," I pleaded to Jas.

"No, I don't think so. It's late, I'm tired, and I think we need to get going."

"Don't be such a party pooper. One more little drink isn't going to hurt."

"If you'll excuse me, I need to visit the ladies room." Jas pinned me with a stare that said I should follow her if I valued my life.

I told Christian I'd be right back and excused myself from the table. When I stood up, I was surprised how light-headed I was. I didn't feel drunk, but the room had a definite tilt to it, which made negotiating my way to the bathroom a bit challenging.

By the time Jas pushed the door open to the Ladies' Room, I was more than a little annoyed. She had been cool all night, and that last display was downright rude. Before I had a chance to give her a piece of my mind she turned on me with barely concealed anger.

"What the hell do you think you're doing?"

"Hey, hold on a minute. What's up with the attitude?" I took a step back.

"It's your attitude that's up. Do you think getting drunk and making out with a stranger is the way to make yourself happy?"

"Excuse me?" I said, raising my voice. "I can't believe you have the nerve to stand there judging my behavior when I saw you doing the same thing yourself with that guy you'd just met."

"The big difference is all I'm going home with tonight is that guy's phone number. You must really be drunk if you think talking to a guy and what you and that sleaze bucket were doing under the table are the same thing."

"I'm not drunk, and how dare you criticize Christian! He's a successful business man, not some greasy low life."

"How could you be so stupid? First, you get involved with Mason, the loser of the century, and now you allow a guy you barely know to play table tango with you. Did you not learn anything after what Mason did to you? This *businessman* plies you with drinks all night and you let him feel you up under the table. What do you think he wants from you?" she said, getting in my face.

"How dare you! Despite what you think, I'm not a slut and I am not stupid! And right now, I don't need you to tell me what to do. You can go home like a good little girl, but I'm staying."

I pushed past her, but she grabbed me by the shoulders and spun me around.

"If you aren't going to be reasonable, at least have the common sense to be safe. You don't have cab fare. Here, take this." Jas jammed a handful of bills into my closed fist. They fluttered to the floor. "I'm too tired to stand here arguing with you. I'm going home. I just don't want to see you hurt again. For your own sake, ask yourself if this guy is worth it." She left me alone in the bathroom.

I stood there breathing hard and trying not to cry.

The door swung open a few seconds later as someone else came in to use the washroom. I quickly picked up the crumpled bills and stuffed them in the pocket of my jeans. I stood in front of the sink looking in the mirror, trying to get my anger under control. My mascara had smeared, creating unattractive dark smudges under my eyes. I ran some water on a paper towel and fixed my face. I put on a fresh coat of lipstick, my hand shaking with anger. I took a deep breath and headed back to the table.

When I returned to the table, Christian sat alone, two drinks in front of him. Jas and Jamie had left. I sat down across from him where Jamie had been sitting. There were a few moments of uncomfortable silence as we sipped our drinks. Christian put his drink down and looked at me. Under his gaze, a pleasant warmth spread up my neck and into my cheeks.

"I can't think of a better way to end my day than sharing a drink with someone I find so intriguing."

"So how long have you worked for Thorpe Industries?" I asked, changing the subject.

"Almost as long as I can remember. My dad didn't believe in handing things to his kids. I had to earn my way from the bottom up. I started working part-time in the mailroom when I was in high school. All through University, I worked summers in the Brook's oil patch as a roughneck. When I graduated, I was hired on in the Acquisitions Department, and over the years, I worked my way up from there." He paused for a moment to take a slow sip of his scotch. "How long have you worked at the spa?"

I should have seen that one coming. "I've been there for three years. I got on with them as soon as I graduated from beauty school."

"Do you enjoy what you do?"

What is it with everyone lately? Why do they all want to know if I like what I do?

I was going to give him a pat answer about liking the people and finding satisfaction in a job well done, but when I looked into his eyes, I didn't want to lie.

"No, I don't. If you had asked me that question even a year ago, I would have answered differently. Now everything seems to have changed." I paused for a moment trying to collect my thoughts. "No, maybe it's me that has changed. It's not enough anymore. Does that make sense?"

"Yes, yes it does, if your work is not what you find fulfilling."

I couldn't believe we were having this conversation. He actually wanted to find out who I was. Jas was so wrong about him.

"I used to think I could spend my life painting. Noni, my grandmother, taught me to hold a paintbrush before I could even walk. She was an accomplished artist, but after she got married, she focused on raising her daughter and running her home. I've never thought about this before, but now I wonder if she was really happy. I mean, she gave up a life of painting, travel and the experience of being on her own with no responsibilities, and for what? For a life of home and family. Of housecleaning and farm duties. She never seemed unhappy or unfulfilled, not like my mother, but it never occurred to me until now to ask her."

I suddenly felt lonely even though I was sitting sharing my thoughts with this amazing man. I missed my grandmother. I wanted her back. I wanted to ask her if she was happy. Now I would never have the chance. A lump closed my throat, and I thought I was going to cry.

"Your grandmother sounds like an amazing person," Christian said, pulling me out of my thoughts.

"She is. I mean, she was. She passed away recently."

"I'm sorry for your loss. It must have been hard on you."

"It was and it still is. Noni was the kind of person that made you believe you could be whatever you wanted to be. She believed in me."

"I know how hard it can be when you lose someone you love," he said softly. "I lost my mom to cancer when I was twelve, and for a long time, I felt like I was just drifting in a horrible sea of pain."

I didn't know what to say.

"So, why aren't you painting?"

"When Noni passed away, it happened so fast we didn't even know she was ill. After she was gone, nothing was the same." I cleared my throat. "My mother said I needed to be more realistic, and instead of working part-time jobs that paid nothing while I painted, I needed to find a career. Being an esthetician was the best thing I could come up with considering how much money I had in the bank. The training only took a year, and it didn't seem like a completely awful job to get into."

That sounded completely lame. Had I really derailed my life because being an esthetician didn't seem awful?

"I guess I really did it just to get my mother off my back and to get away from the farm," I said, finally admitting the truth.

"So do you see your parents often since moving to the city?"

I sipped my drink and lowered the glass slowly and carefully on to the table. "Seeing as I don't own a car and I can't keep asking my da to drive me back and forth to the city, I don't see my parents much lately. I do miss him, but my mother is a different story." I felt guilty admitting this when Christian had to grow up without one. "We get on each other's nerves. We just don't see eye to eye on anything. I mean, we are just so different."

"Or maybe you are too much alike?"

"Oh no, if you'd ever met my mother you'd never even suggest something like that. Do you see your dad much?"

He swirled the scotch in his glass. The ice made a seductive clinking sound. He put his elbows on the table and leaned forward resting his chin on his hands.

"Yeah, I see him quite a bit, actually. Usually once a week I have lunch with him. Although he's retired, he likes to hear how work is going, and I'm happy to oblige. I have a sister, Claire. She lives in Vancouver. She designs one-of-a-kind jewelry, so when she is heading to New York, Toronto, or Montreal to meet with her clients, she usually stops in to see me. I'd like to see her more often, but we're both so busy with our work that scheduling time is almost impossible. I usually head down to see her once a year, get caught up with her, and spend some time soaking up the West coast vibe and relax by the ocean."

I smiled and picked up my drink. I waited to swallow before saying anything, using the time to choose my words carefully. "When your mother died how long did it take for you to feel...normal? What I mean is, when did the—"

"Hurt go away?"

I nodded.

"It never does. The pain of missing her, of wanting my mother back, is always there but the intensity has diminished. I think I was about eighteen and out of the house before I could take a deep breath without feeling intense physical pain. It took longer before I could laugh and enjoy myself without feeling guilty."

"About what? You have nothing to feel guilty about. You didn't cause her cancer."

"No, I didn't feel guilty about that but about living and enjoying my life when she couldn't. Isn't that what you're doing now?"

"Excuse me?"

"You know, not painting, working in a job you hate. Aren't you punishing yourself by denying yourself the things that give you pleasure out of some misplaced feeling of guilt?"

I clasped my hands and rested them on the table as I leaned back in my chair, willing myself not to let my defensiveness show on my face.

"Christian, I'm not holding myself back because of guilt. Following dreams takes money, money I don't have." The muscles in my jaw tightened.

"Please forgive me." He placed his hand on mine. His touch seared my skin. "I didn't mean to judge your choices in life and I don't presume to understand what your grief feels like for you. If I've brought up a subject that makes you uncomfortable I am sorry."

I relaxed my hands. Christian's fingers curled around my open palm and squeezed my hand gently. His touch sent shivers up my arm and my heart raced. I'd never been so physically attracted to a man. Someone who made my body respond as if it was running a marathon, and I liked it. I'd never met a man like him: successful, handsome, thoughtful, and sensitive.

"No, you don't have to apologize. It's just that everyone I know—and even some I don't—has been asking me that very question and it unnerves me. Money is an issue, but it's not the whole reason I still work at the spa. The truth is simple. I'm afraid. I'm afraid that if I pursue my painting as a career and discover I have no talent, that I suck miserably at it, then I'll have no dream left. That thought frightens me. Frightens me into doing absolutely nothing."

I had said more than I intended, and now Christian just sat there saying nothing, his brown eyes gazing intently into mine, still holding my hand. My hand felt clammy and his simple gesture way too intimate. I gently pulled my hand free of his grasp. I hugged myself tightly. I had to get out of here, away from him, before I did something really childish like cry.

"Hey, I didn't mean for this evening to get all heavy," Christian said. "The night's still young. Let me redeem myself. Give me a chance to cheer you up. What do you say we get out of here and head over to my place for a nightcap? The waitress is starting to give us the evil eye. Just one quick drink and then I'll drive you home. It's the least I can do for bringing up such painful memories. And I've had such a good time with you."

I could hear Jas's disapproving voice telling me to stop being so stupid. I should call a cab and go home, but I didn't want to. I didn't see why I wasn't allowed to have some fun, especially when my life sucked so badly lately. And where did she get off telling me how to live my life. Little Ms. Perfect.

"I'd really like that." I gathered up my jacket.

Christian put his arm around me and led me out the door. This time, his touch was comforting.

On the ride to his place, my liquor consumption and the late hour finally caught up with me. My eyelids were heavy, and I fought to keep them open. Soft music floated from the CD player as we drove, and before I knew it, I dozed off.

Someone softly caressing my cheek and neck roused me from my nap. I sighed and opened my eyes. Christian leaned over, cupped my head in both his hands, and kissed me, long and slow.

"Wake up sleepy head. We're here." He brushed a stray hair out of my eyes.

I sat up and looked around. We were parked on a street of brownstones. The large elms lining the boulevard were dressed for the holiday season, their bare branches dripping with tiny white faerie lights that twinkled in the velvety night. Christian's residence had large sandstone steps leading to an elegant black lacquered door sporting a large brass doorknocker. A few lights glowed invitingly behind the sheer curtains that hung in the tall, narrow windows on the main floor.

When I stepped into the small foyer with its high ceiling, my first impression was of a comfortable, welcoming home. A narrow staircase was to the left of the entryway. I leaned against the handrail to unzip my boots. The solid oak handrail was soft and solid under my hand, the wood worn smooth from countless hands running down its length over the years. I removed my boots and placed them neatly next to each other on the white and black marble tile floor.

I followed him into the small front parlor. I was still a little tipsy and held the wall for support. The warm honey-coloured walls and soft lighting accentuated the cozy feeling. The overstuffed maroon sofa almost dominated, but the main feature of the room was the floor to ceiling bookcase that lined the wall opposite the fireplace. An antique oriental carpet, faded with age, covered the deliberately scuffed oak floor.

Christian walked over to the fireplace, which was already stacked with kindling and logs. He lit a long wooden match and touched the flame to the kindling. The fire started effortlessly. He rose in one fluid movement and turned to me.

"May I get you a drink?" He casually draped my coat across the back of the sofa and added his suit jacket.

I was going to suggest coffee to sober me up, but I didn't want him to think I was drunk. "Yes, whatever you're having would be fine."

He headed to the kitchen at the back of the house. While he was gone, I toured the room, letting my fingertips caress the leather spines of the books on the shelves. Chaucer, Byron, the Bronte sisters, a collection of poetry and plays by Shakespeare. I tipped one of the books out to examine it closer but it wouldn't budge. I took a closer look and realized that the shelves weren't stacked full of books after all. These were all fakes, just the covers were real, to create the illusion of a library full of old books.

I looked around at the rest of the room. A large bronze Buddha head took centre stage on the fireplace mantle, complemented by two large chunks of uncut amethyst and a few beeswax pillar candles.

Then I spied the painting on the far wall. It depicted a stand of dark pines bent from the strong ocean breeze. The sky was a moody greenish yellow. I walked over to take a closer look. I couldn't believe it. It was *Pine Island*, by Tom Thomson and it wasn't a print. It was the original.

Christian tapped me lightly on the shoulder and placed a wine glass in my hand. The bowl of the goblet was huge, the crystal impossibly thin and delicate. The red wine tasted of berries and black pepper.

"You like Thomson?"

"Yes, it's beautiful."

"So does it meet with your approval?"

"The wine or your painting?"

"Both."

Instead of answering, I moved closer to him I only intended to give him a quick kiss, but when our lips touched, there was that pull again. He must have felt it too, because he drew me in closer before I had a chance to step back.

He grabbed a handful of my hair and tilted my head back. My lips were only inches from his. The anticipation was unbearable. The heat of the kiss overwhelmed me. I mirrored the hunger and urgency of Christian's kisses as our bodies melded together. When we both came up for air, I was lightheaded. My lips tingled. I stepped away from him trying to catch my breath.

"What's wrong?"

"I was just thinking, maybe this wasn't such a good idea. I have to work tomorrow, and it's already late. I should really get going."

"You're right. It's late. But before you go could I have one request."

"Mm."

"One dance. May I have one dance with you? Then I'll bundle you up and drive you home safe and sound."

I laughed.

He must have taken that as a yes. He took my wine glass and put it down on the coffee table with his own. Then he reached over and picked up a remote from the mantle, hit a button, and Holly Cole's voice floated down from speakers hidden somewhere in the bookshelves. The fire crackled and popped, filling the room with the sweet smell of wood smoke.

Christian gathered me in his arms. We slow danced, my head resting on his broad chest. He drew me in closer. His hands drifted slowly down my back, his fingers tracing the outline of my spine. His touch sent shivers rippling over my skin. He rested his hands on my hips, while we moved to the soulful music.

Lifting my head off his chest, I laced my fingers behind his neck. I stepped in closer, the evidence of his arousal hard against my belly. I swayed my hips in slow drawn out circles. A small voice in the back of my head whispered for me to stop. I'd had too much to drink, it was late, and I had to work tomorrow. I ignored the voice.

When we kissed again, it was full of need and hunger.

The logs shifted, with a whoosh of sparks, and the room brightened as the flames leaped and danced higher.

Christian smoothly guided me backwards across the room to the sofa and slowly lowered me onto the plush, down-filled cushions. Our kissing became more urgent. He tasted of wine. He pulled away grazing his teeth lightly along my jaw, tracing a line down my neck. A sigh escaped my lips.

A raw sexual excitement pulsed from every cell of my being. Mason's adolescent fumbling couldn't compare to the erotic pleasure of Christian's touch. All reason evaporated.

He cupped my breast and made slow torturous circles with his thumb. My nipple was taut, pressing against the fabric of my sweater, making the sensation unbearable. I arched my back as he slipped his hand under my sweater and pushed the lacy fabric of my bra out of his way. The heat of his hand on my bare skin sent new ripples of pleasure coursing down between my legs. He groaned deep in his throat.

After tugging his shirttails out from the waistband of his dress pants, I snuck my hands under his shirt, running my fingers over his sinewy back.

He lifted my sweater up higher, and I helped him pull it over my head and drop it onto the floor. He slipped his hand behind my back and unhooked my bra; the flimsy garment joined my sweater. He looked at my naked breasts and then into my eyes. His lids were hooded, his eyes glazed with hunger. Slowly he lowered his head to take me into his mouth. His mouth hot on my skin, he sucked and teased my nipples, taking his time until I burned with longing.

Everything in the room fell away by degrees. I could no longer hear the crackle of the fire, or the music, or smell the fragrant wood smoke. The lights dimmed; colours blended. All that was left was infinite sensation. The taste of his skin, the pounding of my heart, the quickening of my passion.

I pushed my hips into him, grinding urgently, telegraphing my deepening need. My hands sought the buttons of his shirt and I fumbled to pull it off. I needed to feel his flesh on mine, to feel the weight and strength of his body. He helped me with the last few buttons and we lay down, skin to skin.

All rational thought vanished as our hot bodies collided. Christian slowly, deliberately unzipped my jeans and slid his hand down between my legs. His expert touch made me wet with desire. I held my breath. My pleasure intensified, building wave upon wave, until I thought I would explode into a million sparks of pure bliss. I cried out as I slipped over the edge into ecstasy.

Chapter Fourteen

I rode my horse, Geronimo, at a full gallop through the trees; the wind whipping my hair and the purple scarf around my neck. It felt so good to be riding again. I hadn't been out with Geronimo in such a long time. Although we were hurtling past the trees at breakneck speed, Geronimo didn't slow or break his stride. I glanced down at my naked arms. Not only were my arms naked but so also, it seemed, was the rest of me, with the exception of the scarf around my neck. Tearing through the forest Godiva-like, in the dead of winter didn't seem odd or alarming to me. I was free and it felt exhilarating.

The wind picked up and brought with it an angry blizzard. Moments ago, the sun had been glistening off the snow banks, now the sky turned pitch black—no moon, no stars, just the howl of a vicious wind and the lashing of snow against my naked body. Icy fingers of fear raced up my spine. Geronimo faltered. We were both lost, and I was afraid. The sound of hooves thundered out of the churning whiteness heading towards us.

The joy I had felt moments ago was a distant memory, replaced with blood chilling fear. Whatever or whoever was chasing me was gaining ground fast. Geronimo hurtled us blindly through the trees; the branches scratched my face and tangled in my hair. I risked looking over my shoulder to see how close my pursuer was and I almost lost my seat. I dug my knees into Geronimo's flanks and pulled myself upright.

Geronimo stumbled again but this time he didn't recover. He went down hard, taking me with him. I hit the ground with such force it knocked the wind out of me and left me stunned in the snowdrift. I couldn't see anything but swirling needles of snow. I sensed Geronimo getting to his feet and racing off into the blinding whiteness, leaving me alone to face the evil that was approaching.

The snow burned my exposed flesh. I tried to scramble out of the path of the dark terror, but I wasn't fast enough. A deadly sharp hoof slammed down on my head. I squeezed my eyes shut and screamed.

* * * * *

I sat up in bed clutching the bed sheets, trying to catch my breath. My heart hammered painfully in my chest. I looked around the room, disoriented.

Was I still dreaming? This wasn't my bed, or my apartment. I was in a massive, mahogany, sleigh bed surrounded by a mountain of pillows. Then the events of last night tumbled back into lucid detail.

After our romp on the couch, when the passion had clouded my brain cells and I was at the point of no return, he scooped me up in his arms and carried me upstairs. Our hunger for each other had not diminished as he carefully laid me on his bed.

I blushed when I remembered our lovemaking. Under his skilled hands, I'd climaxed before he even entered me. The second release left me spent and totally blissed out. I'd never had two orgasms in one night. I hugged my knees, smiling at my wild abandon. No guilt here.

I looked around. I was alone in the bedroom but I could smell fresh brewed coffee and hear the muffled sounds of someone moving around downstairs.

I urgently needed to pee. Not able to wait any longer, I slipped off the bed and quickly padded over the thick beige carpet to the bathroom. As I passed our crumpled pile of clothes, I plucked Christian's dress shirt off the top, a smile playing on my lips at the thought of how they got there. Buttoning up his shirt, I caught a faint whiff of his aftershave.

Before I left the bathroom, I placed a blob of toothpaste on my finger and used this impromptu toothbrush to rid myself of my fuzzy morning mouth. It wasn't perfect, but I felt better. While I made my way back to the bed, the door opened and Christian backed into the room carrying a breakfast tray. He turned around and his eyes roamed over me in my improvised nightshirt.

"Good morning." He placed the breakfast tray on one of the nightstands. "That shirt looks ten times better on you."

I crawled back onto the bed and leaned forward to kiss him. Thank God, I used the toothpaste. He reached over and placed the tray on the bed in front of me.

There was a French press filled with a dark fragrant brew, a white plate filled with warm croissants, small crystal dishes with butter and strawberry preserves. I poured two cups of coffee, handed one to Christian, splashed some cream, and added two sugar cubes to mine. He joined me on the bed and we tucked into our little breakfast.

I took another sip of coffee to wash down the buttered flakiness of the warm croissant when I happened to look over at the alarm clock on the nightstand.

"Please tell me that is not the right time."

"As far as I can tell, yes it is." His eyes twinkled.

I pushed the tray aside and scrambled to gather my clothes. "Oh my God, I'm going to be late for work."

"Feel free to have a shower," He said, munching on a croissant and watching me flail around madly.

I took up his offer and jumped into the massive marble walk-in shower. The steamy water revived me, but I was still in a haze of panic. I only had thirty minutes to get to work. I dried myself off using a thick, white towel and stepped into my clothes from yesterday.

Christian knocked on the door as I was trying to brush out the tangles in my wet hair. He handed me a new toothbrush still wrapped in its cardboard tube.

"Found this in the guest bathroom, thought you might need it."

I snatched it out of his hands. "Thanks, you're a life saver."

Having clean teeth made a world of difference in how I felt, but I was still going to be late. I finished detangling my hair and hurriedly brushed my teeth.

Showered, dressed, teeth cleaned, and smelling of Christian's deodorant (I had to use something), I thundered down the stairs to grab my coat. Christian, still dressed in just a pair of his PJ bottoms, followed me. He helped me on with my coat then disappeared into the kitchen.

"Let me drive you to work," he said, returning to the hall. He kissed my forehead and handed me a travel mug full of coffee.

I realized I didn't know where I was. I was asleep when we pulled up last night.

"Where are we, exactly?" I felt stupid asking. I pulled on my dress boots.

He told me his address, and I couldn't believe my luck: I was only four blocks from work.

"Thanks for the offer of the ride, but it'll take longer to warm up the car. I can be there in no time if I hustle."

He pulled me in for a hug and a long kiss. "Have a good day. Call me later."

"Don't you have to work today?"

"No, it's Sunday. I do have some paperwork to look at, but I can do that here in my home office."

We kissed again, then I dashed out the door and down the stairs. I took a quick sip of my coffee and burned my tongue. I waved goodbye to Christian while he stood in the doorway watching me go. He waved back, and I headed off.

The morning sky was low and heavy, the clouds covering every inch of blue. The greyness of the sky bled and blended with the grey of the office buildings. I was breathless by the time I got to work, and, other than that first sip, I hadn't touched my coffee. I had a splitting headache, and, even though it was overcast, the light hurt my eyes. God, this was going to be a long day.

I didn't have my access card with me so I scooted through the salon to get to the back corridor. Jamie fluttered his fingers in a surprised hello. He gave me a quick once over. I knew what he was thinking. I was still dressed in the clothes from last night. I cringed, knowing that with one quick call from Jamie, Jas would be hearing about this by the time I headed down to the break room.

"I'm late, don't have time to talk," I said as I made a quick detour. I headed to the nearest empty hair station and grabbed an elastic from one of the trays, and, without breaking my stride, headed out the back door and into connecting corridor. I raced downstairs and into the break room. Ruth nodded a hello and gave me a smile, but not before I noticed her looking at the clock.

"I know, I know, I'm late." I opened my locker. Thank God I always kept a spare uniform in there. Although I never expected it would come in handy because I had spent the most amazing night having sex with an absolute dream of a man.

"You're lucky you-know-who isn't here today, being his day off. But if you don't hightail it upstairs, someone's going to notice and tattle on you." Ruth closed the washing machine and hit the start button.

I scrambled into my uniform. I was just about to tell her about Christian when one of the laundry staff came through the door, wheeling an empty linen cart ahead of her.

"See you later, Ruth," I called out while I ran down the corridor. I scrambled upstairs, grabbed my schedule, and rushed to my first client.

I thanked my lucky stars that this was Terence's day off. I wasn't naive enough to think I would get off Scot-free for being late. One of his minions would report to him, but I didn't care. What I did care about was getting another cup of coffee at the first available opportunity.

I stumbled through the day, my only focus to make it to quitting time. My headache got worse as the day progressed, and by lunchtime, except for two bites of a croissant, all I had consumed was coffee, gallons of it. My nerves were thrumming from the coffee and emotionally I was a mess. When I wasn't thinking about Christian and our night together, I was fuming about Jas.

What had gotten into her lately? I was getting sick of Ms. High-and-mighty's attitude. Her words last night really hurt. Was that what she really thought of me? That I was a slut? That someone like Christian couldn't possibly be interested in plain old boring me? I know I slept with him on the first date, but it wasn't like I'd just met him.

Since deciding to open her own business, Jas hadn't been dating. She probably couldn't stand the idea that Christian was interested in me and not her. The whole being her own boss thing was starting to go to her head. I wasn't sure if I wanted to call her and give her a piece of my mind or just ignore her.

I pushed these prickly feelings down and focused on getting through the day. I fueled myself with so much coffee that, by quitting time, I still felt like a dog's breakfast—but now I had the caffeine jitters. Not a good combination. I tried to sleep on the bus ride home, but the caffeine jolted constantly through my system. Even my fingers were vibrating. I decided to call Christian as soon as I got home, and since I couldn't sleep on the bus, I used the time to work up my courage.

Once home, I showered, changed into sweats, and warmed up a can of tomato basil soup. While my soup was heating, I pulled out my cell and looked him up on Canada 411. He had told me to call him later, and I figured—in my rush to get out the door—he just forgot to give me his number.

I quickly dialed the number before I lost my nerve. My heart tripped painfully in my chest. His voice came on the line and, for a moment, the sound of his deeply sexy voice had me right back in bed with him. It took a beat before I realized I was listening to his voicemail. I spoke quickly, giving my name and my home phone and cell numbers before I hung up.

My soup was bubbling over on the stove. I poured it in a mug and took it with me as I climbed into bed. I propped several pillows behind my head and slowly drank my dinner. I left the TV and the radio off. My head was still killing me and all I really craved at that moment, other than being with Christian, was peace and quiet.

I listened to my empty apartment—the murmuring of the fridge and the hiss and clank from the radiators. My eyes kept wandering over to Noni's painting. I wanted to reach out and turn it around so she would stop staring at me. I knew that was childish. Besides, Noni wouldn't judge me; she had taken a lover in Paris when she was there studying art. She would understand.

The phone interrupted the whispers of my quiet room, and when I scrambled across the bed to answer it, I spilled soup down my sweatshirt and onto the duvet. I didn't care. I needed to hear Christian's voice.

"Hi." It was Jas. The last person I felt like talking to.

"Hey," I said, getting out of bed.

"I was just calling to see if we were still on for tomorrow."

Shit, I forgot I had promised her I would help move her things into her new place tomorrow. Even though Noni had been a free spirit when it came to many things, the one thing she had been strict on was honoring commitments. She had taught me that along with how to blend colours and creating light and shadows with pigments. God, having a deeply ingrained conscience about keeping promises sucked when it involved the best friend you are currently really mad at.

"Yup," I put my cup in the sink.

"You're still pissed at me aren't you?"

"Yup." I grabbed the dishrag hanging over the sink and proceeded to smush the tomato stain deeper into the fabric of my top.

"Please don't be mad. I was just concerned about you. You'd had too much to drink, and I was worried about your safety."

"You can stop worrying. I'm home, I'm safe, and I didn't do anything stupid. Contrary to what you and Jamie think, I'm a big girl, and I can take care of myself."

"You're right. I went a little overboard last night. I would hate for a rift to happen between us because of something I said out of love for you."

I hated when she did that. She had to play the 'I love you' card. Part of me agreed with her. We'd never had a fight like this. We'd never screamed at each other or called each other names. The thought of not having Jas in my life made me feel hollow.

"Please say something."

"What you said really hurt. I don't want to lose you as a friend, but I think for now I really need you just to drop it, okay? I don't want to talk about last night. I'll see you tomorrow."

I hung up the phone feeling awful. I checked my messages, but Christian hadn't called while I was on the line with Jas. I fell asleep waiting for his call.

Chapter Fifteen

I was having a wonderful dream involving Christian, a sandy beach, and a beautiful sunset, when I awoke to the sound of my door intercom bleating. I tried to ignore it, but then I realized what day it was. Moving day. It was Jas buzzing to come up. I had overslept again. I must have forgotten to set the alarm.

I stumbled out of bed. I threw off my soup-stained sweatshirt and replaced it with a clean t-shirt as I ran to buzz her in. Somehow, I managed to get my arms tangled in the sleeves and I struggled in vain to extricate myself. I ran over to the intercom with my shirt still stuck over my head, my arms raised above me at awkward angles.

"Hello," I said through the fabric of my shirt while I pressed the talk button with my elbow.

"Hi. You ready to go?" Her voice came out of the intercom, crackling with static.

"Yeah, I'm on my way. Did you want to come up?" I asked, finally getting my shirt on.

"No, if you're already on your way down, I'll just wait for you in the van. I left it running."

I dashed to the bathroom, brushed my teeth, downed three extra strength Tylenol, stuffed my feet into my boots, grabbed my coat, and flew down the stairs.

A 15-foot U-Haul truck was idling at the curb when I stepped out onto the street. Jas was already back behind the wheel. She had sweet-talked two burly bouncers from one of the clubs Khandi worked for into schlepping all the heavy pieces of furniture to the salon in another truck. They were probably already on their way. Knowing Jas, she probably insisted she be the one to drive this behemoth because, never having driven a big moving truck before, she thought it would be fun.

I climbed up into the passenger side of the cab. The snow had stopped for the moment, but the early morning air was still bitterly cold. It was just beginning to lighten and a thousand twinkling stars still pinpricked the inky sky. The cab was toasty warm; the heater, turned on high, blasted dry hot air into the space.

"I can't believe this day is finally here," I said as Jas negotiated the merge onto Deerfoot Trail, the main freeway that connected the North and South sides of the sprawling city.

She looked so tiny behind the wheel of the large vehicle. I felt a stab of guilt about all the nasty things I'd been thinking about her. Why was I being such a jerk?

The last time the van had been serviced must have been before I was born. The shocks were completely shot, and when Jas accelerated to the speed limit the truck shook and shimmied. Inside the cab, we were being bounced and jostled over every little bump and dip on the highway.

"I can't believe it either. That come January I'll be opening up my own place," Jas shouted, her eyes focused on the road ahead. "I feel like I'm dreaming, and sometime soon I'll wake up and find I'm still working at The Edge and all this hard work was just a figment of my imagination."

"No, this is not a dream," I said, looking at her profile. My anger lessened slightly. "You have done all the planning, the work. This is what happens when you go after what you want with every ounce of energy you have. This new life is your creation. All yours."

It felt good to be the one giving encouragement for a change.

We drove most of the way in silence, the remnants of our fight still hanging in the air between us. When we pulled up to the back of the building, the bouncers Jas had charmed into helping were unloading her furniture.

The alleyway was too narrow for the two trucks to park together so she swung around to the front. We entered the salon and headed to the back to see how far the boys had gotten with the moving. They were in the process of wedging her sofa through the narrow door to her apartment. After much discussion and trying to shove the couch through the opening at every conceivable angle, everyone agreed that the door and its frame had to come off.

We left the guys to manage the job. Downstairs we met up with Jamie and three girls. Jas introduced me to Christie, Indigo, and Heather. She had hired them, along with Jamie, to work with her.

Once the couch had made it safely into her apartment, the walls suffering only minor dents and a few scraps to the fresh paint, we all pitched in to move her boxes of stuff upstairs. We set up a box brigade on the narrow stairs with Jas waiting at the top. By lunchtime, we had moved every last box and stick of furniture. Jas had pizza and beer delivered. The day took on a party mood as everyone partook of the food and spirits. Jas seemed on top of the world, laughing with the new stylists, flirting with the muscle bound bouncers, and teasing Jamie when she saw him flirting with the guys too.

I, on the other hand, kept thinking about Christian. He had probably called. He might even have wanted to do something with me after he finished work. I kicked myself for forgetting my cell at home.

When I went to get a beer, I realized Jas wasn't in the apartment. I slipped downstairs and found her in the salon, staring off into space, her hands on her hips, her back towards me. She'd obviously snuck down to the salon to have some alone time. I had just turned to go back upstairs when she sighed.

"Hey there." I turned around and walked over to her.

"Hi." She brushed away what looked like tears.

"What's up?"

"God, Hannah. What am I doing? Where did I ever get the idea I could pull this off?"

"Whoa, wait just a minute. You've planned, saved, and worked your ass off to get here. Why all the negative stuff?"

"I don't know. I'm just tired, I guess. I was upstairs listening to the girls and Jamie talking about working here and it just hit me. I'm responsible for these people. They trust me to make a go of this and all of a sudden the thought of that just freaked me out. I had to get out of there before they noticed my panic. That's the last thing they need to see is their boss freaking out and we haven't even opened yet."

I stood there unsure of what to say. Jas had always seemed cool and collected. —I'd never seen her so ruffled. It was a side of her I wasn't sure I wanted to see. If she felt this way about herself, what hope did I have of getting out of my current predicament?

I did the only thing I could think of. I gave her a hug. I was surprised at the fierceness of her return embrace. I murmured reassuring words and was unsettled when this only brought about more tears.

"You're going to make this a success. You have to believe that," I said as she sobbed into my shoulder.

"You're right. You're right. Whew." She ended our embrace. "I probably look like a wreck." She wiped the tears away with the back of her hands. Then she really unnerved me by laughing. "Oh, girl, what a pair we are."

I wasn't quite sure what she meant by that, but at least she wasn't crying anymore.

"Let's go back upstairs and join the party." She squared her shoulders and headed for the stairs.

The party wound itself down by late afternoon. I stayed behind to help Jas unpack some of her boxes. We started in the kitchen. A couple of hours later, we were still unpacking kitchen things, and I was starting to drag. I was tired, and I couldn't stop thinking that Christian had called and I wasn't there to talk to him. I was edgy with anticipation.

About eight, Jas suggested we call it a night, and I had to stifle my eagerness to get home. When I did finally arrive home, I didn't bother taking off my jacket or turning on any lights. I raced over to where I'd left my cell and checked my voicemail. There were no messages.

"He was probably just busy. Who knows, maybe he had to work late," I said to Noni, who just looked back at me with her crooked grin.

I didn't know what to do with myself for the rest of the evening. I showered and changed into my PJs and wandered around my small apartment, rearranging the few knick-knacks, plumping up the pillows on the couch, remaking my bed, all the while pretending that I wasn't waiting for the phone to ring. I finally got fed up with myself and went to bed, where I lay staring into the dark, wondering why Christian hadn't called.

Chapter Sixteen

I rolled over and slowly opened my eyes. I'd tossed and turned the night away trying to find a comfortable position. My brain just wouldn't quiet down. I had finally managed to doze off around four in the morning. Another day of work. Another day with nothing to look forward to unless, of course, Christian called.

The sun peeked through the curtains. At least something was shining today.

Wait a minute. The sun was up and shining into my apartment. When I leave for work, it's still dark out. Christ, I forgot to set my alarm again! It was already 9:00. Even hustling as fast as I could and catching the first available bus downtown, there was no way I was going to make it to work on time.

I swore under my breath while I scrambled to get dressed. No telling what Terence was going to do when he found out. And he would, I had no doubt about that. I had been lucky on Sunday because it was his day off. It was Tuesday; Terence was definitely going to be prowling around checking up on us like he always did.

The ride into work was a nightmare. Construction on the Calf Robe Bridge had backed up traffic, and when the bus finally made it downtown, it stopped at every stop to pick up slow moving seniors. I clutched my purse, nervous sweat trickling down my back and making my shirt stick to my skin. I silently urged the bus to keep going.

When I finally stepped off the bus and tore through the back entrance of the Devonshire building, I was already half an hour late. The adrenaline was sluicing through me as I flew down the stairs and into the staff lounge. I threw my coat onto one of the scruffy couches and whipped my work shoes out of my locker. I slipped them on and pulled my hair back.

"Hi, Ruth."

She didn't answer. I peered into the laundry area. The washers and dryers were silent. Ruth was nowhere in sight and neither was the rest of her staff. Something was wrong, terribly wrong. Unfortunately, I didn't have time to figure it out. I needed to get upstairs quickly.

I didn't see the notice on the white board until I was almost out the door.

STAFF MEETING TONIGHT AT 6:00 P.M. SHARP. Attendance is mandatory.

It was written in big red letters. Underneath it, someone had angrily scrawled the words *Screw You*. The dry erase marker used to write both messages lay on the floor uncapped. What the hell was going on?

I met up with a couple of the girls who were going to get their clients. Beth muttered something under her breath, and Sue nodded in agreement. I didn't have time to talk. I snatched my schedule from its slot in the Prep Room and scanned down the page.

My schedule was packed and definitely overbooked. There wasn't a lunch break scheduled. I had a fifteen-minute break before my last client in the afternoon and that was it. I'd sort it out after my first client, a half-leg wax that I was already late for. I slid my schedule back in its slot and retrieved my client.

I apologized to her for being late, but she wasn't amused. I couldn't even muster the energy to care how ticked off she was. I was just thanking my lucky stars that I hadn't bumped into Terence.

I finished waxing in record time and headed into the Prep Room to grab my pedicure tools for the next client. When I swung open the door, I found another two of my co-workers leaning against the counter. Jill was crying big hiccupping sobs. Nina had her arm around her trying to calm her down.

Had everyone lost their minds? Maybe something bad happened to Ruth and that's why she wasn't downstairs.

"Nina, what is going on around here? Where is Ruth? Is she okay?" I demanded.

Nina glared at me. "Ruth is in talking to Terence. Frankly, after what he did, we should just say to hell with it and all go home. I can't believe that asshole expects us to work and attend his bullshit meeting after what has happened."

"What has happened?"

"What planet have you been on?" Nina turned from consoling Jill to face me, her hands on her hips.

"I had a day off yesterday," I said, bewildered.

"Have you checked your bank balance lately?" Her anger was palpable.

"No."

"Well you should. All of our paycheques bounced. Ruth was furious. She marched right into Terence's office and probably still has him cornered there. Hannah, he had to know about it because the note for the meeting was already on the board before anyone came in this morning. Some of the girls were so mad they just walked out. That's why we're all doing twice as many treatments."

My stomach dropped down to my toes. My paycheque bounced? All I could think of were all the cheques I had written to cover my bills.

"When are we going to get our money?"

"Supposedly, that's what Terence will be telling us at the meeting after work."

"Oh." I picked up my pedicure tools and left the two of them in the Prep Room. I was numb. Shouldn't I feel something in response to the latest disaster in my life?

Five hours later, I managed to get back on track with my schedule by working fast and cutting the odd corner on some of my services. I led yet another client back to the Great Room. I left her looking in satisfaction at her freshly painted toes. I must have given her a pedicure because the evidence of it was staring me right in the face, but I'd no recollection of having done one.

I was officially on my break, so I decided to go check out my financial situation. Maybe only some of the cheques bounced. I double-checked my schedule to make sure I had enough time to zip out and get back for my next service.

My last client was down for a hot rock massage. I peeked into the treatment room to make sure the roaster was turned on and the rocks were heating in the water bath. That done, I went downstairs to get my cell phone. I needed to check my bank balance but my phone was dead. I swore under my breath. I'd forgotten to plug it in yet again. Grabbing my purse, I left the spa without bothering to change my shoes or grab a coat.

Outside, I jogged to the ATM around the corner, panic setting in. Thank God, there wasn't a line. I stepped into the little glass-fronted vestibule. Hot air blasted out of the ceiling vent and relieved the goose bumps on my arms from my frigid dash outdoors, but as I slid my card into the machine, I started to feel sick. The heat was now oppressive, and I couldn't breathe properly. I punched in my PIN number, my hands clammy from nerves. I blindly stabbed the button for account balances and then everything went still. I no longer heard the fan blowing or the sound of my own heart beating. All my focus was on the little grey screen with the illuminated numbers in front of me and the story it told. I was flat broke. My account was overdrawn. I frantically tallied up all the bills I thought I paid. I'd be a thousand dollars overdrawn once all the cheques went through.

"Excuse me," said a male voice from behind me. Although his words were polite, his tone was anything but.

I turned and stared at him blankly.

"Are you going to do something or are you just going to stand there? Some of us actually use the ATM to get money out."

I didn't bother with a reply. I ended the transaction and retrieved my useless card.

"Finally," the man huffed, shoving his card into the machine.

I wandered back to the spa in a daze. I walked right through the front door of the spa. I didn't give a rat's ass about proper procedures. My only hope was Terence would reissue our cheques tonight at the meeting.

I went back to work only because I didn't know what else to do. I picked up my last client of the day. According to my schedule, my client for the hot stone massage was a Mr. Houser. He was a large man, and that was putting it politely. Even the extra-large spa robe barely made it over the circumference of his girth. A large profusion of curly chest hairs peeked out of the gap between the lapels of the robe. The abundance of hair that Mr. Houser's chest boasted wasn't a gift granted to his head. He, like so many men with thinning hair, had made a feeble attempt to hide his bald pate by growing out the hair above his ears and combing the wispy camouflage over his shiny dome.

God, whatever I did in a past life to piss you off, I am really, really sorry.

I escorted Mr. Houser to the treatment room and left him to disrobe and get his bulk up on the treatment table and under the modesty cover. I leaned up against the door and tried to focus on the here and now.

All down the corridor, I spied the staff taking their time getting clients to and from treatment rooms. Some of them looked like they'd been crying, but more of them looked like they were ready to strangle someone. I would hate to be a client who booked a bikini wax today.

I resisted the urge to slide down to the floor in a blubbering puddle. Instead, I took a deep breath, squared my shoulders, and knocked before entering the treatment room.

Mr. Houser, per my instructions, was lying on his back with the modesty sheet draped over his mountain of a stomach. I walked over to the roaster and put on a pair of heat resistant gloves before plunging my hands into the 150-degree water to retrieve the stones. I took out a series of small black stones and placed them on the counter. I dried the stones with a towel and instructed Mr. Houser to sit up. He heaved himself into a sitting position, and I lined up the stones in two parallel lines on the table. I covered the hot stones with two towels and helped Mr. Houser to lie on them.

I put my gloved hands back in the hot water and stared down at the remaining stones resting at the bottom. I was supposed to be taking five stones of various sizes and placing them on the client's body. The first stone was the largest at about six pounds. Instead, I fluttered my fingers in the water creating miniature ripples across the surface.

Why did it seem like life kept throwing roadblocks in my way? More importantly, why did I keep trying so hard to make this job work out when I didn't really want to do it anymore?

Well at least my love life looked more promising. I thought about my night with Christian. I couldn't believe that it had only been three days since I'd been with him. Heat bloomed on my cheeks, I blamed it on the steam rising from the roaster.

What I wouldn't give to be back in that cloud of a bed with Christian lying next to me, instead of here about to run hot rocks over a beached whale. Why was I even doing this when I hadn't been paid? I started splashing the water around creating little tsunamis in the roaster.

A gurgling snort startled me out of my revere. I turned and looked at Mr. Houser. He'd fallen asleep.

I thought about just slipping out of the room and coming back an hour later and he wouldn't even know he didn't get a treatment. I pondered this for a moment and then discarded it as tempting as it was.

I pulled out two heavy stones and dried them with a towel. I took off the insulated gloves and picked up the largest of the smooth dark stones. The gloves were just to protect my hands from the hot water. The stones were supposed to be hot but not hot enough to handle. That is, if the esthetician was in her right mind and hadn't accidentally turned the roaster up too high.

The stone was very, very hot, and I handled it gingerly to try to avoid burning my fingers. I held the stone over Mr. Houser's stomach, watching the rise and fall of his breathing. I tried to time the placement of the stone with his breath, but the stone was really uncomfortable in my hands.

Shouts erupted out in the corridor. The heavy door muffled the voices, but the tone was unmistakable. Somebody was pissed off and didn't care who knew it. The stone was starting to burn my fingers. The shouting escalated and the door to my treatment room shuddered from the force of someone slamming up against it. Startled, I lost my tentative grip on the rock, and it dropped not so delicately on poor Mr. Houser's unsuspecting mid-section.

Shocked into wakefulness, Mr. Houser shouted and reflexively sat up, flinging the stone off his belly and onto the floor. The modesty cover slipped dangerously down his waist. The stone hit the floor narrowly missing my foot.

I bent to pick up the wayward stone, apologizing profusely to Mr. Houser, but he didn't seem to be listening. He waved his arms shouting at me while the modesty cover silently slipped to the floor.

Oh, God. That was more of Mr. Houser than I needed to see. I threw the stone on the counter and bent down again to retrieve the sheet. When I straightened up the door flew open.

I turned still holding the sheet in my hands. Terence stood in the doorway, his mouth hanging open like some dark yawning cavern. His collar was askew and his shirttail was untucked. Peering from behind him was Nina, her cheeks flushed with emotion, her hands bunched into fists at her sides. The three of us stood there frozen, staring at each other.

"What kind of place are you running?" Mr. Houser shouted at Terence. He tugged the sheet from my hands and held it in front of his lap. "Are you all insane?"

Funny that's exactly what I was thinking.

"I came here to get away from the pressures of my job, to get some peace and quiet. Instead this place is full of crazy people shouting and brawling in the hallways...."

I guess he wasn't sleeping so soundly after all.

"And this one," Mr. Houser shook his finger at me, his face turning a dangerous shade of purple, "tried to kill me while I slept. If this is relaxation, you can have it!"

Mr. Houser jumped off the table in a surprisingly nimble fashion for one so large. He wrapped the sheet around his waist and marched off down the hall towards the change rooms. Terence stared at me. I shrugged and braced myself for a dressing down, but Terence surprised me by turning on his heels and following Mr. Houser down the hall.

Nina leaned up against the door jam, her shoulders slumped in defeat. "Looks like I'm out of a job, not that this gig paid that well anyway. Hell, what am I saying, this job doesn't pay anything." She let out a hollow laugh. "I guess there's no point in staying for the meeting. Besides, I have to update my resume. I hear Solace is hiring."

I took a step towards her to offer her some kind of comfort, but she waved me off.

"I gotta go, see ya around." Nina pushed herself away from the doorframe and left without another word.

158

I watched her until she disappeared around the corner. I stepped back into the treatment room and looked around. Without a client, I guess I was done for the day. I quickly cleaned the room, drained the roaster, left the stones on the counter to cool, and shut off the lights. I went to the break room intent on putting my feet up for a few minutes and finding something to eat. I was starving. I hadn't eaten anything all day. I'd no money, so buying something was out of the question. Maybe I could scrounge something out of the staff fridge. I also needed to call Jas and tell her what had gone down.

In the break room, the smell of wet, dirty laundry assaulted me. Maybe I wasn't so hungry after all. When I walked farther into the room, the source of the smell became apparent. The washers and dryers were still slumbering, and there were huge piles of soiled sheets and towels heaped all over the laundry room floor. Ruth, it seemed, was still among the missing.

There was a handful of staff either lounging on the sagging sofa, sitting around the small table, or standing around the rest of the available space. No one lifted a finger to clean up the laundry. The room was heavy with tension, emotions building like thunderheads. The meeting was going to be a doozey. If tempers exploded, Terence might end up getting more than just a shove into a door.

I needed to tell Jas what happened, but my cell was still dead, and with the angry mood in the room I didn't want to try and borrow one. I had to settle for the staff phone, but there was a waiting line. When it was finally my turn, I had to squeeze next to the wall because the break room was full of people waiting for the meeting, bringing with them more accusations and rumors. I dialed Jas's number and got her voice mail. I left a quick message saying I needed to talk to her and that I'd call her later.

Chapter Seventeen

In the time leading up to the meeting, the break room filled with more and more disgruntled employees. The more of us there and the longer we waited, the angrier we became. A few estheticians opted not to come, and from some of the stories going around, the no-shows had decided to cut their losses and start looking for work elsewhere. Six o'clock came and the twenty of us trooped upstairs to the conference room. Terence wasn't there yet. If I were him, I wouldn't show up.

While we waited for Terence, we milled about sharing what we'd heard about our bounced paycheques and our missing Christmas bonuses. Some of the staff said the owners, whom none of us had ever met, had absconded with the spa's money. Some said it was Danielle's fault for not managing the books properly, but most of the blame seemed to land squarely on Terence's shoulders. Not that the majority of us thought he was on the take, but as soon as he and Danielle noticed there was a problem, they should have let us know and done something about it.

Most of the staff were too angry or upset to sit down, but not me. I'd been on my feet all day and standing up shouting about what'd happened seemed like a waste of energy. I sat near the back, turned one of the chairs around, and used it as a footstool. The sound of everyone talking at once reminded me of a hen house, with all the clucking, squawking, and flapping of hands.

I was just going to duck downstairs to call Jas again when Terence finally showed up. As usual, the staff fell silent as Terence crossed the room to take his place at the podium. The only difference today was the accusing stares and angry whispers of discontent that followed him.

"If you will all take a seat we can begin." Terence's voice sounded weak. I detected a hint of nerves.

A few of the staffers joined me in taking their seats, but the majority of them remained standing at the back of the room.

"Just tell us when you're going to pay us!" shouted Carol, her arms crossed in defiance.

Terence scanned the room, pushed up his glasses, and cleared his throat. "This unfortunate incident is being cleared up as we speak."

Unfortunate incident? He made it sound like a social faux pas. Like someone passed gas at a party. I was infuriated.

"I know that it has been an inconvenience for you, but it will be rectified," Terence said, slowly gaining his composure. The haughtiness we all came to expect from him returned. "Danielle will re-issue your cheques next week."

The crowd behind me erupted in frustration and disbelief.

"We want our money now," one of the girls shouted.

"That's not good enough!" someone else shouted.

The angry sentiment echoed around the room as one after another of my coworkers chimed in.

"I need my money now. My rent is due and I've got daycare to pay. I have no food in the fridge. How do you suggest I feed my family when I have no money?"

"What you're doing is robbery. We've all worked for our wages. You can't deny us what we've earned. This is illegal."

"It's bad enough that no one received a Christmas bonus. We depend on that money to live. You cheated us."

"In the meantime," Terence raised his voice over the growing din, "you are still expected to behave in a professional manner when dealing with clients. The reputation of the spa must not be jeopardized. I will be meeting with some of you who have already tarnished the image of the spa with your behavior today. Insubordination will not be tolerated."

"Get over yourself, Terence. What's happened here is not the staff's fault."

Yeah, I thought, *you go sister.* It wasn't until I was only a few steps away from Terence that I realized the voice yelling at him was my own.

"People need to be paid for the work they do, not just because it's the law, but because, for most of us, it means our survival." Anger propelled me forward until I was standing toe-to-toe with Terence.

Life had thrown me way too many curve balls lately, and this one had hit me right between the eyes. I was fed up with feeling powerless in my own life. I hadn't planned on it, but I was standing up for myself. My earlier inertia was blasted away by the pounding of my heart and the fury building in my veins.

"We don't get paid huge dollars. Most of your *employees* are single mothers. They don't have another income to count on." I pointed to my co-workers. "What are Tina, Diana, and Rita supposed to tell their kids when they are hungry?" I stepped closer. Terence took a mincing step back. "What you call an inconvenience means not being able to put food on our tables."

My focus contracted down to a sharp point with Terence as my target. I jabbed my finger into his bony chest. A blush bloomed red hot on his cheeks.

"Next week isn't acceptable. We want and deserve our money today."

Terence batted weakly at my finger, and I jabbed him again.

"You have no right to demand anything from me." Terence smoothed down his cashmere sweater. "You are nothing but a perpetual screw up. Instead of screaming at me, you should be thanking me for not firing you three months ago."

"If you fired me, you wouldn't have all the extra sales I made to help line your greedy little pockets!" I shouted back. "Speaking of which, you also owe all of us the bonuses we earned. Did you think we'd be grateful for getting free movie tickets instead of our money?"

"You had better apologize to me this instant or you can kiss your job goodbye and any hope of working in this industry again."

My laughter echoed in my head. "You don't have to waste your breath threatening me with dismissal because I quit." I yanked my nametag off its magnetic backing and bounced it off Terence's chest.

I turned on my heels and marched out of the meeting. I took great pleasure in slamming the door as hard as I could. The door smacked the frame with such force it bounced back open, the sound echoing like a gunshot down the empty hallway.

I had negotiated my way downstairs to the Staff Room to collect my things, when my legs suddenly turned to Jell-O, and I had to hold on to the railing to stop myself from tumbling down the stairs. My hands shook so badly it took me three times to work the combination on the lock to my locker. I found an empty shopping bag from the cupboard under the kitchenette sink and stuffed my few belongings into the bag. I threw my coat on and laced my boots, feeling the tears building. I squeezed my eyes shut. Two stubborn tears escaped, tickling my cheeks. I angrily scrubbed them away.

I didn't know where to go, and I didn't want go home and be by myself. I wished Jas had picked up her phone. I tried her number one more time—still no answer. I decided to take the bus to her place anyway and hoped that she would be there.

But when I started out onto the street, I walked in the opposite direction from the right bus stop. I wasn't really sure where I was heading; my legs just kept carrying me forward. I passed the storefronts on Seventeenth Avenue, their large plate glass windows decorated for Christmas. Even the trees were sporting Christmas lights. I skirted past several holiday shoppers, their arms laden down with bags and parcels. I glanced at them as we passed each other on the sidewalk. They seemed strange creatures: people living ordinary lives, their only concern finding the right gift for that special person or loved one. The only bag I carried contained a few pedicure tools, a makeup bag, my work shoes, and a pair of flip-flops that I had left in my locker last summer.

It felt like all the bones in my legs had melted away, but they kept carrying me forward, away from the direction I needed to go. I finally stopped walking when I reached the quiet residential streets behind the posh shopping district.

Why am I here?

It took me a moment before I spotted Christian's townhouse. Warm yellow light softly glowed behind the gauzy sheers. His SUV was parked out front. Thank God, he was home. I jogged across the road, the plastic bag slapping against my thigh. By the time I mounted the stone steps to his front door, I was beyond exhausted and shaken to my core. I desperately needed a strong shoulder to cry on and an even stronger drink. Here I would be able to get both.

I rang the bell and leaned against the railing waiting for Christian. I heard the faint chiming of the doorbell followed by the muffled sounds of footsteps coming towards the door. I straightened up and waited for the door to open and for Christian to draw me into the comfort of his arms.

The door swung open, and my heart missed a beat. I looked over to the side of the house eyeing the house numbers and then back to the open doorway. I was at the right address, but....

"Yes?" asked the woman standing in the door, her face pleasantly neutral.

She wore a pale blue bathrobe, one that looked identical to the one I had seen hanging on the back of Christian's bathroom door. She was barefoot and her raven hair was damp; she'd probably just stepped out of the shower. I looked down at her feet. They were so small and delicate. Her toes were painted the softest shell pink. I looked up at her again. Her large almond eyes assessed me, waiting for me to tell her who I was and why I was standing like a deaf mute at the door.

"Uhm." My mind cramped.

"Lu, who is it?" Christian's voice rang out from the back of the house.

"Miss, can I help you?" Her graceful hand fluttered up to her neck.

I stumbled back, away from the exotic creature standing in front of me. I caught myself before I stepped off the porch, backwards.

"Miss, are you okay? Are you hurt? Are you lost?" Lu Lu stepped towards me to offer assistance. She probably thought I was some sort of crazy, homeless person.

"No, no I'm fine," I said, finally finding my voice. Then I did the only thing I could think to do. I turned around and ran.

My throat hurt, and my lungs screamed at me for running so hard in the cold. I clutched my purse and the plastic bag to my chest as if they were my lifeline. The bus to Jas's was already at the stop, and I had to sprint a little harder to catch it before it pulled away. I didn't want to wait another forty-five minutes to catch the next one. I fumbled for my bus pass and flashed it at the disinterested driver. I managed to snag a seat near the back of the bus and collapsed onto the thinly padded vinyl bench.

I focused on breathing. In, out, in, out. I stubbornly refused to allow the images of what just happened to form in my weary brain. Instead, I stared at the graffiti on the seat back in front of me. At the next stop, a man sat down next to me, but I didn't look up. A sob caught in my throat, and the man shifted in his seat. I stared harder at the graffiti and willed myself to keep breathing.

Finally, the bus drove into Inglewood, and I reached up and pulled the stop cord. I forced myself to stand up when the loud hiss of air brakes announced my stop. I said excuse me to the business suit sharing my seat hoping he would stand up to let me get past him. Instead, he simply turned his body so that his legs poked into the aisle. I squeezed past. If I had any fight left in me, I would've accidentally elbowed his head or hit him with my bag on the way past. As it was, I had to push myself forward using all my willpower just to get off the bus.

I almost wept with relief when I saw the salon. Darkness cloaked the lower level but I banged on the door anyway. No answer. A small sliver of light sliced through the curtains on the second floor. She must be home. I walked around the block and headed down the alleyway. The alley was treacherously slick; a thin layer of ice crusted the pavement. I slowed my pace to a crawl, testing my footing, tentatively putting one foot in front of the other. When I reached the back door to the salon, my back was stiff from the effort to keep from slipping on the ice. I leaned on the newly installed doorbell.

The light over the door cast a sickly yellow pool on the new unpainted metal door. The door looked like the colour of dried blood in the wan light. I leaned on the bell again. When I heard the deadbolt snap open, I let out a sigh of relief.

"Hannah?" Jas reached for my wrist, my hands were still firmly clutching the bag and my purse to my chest. "Girl, what are you doing here? You're freezing."

Her hands were so warm against my wrist it made me shiver. She pulled me into the back room. I followed blindly, stumbling over the threshold.

Her eyes were big and full of concern. She quickly looked me up and down to see if there was something physically wrong with me. "Please talk to me. You look like you've seen a ghost, and you're really starting to scare me."

I opened my mouth to reassure her, to let her know that I hadn't sustained any life threatening injuries, but nothing came out. She tugged at my purse and bag and I absently let them drop.

"I got your message to call you. You sounded upset so I called your cell but you didn't pick up, which was strange in itself, and when I called the spa, no one answered. What's going on?"

I swallowed hard around the lump in my throat.

"You're coming upstairs with me. You need to get warm."

Unable to get me to tell her what happened, Jas guided me to the apartment stairs. The steps were ridiculously steep, and I was so tired I didn't think I would be able to make the climb. In the end, she resorted to tugging me by the arm. It took an inhuman amount of energy for me to lift my boot-clad feet up each step.

Once we negotiated the Mt. Everest of staircases, I sank gratefully into the squishy cushions of her overstuffed couch, shivering uncontrollably. Jas draped a blanket over my quaking shoulders. I clenched my teeth to stop them from chattering. I felt a tug at my left ankle as she unlaced my boot and pulled it off my frozen foot. I sat back and let her take off the other one.

Wordlessly, she headed into the kitchen. I curled up on the couch and closed my eyes, tucking my feet underneath me. Jas's stocking feet padded across the hard wood. She put her hand on my shoulder. I forced my heavy lids open and gratefully accepted the wine she held out to me. I took a deep swallow, it burned slightly as the blessed warmth hit my empty stomach. She sat down next to me holding her own glass of wine.

"Do you think you can try this again and tell me what's happened?"

I nodded and took another drink. "I...."

That was as far as I got. Huge sobs racked my body. I put my wine down on the coffee table and hugged a throw pillow while I continued to let the burning tears flow. Jas stroked my hair and waited, gentle and patient, while I cried myself out.

Through hiccupping breaths, I managed to tell her what happened at work: first my paycheque bouncing, then me stoning a client, shouting Terence down, and quitting. The next part was harder, much harder. Feeling the shame tighten my throat, I told her I went home with Christian after the night at Karma. I glossed over the details, but I did tell her I had slept with him. I couldn't look her in the eye when I said it. Harder still, was telling her about finding a woman at his door just mere days after he had been with me. I spoke quickly, letting the flood of words pour out before I had a chance to chicken out and not tell her. When I finished, all I felt was empty.

I expected her to give me the old 'I told you so' routine. Instead, she just squeezed my hand. That's when I knew things were really as bad as I thought they were.

Jas finally broke the silence. "Why don't you stay here tonight? It's late and cold, and after the day you've had, I would feel better if you just crashed here."

Great, the one person I could always count on to look on the bright side of things was now worried about my mental stability.

"Now, knowing you," she continued not waiting for me to reply, "you probably haven't had dinner yet."

"No, I haven't." I felt like a little kid. I guess I was staying the night, not that I was going to protest. I didn't have the strength to negotiate the trip home anyway.

She gave my hand a motherly pat and went to put dinner together. I finished my wine, resting my chin on the back of the sofa and silently watched her work in the kitchen. She rummaged through the fridge and found enough food to whip up a stir fry with steamed rice. She talked to me while she browned the meat in a wok and chopped vegetables. She brought me up to speed on what remained to do in the salon before the opening. Thankfully, she kept up her running monologue through the dinner preparations and didn't expect me to hold up my end of the conversation.

I hadn't thought I would ever feel hungry again, but once I caught the savory aroma wafting from the kitchen, my stomach started to grumble painfully.

We ate sitting on the sofa. Despite my emotional state, I still managed to put away two bowls of food and a few more glasses of wine. It occurred to me that I should really cut down on the booze. I seemed to be pounding back quite a bit lately.

With my stomach full, the rest of me decided that I had enough excitement for one day. I curled up on my end of the sofa as Jas picked up the bowls to put them in the kitchen sink. I was asleep before she made it back into the room.

Chapter Eighteen

I awoke to sunshine streaming through jewel-coloured curtains. The bright light transformed as it filtered through the Sari fabric drapes, splashing bands of red, purple, and orange across the pine floor. When I stretched to work out the stiffness in my legs, my feet hit something solid—the armrest of the couch I was sleeping on. I yawned, stretched again, and looked around.

Yeah, last night. I spent the night at Jas's because....

All the events of yesterday came back in a flash of pain so intense that I curled into a fetal position, wrapping the blanket tightly around me for protection.

I wasn't panicked about being unemployed. No, it wasn't that at all. Well maybe a little, but mostly it was what Christian had done that made my heart ache. He was with another woman only days after sleeping with me. How could I have been so stupid? I wished I could step out of my body and away from the hot poker stabbing my chest.

A wave of nausea washed over me, and I thought I was going to be sick. Slowly, I pulled myself into a sitting position and tried to ignore my aching head and churning stomach. I stood up carefully, blinking at the stars dancing in front of my eyes. I felt like I was made of glass. I eased myself into the tiny kitchen, making sure not to move my head too quickly in case the jackhammer behind my eyes caused the bones in my face to shatter.

Coffee. I needed coffee. I rummaged around for the tin of Kicking Horse and filters and instead of waiting for the machine to finish brewing, I decided to take a shower. I reeked of fear and sweat, and the smell wasn't helping me feel any better. I'd have to wash my clothes but I'd deal with that once Jas was up. I'd just have to wear a towel or maybe borrow a bathrobe.

I stepped quietly down the hall to the bathroom, trying not to wake her, but the old wooden floor creaked and popped at my every footfall. The bathroom was small but sparkling, with its new coat of white paint, chrome fixtures, and refurbished claw foot tub. I ran the water as hot as I could stand, stripped off my filthy clothes, and stepped into the steamy spray. The shower curtain smelled brand new, like Barbie dolls fresh out of the package. I leaned into the water, the hot needles working on the knots of tension in my neck and shoulders. I breathed in the thick steam, letting it relax my overwrought body, pinking my skin. I stifled my sobs, but I didn't move until the water started to cool. I used Jas's shampoo and conditioner on my hair and her French milled soap to wash away all the grime of yesterday.

I finished my ablutions just as the water turned icy. Wrapping myself in a white bath sheet, I stepped out of the tub onto a shaggy bath mat, plush and soft under my feet. I snagged a smaller towel from a wicker basket on the floor and twisted it around my head like a turban. The bathroom was full of steam, so thankfully I couldn't see my reflection in the fogged mirror. I wanted to stay in there all day—and I could. It wasn't like I had a job to go to or a boyfriend who would want to see me.

I looked down to find my dirty clothes, but they were gone. Jas must have popped into the bathroom and taken them while I was zoning out under the water. Instead of my clothes, a folded, white bathrobe was on the vanity counter. I put it on and towel-dried my hair before heading out to the kitchen to find my thoughtful friend and snag a cup of coffee.

Jas was standing in the kitchen, pouring the freshly brewed coffee into two oversized white mugs. She was dressed in a purple tank top with an Ohm sign printed on the front and a matching pair of yoga pants. Her platinum tresses were piled haphazardly on the top of her head. She looked way too perky and awake so early in the morning.

"How did you sleep?" She handed me a mug.

"Like the dead." I took a seat at the vintage Formica and chrome kitchen table. I drew lazy circles with my finger on the bright lipstick pink top while I sipped my coffee.

"I threw your uniform in the washer while you were taking a shower. It's in the dryer now. I tried to find something of mine that would fit you, but we're such different sizes, so I figured the robe would do until your clothes were dry."

I cleared my throat. "Thanks for washing them."

"You're welcome." She joined me at the table, taking a seat across from me on a matching chair, upholstered in bright orange vinyl. "You probably don't want to talk about yesterday, but are you sure about Christian? I mean, are you sure that he, the other woman—that they were up to something? You were very upset yesterday after quitting, maybe you just jumped to conclusions, and there's really a perfectly reasonable explanation for that woman to be at his door. Maybe she was his housekeeper or maybe he has a sister."

"Thanks for trying to sugarcoat this one. If it was his housekeeper, she sure wears a strange uniform to work in. And, I highly doubt she was his sister. She definitely wasn't giving off a sisterly vibe. Also, this woman was Asian. Small, exotic, beautiful." Everything I wasn't. I stared into my coffee mug.

"You can't take this personally. I mean the thing with Christian. You made a bad choice that's all. Now it's time to make another choice. I know it must hurt, but you don't need someone like Christian, or even Mason for that matter, to feel like you are worth something."

"Please don't remind me about Mason."

"Sorry, it's just that I don't understand why you keep putting yourself in a position to be hurt."

"Neither do I. Maybe I was born under an unlucky star, or maybe I was a mass murderer in a past life."

Jas pursed her lips.

I cradled my coffee mug in both hands and looked her squarely in the eyes. "Enough about my bad choices in men." I quickly stood up and poured myself more coffee. "I don't want to talk about it anymore. Besides, I have more pressing matters to deal with. Like finding a new job and scrounging up money for rent before my landlord has a coronary. Speaking of which, I'd better call him." My stomach churned acid.

"Sure, I'll take my turn in the shower while you're on the phone."

She held up her empty mug, and I refilled it. She handed me her cell phone then took a sip of coffee while she ambled down the hallway towards the bathroom. Moments later water gurgled through the pipes. I sat on the couch and dialed my landlord's number.

"Please, please let his answering machine pick up," I prayed to the phone gods.

Mr. Stevenson picked up on the second ring. Damn. The sound of his gravelly voice made my hands slick with nerves. I hoped I hadn't woken him up.

I blurted out why I called. Like taking off a bandage, I figured the faster I did this, the less painful it would be. I told him why his rent cheque bounced, emphasizing the fact that it was the spa's fault, not mine. I didn't mention I was unemployed.

Mr. Stevenson listened quietly as I raced through my explanation, the sweat trickling down my back.

"Ya know, Hannah, ya seem like a nice girl, a bit scatterbrained, but nice. The problem I'm having is that this is not the first time you've been late with the rent. I've given ya room in the past to make it up, and every time I do, ya promise not to do it again." He cleared his throat. "I'm not a charity, girl. This is how I make my living. If you can't pay the rent then you can't be livin' in my building.

"I'll give you until the end of today to get me cash or a certified cheque for the rent plus fifty for the bounced cheque. If I don't get the money, consider yourself outta here. Two weeks is what I'll give you to get your stuff out. Understand?" He barked and hung up the phone before I could reply.

"Yes," I whispered to the dial tone.

I turned off the cell and carefully placed it on the coffee table. I rubbed my hands together and jumped up from the couch. I paced Jas's tiny apartment, sipping absently from my cold coffee, as my mind raced around for possible solutions to my cash problems. I kept coming back to the same answer. I was going to have to call my parents and ask for help.

The coffee turned sour in my stomach. I poured the cold dregs down the kitchen sink just as Jas appeared from the bathroom. She had braided her hair into one thick plait down her back and she had changed from her purple yoga gear into a black t-shirt and jeans. She smelled faintly of coconut.

"How did it go with Mr. S.?"

"Not so good. If I don't get the money to him by the end of today, consider me homeless. I'm going to have to ask my parents for a loan." I leaned up against the kitchen counter. I could feel the tears wanting to come. I closed my eyes.

"I don't think you do."

"Excuse me?" I opened my eyes and looked at her.

"At least, not for the rent. While I was in the shower I had a truly brilliant idea." Her face beamed with excitement. "You, my little pumpkin, are going to room with me. I've an extra bedroom; you just need to supply the bed. And the best part is the rent fits your current budget."

"I can't possibly—"

"This isn't a hand-out, Missy. Until you get another job, you don't have to pay rent, but I will make you work for your keep by helping me get ready for the opening. There is way too much for me to do, and I really do need the help. Besides, I'm kinda lonely living here by myself after living with two other women for so long. I've always thought it would be cool for us to be roomies, anyway."

"Well roomie," I smiled back. "Let's get to work."

We worked for several hours. Nicki Minaj blasted from the portable stereo, which sat on the reception desk. We tackled the wooden shelving units first. After a few false starts with the first one—we put the shelves on backwards and had to dismantle it and start again—we managed to put together five more before lunch.

I was grateful for something to focus on, something to distract me from what I felt. Eventually, the extra-strength pain pills kicked in, and my headache went away, but nothing could completely take away my humiliation. I held it together for most of the day, but every so often, the image of that woman standing half-dressed in Christian's front hall replayed in my mind and it would slam me back into feeling miserable. I ducked into the bathroom a few times to cry, blow my nose, and pull myself together.

After a quick lunch of sandwiches and coffee, we were back at it. We unpacked box after box of product, carefully arranging shampoo, conditioner, hairspray, mousse, lotion, nail polish, and hairbrushes on the spanking new shelves. We stocked about half the shelves and polished the hair station mirrors by three in the afternoon. I was bushed. My body ached, and I felt bruised on the inside—raw and tender.

Jas straightened up from cleaning plaster dust off one of the hydraulic chairs, dust rag in hand. "Let's go get your stuff from your apartment before we're too tired to move."

"Sounds like a plan. My only question is how are we going to schlep all my stuff on the bus? Even though it's a furnished apartment, I'm still going to end up filling most of the boxes we just unpacked. I don't have money for a taxi, and I can't ask you to pay for that after all that you've done for me." God, I sounded like such a loser.

"Oh yeah, I haven't told you my little piece of news. Last night didn't seem like the right time, and today we've been so busy I completely forgot."

She put her rag down and motioned for me to follow. She opened the back door and stood back.

"Voila, my new wheels." Jas flourished her hands like a Price Is Right model.

It was the truck that I half remembered seeing last night when I made my way over the icy road to her back door. The truck was a 1974 Ford Ranger. Primer and rust covered most of it; what was left was the colour of a school bus. That orangey yellow colour that wasn't either orange or yellow.

"Where and when did you get that?"

"I picked it up yesterday. I knew I would need a set of wheels, and I found this baby on *Kijiji*. Seems to work and the price was right."

We filled the bed of the truck with the empty boxes and covered the cardboard mountain with a blue plastic tarp, securing it down with bungee cords Jas dug out of the cab. The last thing we needed was to have boxes take flight as we motored down the Deerfoot.

My apartment was just as I left it, my dirty clothes strewn all over the unmade bed, dishes piled in the sink. Everything was the same, except for the heat. My apartment was always cold. The heat never seemed to work properly except for today. Hot air blasted from the radiators and the apartment was stifling.

"God, it feels like a sauna in here." Jas waved her hand in front of her face.

She put down the empty boxes she was carrying and went downstairs to get another load. I started stuffing my clothes and anything that was unbreakable into garbage bags. Although, I didn't have many things, we still managed to use all the boxes we brought plus four garbage bags. Jas offered to give the place a quick going over, while I went down to face Mr. Stevenson. I told her not to get too crazy because I wasn't going to be seeing my damage deposit anyway.

I made my way downstairs to the landlord's suite. It was the first apartment on the left from the main door of the building. The stairwell smelled of disinfectant and cabbage and onions from someone's dinner. I had butterflies in my stomach. I felt like I was back in high school and going to see the principal for something I'd done wrong.

I knocked on the steel door of #101. The TV blared through the door. It sounded like a hockey game. No one answered. I knocked again, louder this time.

"Yah, Yah, I'm coming. Don't have to bang the friggin' door down."

Great, now I pissed him off. *Way to go, Hannah.*

The door opened, and Mr. S. glared at me. Not only had I interrupted his hockey game, but by the look of irritation on his face, I was also the last person he probably wanted to see right now. Wait until he found out I didn't have the money.

"I see ya made it here before six. You'd better have the cash, Missy. I'm not taking any promises from you anymore."

"Actually, Mr. Stevenson, I don't have the money. I just came down to tell you I've moved my stuff out."

"He shoots! He scores!" screamed the sports announcer.

Mr. S. turned to look at the TV and then back at me. He scowled. Was he angry that I made him miss a goal or for not having the money?

"Humph," he grunted. "Figures, and don't ya be expect'n your damage deposit because you ain't getting it." He slammed the door in my face.

I guess that settled it. Everything in my life seemed to be punctuated by the slamming of doors.

Jas did a terrific job giving the place one last dust and polish. It smelled fresh.

My place. Not anymore. When I thought about it, the apartment was nothing special. Used, uninspired furniture, a plain bed, a postage stamp of a bathroom with no tub. Hot water was always a scarcity, the fridge hummed too loud, the faucet in the kitchen dripped, and the windows were drafty. Bit of a dump really.

But, it had been my dump.

"You ready to go?" Jas asked.

I nodded and followed her to the door. When the door swung closed behind us, the lock automatically engaged. I dropped my keys in Mr. Stevenson's mailbox and left my apartment building for the last time. I didn't bother to look back.

Back at Jas's place, we hauled all my boxes into the spare room. I decided, for now, they could stay packed.

I had a place to sleep, but I still had quite a few outstanding bills that were collecting interest by the minute. As much as I would like to put off calling my mom, I didn't have a choice. I took my cell phone into my new room, sat on the floor, and dialed the number.

It was after nine. She was probably watching TV. Da was most likely reading in the chair next to her. I hoped Da would answer the phone. It would be so much easier to ask him for the money.

"Hi." I rubbed the palm of my free hand up and down the leg of my pants.

"Why are you calling so late?" Mom actually sounded concerned.

"I need to ask a favor."

"If you've met someone and want to bring him for Christmas dinner, it's a bit last minute. I've only planned for five people. I don't know why you always leave things to the very end. It always ends up inconveniencing someone."

"No, I'm not calling to ask if I can bring a date. I'm not seeing anyone right now. What I need to ask is kinda important."

"There is no need to snipe at me."

"Mom," I continued, ignoring my irritation, "the spa is having financial trouble and my paycheque bounced. My boss says we won't see the money until next week."

"Oh."

"I was wondering if you and Da could float me some money. I'll pay you back as soon as I can. I promise."

"How much do you need?"

"I was thinking eight or nine hundred dollars ought to cover my bills. I promise to pay it back."

"Well now, I'll have to ask your father about that. A few hundred dollars I would say yes to, but nine hundred dollars is a lot of money."

I rolled my eyes up to the ceiling. *No kidding mom.*

"I'll let you know tomorrow."

"Thanks." I wasn't sure what I was thanking her for.

I said goodbye and hung up. There was one more call that I needed to make before heading to bed. I dug the card out of my purse and dialed the number before I changed my mind. I needed money desperately, and I knew where I could make some in a hurry.

Aaron answered on the fourth ring, just when I anticipated his voice mail picking up.

"Hello." He sounded annoyed. Maybe this wasn't such a good idea.

"Hi, Aaron, this is Hannah. I hope I didn't catch you in the middle of something. If this isn't a good time, I can call back later." My words came out in a rush.

"Hi," his voice softened. "I didn't think you would actually call me."

"My work schedule opened up suddenly, and if you are still interested in having me sit for you, I'm available."

"Sure, sure I can still use you." I winced at his choice of words. "What day would be good for you?"

We arranged a time for the photo shoot, and he gave me directions to his studio. He asked for my phone number in case he had to reschedule the shoot. I gave him my cell number because I didn't know where or what I would be doing in the near future. We ended the call, and as I settled onto Jas's couch for the night, I felt just a sliver of hopefulness. Maybe things would work out all right after all.

* * * *

After three days, I got tired of digging my clothes out of the garbage bags I had thrown them in when I moved. I needed to feel like I belonged somewhere even if it was temporary. It was time to unpack and settle into my new digs. I looked at the mountain of boxes jammed into the corners of the small room. I needed to clear some floor space for my old bed, nightstand, and dresser that I planned on picking up from my parents' house.

Telling my mom why I needed my old bedroom furniture was humiliating. At least she came through with the money to cover my bills, and I was meeting with Aaron in a couple of days so I'd be getting yet another small injection of cash.

I flipped open the top of the nearest box. When I left my apartment, I had just thrown everything willy-nilly into boxes and bags. There hadn't been time to label anything. I opened the nearest box and looked inside. The past floated up, uninvited. I reached inside and lightly touched the chest that lay within. I didn't want to take it out, but now that I saw it, I couldn't just close the flaps of the box and shove it into the closet like I had in the past.

Slowly, carefully, I lifted the wrapped package out and placed it gently on the floor. It was heavier than I remembered. I got down on my knees and gingerly removed the yellowed and crinkled shroud of tissue paper that surrounded it. I didn't know why I took the extra precaution of wrapping it in tissue because the box wasn't breakable. I put the tissue paper aside and held the carved, wooden chest in my hands. I held it close, trying desperately to feel the woman it had belonged to, to sense her energy, her vibrancy, anything that felt like her. There was nothing there but the faint smell of sandalwood from the chest itself.

I sat down cross-legged on the floor and placed it in front of me. I traced my finger over the finely detailed image of the Indian Goddess Ganesh carved into the lid. Before I changed my mind, I released the brass catch and opened it. A jagged sigh escaped my lips. It sounded far away.

This was one of the things Noni had left me in her will. A month after her funeral, I sat with my parents while the lawyer parceled out her possessions. None of it was a surprise. She had signed over the farm to my parents years ago, so all that was left for her to bequeath were her personal belongings.

I had only vague memories of the funeral, but I remembered that horrible day at the lawyer's office so clearly. My mother had worn a black crepe dress and matching silk scarf knotted at her throat. She had held herself ramrod straight, distant in her unexpressed grief and unshed tears. My father had dressed up in his only good suit, looking uncomfortable in his tight collar and tie. I remembered the texture of my grief, the coarse fabric of it rubbing my nerves raw. The weight of it pushing me down and away from the world around me. Nothing felt real, nothing made sense. It still didn't.

The conference room we'd been led into made my skin crawl. The whole room was wrapped in dark wood—the floors, the walls, even the furniture. I struggled not to hyperventilate as I followed my parents into the room-sized coffin.

We had sat at the conference table with the lawyer across from us reading out the complicated lengthy legalese. The words didn't sound like English. All those words to describe so few material things and not enough about the life Noni had lived. Is that what it all comes down to—her talent, her smile, her sense of humor, her gift of seeing the world—all condensed, abbreviated into a few trinkets and bobbles?

My mom and da were given the family photo albums, Noni's antiques that were scattered about the farm house, the few pieces of jewelry that were actually worth something, and the three thousand dollars Noni had in her savings account at the time of her death. Noni gave me all of her paintings, brushes, sketchbooks, art books, and the box that now sat on the floor in front of me.

At the time, I was so angry with Noni for leaving me, for not telling me she was sick, for not preparing me for a life without her, that I couldn't, wouldn't, look past my rage to go through any of the things she had bequeathed to me. The only things I took with me when I moved were her self-portrait and the wooden box. I'd left the box in its cardboard container and put it in the back of the closet, not discarded but hopefully forgotten.

Now I faced it again. With the lid raised, the smell of sandalwood was stronger. I lifted out a pair of jet earrings. I held them up, the light dancing off the surface of the shiny black beads. Noni had worn these to my high school graduation.

I shook the earrings, making the beads dance and shimmy. Putting them aside, I pulled out a small, black, travel diary, its leather cover scuffed and scarred, the edges worn smooth from handling. The box held five other diaries just like this one.

Just seeing her handwriting, her quick sketches in the boarders of the page, and the postcards she had affixed to the yellowed pages with little, black photo corners made her absence a searing pain. A thousand panicked sparrows frantically beat their wings trying to escape my chest. I wouldn't grant them freedom.

I flipped to the front page of the first diary. This journal was the one she started when she first set out to study art in Paris. She had taken four months before beginning her time at the École des Beaux-Arts to travel around France with a girlfriend. I read her thoughts and secret desires, all written in her elegant handwriting. I studied the black and white photos of her. In one she stood in a field of lavender, her head thrown back catching the heat of a summer afternoon on her face. Another showed her and her girlfriend standing on the lookout of the Eiffel Tower, the iron railing behind them and the city spread out below them. Yet another picture showed her at a small outdoor café. She was looking straight at the lens, and the camera had caught her taking a sip of something from a large white cup, her short hair caught in the breeze, her mouth obscured by the mug, but her eyes twinkled with a secret.

It struck me how young she looked in all the snap shots. I looked at the dates of her journal entries and was amazed to realize she was young, younger than I was now. I was still working at a tack shop and dreaming about being an artist when my grandmother, at the same age, had headed off to Europe and was having the time of her life.

Over the years, Noni had told me stories about her travels, but reading about them in her own words, hearing the echo of the young girl she had been, her fearlessness, her excitement at studying what she loved, her complete joy in discovering new places, was such an odd experience. It was like meeting my grandmother for the first time. I had always thought Noni was beautiful, but in the way a child sees beauty — in the soft focus of love and affection, not in the assessing of physical attributes. For the first time, looking at the photos, I realized she really was an extraordinarily beautiful young woman.

Vague questions that had started the night Christian and I had talked at the club loomed in the back of my mind. While I read Noni's journal, they grew into fully formed mysteries that I needed to answer. Had my grandmother been happy in her later years? Did she regret giving up this vivid life, outlined in her own hand, to become a farmer's wife, a mother, and a grandmother?

I had read only half of the first journal when I called it quits. It was late. I was exhausted, my back was stiff, and my butt had gone numb from sitting on the hard floor. I carefully replaced the journal and closed the lid on the keepsake chest. I wasn't going to find the answers to my questions tonight, and I needed to get a tiny corner of my life in order.

In the end, I unpacked only two more boxes. The only two I really needed now that I was rooming with Jas. One of the boxes contained my toiletries, hair dryer, make-up, and some costume jewelry. The other box held bills, papers, a few books, and Noni's painting, wrapped in a bath towel for protection.

I pulled out the painting and carefully unwrapped it, then set it leaning on the top of a stack of boxes with her keepsake chest next to it. After hanging my clothes on the wooden rod in the miniscule closet and stacking my sweaters on the shelf above, I surveyed my new bedroom. Everything that defined who I was fit into the tiny space.

The wings of those lost birds began to beat in frantic rhythm again. I needed to find Jas and be in her company for a while. I needed to get away from my thoughts. As I turned out the light, I realized I had lost something, something that wasn't hanging in the closet or packed in a box, and I wasn't sure how I was going to get it back or if I even could.

Chapter Nineteen

On the day of the photo shoot, I drove Jas's truck to Aaron's studio. I gave myself plenty of time to get there in case I got lost, but, because of Aaron's detailed directions, I arrived ten minutes early. I was having second thoughts about the shoot, so instead of going in right away, I sat in the truck with the engine running and waited to see if the feeling would pass.

His offer sounded legit, and looking around, the area didn't look seedy. I mean, it wasn't an upscale part of the city by anybody's standards, not that I expected a young artist to be able to afford much. The building looked well kept, and it wasn't too far from the museum even if it was directly in front of the CN rail yard.

His studio was the middle unit of a warehouse-type structure. The façade was clad in tin pressed to look like brick and had been painted red to further the illusion. Each unit had oversized windows and large industrial doors with wooden side steps leading down to a gravel-strewn yard. At one time, the warehouse probably stored the goods that came off the trains. Now, arched canopies hung above each door, declaring the varied proprietors who worked there. There was a graphic artist, Aaron's studio, a web designer, and a glass artist.

What would it be like to have a place of my own in a building like that, surrounded by other artists and creative types? I couldn't imagine what it would feel like to have a whole space dedicated to painting, to be a full time artist, a professional. What would my life look like if I were a real artist instead of wishing I could be one?

Why did I keep doing this to myself? Why did I waste my time daydreaming about being an artist when the thought of picking up a brush right now hurt beyond belief? A painter needs to paint and I couldn't. Instead I should be dealing with the disaster that was my life. My reality was that I was cash poor, and at least this gig paid. I made my decision despite my nerves, turned off the engine, and headed in for the photo shoot.

From the entrance, I stepped into a small room. Compared to the brightness of the afternoon sun reflecting off the snow-covered streets, it was as dark as a cave. I stood for a moment, letting my eyes adjust to the low light. The room was deserted.

There were two doors leading off the space, one at the back and one to the right. The room had several pieces of furniture crammed into it. In the back corner was a desk and chair. The desk was home to a state of the art computer, laser printer, and phone. There were notepads, pens and pencils, and empty paper coffee cups strewn about the surface. Mounted on the wall behind the desk were a myriad of frame samples in every colour and material imaginable.

At the front of the room, two black leather tub chairs and a chaise lounge covered in a leopard print fabric were grouped around a coffee table. The chaise looked like it belonged more in a brothel than a photographer's studio. Something a Lady of the Evening would lounge on while she waited for her next client. That uneasy feeling returned.

I called out but no one answered. I didn't want to knock on the doors in case Aaron was in the middle of a session. There was nothing to do but take a seat and wait. I'd give him ten minutes, and, if no one came out, I was going to head home. I skirted the chaise and sat in one of the black chairs.

While I waited, I scanned the photographs hanging on the walls. When he still hadn't appeared, I picked up a large album from the stack on the coffee table. I flipped through the pages looking at his work. I went through two more albums and had just decided to cut my losses and go home when the door at the back of the room opened and Aaron walked in.

"Hi. Is it that time already?"

"Actually, it's after *that* time, and I was just about to leave. I thought maybe you forgot about our appointment." Even though he was paying me to be here, I was annoyed that he had kept me waiting.

"Sorry, I was in the darkroom developing some film, and the time just got away from me."

"Do you make it a habit to keep clients waiting too?" I wasn't going to let him off the hook that easily.

"I hate to admit this, but yeah, I do. I wish I didn't but, according to Sandy, I do it all the time."

"If you know you have a client coming and you want to work in your darkroom, set the timer to go off a few minutes before they are scheduled to arrive and you will never keep them waiting."

"That's a good idea. I don't know why I never thought of doing that. Now, I've kept you waiting long enough, shall we get started?"

I followed him through the door on the right and into the studio itself. It was a much larger room than the front room. Two floor-to-ceiling windows had their blackout shades drawn, throwing the room into an unnatural gloaming considering the time of day. The studio was much warmer than the anterior space, and the heat reminded me he'd told me not to wear underwear. That only added to my nerves, which were already making me slightly nauseous.

Against the far wall, an area had already been set up for the shoot. Situated on either side of a three-foot white wooden box were two bulky lights on tripods, and nearby, several cameras and assorted photography paraphernalia covered a table's surface.

"For today's shoot, I'm going to have you pose on the box. I think I'm going to shoot your back, neck, and shoulders but we'll see if I want to do something else as the shoot progresses."

"Okay" was all I could think to say.

I was really starting to lose my cool at this point. Now that I was standing in the room and looking at where I would be doing a nude photo shoot, the money didn't seem all that important. I could just imagine what my mother would say if she knew what I was doing. She would have freaked. Now, I was doing a little freaking of my own.

As if reading my thoughts, Aaron spoke up. "Look, I know you haven't done any modeling before, and if you don't feel comfortable about it, you can still say no. I mean, don't get me wrong, I think you would make a great model, that's why I asked you, but if you are having second thoughts, it's okay to change your mind about doing this."

"No, I'm fine. Just a little nervous is all." I tried not to choke on my words.

"Let's get down to work, then. You can change in the bathroom. It's in the back next to the darkroom. There's a robe hanging on the door. You can slip into that."

I made my way back through the reception area and through the door Aaron had come out of earlier. It didn't take long for me to change into the thin cotton robe and within minutes, I padded back to the studio in my bare feet.

It wasn't a long walk back, but the floor was cold, and I was shivering by the time I entered the studio. The first time I stepped into the studio, I thought it was too warm. Now standing in my bare feet, wearing only a thin cotton robe, the temperature in the room was a welcome balm. Aaron's back was towards me while he fiddled with his cameras laid out on the table. I cleared my throat to get his attention.

He turned and gave me smile. "That was quick."

"There wasn't much to do to get ready," I said, trying to make light of how nervous I was.

"Shall we?"

"Sure." I wrapped my arms around myself.

"Could you take a seat on the box? I'm going to take a few test shots before we get down to business."

I followed his instructions, perching on the edge of the box and holding the corners of my robe tightly together. He picked up a light meter and held it close to my face. When the lights flashed, I jumped.

"Did you want me to put some music on?"

I nodded, and he picked up a remote from the table and loud aggressive rock filled the air. I flinched and shook my head. He hit the remote again, and a new age soundtrack complete with birdsong and a burbling stream replaced the rock music. It reminded me of the saccharine stuff they played at the Serenity. I vigorously shook my head holding up my hand for him to stop. He laughed and hit the remote again. Debussy's *Prélude à l'après-midi d'un faune* hit all the right notes. I nodded, and Aaron put down the remote.

He picked up the smallest of the cameras and instructed me to sit in the middle of the box. I did what he asked and sat with my legs tucked underneath me. He took the pictures quickly. Every few shots, he would stop and view the images on the screen of the digital camera. By the time the test shots were done, I was used to the popping sound when the flash went off and the small whine as it recharged. Whatever he was seeing on the camera must have satisfied Aaron because he put the camera down and picked up a folded white sheet from the table.

The moment of truth. Could I do this? Would I do this?

I climbed off the box and took the sheet from him. It was soft under my fingertips and smelled of fresh laundry soap.

"I'm going to step outside while you change. You can just leave the robe on the chair and wrap yourself in the sheet. Then sit in the middle of the box just like you did before."

"Sure, no problem," I said as he stepped out of the studio and closed the door behind him.

I exchanged the safety of the robe for the white sheet. It more than covered me, with fabric to spare, but it still felt too flimsy for comfort. I wrapped the sheet over one shoulder and gathered the extra fabric that pooled at my feet in my left hand. As gingerly as I could, I sat on the corner of the box and scooted myself over until I was in the middle.

Moments later, Aaron tapped on the door before walking in and heading directly to the table. He picked up one of the large black cameras.

"I know being vulnerable like this isn't easy, but try to relax. If you feel uncomfortable at any time, you can just say stop, and we'll call it a day. Okay?"

"Okay."

"First, let's get you so that you are sitting with your back to me. Yeah, that's good, sit like that on one hip. Great. Now turn your head to the left. No, that's too far. Turn your head back a little. Good." He stepped closer. "Now hold onto the sheet with your right hand and put your other hand here," he guided my hand to rest on my knee. "Now, I'm just going to adjust the draping of the sheet."

Aaron's hand lightly brushed against my back when he lowered the sheet so it sat just a hair's breadth above my butt. I tried not to think about his hand touching my bare skin.

Satisfied with my pose, he stepped back, picked up a camera from the table, and began shooting. There was a rhythm to the work that relaxed me—the pop, click, and whirr of the equipment, his voice calling out positions, his touch when he rearranged the drape around my body.

I didn't know how long we had been at it—I had no sense of time, but after a while, my back began to ache and the leg I was sitting on fell asleep. I tried to adjust my sitting position to ease the ache when Aaron put down his camera and said we should take a break. He handed me the robe and left to get us both some water.

While he was gone, I changed back into the robe and stretched out my back. I had no idea being a model was such hard work. I wasn't moving around much, but holding each pose and trying to remain as still as possible took a great deal of focus and energy. I was quite warm from sitting under the hot lights, and I welcomed something cold to drink. When he came back with the water, I drank half the bottle in one greedy gulp.

"How are you holding up?"

"Good, it's harder than I thought it would be, but I'll be fine. This is just what I needed." I held up the almost empty bottle of water.

"I'm glad you changed your mind about doing the session. These are going to be great."

"I'm glad too. It's not what I thought it would be like. Do you always shoot with film? I would have thought that you'd be using digital cameras. Wouldn't it be easier and faster? You could tell right away if you had a good shot."

"Yes, but easier and faster are not always better. I prefer to use film when I'm shooting medium format." I gave him a puzzled look. "Medium format uses larger film than most cameras and gives me a higher resolution. Basically, it allows me to print bigger enlargements without any blur or fuzziness I would get if I used a smaller format film. But getting back to your question, I feel the process of creating art is not just in the shoot, but in the developing. I like to get my hands into it, to be a part of the process on a basic level from start to finish. Sure, I use digital but mostly for client work, headshots, things like that. The images I create for my own art and pleasure, I like to use film."

"I get that. I'm not a photographer, but I used to paint. I loved the process of preparing the canvas and mixing the paints. Painting is not just about the end result but the process too. It's like a part of me gets imbued into the work, into the layers of pigment. I also understand how you have a tendency to lose track of time. That happens to me a lot too. Used to annoy my mother to no end."

"Is that where the timer idea came from?"

"Yeah, but I only used it when I absolutely had to because part of the joy of painting was losing myself in it, to be in a place where nothing existed but the pure joy of creating."

"That's it exactly. I guess it takes another artist to understand that. That's one thing I couldn't get Sandy to understand; I wasn't ignoring her on purpose. It's one of the things that finally broke us up."

"I'm sorry to hear that," I said, though I was surprised to discover I really wasn't. In fact, Aaron's newly revealed single status gave me a strange, little thrill. *Hannah, give your head a shake!* Did I need to call Jas so she could remind me what happened the last time I fell for a hunky stranger?

"Don't be. In the long run, we really weren't suited for each other."

"I can relate to that. It's been a hobby of mine to pick completely unsuitable people to date, with similar results. I just recently decided that it's not a great way to spend my time." I finished my water and put the empty on the table.

"Ready to get back to work?"

"Sure."

When he started to leave, I stopped him. It seemed silly to have him leave every time I needed to change. I asked him to turn his back while I swapped the robe for the sheet again. I got back into position on the box and told him it was okay to turn around.

Aaron wanted to focus on my neck and shoulders so he had me kneel on the box and hold the draping in both hands at my chest, exposing both shoulders. He made some small adjustments to my pose and then, picking up a camera, he climbed up the ladder. He checked the shot and quickly climbed back down. He made a few more changes to my pose and gently brushed my hair to one side, his fingertips on my neck sending shivers down my spine. I tried to ignore the sensation and focus on holding my pose.

He climbed the ladder again and began shooting. The second part of the session went as quickly as the first. We only stopped when Aaron had to reload his camera or when he needed me to change a pose. Before I knew it, he'd taken all the shots he wanted, there was no more film left to load into the cameras, and the session was over.

I changed back into my street clothes and joined Aaron in the reception area of his studio. Every muscle in my body ached from holding poses for so long, but it felt good. It wasn't sleazy or anything like I had feared it would be. Aaron was who he said he was, a fine art photographer who loved what he did. Not once during the shoot did he try to do anything indecent or take advantage of my vulnerability. I had felt safe and relaxed during the whole session.

"Here you go," Aaron handed me a cheque. "Thank you for your work today. You were really great."

"No problem and thanks for this." I held up the cheque. "I'm between jobs right now so this is really going to come in handy." I carefully folded the cheque and put it in my purse.

"If you're looking for work, you could model full time. You're really a natural at it, and there is always a need for more artists' models. In fact, I could make a few phone calls if you want."

"I really do appreciate that, but right now I think I'll pass. I'm helping my girlfriend, Jas, set up her new hair salon in Inglewood, and I may end up working there after Christmas. I'm not really sure; things are a little up in the air right now. Anyway, I should get going." I started for the door.

"Before you go, I have something to ask you."

I turned to face him, "Sure, ask away."

"I was wondering if maybe I could call you sometime. I mean, not right away. I'm leaving for Australia for a few months, but I was thinking maybe when I get back? I know you said you've sworn off dating, but a lot can happen in a couple of months, and maybe you'll change your mind by then." He shoved his hands in his pockets and glancing down at his feet.

He made me want to giggle. During the photo shoot, he was so in control and in his element, but asking me out, he became all nervous and awkward. He looked so sweet standing there.

"Sure, I'd like that. You've got my cell number so call me when you get back." His face relaxed with relief.

Once inside the truck I pulled the cheque out of my pocket. It was made out for $150 just like he promised. I finally meet a sweet guy who keeps his promises, and I've put myself off the market. I couldn't help but smile at the irony. But, like Aaron said, a lot can happen in a few months. I left the studio and headed home feeling a little bit lighter, sensing that my life might finally start heading in a better direction.

Chapter Twenty

Christmas was just around the corner, and since I was planning to spend the holiday at my parents' place anyway, I decided to head there a little early. Jas and I had done all the salon set-up we could do for now, and there really wasn't much for me to do until the New Year. She was busy buying Christmas presents, securing her licenses and permits, and interviewing receptionists for the shop. I couldn't really help her with those things, and I felt like I was just getting in the way. If I went to the farm, I could at least ride my horse and help my da with the chores. I might even stay with my parents until after the holidays, depending on if Jas had anything for me to do.

I still hadn't retrieved my bed and night stand from my old room at home, but I figured if I was going home early, I'd just wait to take them with me when I headed back to the city in the New Year. I also decided to take all my unopened boxes and store them in the attic at the farm. They were just taking up valuable space. Jas offered to drive me and my surplus stuff to my parents' place, and I took her up on the offer.

She had christened her odd little truck "Duckie." The ride through the city was uneventful, but when we hit the country roads, the truck began to show its true nature. Duckie vibrated ominously when she pushed the safe speed limit for traveling backcountry roads in winter. My lower back ached from bracing my feet against the floor of the foot well. Jas's love for speed reduced the normal hour drive to my parents to a mere forty-five minutes.

The snow was blowing hard. The truck had its problems, but thankfully, Duckie's heating worked, and it was nice and cozy inside the cab. Katy Perry's "Roar" blared on the tinny radio, and we sang along just as loudly. Jas kept time with the song, her fingers tapping out the beat on the steering wheel. Neither of us would ever make it through a *Canadian Idol* audition, but that didn't stop us from trying to hit all the high notes.

She took the left turn onto my parents' winding driveway a little too sharply, and Duckie's wheels started to slide on the hard packed snow. I pushed my feet even harder into the floor of the truck. She corrected her steering, and the truck straightened out. She didn't miss a beat of her singing. She gunned the engine for the last sprint up to the two-story farmhouse and braked the truck to a shuddering halt at the side of the house.

We jumped out of the truck and headed for the house. After listening to the music blaring and the truck rumbling for three quarters of an hour, the quiet of the country was deafening. We clambered up the front porch, our boots thudding hollowly on the wooden planks. I was just about to open the door when it swung open. Da stood there welcoming us in.

He gave me a bear hug. "Hi, princess."

"Hi, Da."

His old, grey cardigan was scratchy against my cheek, and he smelled of Old Spice and pipe tobacco. He gave me a kiss on the forehead.

"Hello Mr. M.; good to see you again."

"You're not getting off that lightly. You and your polite talk. Come here." Da gathered Jas into a hug. When he let go, she was smiling, and a soft blush brightened her cheeks.

The house smelled like all the family dinners of my childhood: pot roast, potatoes, and the tang of freshly peeled apples.

"That's some truck you got out there." A playful grin lit up Da's face.

"Isn't she something? I just love her. Do you want to go check her out?"

Da grabbed his parka from the hook by the door.

"I'll join you guys in a sec; I'm just going to say hi to Mom."

He nodded and went outside with Jas. I followed the trail of delicious smells past the living room and into the kitchen. The living room hadn't been redecorated since the eighties. It was a time warp of peach and seafoam green right down to the curtains. Everything matched except my da's battered leather recliner, which sat next to the brick fireplace. Mom had threatened to throw it out, but Da, on that rare occasion, wouldn't give in to her wishes and the recliner stayed.

The kitchen had escaped the fate of the rest of the house and still retained a country charm with its faded linoleum floors and butcher-block counters. The clinking music of metal lids dancing on boiling pots and the bland melody of easy listening music, turned down low, filled the room.

My mom stood at the counter, her face in profile. I silently watched while she cut strips from a round of pie dough she had rolled out on the flour-dusted counter. She looked so small standing alone in our kitchen. The room used to seem full with the three of us, the women of the house. If I listened closely, I imagined I could hear the faint echoes of our voices picking up the threads of everyday life and weaving our female tapestry in the colours of love, pain, and unexamined truths. Without Noni's contributions, her peacemaking presence, Mom and I were just loose threads unable to maintain the whole of what used to be.

I stared at her hands, fascinated by their strength, the deftness and precision of her movements, as she placed the final strip of dough on the top of the pie, completing a perfect lattice. My fingers itched to hold a brush. To capture the texture of her skin, the grainy flour dusting her knuckles. I ignored the sensation.

"Hi." I walked into the kitchen as she turned from the counter.

Her crisp apron was pristine. How did she manage to make a pie without getting flour all over herself?

"I didn't hear you come in." She looked past me. "Where's Jasmine?"

"She's outside showing Da her new wheels."

She stepped forward, presenting me with her cheek while holding her hands up and away from her sides. I kissed her cheek. Her skin felt dry and papery and smelled of her face powder. "You look great."

Her gaze travelled down from my head to my toes. "You look nice too. You'd look prettier if you wore a skirt and put on some lipstick, though."

Thanks, Mom.

I walked over to the stove, lifted up the pot lids, and peeked inside. Potatoes, turnips, and carrots. The same kind of family meals she had made for as long as I could remember.

"Thanks again for the loan." I dug into the front pocket of my jeans and fished out a folded cheque. "I got this in the mail the other day. It's not all of what the spa owes me, but at least it is something. One of the girls from work says the spa is in receivership, so I guess I should be grateful for what little they paid me. I'll get the rest of what I owe you as soon as I can." I held out the cheque.

Mom washed the pie dough and flour off her hands and dried them on a faded dishtowel hanging on the oven door. She plucked the cheque out of my fingers and it disappeared into the pocket of her apron.

"So you're unemployed, then." She turned to the stove so I had to move out of her way.

I talked to her back while she pulled the roast out of the oven and slipped the pie in its place. "I updated my resume, and I've already applied at a few places," I lied. "In the meantime, I'm working for Jas."

She turned to me, her gaze steady. "You'll find another job. You just need to commit yourself to the task."

I nodded. "I'm going to go bring my stuff in," I said, escaping as fast as I could.

I avoided her until we all sat down to eat. Dinner was wonderful, as always. Mom had never tried her hand at anything she considered artistic because she believed art was a waste of time. It was more practical to put her energies into things she deemed important, like running the household, taking care of our family, and helping out with the farm. She would never admit it, but her artistic flair came through in the food she prepared. She cooked simple meals, but it was always infused with exotic seasonings and precise presentation.

During dinner, Jas entertained everyone with talk about her salon, taking the focus off me. When everyone had eaten their fill, Jas and I cleared the table. She offered to help with dishes, but Mom wouldn't hear if it. So instead, Jas and my da went out to take another look at Duckie. He wanted to do some minor tinkering with the engine. He thought he could stop the truck from shaking when it went over forty kilometers.

That left me alone with Mom. Without saying a word, we each slipped into the roles we had always had in the kitchen. She washed, I dried and put away the dishes—all in silence. Whenever she wasn't telling me what to do or commenting on how I was doing something wrong, my mother would disappear inside herself and wouldn't talk to me. I didn't know where she went or what she was thinking, but I knew from experience not to try engaging her in conversation because she just wouldn't respond.

Jas left for home at ten, and my mother headed to bed shortly after that. Da and I decided to haul my boxes up to the attic for storage. We put all my things except Noni's self-portrait and her keepsake box in the attic. Those two treasures went in my bedroom.

I hadn't been up to the attic in ages. After helping me with the last box, he kissed me good night and gave me strict orders not to stay up too late.

Before heading downstairs, he turned to me. "You okay?"

"Yeah, Da, I'm fine." I gave him what I hoped was a cheery smile. "Sleep well."

"You too." He shut the door. It closed with a soft click. I walked the perimeter of the attic. It wasn't just a place to store junk: this had been Noni's and my painting studio. Unframed canvases were stacked in layers against the walls, and a few hung alongside tacked up pencil and charcoal drawings. I wandered over to the charcoal drawing I'd made of our dog, Chipper, when I was six. When I got older, and Noni helped to refine my skills as a painter, charcoal on paper was replaced with oil on canvas. Pictures of our farm animals and my family evolved into still life studies, moody landscapes, and more complex portraits of my family and friends.

I looked around. Something wasn't right. These were all my paintings. Noni's work wasn't here. I stopped my tour of the studio in front of my easel, still set up in the middle of the room, like a loyal pet waiting silently and patiently for my return. Noni's easel was missing from its customary place next to mine. I found it propped up under the east dormer next to a large canvas tarp. I pulled back the musty tarp, revealing the stack of paintings beneath. These were all Noni's. Mom must have put them here. Resentful, I kicked the drop cloth out of my way, sending up a cloud of dust in the process.

I lingered over the paintings, hauling each one out and placing it on my knees while I crouched on the dusty floor. Each possessed a secret life that shone from the layers of pigment. A clarity of detail, a richness of texture. These were good enough to be hanging in any high-end gallery in town. And that's where they should be, not discarded in the dark, lonely corners of this forgotten place.

"Noni, I miss you so much. My life's become unraveled without you, and I don't know what to do. Please, Noni, I need your help," I whispered to the empty room.

Chapter Twenty-One

The next day, I didn't want to get up. I'd had a restless night of tossing and turning and even though I was physically tired, when I closed my eyes, they kept popping open. When daylight finally started to peek around my closed curtains, I finally felt ready for sleep. I wanted to stay buried under my comforter forever.

As I contemplated that idea, my mother barged in, turned on the lights, and flung back the curtains. "Time to get up or you'll be late for church. Breakfast will be ready in fifteen minutes."

I dragged myself out of bed. I didn't have a choice.

I waited until we were almost finished with breakfast before I told my mother I wasn't going to join them at church. I spread homemade strawberry preserves on my toast to avoid my mother's disapproving stare.

"I don't understand what you have to do around here today that's more important than going to church," Mom sniffed.

Da poured himself another cup of coffee, carefully stirring in the cream.

I wanted to spend the day in the attic, and I didn't feel up to defending myself or dealing with my mother's disapproval. Having her label me a sinner and a lazy heathen seemed easier than trying to explain.

"I just need some time to make some plans, make a few phone calls, and check out some job opportunities. Besides, I think I'm coming down with a cold."

"Can't you call people on Monday? Surely most places would be closed today. And if you're getting sick, you need to drink more orange juice and get some fresh air, not stay inside."

"Mom, please. I have things that I need to do." I picked up my plate and started to fill the sink with hot water and dish soap. "I'll do the dishes and clean up the kitchen while you get ready." I kept my back to her, watching the sink fill with bubbles. I tried to ignore the angry slash of her knife on her plate as she savaged her innocent breakfast sausage.

When she finished eating, she slapped her napkin down on the table and stood up. "Frankly, Hannah, I think you like to disagree with me because you enjoy being contrary." She left the room and went upstairs.

Da finished his coffee in silence. When he was done, he grabbed his coat and headed outside, but not before giving me a gentle squeeze on the shoulder. I smiled up at him. Alone in the kitchen, I lost myself in the soothing repetitiveness of domestic chores while I went about clearing the table and washing up the dishes. Mom came back down a few minutes later. When I heard her footsteps on the stairs, I focused on scrubbing the grease-coated pan I had in my hands.

The back door opened and a gust of icy wind followed my da in, swirling around my ankles and ruffling the edges of the blue gingham tablecloth.

"Margaret, are you ready to go?" He called out, brushing snow off the front of his jacket.

Mom appeared wearing her Sunday wool coat and a paisley silk scarf knotted at her throat. "George, there is no need to yell like that. We may make our living off the land but we're not a bunch of uneducated rednecks."

Snapping her purse closed she walked past me to put on her winter boots. On her way out, she picked up a cloth shoe bag containing the black leather pumps she'd put on in the church parking lot before heading into the service.

"Drive carefully," I said to Da as I pulled the plug in the sink. The greasy water slurped down the drain.

"Always do. See you later." He stepped back outside into the frigid morning air.

"Don't forget to wipe down the counters and hang the dishcloth to dry. Don't leave it in the sink to get musty," Mom said, and shut the door behind her.

When I heard the truck rumble down the drive, I hastily wiped off the counter, rung out the dishcloth, and hung it on the little hook under the sink. I headed upstairs, but instead of going directly to the attic, I ended up in front of the door to Noni's bedroom. The dull brass doorknob was cold under my hand. I turned it and was surprised when it resisted my efforts. I rattled the doorknob in frustration. None of the doors in this house had ever been locked, not even the door to my parents' room.

I hadn't wanted to go into Noni's room after she died—not even after the funeral. I didn't need or want to be reminded she wouldn't be coming back. Ever. Now, as I stood staring at the unyielding door, I was possessed with the urgent need to be close to her things. Having read her journals, I now looked at her life differently. Now, I needed to see her room, to look into the shrine of her life and find out if it felt different, if there were clues to her truth that I hadn't noticed before.

But I was locked out, and removing this barrier was now more important than stealing a few hours of quiet time up in the attic. I searched all over the house looking for the key. The house was old, and the keys that fit the locks were large, heavy, and easy to spot. I peered into kitchen cupboards and in the small drawers and cubbies of the old roll-top desk in Da's study. I checked the obvious places like the key hooks at the back door.

I even ventured into my parents' room. I felt like I was twelve again stealing into the most forbidden place in the house. Although I was alone, I still tiptoed quietly across their bedroom carpet to the bureau. I carefully lifted the precisely folded underwear and socks, the soft cotton T-shirts and sweaters, but no luck. The dresser held no secrets, and I gave up. But before leaving the bedroom, I snuck into their bathroom. I stole a hairpin from my mom's stash she kept in a glass jar on the counter. Weapon in hand, I marched back to Noni's door and prepared to do battle.

I straightened out the hairpin and slowly began working the lock. The pin kept slipping off the tumblers inside. Then, just when I thought I had it, half of the pin broke off in the lock. I pounded on the door in frustration rattling it in its frame. It didn't care and remained locked and stubborn. I headed back to my parent's bathroom in search of a fresh hairpin and a pair of tweezers to pry out the broken piece.

Once I removed the broken bit of pin, I carefully straightened out the second pin, took a deep breath, and wiggled it around inside the keyhole. I focused on the feel of the tumblers, pushing firmly as the mechanism finally gave way with a satisfying click. I dropped the pin and turned the knob. The door eased open with a sad sigh, and I slipped inside, closing it behind me.

The first thing I noticed was her perfume, *Opium*. It lingered in the room, whispering in the corners, clinging to the walls. I breathed in the shadow of the spicy, thick scent. Noni had worn it every day that I'd known her. Underneath the scent of *Opium*, the room smelled only faintly of dust and abandon. Not the heavy quietude of neglect I expected from a room entombed for almost four years.

I leaned against the door, covering my eyes and peering through my fingers. Little glimpses, small doses of pain. Why did I want to be in here so bad?

The room looked like it always had. A cruel illusion of her presence that mocked me. The walls were the same vibrant purple, the familiar red velvet drapes closed tight against the insolent morning sun. Her bed was made, the pink silk duvet smoothed over the bed, the top folded neatly over to reveal the vibrant orange silk of the other side. The purple and gold banner of fabric suspended over the bed like a canopy, swayed slowly from some unforeseen breeze.

Lined up all around the perimeter of the room and piled on the dresser and nightstand were Noni's art books, her sketchpads scattered among them. These were mine now, but I had no desire to remove them. I wandered around the room, running a finger across the top of the dark wood dresser and looked at my dust-free finger. There were no sad cobwebs weeping from the corners of the ceiling, either.

Puzzled, I opened up Noni's closet. Her clothes hung neatly on the rod. Her scent was stronger in here. I touched the slithery fabrics of her dressing gowns, the fur collars of her coats, and the soft cottons of the flowing ethnic dresses she favored. I longed to take the silk scarf draped over a hanger. I wanted this bright and sensuous relic of my grandmother, but I knew the caretaker of her shrine would miss it. I reluctantly closed the closet and quietly left Noni's room, making sure that the door was firmly locked behind me.

My little excursion had left me feeling paper-thin. I headed to my room and lay down. I fell asleep and dreamed of empty churches and violent orange sunsets. I woke up when I heard my da calling out my name.

* * * *

Over the next two days, I filled my time helping my da around the farm; my desire to spend time in the attic was gone. I knew he really didn't need my help, but I appreciated the distraction. The work was mostly minor maintenance on the farm equipment, mending the odd length of fence, fixing a loose hinge on one of the stalls, and the general care of the few cows and chickens he still kept.

I also reacquainted myself with Geronimo, my horse. It had been awhile since I'd taken him out for a ride. My mom didn't ride, but Da made sure Geronimo had adequate exercise. Under his care my horse was fit and healthy and looked more like an energetic seven-year-old than the sixteen years he was. I felt guilty because I hadn't been there to ride him or take care of him myself. He let me know he resented my neglect, rebuffing me when I went to see him for the first time. It took some coaxing, a lot of time gently grooming him, and a few handfuls of carrots to win him over.

I took him out riding and ended up in an empty pasture as far away from the house as I could get. Geronimo's progress across the field was slow, but I didn't push him. Our breath plumed out into the crystalline air. His hooves made a crunching sound as they broke through the thin crust of ice that covered the powder below.

I looked out onto the never-ending whiteness, the split rail fence and the poplar windbreak surrounding the fields were the only dark strokes on an otherwise blank canvas. The wind picked up, whipping my hair into my eyes. I tucked the strays behind my ears and pulled my wool cap down lower over my ears. I reined Geronimo in, and we stood silent in the dead landscape. I listened to my horse's rhythmic breathing, the cruel moan of the wind, and the squeak of saddle leather when Geronimo shifted his weight.

Emptiness, biting wind, blowing snow. A sudden blind rage fractured my thoughts. Everything hurt; a pain long ignored drove needles into my heart. I tightened my grip on the reigns.

I threw my head back and screamed. "Why did you leave me all alone, Noni?! Why didn't you tell me you were so sick?! I had a right to know!" Hot tears streamed down my cheeks and froze salty tracks of grief on my wind-bitten skin.

Geronimo turned to look at me, his ears laid low. My screams startled a congress of ravens nesting in the nearby windbreak. They erupted into the air, a black smudge against the grey sky, cawing and chortling back at me. They wheeled in the air and then settled back down into the naked poplar branches.

I calmed my anxious horse. My throat hurt, and I felt ridiculous sitting in the middle of a field screaming at nothing and scaring my horse. I craved the darkness and comfort of my bed. I apologized to Geronimo as I turned him around and headed for the barn.

After I groomed and fed him, I walked inside the house, went up to my room, and shut the door. I changed into my PJs, climbed into bed, and stayed there. When my da came looking for me, I told him that the cold I felt coming on earlier had finally hit. I endured my mom telling me that was my own fault for getting sick because I didn't drink enough orange juice or get the right amount of fresh air before she left me alone.

On the third day, I was still in my bedroom, but I was bored. I had nothing to do in my room, so I pulled out Noni's journals. Reading her journals was fascinating but jarring at the same time. The pages revealed a side of my grandmother I hadn't known. I felt a little like a voyeur reading her private thoughts, but I couldn't stop myself from wanting to know more.

I read about her wanderings through Germany on one of her summer breaks. She spent three weeks traveling before heading back to Canada for the summer. She had met up with a man and was thoroughly enjoying his company and, by her own words, the sex was great. I blushed when I read these entries. She may have been a young woman when she was writing about this, but she was still my grandmother.

I read on in rapt attention as she had her heart broken by her German man. I even cried a little when I read her anguished words. We'd both had had our hearts trampled on. Maybe this young adventurer wasn't such a stranger after all.

When I turned the page to read what happened next, I found it blank. I flipped through the remaining pages but they were all clean and unblemished by the touch of a pen. I opened the chest to find the next journal but there were no more small black books left. I gathered up all the journals that were scattered about my bed and flipped through them again, lining them up in chronological order. Her adventures in Europe had ended abruptly that summer, her third year abroad.

I looked into the chest to see what else was there. I found a pile of loose photographs, birthday cards, ticket stubs from museum exhibitions, and invitations to gallery showings. I pulled them out, one by one, and put them in a neat pile next to Noni's journals. I opened a large birthday card and a crisp, white envelope fell into my lap.

My name was written across the front in Noni's elegant cursive. I carefully opened it and pulled out several sheets of paper. I put the envelope aside to save it because it had her handwriting on it. The letter was dated just a few weeks before her death.

Tears clouded my vision, and I couldn't read her handwriting. I just sat there breathing hard and trying to make sense of what I'd just found. Noni had obviously put the note in the box expecting it would be the first thing I found when I received the box after her death. But I hadn't had the courage to open the box until now. The letter must have gotten wedged inside the card when I moved to the city.

When I finally got control over my emotions, I read the letter. I consciously slowed down my reading; my eyes wanted to jump over her words to read the letter as fast as I could to reconnect with Noni one last time.

My dearest Hannah,

If you are reading this, then I am no longer with you and you are probably furious with me. My little one, the last thing I wanted to do was cause you any pain. I love you so very much.

It hurts me more than you will ever know to leave you, to miss out on the rest of your life, to not be there when you graduate from art school, to not be standing next to you at your first gallery opening. I won't be there to witness when you fall in love, get married, all the milestones that I just assumed I would be around for.

I hope with time you can find it in your heart to forgive me for not telling you about the cancer. I had my reasons, but now, as I try to write them down, I realize how selfish they are. The truth is, I am a selfish person and not a very courageous one either. There it is, down on paper, the truth, my truth.

At first, I didn't know I was ill. I had been feeling a little under the weather, but I delayed going to the doctor because a part of me knew something wasn't right but I didn't want to know. By the time I finally went and had the tests, it was too late to do much of anything. That's when I decided not to tell anyone, not even you.

I was a coward, my dear. I didn't tell you because I didn't want to spend my last days in the hospital pumped full of drugs and, worst of all, having to witness your grief. I didn't want to see your pain when you found out I was dying, time enough for that when I was dead. I wanted my last days to be normal everyday moments with my family. I wanted these memories, untainted by anything as melodramatic as grieving my death while I was still here.

I am also writing to you because I need to tell you about my past, in the hope that you don't make the same mistakes I did.

Hannah, I see a talent in you, a talent that surpasses mine, but I also see the doubt and the fear of what it means to follow your heart. That is why, even if you are angry with me, you must at least think about what I have to say. If you have read my journals, you will understand what I gave up, but not why.

I met up with a man in the summer before my final year at the *École des Beaux-Arts*. At the time, I thought he was my true love, and when he broke my heart, I was truly devastated as only someone in their early twenties could be. I was coming into my final year of school, and I realized that when I graduated I would have to be an artist in the real world, not in the sheltered environment of school. So instead of following my passion, I looked for it in men; it was easier, safer.

I went back home, and that is when I met your Grandfather. I got pregnant shortly after meeting him, and we married that fall. It was a shame that you were just a baby when he passed away and that you never really got to know him. He was a kind man, a gentle man, and over time, I came to admire and respect him, but I didn't love him. My true love wasn't a man, it was painting, and I threw it away because I was scared.

When I got pregnant, which really wasn't so much an accident as it was an unconscious way out, a large part of me was relieved. There was no way I could go back to school.

This next part is harder to admit even to myself. For the first three years of your mother's life, I didn't paint. Even though I had chosen my circumstances, I was angry and frustrated with my life, and I took it out on your mother. I never raised a hand to her or yelled at her, but I did something just as wicked. I withheld my love, my attention, my affection.

When you were born, I saw a chance to make amends, to give to you what I didn't give to my own child. When I saw you had a natural gift for drawing and painting, I became your teacher and gave you encouragement whenever I could. A part of me hoped that you would be different than me. That you would have the courage to live a big life, to stand in your own power and own it, as scary as that can be at times.

I have seen and felt my own daughter's jealousy of who you are, and regrettably it is because of me it exists. I never knew how to undo the damage I caused her, but I had hoped I could make a difference with you. I hoped I would be around, and when you hit that wall of fear, when you doubted your own path, I would be there to help you along the way. Unfortunately, my wish is not to be granted. So instead, I need you to promise me something. If it sounds like emotional blackmail, perhaps it is, but I'm your Grandmother, I'm entitled.

Promise you will follow the whispers of your secret heart. Please, don't fold your spirit down to fit into a safe, acceptable corner in your life. Be fierce in your passion, in your life, and in your love.

I reread the letter several times. Everything I thought I knew jumbled inside my head. Now that I knew about how she treated my mother, what did that make her? Did it change the way I saw Noni? How would this new insight change my relationship with my mother? Or would it? It freaked me out to realize that, without knowing it, I was following in Noni's footsteps, running away from my truth.

The one thing I did know was that I couldn't find my own answers to these questions by lying in bed. I needed to get out, get some fresh air, and maybe a fresh perspective.

I picked up all the used Kleenex off the floor, made my bed, opened the curtains, showered, and changed out of my PJs. Then I went looking for my da. I found him in the barn, throwing down new bedding in the stalls.

"Hey, let me do that for you." I opened the gate and stepped into the stall.

"You finally over your cold?" He handed me the bedding fork.

"Yeah, I'm over it. I feel much better."

"Good to hear. Colds can be nasty." He chucked me gently under the chin. "And if you ever want to talk about it, I'm willing to listen."

I smiled. "Thanks, but really, I'm fine."

He left it at that and went to get another bale of straw.

The days fell into a rhythm of getting up early with my da, the morning sky still dark and sprinkled with stars. We'd have coffee at the worn kitchen table before heading out to see to the livestock. Then I helped him out in the heated Quonset where the machinery was stored. When we came in for the hearty breakfast Mom had prepared, the kitchen smelled of bacon grease and frying eggs. I'd forgotten how much I used to eat at breakfast.

I took Geronimo out for long rides covering the twenty acres of what was left of our homestead. I felt a touch of sadness looking at the surrounding land that had been Da's. Now, our nearest neighbor, Mr. Jensen leased most of it. The livestock grazing the pastures were no longer ours. After riding, I returned home tired, sweaty, and ready for a shower.

The rest of the long day, I really had nothing to do—except think about my relationships with my mother and Noni. Why we never shared our fears, our hopes, and dreams. Why Noni never tried to make up for what she did to my mother. I couldn't reconcile the warm, nurturing, supportive Noni, who had helped me grow into an artist, with the mother who withheld her affection from her only child. How could these seemingly opposite people both be my Noni?

The afternoons were hard enough to get through, but the evenings were worse. Da liked his time alone in his study with his books, and I tried to limit my contact with mom to spare us both the tension that inevitably built between us if we spent too much time in each other's company. It was close to Christmas and I didn't want to blow it by having a screaming match with her. That left me with few engaging activities to fill my time. I tried to focus on reading, but I was too restless to sit for long, and I could only force myself to take so many naps.

I came in from yet another long ride. The snow started falling again, adding to the already three foot deep drifts. I settled Geronimo in his stall and headed back to the house to change my jeans, which were wet up to the knees.

Mom and Da were in town picking up a few groceries for the impending Christmas feast and to do some last minute Christmas shopping. The last minute shopping was because of Da. He was notorious for leaving it until the very end. He asked me if I wanted to come along, but I said no. Mostly because I had no money to buy presents, and the thought of being trapped in a vehicle with my mom didn't thrill me.

I stepped into the front hall and was struck by the emptiness. The house creaked and moaned softly in its slumber. The ride hadn't helped burn off the restless feeling in my bones. Between my mother and everything else going on in my life, my nerves were strung tight and the silence made it worse.

I snatched an apple from the bowl on the kitchen table and absently munched it as I made my way upstairs to the attic. At the top of the stairs, I gently pushed the door open. The mid-morning sun was streaming through the dormer windows, washing the whole room in its clear yellow light. The sun cast thin, translucent shadows at the far end of the room. I gazed out the window, watching the wisps of exhaust from the chimney scuttle across the slice of blue sky framed by the window.

I made my way over to my easel, eating the last of my apple. I tossed the core into the empty wastebasket under the nearby worktable. Everything was coated in a fine layer of dust. The worktable was a mess. A few mason jars that once held turpentine to soak brushes now contained a gooey paint sludge encasing the brushes. They were ruined. Suddenly, I knew what I needed to do and there was no better time to do it.

Two hours later, the studio was almost back to the way I remembered it, and I was a sweaty, dusty mess. I couldn't save my brushes, they were beyond fixing, but I managed to find quite a few tubes and jars of paint that were still good. I felt guilty that I hadn't taken better care of my brushes. I could hear Noni admonishing me as I threw my ruined brushes into the trash bin.

There were a few blank, pre-primed canvases stacked in the corner. I selected a small one and positioned it on my easel. I found Noni's canvas brush holder and carefully unrolled the cloth, revealing her brushes all lined up in their little fabric pockets, the bristles clean and perfectly shaped. My heart pounded. I placed a small table to the left of my easel for the brushes, paint tubes, and a palette. I picked up a piece of charcoal. Its silky texture was cool under my shaking hand. I breathed deep and let my mind reach out and touch the white void in front of me. A chill ran through me. And then there it was—an image brilliant and clear in its detail.

I let out a whoop of delight. "Noni, I've still got it!"

I sketched the image from my mind and watched in awe as it was reborn on the snow-white canvas. There was no pain or sorrow in my heart, as I continued to draw, only that long forgotten joy of creating. I grabbed the tubes of oils, squeezed out lines of glorious pigment, and began to mix my colours. I didn't stop until the light began to fade. I stepped back and examined my work, and then smiled, satisfied. Not bad considering I hadn't picked up a brush in over four years.

The door creaked and I turned around. No one was there.

I thoroughly cleaned Noni's brushes, reshaped them, and left them to dry. I tidied up my workspace and scrubbed at the paint splotches on my hands with an old rag. In my haste to put paint to canvas, I hadn't put on a smock and now I had paint all over my shirt and jeans.

I quickly changed my clothes and went in search of my parents. I checked the time when I was in my room changing and was amazed to see that it was 4:30. Mom and Da must be home from shopping. I found them both at the kitchen table having a cup of tea. The Brown Betty sat between them on the table, a plate of cookies next to it.

"Get all your shopping done?" I asked.

"Almost, I've got one more thing to pick up." Da poured himself and mom more tea. He lifted the pot. "You joining us?"

"Sure." I grabbed a mug from the cupboard.

"Don't use a mug, Hannah, those are for coffee, use a proper tea cup," mom snapped at me.

I replaced the coffee mug, took a teacup to the table, and sat down. Da poured me some tea. We made small talk for a few minutes then mom asked me about my job hunt. She just wouldn't let it go. I was vague with my answers but could feel my cheeks getting hot. I sipped my tea and munched on a ginger snap.

"You've got to get back out there." She peered over her cup. "As much as we love having you come down over Christmas, you are not going to find another job riding Geronimo all day."

"I know that." My back stiffened.

"No, I don't think you do, otherwise you would have been sending out resumes and going into town for interviews, not hanging around here doing nothing."

"Can we talk about this later?"

221

"Dear, how do you expect to keep a boyfriend if you can't even keep a job? Men these days aren't willing to take care of a woman. They expect to have partners who have drive and ambition, like Jasmine."

"So is that what you're really worried about, whether or not your daughter can keep a man? Getting married and having kids isn't my life's goal!" I was shouting, but I couldn't seem to stop myself. Just what she wanted, me losing my temper and showing her that I was an unreasonable, difficult child.

"And it's obviously not doing the work you were trained for. Hannah, you have to start applying yourself."

"I don't want to be an esthetician for the rest of my life."

"What exactly do you want?"

"To paint, Mom!" I screamed. "To paint!"

"Of all the ridiculous ideas." She threw her hands up in the air. "You can't make a living at that. Sometimes I wish Noni had never taught you to paint. It's done nothing but put unrealistic ideas in your head." She pushed away from the table. "You talk some sense into her; she obviously won't listen to what her mother has to say, and I have dinner to start." She walked past me as if I was invisible and started pulling pots out of the cupboard, banging them down on the stove.

"Why don't we go see to the cows while Mother makes dinner?" Da got up from the table and gently steered me to the back door.

I followed him. I knew it was useless to try arguing with my mother. She banged around in the kitchen while Da and I headed out into the yard. He didn't walk to the barn though; instead, he ambled towards the small woods at the back of the property. The light post in the backyard barely cast its pale glow to the edge of the trees. I followed along in silence. We trudged through the deep snow, our footfalls muffled by the white drifts, staying along the perimeter of the backyard light.

"She does love you, despite what you may think."

"I know Da, but I get so frustrated with her. She never listens to what I say. She has a plan for my life whether I want it or not. I don't think getting married and having children is the right thing for me. It's my life, shouldn't I have a say in it?" I knew I sounded whiney.

"So were you telling the truth in there? Do you want to paint?"

"Yes, I do. I'm miserable being an esthetician, and honestly, I'm not very good at it." I couldn't believe how easy it was to finally admit it—I sucked at being an esthetician.

"Well, you're just going to have to figure out a way to do what you love. You have my support, and your mother will come around, just give her time."

We walked a full circuit around the back yard and ended up where we started. We stood under the shelter of the back porch and looked out into the inky night. A solitary owl called out from the darkness. I leaned into Da's shoulder and he wrapped his arm around me.

"You'd better hope she hasn't put any of that anger into her cooking or you and I are both going to be up all night with indigestion."

Chapter Twenty-Two

I spent the rest of the week leading up to Christmas avoiding my mother, which was hard to do. We were stuck in the same house. When I wasn't hiding out in the attic studio painting, I looked for ways to get away from her. I exhausted all of my reasons for taking Da's truck and escaping. Even he couldn't think of any more errands for me to do in the city. We had already brought home the Christmas tree and set it up. There was no place else for me to run.

When Mom and I found ourselves in the same room at mealtimes, we were both painfully polite. I didn't bring up our earlier conversation and neither did she. The only time my heart didn't feel heavy was when I was up in the studio.

Christmas Eve finally arrived. Before dinner, I holed myself up in the attic, wrapping up my Christmas presents in brown craft paper that I had hand painted. I was putting the finishing touches on the last present when the smells of frying pork chops and scalloped potatoes drifted up the stairs and through the vents.

When I finished cleaning up my mess, I looked out the dormer window at the full moon. It was only six in the evening, but the moon already hung heavy in the night sky. I turned out the lights in the studio. The moon cast its slivery light over the painting on my easel. I was so pleased that I finished it in time. My heart swelled with love and ached with sadness. I reluctantly headed down to the kitchen to see if Mom needed any help putting supper on the table.

Our family always has a modest meal Christmas Eve; the traditional turkey dinner with all the trimmings would be served tomorrow. Jas and her mom would be coming over in the morning to open presents and join us for afternoon supper.

After dinner, the three of us settled in the living room to play cards in front of the fire. *It's a Wonderful Life* was playing on the TV, but no one was really watching it. Da turned on the Christmas tree lights, and they shed a glittering wash of colour over the room. I couldn't help but get nostalgic about all those childhood Christmases, the delicious excitement of Christmas morning. The simple enjoyment of opening presents that I believed were delivered down the chimney by Saint Nick, Mom and Noni in the kitchen preparing the feast, the smell of cinnamon and cloves in the air. My thoughts were in the past, my mind just dimly aware of the card game, so when my cell rang, I was so startled I dropped my cards.

I had left it charging on the kitchen counter, so I excused myself and quickly went to answer it. I hit answer without looking at the caller id, expecting Jas on the other end.

"Hello, Morgan House of Ill Repute"

"Hey, babe. That's my kinda hello."

My stomach clenched and my jaw tightened in irritation.

"Hey baby, you still there?"

I cleared my throat, "Yes, I'm still here. Mason, why are you calling me?" I tried to sound cool and disinterested.

"What's with the attitude? It's Christmas and I just wanted to call you and wish you a Merry Ho Ho and all that. Thought maybe we could hook up for old time's sake. Maybe have a drink or something." Mason's words were slurred, as if he had already started drinking without me.

I didn't have the patience to talk to him when he was sober and even less when he was drunk. "Mason, you haven't bothered to call me in months, and then out of the blue you call to say Merry Christmas. Give me a break. Why did you really call? Did your latest tart suddenly come out of her coma and dump you?"

"I see some things haven't changed. You know, you always were a piece of work. If you weren't such a frigid bitch, you might actually be able to keep a man," Mason growled.

I hung up while Mason was still ranting. I had enough of being lied to and used. I held the phone to my chest, willing my heart to slow down, when it started to ring again. Was Mason completely stupid?

I angrily jabbed the phone ready to tell him off again. "Look here, asshole, you call me one more time and I'll star fifty-seven you and charge you with harassment so fast it will make your head spin. Do I make myself clear?"

"Yes, perfectly clear." Came the reply, but it wasn't Mason's drunken voice on the other end.

"Aaron? Aaron, is that you." There was dead air and then a faint click.

"I'll stay on the line and answer that question if you promise not to send the cops after me."

"I'm so sorry. I thought you were someone else. Where are you? Are you in town? I thought you were in Australia."

"I am, but I just wanted to call you and wish you a Merry Christmas. It's actually Christmas day here and thirty degrees in the shade. It's the strangest experience, celebrating Christmas in a heat wave; people are walking around in shorts with not a snow flake in sight."

"It's snowing here—big, fat, fluffy flakes and cold, bitterly cold."

"Strangely enough, I miss the cold and—I miss you. I know that's a strange thing to say as we've only met a couple of times but it's true. That's why I called. I just wanted to hear your voice."

"Yes it is strange. Weird, in fact.

"But Hannah, I won't lie to you. I was attracted to you the moment I saw you at the Albright Gallery."

I started to protest, but he cut me off.

"No, don't interrupt, let me finish and then you can hang up and never speak to me again, if that's what you want. You're right when you say I don't know you, but I want to. I want to know what makes you happy, what pisses you off, and, most importantly, what that terrible sadness is that you are holding on to so tightly. But I can't know any of these things if you won't let me in."

"I can't. I just don't have it in me right now to let anyone in. I hope you understand."

"I'm not going to give up on you that easily. You already agreed I could call you when I got back to town. Maybe by the end of February, you will have changed your mind."

"You're very persistent aren't you?"

"I'll take that as a yes. Could you hold on a second?" Aaron spoke to someone and came back on the line a moment later. "Unfortunately, I have to get going; otherwise I'd work a little more on wearing down your resistance. I hope you have a good Christmas, and I'll call you when I get back."

We said our goodbyes and ended the call. I didn't know what to think about Aaron. He made me all mixed up inside. I was still so confused about my life, and my lack of discretion when it came to picking men made me question if I should ever date again. I didn't trust myself anymore. I turned off my cell phone and left it on the counter before I joined my parents in the living room.

"Who was that on the phone?" my mother asked.

"It was just Jas calling about tomorrow," I said as I picked up my cards and tried to stop thinking about what Aaron had said.

Chapter Twenty-Three

Christmas day dawned clear and cold. The thermometer hanging outside the kitchen window read a teeth chattering minus thirty-two degrees Celsius. The sky was an endless blue; the sun sparkled on the fresh snowdrifts dusting the white fields with diamonds. The world was new and clean.

I got up early, but instead of helping Da out in the barn, I spent my morning helping my mother put together the final preparations for the afternoon's dinner. My mother and I worked silently in the kitchen, except when I needed to ask what she wanted done or what serving dishes she wanted out to use later. She replied in terse one-word answers. I tried not to let her coldness bother me, but after several attempts to carry on a conversation with her, I gave up. Together in the heavy stillness we assembled the bread stuffing and peeled potatoes and turnips. The pumpkin pie was baked, and the rhubarb and strawberry pie sat on the counter waiting its turn in the oven after the turkey. We also had fresh brewed coffee and made from scratch cinnamon rolls cooling on the counter.

Mom slipped the huge bird in the oven just as the doorbell rang. It was ten o'clock. Khandi and Jas were right on time. I went to let them in while mom placed the cinnamon buns on a serving platter. The only time mom allowed us to eat in the living room was Christmas morning.

I threw open the door and was blasted by a wall of frigid air followed by a warm embrace from Khandi. She wore a leopard print coat with matching earmuffs and fashion boots with three-inch heels. Her auburn hair was pulled into a girlish ponytail and the only makeup she wore was bright pink lipgloss. Her cheeks were flushed from the cold.

"Merry Christmas, kiddo."

I took a large duffel bag from her and helped her with her coat. Jas followed her mom, carrying a casserole dish covered in tinfoil. Khandi was dressed in baby blue flannel PJs with polar bears cavorting across the fabric. Our Christmas morning tradition was to wear pajamas while we opened presents, ate cinnamon buns, and drank Mimosas. Even Da, when he came back from taking care of the livestock, would change into a new pair of plaid flannels and his old dressing gown. Mom, on the other hand, dressed this morning in black dress pants and a green silk top that she covered with her apron while she cooked.

Jas handed me the casserole dish so she could hang up her coat. Her mom removed her boots and slipped on a pair of dainty heeled mule slippers covered with fuzzy blue marabou feathers. Jas giggled at her. Shoes clicking on the hardwood, Khandi ignored her daughter's laughter and headed for the kitchen, holding a bottle of champagne under her arm.

Jas put on a pair of pink slippers with rabbit ears on the toes and followed me into the kitchen. I deposited their contribution to our feast on the counter.

"Merry Christmas, Mrs. Morgan," Jas sang out. She gave my mom a hug.

"Merry Christmas. Congratulations on your new business. Your mom certainly has reason to be proud of you."

"Yes, I am," said Khandi, "but I'd be proud of her even if she didn't start her own business. She's a great kid." Khandi poured champagne and orange juice in the water goblets mom had set out earlier.

"Thanks, you two. And, Mrs. M., since we're on the subject, I'm planning the grand opening at the end of January, and I'd like to invite you and Mr. M. Do you think you could come?"

Were my eyes playing tricks on me or were Mom's eyes misting up?

"Of course we'll come." Mom untied her apron, folded it over the handle on the oven door, and gave Jas a hug.

A surge of jealousy washed over me. I clenched my fists, digging my fingernails into my palms.

Leaving our moms in the kitchen, Jas and I kicked off our slippers, bundled up and dashed outside to bring in the presents sitting in her truck. We had just finished putting the last present under the tree when Da came in from the barn. He said a quick Merry Christmas and ducked upstairs to change into his PJs. His cheeks and nose were red from the cold, and his eyes sparkled like a mischievous child.

We gathered in the living room to open presents. Da was delegated the official job of handing out the presents. My gifts to everyone, except my mother, were already under the tree. I chose paintings I had done years ago to give to everyone and had snuck them down last night when my parents were asleep. He handed out the presents, each of us taking turns unwrapping, admiring, and thanking each other.

Halfway through the gift giving, Da turned to me, just like we had planned last night. I ran up to my room and brought down my mother's present.

"Mom, close your eyes," I called out from the hallway. I walked into the living room. "I didn't have time to wrap it." I stepped in front of her.

"How could you not have time to wrap my present? You've been home for over two weeks," she said, her eyes still closed tightly.

"Okay, open your eyes."

I watched her face as her eyes settled on the painting in front of her.

"The paint's still wet so be careful when you hold it."

She kept her hands clasped in her lap. Her face drained of colour. She looked at me and then back at the painting of Noni and her I still held. I willed her to take it.

"Mom?"

"It's beautiful. Amazing," Jas and Khandi said in unison.

My mother blinked her eyes furiously. She opened her mouth and then snapped it closed. I felt stupid standing there holding her present. Why wouldn't she take it?

"If you'll excuse me." My mother got up from the sofa. She bolted out of the room pushing past me, the sleeve of her blouse brushing against the wet canvas.

I carefully leaned the ruined painting against the coffee table. Jas and her mom exchanged a quick glance.

Da spoke first. "I'll go up and check on your mother."

I put my hand on his to stop him. "No, let me handle this."

I apologized to the three of them and left the room. The blood thrummed against my temples, as I climbed the stairs. Outside her door, I could hear muffled sobs.

I thumped on the door and flung it open before she could tell me to go away. She was curled up on her side of the bed, her back towards me, her face squished in the pillow. Her shoulders shook with each sob.

I wanted to slap her face until she stopped crying. I wanted to scream at her to grow up. Instead, I took a deep breath. "Why are you crying?"

She turned to face me. "I don't recall giving you permission to come in."

"You didn't."

"Then I'll ask you to leave."

"You can, but I won't. Why can't I ever do the right thing by you? I gave you a gift from my heart, and you make a huge ugly scene. Couldn't you even pretend you liked it?"

"I don't have to explain my behavior to you, and I never asked you to paint that for me. You embarrassed me in front of our guests."

"No, you didn't ask me to paint that for you. I painted it for you to remember her by. I know you miss her too." I sat down on the corner of the bed, all the fight had gone out of me. "How could you be embarrassed by my painting?"

"You painted Noni and I like a loving mother and daughter. We never had that, that's why. Do you think I don't know that you were making fun of me, painting us like that? You're just being spiteful."

"I'm being spiteful?" The anger returned at full throttle. "At least I'm not a mean-spirited woman who thinks she is the only one going through something. One who lashes out at the people who care about her. I miss her too. I also know that without Noni here, you and I don't seem to have much to hold us together."

"You have no right to speak to me that way." Her anger radiated off her like a blast furnace. "You have no idea what I'm feeling or what I'm going through. She may have been your grandmother, but she was *my* mother. She never encouraged me in anything. Never said I was special or good. Instead, she gave all that to you. She never once took the time to show me how to paint. And the two of you, thick as thieves, would hole up in that damn attic or shut yourselves up in her room having fun, sharing your secrets. I was left to keep the house and run the farm like some kind of servant who wasn't worthy of belonging to your little club." Her eyes were wild, her fists clenched at her sides.

I wanted to tell her about the letter I found. About Noni's regret at how she raised her daughter, but I wasn't sure if it would make things better or worse. Before I could decide what to do, my mother decided for me.

"Get out, get out, get out!" She pounded her fists on the bed.

I scrambled off the edge of the mattress, backing out of the room. Mothers aren't supposed to be jealous of their children. She started to sob again.

When, I returned to the living room, alone, no one looked at me. I didn't need to explain what had just happened; no doubt they had heard it all. I sat on the couch and avoided looking at the painting. It was where I left it, leaning against the coffee table.

"Anyone want another Mimosa?" Khandi didn't wait for anyone to reply before she stood up. "Honey, why don't you come and help me with the drinks."

"Sure, Mom." Jas left too.

I looked at Da. "I don't think she's coming downstairs anytime soon."

"I'll go see to your mother. I'm sorry, honey." He gave me a hug and went upstairs.

Khandi and Jas returned with our drinks. I sipped mine. My stomach clenched and I put the drink down.

"Sorry."

"Don't be. There is nothing to be sorry about," Khandi said.

"But I've ruined your Christmas—"

"No you haven't," Khandi said. "Your mom is just going through an emotional time. When people are hurting they tend to lash out at the people they love. That's normal."

No, I didn't think my mother was normal at all.

We sipped our drinks in awkward silence. Khandi picked absently at her cinnamon bun while we all pretended not to listen to the muffled voices coming from upstairs. Minutes ticked by and my parents hadn't returned.

The three of us finally decided to go check on the turkey and set the table. An hour later, Da appeared in the kitchen looking haggard. We'd kept ourselves busy while we waited for my mother to come back down, so we could resume our Christmas, but it looked like there wasn't any point.

"Margaret has got one of her migraines," he announced. No one believed this flimsy excuse. "She extends her apologies for not being able to join us for dinner, but she wants you to stay and enjoy yourself."

We were all desperate to cling to this charade. Khandi reassured Da that we all understood the situation. Jas mumbled something about hoping my mother would be feeling better. I stared at the handful of cutlery I was holding. I finished setting the table. My back was to everyone and I squeezed back tears.

"I see you ladies have everything under control." Da cleared his throat. "Why don't we finish opening up our presents?"

There was nothing left to do, so we all filed back into the living room. With painfully bright enthusiasm, we finished opening the rest of the presents still left under the tree. Then we went outside to partake in the next part of the Christmas day tradition. Jas retrieved the duffel bag I left in the front hall, and she and her mom changed into jeans and sweaters. I joined them after I had changed into similar clothes. The three of us put on our coats, scarves, and mitts, and, holding our skates by their laces, we walked down to the frozen pond. Later, Da joined us by the pond's edge. He had brought down a large thermos full of hot chocolate. He built a cheery fire in the nearby stone fire pit, and we sat with him by the fire, warming our feet and sipping sweet, hot chocolate.

My mother, true to her word, stayed in her room even when we sat down for dinner. The four of us made the best of it, trying to be happy, not mentioning the missing person at the table. Da took my mother a plate of food before we sat down to eat. I had no idea if the meal was any good, I couldn't taste anything. The turkey was sawdust in my mouth. The mashed potatoes were like glue clogging my throat. I drank too much wine.

After the meal, Khandi and Jas stayed only long enough to be polite. Da and I helped them pack up their gifts, and I put together an armload of leftovers for them to take home. When they left, Da headed outside, and I went around the house and tidied things up before hiding in my room.

It was still early in the evening, but I was exhausted. I had just slipped under the covers when there was a knock at my door. It was Da, holding a large box wrapped in red paper and topped with a large green bow. I stepped back and invited him in

"I forgot about this one. Here, open it."

The box was heavy, so I put it down on the bed.

Da settled on the corner of the mattress and watched me tear off the paper. "It's from me and your mother. I forgot to put a tag on it."

I ripped the last bit of wrapping off the box. The top was stamped with a TriArt logo. I slowly opened the lid of the large, wooden box. Row upon row of pristine tubes of pigment greeted me. Taped to the inside of the lid was an envelope. It was a gift certificate from an art supply store for an outrageous amount of money.

I searched my da's deeply lined face for the meaning behind such an expensive and extravagant gift. "This was the one last gift you had to get, wasn't it?"

"Yes. If you say that painting is what you want to do, then you must do it."

"Does she feel the same way?"

"Although you may not see it, your mother only wants you to be happy. There are things about your mother's life that you aren't aware of that make her relationship with you difficult. She does love you, honey. Just give her some space and time to heal." He kissed my forehead and said good night.

I propped the paint box on my nightstand so I could see it when I lay down. I thought about what he had said. I thought about my mother, what she'd said. I didn't know what stopped me from telling my mother about Noni's letter. I understood my mother's anger, but it wasn't my fault. Surely, she could see that. Punishing me wasn't going to change that. She hurt and humiliated me, for the last time.

I managed to stick it out at home for two more days before the tension between my mother and me became unbearable. She wouldn't speak to me or look at me and would leave the room if I walked in.

Da helped me pack my bedroom furniture, my new paint box, my Christmas presents, a handful of my canvases and Noni's easel in the back of his truck. I set up my stuff in my new bedroom over the salon and thought only of starting my new life. I knew what direction I was headed in.

Chapter Twenty-Four

On New Year's Eve, Jas and I hosted a party at the apartment. We invited Christie, Indigo, and Heather, Jas's new staff, and their respective boyfriends. Jamie had to pass on our little soiree because he had plans to attend a costume party. Jas and I were the only ones not paired up for the night. Jas because she was too focused on the salon to have time to date, and me because my latest dating endeavors only proved to me, yet again, how much I sucked at picking men.

But it was still a nice night. And I managed to hold off any feelings of despair by downing way too much champagne. After midnight, I stumbled incoherently to my bed and tried to remain motionless to stop the room from spinning. While I waited for sleep to come, I thought about the past year.

At this point, I didn't have a boyfriend, my mother wasn't speaking to me, and I only had twenty-five dollars to my name, but I still had several blessings to count. I had a place to stay and a job as a receptionist at the salon, both thanks to Jas. The last blessing was one I bestowed upon myself: I was going to follow my dreams. I had Noni's letter, my mother's meltdown, and my da's gift to thank for my newfound courage.

As the New Year dawned, I shed any lingering doubts about what I wanted to do with my life. I felt a lightness of being that I hadn't felt in a long time. I needed a cave to retreat to, to unearth the truths about who I was and what I wanted to be in the world, and the salon proved to be that place for me. Jas never questioned me or made me feel the least bit guilty when, after working all day, I would disappear into my room for the rest of the evening to sketch, think, sleep, and think and draw some more. Then one day I filled out the admissions forms for the art college and mailed them off without a moment's hesitation.

While I put the pieces in place to become who I wanted to be, I was also busy at my new job. The salon had just opened, and already the phones were ringing nonstop. Jas had sent off the invitations for the grand opening, and the new stylists were all working out fabulously. We made a great team. I helped Jas with her dream while working on my own, and that was exciting.

January fell into the comfortable rhythm of a life with few responsibilities—the camaraderie of the new girls, Jamie's humorous banter, and the bustle of the salon. I welcomed the simplicity of the hours I spent taking appointments, washing hair, sweeping up the salon, and doing laundry in the back room. There was no pressure to make a quota, and I no longer had to expend so much energy making myself believe that being an esthetician was my life's dream. There was no last minute scramble to pay my bills. Even my mother's refusal to talk to me was a hidden blessing—I didn't have to deal with her anger any longer.

* * * *

On the night of Blue Funk's grand opening, the salon looked spectacular. Jas didn't have the budget to pull off an event like the Thorpe function at The Serenity, but to my eyes, it was better. The room sparkled from the hundreds of tea lights placed around the shop. We bought the candles at a dollar store, but the effect was anything but cheap. Jas had negotiated with several of the small businesses on the block to give her a discount on their merchandise. In the spirit of the new revitalization of the area, the other Inglewood merchants were glad to lend their support to Jas's opening. The fresh flower arrangements resting on each hair station came from the florist next door, and the platters of finger foods set up on the reception desk had been donated by the local deli. We had bottles of red and white wine to serve our guests, compliments of the wine boutique two doors down. Khandi managed to snag us some real wine glasses for the night from one of the clubs she did the books for. It meant we needed to hand wash all the glasses the next day, but it was a small sacrifice to make if it meant none of our guests had to drink wine out of those dinky, plastic things.

It was almost time for the guests to arrive, so I positioned myself behind the reception desk and started opening the wine. Jas fussed over the swag bags she artfully displayed on a low table near the door. Each blue bag carried the *Blue Funk* logo and contained a generous selection of travel-sized hair and body products plus a discount coupon for a haircut. She looked calm and collected, but I knew better. I could tell by the way she kept repositioning the swag bags and tweaking the tissue paper that she was nervous. Even though we were already getting steady bookings, I could understand the fear of not having anyone show up for the party.

This event marked the realization of a dream, and the crowd that came to share in the celebration was a sign of approval that meant a great deal to Jas. I knew how she was feeling as she darted over to rearrange a vase of flowers that already looked perfect. I would have felt the same way.

It didn't take long for the guests to start arriving, and almost immediately, the small shop was packed. The guests mingled with the stylists, some of them getting free hair consultations while they sipped their wine and nibbled on the finger food. I was thrilled for Jas.

I opened more bottles of wine and rearranged the platters to replace the quickly disappearing food when Jas ducked behind the reception desk to grab the appointment book. She squeezed my arm and flashed me a radiant smile then zipped back into the crowd to book one of the guests for an appointment.

Just when things couldn't get any better, I noticed Hilary Duncan, from *The Calgary Chronicle's* lifestyle section, enter the party with a photographer in tow. Jamie made sure that Hilary always had a drink in her hand, and Jas introduced her to all of us. The publicity would go a long way to ensure that the stylist's chairs were always full.

Her fears about the party had started to surface last week, and I didn't want my problems with my mother to add to her stress. I cornered her in the back room of the salon and told her that inviting my mother to the opening was okay with me and that she shouldn't let my relationship with my mother make her feel uncomfortable. She had looked visibly relieved.

Still, for me the only blemish on the evening was the appearance of my mother, despite what I had said to Jas earlier. She was all sweetness and light to Jas and in fact everyone else in the room. To me she was barely polite, and only because she didn't want to ruin Jas's big night. I didn't either, so I bit my tongue and smiled until it hurt. Da tried to take the sting out of my mother's behavior, and I appreciated the effort, but it didn't help.

I finally couldn't take it anymore and asked one of the stylists to cover for me, telling her that I needed to wash some of the glasses because we were running low on clean ones. I filled a tray with dirty glasses and made my escape. It didn't take long to wash and dry the glasses but I stayed upstairs and hid like a child. As I'd hoped, when I finally returned downstairs, my parents were gone.

* * * *

Over the next month, things looked pretty much the same on the surface; but there was a subtle shift in the texture of my days, an undercurrent of something new taking shape in my life and making the time slip away faster and faster. I didn't panic, watching the hours fly by, I felt exhilarated. For one thing, after I applied to art school, turned in my portfolio, and had my admissions interview, my confidence had peaked. I felt sure I'd get in. Plus, I knew Aaron would be home soon, and I looked forward to seeing him again with happy anticipation.

Sometime between sweeping endless piles of hair from the salon floor and disappearing into the glorious world of creating art, I decided I wanted Aaron as a friend. I didn't think I was ready for a boyfriend, but a friend, most definitely. He was the first person I'd ever known who was an artist—a full-time artist. He followed his passion and spent his days creating his art as a living. I would be a fool if I didn't at least explore a friendship with him.

The letter from the college came in the third week of February. Jas brought it in along with a tray of Starbucks coffee before the salon opened for the day. She quietly slid the large white envelope across the reception desk towards me and gave me a wink before she handed out coffees to Jamie and the girls. I picked up the envelope, my heart hammering in my chest.

Ignoring the letter opener lying on the desk, I used my fingers to rip a jagged tear in the top of the envelope. I slid the contents out onto the desk and picked up the official looking document. My eyes scanned the words faster than my brain could register what I was reading. I took a deep breath and tried to slow myself down. I read the words twice before it made sense. I got up from the desk and went to Jas, a smile on my face as I handed her the letter.

"This comes as no surprise. Congratulations, Peanut!" She threw her arms around me and gave me a big squeeze. Then she turned to the girls, holding the acceptance letter high in the air like a holy relic. "Ladies, you may not have realized it, but the girl who has been washing your clients' hair and attending to your needs is none other than Hannah Morgan, the famous *artiste*, soon to be studying her craft at the prestigious Western Canadian College of Art and Design."

I blushed from the clapping and cheering that followed.

"And to think we have an original Hannah hanging in our own little shop." She flourished her hand towards her Christmas gift—a sharply rendered botanical enlargement I did of a magnolia—that she had hung behind the reception counter. "When you're famous, maybe I'll sell it and retire on the proceeds."

I wanted to call my da to share my news, but it was only Tuesday; I would have to wait another day. Since the awful scene on Christmas day, every time I called home and my mother answered, she would pass the phone to Da without saying a word, or when she was feeling especially cruel, she would just hang up on me when she heard my voice. Da made a point of calling me every Wednesday after dinner. He still held out hope my mother would come around and start talking to me. I was not so optimistic.

When he called the next day, he was as thrilled as I was. We talked about the classes I would be taking and how proud Noni would have been. He didn't bring up what my mother's reaction would be to my news, and I didn't ask. Even Khandi had given me a call to say congratulations, but my own mother didn't even bother. Thinking about her left me with a dull ache in my bones. I didn't know what to do with how I was feeling, so I shoved the heavy sorrow down as deep as I could.

After being accepted into the college, everything else started to fall into place. I applied for a student loan and anticipated being accepted for the full amount. Thanks to Jas's continued generosity, I still didn't pay rent, but I did chip in for my portion of the food and household necessities. Because of this arrangement, I managed to pay off a great deal of my remaining debt. She said when I started school, she would find someone to replace me as the receptionist during the day, but I could continue to work evenings and Saturdays. The college was close enough to the salon that I could walk on nice days or take a fifteen-minute bus ride to its doors. All that was left to do was start classes, and those began in just a few short months.

"Look at me go," I giggled to myself as I crossed out the days on the calendar.

Goddess Magazine
> We are all women
>> Everywhere

February Issue

Take our TRUE LOVE questionnaire:
Find out if your match is made in heaven or if you're headed for heartache!

PSSST!
WHY GUYS LOVE YOU JUST <u>EXACTLY</u> AS YOU ARE

Sultry makeup in 15 minutes (or less)

Our readers share their most romantic Valentine's Day memories

50 questions no one's ever asked men before. Find out what makes them tick and what ticks them off. Our most revealing survey, p.132

Chapter Twenty-Five

On the last day of February, I closed up the shop alone after a long and busy day. The stylists had all gone home, and as soon as Jas finished her last client of the evening, I shooed her upstairs so she could get ready for her date. She was going out for drinks with a guy she had met a couple of days ago at the organic market. I busied myself with tidying up and trying not to think about what this day meant.

Aaron hadn't called. For a whole month, I made sure that my cell phone was fully charged and with me at all times just so I wouldn't miss his call. He'd sounded so sincere when he called at Christmas, but he had broken his promise.

I told myself not to get down about it and turned my attention to cleaning up. I tidied up the hair stations, lined up the bottles of hair products, put brushes away, and made sure all the hairdryers and flat irons were unplugged.

It wasn't like we had a relationship anyway. Wasn't I the one who'd told him I didn't want to see him, that I wasn't ready? I guess I had been right about that after all. He really wasn't worth getting upset about.

I glanced up at the clock on the wall; it was a little after nine. If he was going to call, he would have done it by now. I turned off my cell and threw it on the counter. I wasn't sure who I was more disgusted with, Aaron or myself for being fooled yet again by a smooth talker.

I finished sweeping the floor, then locked the front door, flipped the sign over to "closed," and pulled down the shade that covered the door glass. I started counting out the float when the salon phone rang. I ignored it and let the call go to voice mail. Twenty minutes later, I was turning out the lights when someone started banging on the door.

My first thought was that someone was trying to break in. I grabbed the phone and started to dial 911 when I realized most burglars don't knock first. I hung up the phone, laughing at myself, then crossed back over to the door to see who it was, fully expecting to see Jas standing there. In the rush to make her date, she probably forgot her purse or her keys. I pulled up the shade ready to razz her for forgetting her purse, but it wasn't Jas standing on the other side of the door. It was Aaron.

I slid the deadbolt and opened the door. He looked even better than I remembered. My heart picked up its pace and my stomach did that strange flip-flop thing. His brown hair had been streaked lighter by the sun and his tan made the strange icy blueness of his eyes stand out even more. It was a cold night, but all he had on were a pair of worn jeans and a heather grey sweater with a hole at the collar. He must have been freezing.

I motioned for him to step inside, trying to hide my excitement at seeing him again. Wasn't it just a few minutes ago I was angry with him for not calling? But here he was, in person, and it was still February.

"I'm so glad I caught you before you left." He stepped into the salon.

I closed and bolted the door behind him.

"How was your trip?" I picked up the broom and swept the floor I just finished minutes earlier.

He ignored my question. "I know you're probably upset because I didn't call you. That's why I came here instead. I didn't want you to think that I didn't mean what I said at Christmas. I was in the outback longer than I expected, and I didn't get back to civilization until the day my flight left. I called you on your cell from the airport lobby as soon as my flight landed but you didn't pick up. I remembered where you worked, so I looked it up in the yellow pages and tried calling you here. When no one answered, I took a chance you'd still be here, hopped a cab, and here I am."

I stopped sweeping the floor. It was still February for another three hours. He'd rushed over here to keep his promise to me. He came here not knowing if I even wanted to see him again. I didn't know what to say. A part of me wanted to reply with something witty and nonchalant, to make him think his gesture didn't mean as much as it did; the other part of me wanted to rush into his arms. I settled for something in between.

"I'm glad you came by. It's really good to see you."

"Does this mean you are willing to give me a chance?" He took a step closer to me.

"It means that I missed you, too. I thought a lot about what you said, and I realize what I really need right now is a friend. I don't know if I can give you more than that, but I also don't want you to leave."

"If that's all you can give right now, then I'll take it." Aaron gave me a smile that made my legs weak. "The cab is still waiting for me outside. Did you want to go for coffee or a drink or something?"

"I'd love to, but why don't we have it upstairs. It's where I live now. You're probably tired from the flight, and I don't really feel like sitting in a room full of people. How does that sound?"

"Sounds great. Just let me go pay the driver and pick up my bags. I'll be right back."

When he left, I couldn't stop myself from doing a little dance of joy, laughing and twirling the broom as if it was my partner. I felt ridiculously happy.

He was back a few minutes later. I told him to put his bags and camera equipment behind the counter. I relocked the door for the final time and set the alarm while he looked around.

"So this is where you work. Your friend did a great job with the space. This is one of yours, isn't it?" He pointed to the canvas I gave Jas for Christmas.

"Yes it is."

I held my breath when he took a step closer to the painting. I knew I shouldn't care if he liked it or not, but I did. What would be worse was if he just pretended to like it.

"It's incredible," he said, his voice just above a whisper. "Incredible. Do you have any more of your work here?"

"No, I gave that to Jas as a Christmas present. All of my stuff is still at my parents' place. All I have here are the sketches I've been working on. There just isn't the space for me to paint here."

"I would love to see more."

The sincerity of his words turned my insides to mush. "Sure, but for now why don't we head upstairs and see about that drink. I could put together something for you to eat; you probably haven't had much on the plane. Are you hungry?"

"I wouldn't say no to some food. Actually, I'm starving, now that you mention it," he grinned.

I turned off the salon lights and led Aaron upstairs. While he washed up, I scrounged through the fridge for something to feed him. Thank God Jas shopped the organic market just the other day. I set out fresh strawberries and cream. I warmed up some Brie and sun dried tomatoes and sliced a fresh baguette. I arranged green and Kalamata olives on a dish and transferred some antipasto into a bowl. I was slicing a pepper salami when he came into the kitchen.

"Is there anything I can do to help?"

"I've got the food end of it under control, but if you wouldn't mind, there's a bottle of wine in the cupboard to the left of the sink. You could open that. The corkscrew is in the top drawer." I placed the sliced salami on the table with the rest of the food.

He poured the wine, and we sat down at the kitchen table. He piled his plate high and dug into his food like a man who hadn't eaten for months. I nibbled at a strawberry and sipped my wine while I watched him eat.

"This is really good," he said between mouthfuls.

Jeez, if he's that impressed with throwing together snacks out of the fridge, what would he say if I actually cooked him a meal?

He finished his first plate of food in no time and proceeded to pile it high with seconds. While he ate, I asked him about his trip.

He described the beauty and spirit of the indigenous people that he met. He told me about the stark contrasts of the landscapes, from desert to lush tropical forests and the vastness of the ocean. And all the while, he talked about the colours he'd seen as if they were rare jewels that could be held in his hand, tangible objects of red and orange, of deep shimmering greens and opalescent tropical blues. I could see the colours like swirls of pigments laid out on my paint palette.

He told me of his unplanned adventure in the outback when the jeep he and his guide had been traveling in broke down. I knew how the story ended as he was sitting here with me, safe and sound, but hearing him recount walking to the closest habitation with limited water and almost no food in the blistering heat of summer had me on the edge of my seat.

I've never had wanderlust, even though by Noni's example it was in my blood. But hearing Aaron describe his journeys through Australia, I wanted to go there, to experience the beauty and strangeness first hand. That is, if I could go first class and be absolutely sure I wouldn't be stranded in the middle of nowhere. Of course running water and room service would be a must.

"So, when we last spoke, I told you that I wanted to get to know you. I've talked about myself for the last hour and a half, now it's your turn," he said.

"What do you want to know? There's really nothing special about me."

"Can I be the judge of that?"

"Sure, but don't be disappointed when you find out I'm pretty ordinary."

"Okay, what's your favorite colour?"

"Well, that depends. If you're talking about what colour I like to wear, that would be blue. If you mean what are my favorite colours that I see around me, then I'd have to say the deep violet of a winter's night sky, or the intense oranges and reds of a summer sunset, or the soft pink of a baby's cheek. If you mean, what colours do I like to paint with, I couldn't say. I love them all."

"And you really think that you are uncomplicated and ordinary?"

He continued to ask me questions like what was my favorite music, what was my favorite food, what were my favorite flowers, and what did I do for fun. I answered each question unselfconsciously, probably for the first time in my life. I talked to him the way my thoughts flowed, no censoring, no editing, no judgments. I felt like I was analyzing myself for the first time and Aaron was along for the ride.

When he asked what I'd been up to, I told him about Christmas and the fight with my mother. He only interrupted my narrative to ask how it made me feel and to murmur words of understanding. I shared with him my fear about being an artist. I told him about starting at the college in the summer, and to my surprise, he started to laugh. It was not the reaction I expected.

"What's so funny?" I asked, unable to keep the irritation out of my voice.

"The fact that even if you had said no to seeing me again, you would have anyway."

"I don't understand."

"I teach advanced photography classes at the college during the summer session. It's a small campus, so you see, chances are you would have bumped into me at some point. You know what they say about messing with fate," Aaron said, and we began a long discussion on destiny, fate, and whether or not free will plays a part in life's journey. Our discussion flowed easily, both of us arguing our points and agreeing to disagree on a few issues. I felt so comfortable talking with him. I didn't have to pretend to be anyone other than who I was.

He was just pouring the last of the wine when the backdoor alarm chirped followed by a second chirp indicating that Jas had come home, disengaged the alarm, and then reset it. Within minutes, her footsteps sounded on the stairs, and the door opened as she poked her head in.

"Hi. I didn't know you were having company over tonight," she said, not even trying to hide the huge smile on her face.

I knew what she was thinking. "It was kind of a last minute thing. Jas, I'd like you to meet Aaron."

"Nice to meet you. You're the photographer that Hannah posed for right?" She tugged off her coat and threw it over the back of the sofa.

"Yeah, I am. Hannah's a great model, and the pictures turned out amazing. I'll have to have both of you over to the studio so you can see them sometime."

"That would be cool." Jas took a seat at the table. She reached for my glass of wine and waited for me to nod before she picked it up and took a sip.

"You're home early. Does that mean you didn't hit it off with 'granola guy'?" I asked.

"Actually, I had a really good time. In fact, we are planning on going out on Sunday. And I'm not home early, it's after midnight," Jas replied.

"Oh my God, you're right." I checked the time on the clock above the sink. "I didn't realize it was so late."

"You must have been having a good time. At least that's what they say about time flying." She gave me a wink and popped an olive in her mouth. "It was nice meeting you, but I'm going to toddle off to bed now. I'm bushed, and I have a full day tomorrow. Good night, kids." She got up from the table and pushed her chair in.

We said good night to Jas, and, as soon as she went to her room, Aaron stood up and started removing plates from the table and stacking them in the sink.

"I didn't realize it was so late either. I should get going."

"You're probably right. I have to work tomorrow, and you must be exhausted from the flight home. Just leave the dishes, Aaron, I'll do them tomorrow." I led him away from the sink.

We collected his bags from the salon, and I drove him home in Jas's truck. The streets were deserted, and we hit all the green lights. The ride over was so short. I wanted to keep talking, but when I parked in front of his apartment, I was betrayed by my uncontrollable yawning.

We said good night. Aaron opened the passenger side door to leave, then he stopped and turned to face me. He leaned in and, for one crazy moment, I thought he was going to kiss me. I closed my eyes and angled my head in anticipation. I really, really wanted him to kiss me despite what I had said to him earlier. Instead, he gave me a one-armed hug.

"Sweet dreams, Hannah. I'll talk to you tomorrow," Aaron said as he got out of the truck.

He collected his bags from the back. I stayed parked on the curb, giving him a wave as he disappeared behind the door of his apartment.

On the ride home, I pondered my feelings for Aaron and the truth that I really wanted him to be more than a friend. I wasn't sure if my sudden reversal was a real desire and connection, or whether I was following my old patterns of throwing myself into a relationship before I even knew the person or knew if that was really what I wanted. What was even more confounding to me was that he respected my wishes to go slow and just be friends more than I did. I knew I needed to sort out my feelings, but I was too tired to deal with it. I knew I couldn't put off taking a hard look at my behavior, but it was going to have to wait until the morning.

Chapter Twenty-Six

Aaron called me Saturday evening to invite me out the next day. The salon was closed Sundays, and I had nothing more pressing than laundry and house cleaning to do.

"Just so that we are clear, this is just a friendly outing. This is definitely not a date," he said as soon as I agreed. "I don't want you to get the idea that I'm disregarding your wishes. This is just what friends do; they go out and enjoy each other's company."

I wasn't a hundred percent sure, but I thought I detected a hint of playfulness. "No, the thought never occurred to me. Just friends. Where are you planning to take me on this friendly outing?"

"That's for me to know, and for you to experience. Just make sure you're dressed for the elements. See you tomorrow at one. I'll come by and pick you up."

* * * *

I needled Aaron while he drove his Honda Civic, but he kept mum about our destination. It didn't matter how many questions I asked, he just kept replying, "You'll see when we get there."

"There" turned out to be in front of Olympic Plaza. The Plaza was built for the 1988 Winter Olympics and included an outdoor amphitheatre and stage, landscaped terraces, a brick plaza, and a central shallow pool. The park was primarily used for the medal presentations during the games. Now the park hosted several festivals and concerts throughout the year. In the summer, the large pool was opened to the public to wade in during hot sultry days. In the winter, it was maintained as an outdoor skating rink.

I had an idea what he had planned when we parked the car next to City Hall. Its geometric design made it look like giant azure steps leading to nowhere. We got out of the car, and Aaron led me through the wrought iron carriage gate and into the plaza. We walked through the stone arches and down the steps of the amphitheatre towards the skating rink.

Despite the skin numbing temperature, several hearty souls were out on the rink enjoying the day. I saw a mom and dad teaching their toddler how to skate, each one holding one of her little, mittened hands while she tried to master skating on wobbly legs. Several teenaged boys skated effortlessly around the rink, checking out the girls clustered in groups around the ice, feigning boredom and disinterest, but fooling no one. There were also couples of all ages leisurely skating hand in hand.

"We're going skating for our date?" I asked.

"Yes, and it's not a date, it's an outing with friends, remember."

"Right, just friends hanging out." I stopped at the edge of the rink. "I'm so glad you picked this, I love skating. I wish I had my skates, though."

"That's okay, we can rent some." He pointed to a trailer set up near the rink.

"You live in a province that gets eight months of winter and you don't own skates."

"Nope, I never had the need because I never learned to skate."

"You don't know how to skate? Then why did you bring me here?"

"Because you mentioned the other night that your two favorite outdoor activities were skating and horseback riding, which I also don't know how to do. I figured my chances of getting seriously hurt were lower with skating. I'll need some time to work up the courage to climb on the back of a thousand pound animal that can smell fear and incompetence. Besides, with skating I figured you could teach me."

"I'll do my best." I smiled.

I gave Aaron my shoe size, and he went to the rental trailer and picked up our skates. We sat side by side on a nearby bench, taking off our boots and tying up our skates. I laced mine up in no time and watched in amusement while he struggled with his laces.

I leaned into him and whispered in his ear, "Need some help?"

"Yes, God yes." He threw his hands up in the air. "I seem to have made a complete mess of this."

Laughing, I got down on my knees in front of him and examined what he had done. I retightened the laces on his left skate and had to re-lace his right one because he missed an eyelet. In no time, I had Aaron and his skates put to rights.

"There, you're good to go," I said.

Slowly he stood then reached down and helped me up. We were standing inches apart, so close I had to crane my neck to look up into his face. We stood like that, neither of us moving, until a teenaged boy stopped abruptly at the edge of the rink, close enough to spray us with a plume of slushy ice from his skate blades

I bent down to brush the slush from my pant legs, but Aaron stopped me by gently placing his hand under my chin.

"You've got snow on your face." He took off his glove and wiped the ice off my cheek. His fingertips felt hot against my cold skin.

My stomach fluttered. What was I doing? I didn't want to get involved in another relationship. He agreed to just be friends and here I was having these feelings. What was wrong with me? Why was I always doing things backwards? Wanting things that I knew I couldn't handle.

I stepped away from him and onto the ice. I skated backwards, spun around, and headed back to the edge of the rink where he waited.

"You make that look easy." He stood where I'd left him.

"It is, once you get the hang of it. Here take my hand."

He stepped onto the ice, his skates immediately sliding out from under him and he started to fall backwards. I held on tight and Aaron righted himself holding on to me for dear life.

"Okay, maybe this wasn't such a good idea after all. Maybe I should have picked horseback riding."

"No, you're doing just fine. The trick is to stay relaxed and bend at the knees." I let go of his hand and demonstrated. "Remember, push off your blades from the side, keep your knees bent, and don't tense up."

"Right, keep my knees bent, push off from the sides of the blades, and stay relaxed," he repeated under his breath as he followed my instructions.

He pushed off and away we went hand-in-hand. I slowed my pace so Aaron could keep up as he skated on unsteady legs much like the toddler I had seen earlier. It only took a couple of laps around the rink before he got the hang of it. By the end of the afternoon, he was skating pretty good for a newbie. We only fell once when someone cut in front of us and Aaron forgot how to stop. He lost his balance and took me down with him, and we fell in a heap on the ice, me on top and laughing so hard my sides hurt. We were still laughing, even after we picked each other up off the ice and headed to the safety of the benches.

We took off our skates and put on our ice-cold boots. I jumped up and down to warm up my toes while Aaron returned our skates.

"Are you hungry?" He asked when he came back.

"Starving."

"I know just the place." He led me down into the park.

We stopped at a vending cart and Aaron bought us smokies on a bun and hot chocolate. We sat on a bench and ate our lunch. I was chilled to the bone, but the hotdogs tasted so good and the fresh air was invigorating. We finished sipping our cocoa while we walked back to the car. It was only 4:30 in the afternoon, but the sun had already started to set.

On the way home, he turned up the heat in the car, and by the time he pulled up to the back of the salon, I was toasty warm. Aaron got out and walked me to the door.

"Did you want to come up?"

"I'd love to, but I have to get some prints ready for a client tomorrow, which means I'll probably have to work most of the night. I'll call you tomorrow, though."

"Thanks for a wonderful day. I had so much fun." I stepped into him and gave him a hug.

He wrapped his arms around me returning the embrace. His arms felt so good around me, strong and safe. I kissed him lightly on the cheek, just a friendly peck.

I went inside and practically floated upstairs. Jas was cooking dinner, and I helped her get it on the table while I recounted how much fun I had with Aaron. I couldn't wait to talk to him tomorrow. I knew we had begun something special, even if it would only be an exceptional friendship.

Western Canadian College of Art and Design
Nurturing Artists, Expanding Possibilities,
Supporting Culture

For more than 95 years, the college has created an
environment that has produced many of Canada's award-winning
designers, renowned artists, and innovative minds. As one of
only three degree-granting institutions of art and design
education in Canada, we take our unique responsibility very
seriously. Our professors offer the highest level of instruction
available. We have created a learning environment and designed
our degree programs around the unique needs and requirements
of our student body.

Admission Deadlines:
Spring/Summer Term (accelerated studies): see pg. 5
Fall Term: see pg. 7

Chapter Twenty-Seven

May finally arrived. It was my first day of class, and I was nervous as hell. I felt like I was back in elementary school. Would anybody like me? Would I like my classes? Did someone make a horrible mistake and let me in by accident? Would I be the oldest student there? Would anyone sit with me at lunch, or would I be the geeky kid sitting by herself?

At least I knew one person on campus. Aaron had offered to come with me, but I had told him no. I wanted to start this adventure on my own. Just knowing I would see a friendly face today was enough.

And what a face it was. The body wasn't half-bad either, from what I could tell with his clothes on. Even though we'd gone out on several 'friendly' dates and spent many evenings talking until dawn, we hadn't taken the next step. It frustrated me sometimes, but I was enjoying getting to know him and just spending time with him.

Aaron, true to his word, did go horseback riding with me. I took him to Rafters Six, a dude ranch just west of the city on the Trans-Canada Highway. I picked the ranch because of its reputation of caring for their horses and the caliber of their wranglers. The wrangler who led our group selected a calm, sweet-natured mare for Aaron. Instead of fear and incompetence, I think the mare sensed his gentle character, and they got along famously. He did far better on his first horseback ride than he did on his first skating attempt.

I finally meet a guy who wants to take the time to get to know me before having sex, and all I can think about when I'm around him is getting hot and sweaty between the sheets. I knew he was feeling the same urges, it was hard not to notice, but other than hugs and chaste kisses on the cheek, he never took things any further.

Damn him and his promises.

And here I was doing it again. My first day of school, the beginning of my new adventure, and I was standing on the steps thinking about being with Aaron. Over the last week, I hadn't been able to see him as much as I would have liked because I'd had too much to do to get ready for college. For instance, getting supplies.

When I went to the art supply store with my gift certificate and list of supplies from the college tucked safely in my purse, I hadn't felt fearful or nervous, just excited and overwhelmed. It had occurred to me that, in the past year, I had unconsciously retraced all the places Noni and I used to frequent. This place had been one of my favorites. It was crammed full of lovely things. Narrow aisles with shelves stocked with every conceivable art tool—paint, stretchers, papers, inks, charcoals, pens, brushes, brush cleaners, palettes, and other items for just about any type of art one would want to create. Along the back wall, primed canvases of varying sizes were stacked three feet deep and easels hung on the walls. Noni and I used to spend hours exploring the wonderful items that held the potential for so much creativity.

When I walked into the store, I felt like I had stepped back in time. Even Jeff, the owner, was standing behind the counter as he always was when Noni and I had visited. He waved me over to say hello. He gave me his condolences over my loss, and, although I was uncomfortable, I was touched by his heartfelt words.

My hands shook slightly as I pulled out my list and got down to business. Jeff was more than happy to help me collect the things on my list. I wandered behind him while he placed the items in the wire basket I carried. I let my fingers float over the stacks of pastels and charcoals. I picked up a badger-hair brush and stroked its silky hairs under my hands. When I had paid for all my purchases, Jeff helped me load everything, gave me a hearty handshake and wished me luck.

Now here I was, still standing on the steps, feeling like a scared little girl.

Enough, Hannah.

I was determined not to let my niggling fears get the best of me. Not again. Not this time. Besides, if I didn't hurry up, I was going to be late for my first class.

I pulled back my shoulders and dashed up the wide steps and through the heavy oak doors. Once inside, I stopped in my tracks again. The air was fragrant with the wonderful perfume of old schools: chalk, paper, old wood, lemon polish, and a warm dust-motey smell. Mingled in the air was the unmistakable aroma of linseed oil, turpentine, and paint. Other students making their way to class had to walk around me as I stood there soaking up the atmosphere. My schedule said my first class, Art History, was in room 215A. I headed down the hall, unsure of where I was going.

Tall glass display cases lined the main floor hall. Some of the cases contained clay and porcelain pieces ranging from large urns to teapots and small decorative plates. Others held bronze statues and gigantic blown glass vessels which came to life with cleverly placed spotlights.

I proceeded upstairs and wandered around the second floor, but I couldn't find the room. In a panic, I retraced my steps back to the main administration office.

The front of the office was separated from the main foyer by a counter with sliding glass partitions. The partitions were open and revealed a secretary sitting at a desk talking on the phone. Behind her was a very old Xerox machine and a wall of mail cubbies labeled with instructors names.

I stepped up to the counter. Aaron stood there, his back towards me, feeding a stack of papers into the copier. He turned around when I called his name, a smile spreading over his face when he saw me. He put the papers down and walked over the counter.

"Hi. How's your first day going?" He had a terrific smile.

"Great. I'm so excited, but I'm feeling like a bit of a geek because I can't find my first class."

"You certainly don't look like a geek." He gave me an appraising look. "What room are you looking for?"

"Room 215A."

"Yah, you're not the first one to get stumped by that one. It's in the annex; that's what the A stands for. It's not connected to the main building stairwell, which you probably already tried, right?"

"Yup."

"Just head down the hall," he pointed to the hall I had just come down, "and go past the main staircase, take a right, and at the end of the corridor you'll see another set of stairs. That will take you to the second floor of the annex."

"Thanks."

"Hey, anytime. What time do you get lunch? Maybe I could join you."

We made plans to meet up during my lunch break, and I headed down the hallway.

The walls of the second floor annex were home to artwork created on canvas. I slowed my pace, forgetting for a moment that I was already late for class. I couldn't help but cast a judgmental eye towards some of the paintings. Other pieces, however, showed a skill and talent that far surpassed mine. A bitter pill of insecurity flowed through me, and I could taste the acid in the back of my throat. Finally, I saw the door to my classroom and quickly walked through it before I gave in to the urge to high-tail it out of there.

As it turned out, my insecurity and uneasiness were unfounded and soon evaporated. I had been starving for this for so long that I gobbled up every word, every idea, every experience. I wasn't the oldest student in class but fell somewhere comfortably in the middle. By lunchtime, my head was buzzing pleasantly, so drunk on all the new experiences that I barely touched the lunch I'd so carefully packed the night before. I ate, or rather sat, in the cafeteria, with a few of the students from my Perspective Drawing class sharing our histories, our opinions on art, and our experiences.

I was the last one to leave. Aaron hadn't showed, and I still had a few minutes before my next class. I was just packing up my uneaten lunch when I spied him walking across the cafeteria. I could feel the smile spreading across my face.

"Sorry I'm late. A couple of students had questions after class. How's it going so far? You surviving?" He carried a lunch tray piled high with lasagna, salad, and bread.

"Good, great actually." I stared at him while he ate.

He looked from his plate catching me in the act.

"What? You look like the cat that caught the canary," he said through a mouthful of food.

"I'm so happy. I really didn't think I could feel this way: that my life could be like this. The moment I stepped through the doors of the college, I felt like I belonged. It's everything I'd hoped for and more. The teachers are great, and to be surrounded by other artists, all of us striving for the same thing, is almost surreal. I keep thinking this is a really great dream and I don't want to wake up."

"It's pretty heady stuff isn't it? And, it's not a dream. Life is supposed to be filled with joy. As long as you have the courage to go after what means something to you, it will always feel joyful, even when the day-to-day stuff gets tedious or you run into a few obstacles along the way." He put his fork down to reach across the table and squeeze my hand.

I had said almost the exact words to Jas as we were driving to her salon for the first time. Now I understood what she had gone through: the fear, the elation, the wondering if she really had the right to be happy and successful doing something she loved.

"That means a lot to me, not just the words, but the understanding. And on that note, I'd better skedaddle. I was late for my first class and if I don't get going, I'm going to be late for another. I don't want to get a reputation as a slacker." I stood up.

"Enjoy the rest of your day. I'll see you soon."

When he smiled, his eyes lit up. My heart fluttered pleasantly in my chest, and I went off to my next class, feeling a warm glow and a joyful anticipation of what the rest of the day would bring.

I never dreamed the secret and sacred world that Noni's paintbrushes and patience revealed to me in my childhood had so many more landscapes and textures and deep pools of knowledge and expression yet to be explored. Each day, as I made my way up those stately stone steps into that world of mystery, I traveled new roads that delighted and enthralled me. So wrapped up in these discoveries, I didn't notice spring quietly slipping into summer. Some of the work and assignments were embarrassingly easy; others were frustratingly challenging. But I welcomed everything with an ecstasy bordering on the religious.

Although the majority of my classes pertained to painting and drawing, I also had to take elective courses in other areas of art. I tried my hand at silk-screening, printmaking, sculpting and throwing clay on a potter's wheel. I had no aptitude for sculpting but I loved pottery. I reveled in the smell of the dark earth and the slippery wetness as the mound of clay spun and moved on the wheel.

After my first Art History exam, the professor asked me to see him after class. He said, based on my written assignments and my grades so far, I should take the equivalency exam. If I passed the exam, I wouldn't have to sit through the rest of the course. That would give me more time in the studio. I hadn't realized how much Noni had taught me and how much had become part of the things that I just knew.

In my childhood, when we weren't painting or exploring art galleries and the museum, Noni would take me to her room and pull out her large art books from an old steamer trunk that sat at the foot of her bed. The trunk smelled like mothballs and cedar and so did the books that were kept there. The two of us would nestle down on her large feather bed and flip through each of the thick volumes while Noni described what we were looking at. Later, when I was old enough to understand what I was reading, I would ask to borrow these well-traveled tomes and spend hours poring over the images and reading every word of text. At the time, I didn't think of this as part of my education but as another extension of the art that I loved and the woman in my life that I loved even more.

I took the Art History exam and passed. It wasn't even a stretch for me. That left me with three extra hours a week to spend in the studio.

The airy, well-lit studio was completely outfitted with easels, pre-stretched canvases of every size imaginable, community brushes, and paints. I loved the counterpoint of scents —oil and pigments beneath sun-warmed pine beams. An artist's dream. I preferred to use the set of paints that Da gave me and, after a couple of weeks, I brought Noni's easel to the studio, labeling it with a piece of masking tape on which I had written my name.

July arrived, bringing hot, desert-dry weather. On one such day, I decided to eat my bag lunch outside. The sky was clear and blue with just a few billowy clouds dotting its expanse. The plants and trees were at the height of their lushness, showy in their colours and heady in their scents. This far north the sun's heat was fleeting, and we had to enjoy it before our short summer disappeared into cold and darkness again.

I ambled across the green space, looking for a place to sit, occasionally having to dodge fat bumblebees weighed down by dusty clumps of pollen clinging to their back legs. I spied a spot under a huge elm but it wasn't until I approached the tree that I noticed a pair of legs sticking out from behind the other side of the trunk. I felt disappointed. The tree looked so inviting, the shade sweetly soothing, but I wanted to be alone. I'd started to head off in the other direction, when the owner of the legs leaned over and called my name.

"Hi, Aaron." I walked back over to the tree.

"Hey you!" He patted the ground next to him.

I sat down on the grass and leaned against the gnarly tree trunk, hyperaware of his body so close to mine. We had continued to see each other on a regular basis over the summer and become great friends. He was as dear to me as Jas and Noni, except my friendship with him held a thrilling undercurrent of attraction. I still wasn't sure what I was going to do with this attraction, but I swore to myself that I wasn't going to screw up what we had. This time I was going to lead with my head and not my heart, or my libido for that matter.

Aaron flipped through a stack of proofs that rested on his lap. "Seeing you is the kind of interruption I look forward to."

"What are those?"

"Proofs for my upcoming show, in fact these are from the series of photos you sat for. I was just going through the final selection." He handed me a smaller stack of photos that were nestled in a box on the grass beside him. I wiped my hands on the sleeve of my shirt to brush off any stray breadcrumbs and took the photos.

They were black and whites. Not full on pictures of women but close up studies of body parts—the curve of a hip, the roundness of a shoulder, graceful hands. Each photo, lit to enhance the texture of its subject, evoked a sense of wonder and sensuality.

"These are stunning."

"I'm glad you think so. I particularly like this one and the model that sat for it." He pointed to the photo I held.

It showed the bust of a woman turned away from the camera so all she revealed was the curve of her neck and slope of her shoulder. It was one of the photographs from my sitting.

"And I also think this one is amazing." He pulled out the next shot.

Again, it was me in the photo but just my eyes. I didn't realize he had taken that picture. It was strange to see how much sorrow there was in my eyes. Who was that person?

"Where's your showing being held?"

"At Bernie's. He was the one that gave me my first break and he's helped my career immeasurably. I wouldn't think of showing with anyone else. Would you come to the opening? I'd really like you to be there."

"I'd love to. When is it?"

"In three weeks. It's a Friday at seven."

"I can't wait."

"You know, one day, Hannah, maybe you and I could actually spend a whole lunch hour together. But for now, I have to get back to work, I only snuck out for my coffee break and my fifteen minutes are up. I'll see you tomorrow." Aaron gathered his photos into the boxes.

I watched him wander back towards the school, and I finished my lunch alone under the tree contemplating what a wonderful turn of events life had presented me recently. I didn't recognize the unhappiness in the eyes of the young woman in the photo. The only part of my life that continued to cause me any angst was my relationship with my mother, who still wasn't speaking to me. At least my da was supportive. In fact, I still spoke to him every week.

When he called, I would recap what I had done at school, what I'd learned, and what was frustrating me. Da, on his part, kept me updated as to what was happening on the farm—what cows from the Jensen's herd had dropped their calves, how his small crops and kitchen garden were progressing, and what books he was reading. The one thing, the one person who was conspicuously absent from our conversations was my mother. It left a tender bruise on my feelings. But if Da, the great mediator, wasn't willing to bring up her name, it only meant one thing: she was still angry with me.

My strained relationship with my mother had me terribly confused as a young child and resulted in my turning even more to Noni for comfort. I didn't want to find out. Did my mother really feel it was better for me to have a small life that didn't suit me than go after my dreams? Her silence told me that's exactly how she felt. Now, I felt our mother-daughter bond might shatter completely. Did Mom really think I should settle for a life that didn't suit me rather than go after my dreams? I didn't want this to be true but her silence only confirmed it. How would I ever pick up the pieces then?

Along with his weekly calls, Da unexpectedly started showing up in town. At first, he pretended he needed to come to the city on important errands, but eventually he dropped the pretense and admitted he was coming to see me. He and Aaron finally met on one of his visits.

Over lunch in a little Italian bistro, I introduced Aaron to my da as a dear friend. Really, that's what he was, even if a corner of my heart kept insisting that I wanted it to be more. I was nervous about them finally meeting and the slim chance that they wouldn't like each other. I had no reason to worry. Aaron was at ease with Da, and Da showed an honest interest in what Aaron did for a living.

The lunch felt easy, comfortable. While we finished our after-lunch coffees, I was overcome by a feeling of such love for these two men sitting at the table. They were so different physically, in their ages, and in their chosen paths in life; but at their core, they shared the same mix of quiet courage, loyalty, honesty, and gift of compassion. I felt so blessed to have two men in my life that I could depend on.

One sunny afternoon after class, I met up with Da to give him a tour of the campus. I was excited to show him around and have him see what my new life looked like. I introduced him to a few of the students and teachers we met along the way, we toured the painting studio, the cafeteria, past the classrooms, and finally the Art Space where we showed our work.

After the tour, we grabbed a fast-food dinner before he headed back home. Over hamburgers and fries, we talked about the upcoming show and which of my paintings he liked the best. In the middle of our conversation, I realized how much more grey he had at his temples, and dark circles shadowed his eyes. It clutched at my heart.

"Da, are you feeling okay?" I put down my burger.

"I'm fine, Hannah. I'm a little tired is all. Takes a lot to keep even our small farm running, and I'm not as young as I used to be. Nothing a couple of good night's rest won't cure."

He looked so worn, so old. The feud between my mom and I seemed to be taking a toll on him, too. I felt childish and selfish; when I kissed him goodbye, I made a silent pledge to do whatever I needed to do to stop this stupid fight. I just needed to suck it up.

After dinner, I kept thinking of ways to make my mother come around to accepting the choices I'd made, to help her understand her anger was with Noni, not me. Since she still wasn't taking my calls, I had to think of more creatively to get through to her. I kept coming up with ideas and rejecting them. How do you say you're sorry for something you didn't think was wrong? I wasn't sorry for the relationship I had with Noni. My feelings about Noni would never change, but I needed my mother—and not only for Da's sake. I wanted some kind of connection with her. I wasn't sure it was possible, but I had to at least try to break through the silence between us.

Chapter Twenty-Eight

The day of Aaron's exhibition arrived. The exhibit was called "Essence." He wouldn't allow me to go to the gallery with him to see the set up; he wanted me to see it when everything had been hung and lit properly. I'd only seen the proofs that one day under the tree in the quad. I had my dress picked out, and it was laying on my bed waiting for me. It would be hours before time for the opening, In the meantime, I was busy hanging my paintings in the students' gallery because my turn on the schedule had come around.

Celia, another student who shared most of my classes, agreed to come down that afternoon so we could help each other put up our work.

We finished hanging all of her pieces and started on mine. Just as we were going to hang my biggest one, her cell phone rang.

It was her boyfriend. They'd had a huge fight the night before—Celia had filled me in on all the gory details while we were putting up her paintings. She motioned that she would be just a minute and left the room, with her phone pressed to her ear.

I stood alone, looking at my work. Up until this year, the only people who had seen my paintings were my family and my small circle friends. Now strangers would see them and judge a part of me hanging on these walls. I wasn't sure how I felt about that. In a way I was glad that it was just the student gallery, and not that many people would see my work.

"Need some help?"

Aaron had come up behind me so quietly I jumped when he spoke.

"Sure, if you don't mind," I said, regaining my composure. "I seem to have lost my help. She had a boyfriend crisis to sort out."

Aaron helped me lift my canvas in place. We stepped back to make sure it was hanging straight.

"That one's my favorite." He pointed to my painting he had just helped put up. It was of a stand of poplars in winter and it had a stark and eerie quality to it. I called it "The Sentinels." "You know, I just might have to buy that one before someone else snatches it up."

"You say that about all my pieces."

"But it's true. Hey, do you need help with anything else before I get going?"

"No, that about does it."

"Okay, I'm off to the gallery to see about the final touches to the exhibit. I'll see you there at seven?"

"Seven it is. I'm really looking forward to tonight. Maybe I'll even have to buy a piece before someone snatches it up." I laughed as he gave me a playful punch in the arm.

I had just turned to leave the gallery, intent on getting home and soaking in a hot bath before getting ready for the evening with Aaron, when Elizabeth Beddoes, the director of the college, walked in and headed in my direction.

"May I speak with you for a moment, Hannah?"

I had met Elizabeth at the meet-and-greet wine and cheese party held during the second week of school. Since then, our paths hadn't crossed and I was surprised she even remembered my name.

"Sure," I replied.

"Why don't we head to my office?"

278

I followed Elizabeth into her office. She shut the door behind me and turned to face me with what looked like sympathy in her eyes. A bubble of fear formed in the pit of my stomach.

"I just got a call from the Rocky View Hospital." She leaned up against her desk. "I'm sorry to have to tell you this, but your dad's had a heart attack. I don't know all the details but the nurse I spoke to said your mother is already there and you should get to the hospital as soon as you can."

I watched her mouth as she spoke, but I couldn't make sense of the garbled nonsense tumbling out of her. Suddenly all the air in the office was sucked out and I couldn't breathe, I couldn't hear, I couldn't talk.

"I think you had better sit down." Elizabeth guided me to a chair as I desperately tried to breathe. "Is there someone I can call? Someone who could go with you to the hospital?"

I couldn't think. My mind was racing over the words "your father" and "heart attack." This couldn't be happening. I wanted to call Aaron. He'd just left the college and could be here in no time. I wanted to call Jas too. She was only five minutes away by car. I needed them both. I needed to get to the hospital and I needed to get there now.

"Uh—yes, yes my friend, Jas."

Chapter Twenty-Nine

I remembered getting into Jas's truck and racing off in the direction of the hospital, but the ride was a blur. I don't know if I said anything to her. I just kept thinking that this wasn't really happening. This was all just a horrible dream, and soon I would wake up and everything would be just as it was supposed to be. My da would be fine, puttering around the farm, calling me on Wednesday night, and coming into the city for his visits.

Jas pulled into the visitor parking lot at Rocky View, came around the truck, and opened my door. I stepped out onto the pavement and looked around. I didn't know where to go, so I followed Jas. The large automatic doors swooshed open and closed behind us as we stepped inside. I stood in the lobby while she approached the information desk. Water dripped off my nose and hair.

It must be raining, I thought absently. Everything around me seemed distant and faded as if I was wrapped in cotton.

"Hannah, we have to go to the third floor."

I wiped the rain off my face with the sleeve of my jacket. When I moved to the elevators, a sudden rushing sound, like a gale force wind, pounded my eardrums. Sounds exploded around me, voices of people talking, the tapping of high-heeled shoes on the linoleum floor, a distant phone ringing, the metal clang of a gurney being wheeled down the corridor. With the sounds came the feeling of a hand pushing me forward, urging me on. I rushed to the bank of elevators. I pressed on the call button several times and paced until, with excruciating slowness, the elevator doors finally opened. I jabbed the number three button on the panel and hit the close door button without caring if anyone else needed to get on.

As soon as the elevator deposited us on the third floor, I ran down the corridor following the signs to the ICU waiting room. I found my mother sitting all by herself on a dreary green couch. Her hands were in her lap shredding a tissue while tears rolled unchecked down her cheeks.

"Mom?"

She looked up at me, her eyes red rimmed and unfocused. She stood up slowly. I ran to her and wrapped my arms tightly around her shaking shoulders. She felt so small. Through tears, and still holding onto her tightly, I asked her how Da was doing. She smelled faintly of White Linen, sweet and cloying.

She straightened up and away from me, using her shredded tissue to dab at her tears. "He's had a heart attack."

"Yes, I know."

She continued on, as if I hadn't spoken. "They took him into surgery twenty minutes ago to do an emergency bypass. The doctor said he would be back to see us when it's over."

This couldn't be happening. Not to my da. The room tilted dangerously and I reached out for the wall to steady myself. My mother hugged herself and looked past me into space. There was nothing to do but wait for the doctor. We both sat down on the hideously uncomfortable couch. The cushions sighed under our combined weight.

"I thought you guys could use some tea." Jas held a tray with three Styrofoam cups, steam trailing out of the tops. She handed one to my mother and then me. I didn't even know she'd left.

"Thank you, dear, that's very thoughtful of you." Mom took the cup and held it in her lap.

The tea was weak and tasted like Styrofoam. I took another scalding sip and settled down again to wait.

We sat in silence, Mom still as a stone, holding her tea until it went cold. I had my arm around her, but I couldn't think of anything to say. I just kept silently praying that Da would be okay.

When Khandi arrived hours later, we still hadn't seen the doctor. She looked at the three of us before speaking.

"You need to eat," she said to me. I opened my mouth to tell her I wasn't going anywhere but she wouldn't give me a chance. "You aren't going to be much help to your mother if you pass out from hunger. And bring your mother back a muffin and some strong, sweet tea. I'll call you on your cell if anything changes. Now, go!" Khandi kissed me on the cheek and gently pushed me towards the elevators like a small child.

I was going to argue with her, insist that I was going to stay, but, when I watched her comfort my mother, I stifled my anger. My mother had sat with me not saying a word. As Khandi approached her, she started to cry again, telling Khandi, through her tears, how Da was just leaving the house when she heard him collapse in the living room. She told Khandi how scared she was that she was going to lose him.

"Let's go, Hannah," Jas whispered in my ear. "My mom will look after her."

Weighed down with too many feelings to understand or even name, I followed her down the elevator to the small coffee shop on the main floor of the hospital. I drank a Coke and picked at my egg salad sandwich. I kept willing Jas to hurry up and finish her food so we could get back upstairs.

When we finally headed back with the tea and a cheese scone for my mother, a doctor was walking ahead of us towards the waiting room. He wore green surgery scrubs and a funny little hat with the strings hanging down loosely on either side of his head. We followed him into the waiting room.

"Mrs. Morgan," he said.

"Yes?" My mother stood up.

"I'm Dr. Vincelli. Please take a seat." His voice was soft and kind.

My mother sat back down, her face turning a pasty grey. The doctor sat down in a plastic chair across from her, resting his forearms on his knees. I remained standing.

"I have good news. The surgery went even better than expected. There were no complications, and with time and rehab, I am confident he will make a complete recovery. He needs to be monitored for infections. The chances are slight, but we want to be on the safe side. He'll have to spend a few days in ICU for observation. If everything looks good, he'll be transferred down to another nursing unit."

"Thank you, thank you," my mother whispered. She started crying again.

The doctor patted her gently on the leg.

"May I see him?" She asked, looking like a lost little girl.

"Yes you can. He is in the Recovery Room. A nurse will be by shortly and take you to see him. He'll still be groggy from the surgery so he may not be coherent. Do you have any other questions?" When he'd answered them all, he excused himself from our little circle.

A wave of relief flooded over me and my knees buckled. I sat down hard on the chair, the doctor had just vacated. Da was going to be all right. My mother excused herself to use the washroom.

Before she left, Khandi took my hand. "He's going to be okay."

I knew that, but I was still anxious. I wanted to see my da with my own eyes, to touch him, to tell him I loved him so very much.

At last, the nurse arrived and escorted my mother and me to Da's room. He looked so small lying in the hospital bed, the blanket tucked tightly around his still form. He had tubes up his nose and he was hooked up to monitors that beeped and chirped. Fresh tears sprang into my eyes. I wanted to rip the tubes and the wires off him and shake him awake. I wanted him to look like he did just a few days ago, with his sturdiness and his strong quiet presence, not like this, not this small frail old man.

During the whole time in the waiting room, I had prayed that he would be all right, that I would get to see him again. Now that we were standing in his room, I was afraid. I hung back at the foot of the bed as my mother approached him. She tenderly placed his hand in hers and stroked his face speaking softly to him. Da slowly turned his head towards the sound of her voice. His eyes fluttered open and rested, slightly out of focus, on her face. My mother cupped her hand on his cheek and leaned in to kiss him on the lips. Her face was close to his, looking into his eyes. She kept saying I love you.

I never saw my parents kiss or be intimate in front of me in any way. I felt like a voyeur, an intruder witnessing an emotionally raw moment between husband and wife.

"I love you too," he managed to whisper. Exhausted from this small effort, his eyes closed and he drifted off into a drug-induced sleep.

My mother caressed his hand being careful not to knock the IV sticking out from his thin, age-spotted skin.

I walked to the other side of the bed and kissed him lightly on the cheek. "I love you, Da, please get better soon."

He didn't respond. I watched his chest slowly rise and fall with each soft snore.

It felt as if we had just stepped into Da's room when the same nurse that had brought us in came back. She said Da needed to rest. She took my mother aside and told her she could spend the night if she wanted. There was a small couch in the room for her to rest on if she needed to.

"Mom, I want to spend the night too."

"No, there is no need. He's out of the woods now, and there really isn't room for both of us. Besides, you would just be in the way of the nurses who need to focus on taking care of him." My mom walked over to Da and gently brushed his hair out of his closed eyes.

I didn't have the desire or the energy to fight. She didn't want me there, so I left.

Jas and I, per my mother's instructions, headed out to find a late night drugstore to buy her some toiletries. Tomorrow, I would go to the farm and pack my mother a suitcase and a few things for Da.

On the way over to the drugstore, I realized, in a panic, the livestock and Geronimo hadn't been seen to since morning. I pulled out my cell and dialed our neighbors, the Jensen's.

To my relief Mr. Jensen had already taken it upon himself to see to our animals and make sure the house was locked up for the night. He had heard the ambulance sirens, and he and his son, Eric, drove over to see what was happening. In her panic, my mother must have forgotten she had seen them and apparently spoken to them. Mr. Jensen assured me all was looked after and would be until Da was feeling better.

It was close to ten at night by the time I headed back to the hospital. I convinced Jas to go home.

"I want to be with my da for a bit. You need to get some rest and I promise to take a cab when I leave."

I found my mother in Da's room exactly where I'd left her, sitting next to the bed and holding his hand. The only light came from the fixture over the bed. It was turned to its lowest setting, casting a faint light over his drawn face. I put the bag of toiletries on the night table, and told her I would be back first thing in the morning. I wanted to hug her and tell her how much I loved her, but I just couldn't. Instead, I said good night, and left her sitting in the gloom keeping watch over her husband.

I stood outside the room, taking one last look through the large window that faced the nurses' station. I leaned against the window; it felt cool on my skin.

"Your father is doing remarkably well. He'll be as right as rain in a few days," the nurse at the desk said to my back.

I was instantly and irrationally angry with her. I bit my lip to stop the words that wanted to come out.

"Hannah."

I looked up. Aaron was hurrying down the corridor, a look of worry on his face, his arms open wide to receive me. I ran into his arms and held tight. He held me while I sobbed uncontrollably into his chest and the sound of his heartbeat kept me from losing my grip completely. He stroked my hair and murmured sounds of comfort in my ear. When I had cried out all my fear, he still held me safe in the circle of his arms, his head bowed down close to mine.

"Come, let me take you home," he said softly into my hair.

He started to lead me down the corridor, his arm wrapped reassuringly around my waist, until I stopped in my tracks.

"How did you know about Da? How did you know to come to the hospital?"

"Jas came by the gallery on her way home and told me what happened. She figured you might want me here. I came as soon as I could."

"Your opening. I'm so sorry —"

"Don't be. I had more than enough time to schmooze with all the guests, and it's just an opening. Besides, I'd rather be here with you."

His words pierced my heart, and tears welled up in my eyes again. I swayed slightly as a wave of light-headedness washed over me.

"Let me take you home." He said again, starting down the hall.

Jas was waiting for us. She gave me a hug as I stepped through the door. I told her Da was resting and things looked good. She said good night to Aaron and me and headed to her room.

"You want something to drink? Coffee, wine, or some herbal tea? Or maybe a glass of water?" I asked Aaron as he slipped off his jacket.

I knew I was babbling, but I couldn't stop. I kept seeing Da lying in that hospital bed with all the tubes and the machines coming out of him. It made me sick. I had come so close to losing him. I opened cupboards not sure what I was looking for, only to turn around and open the fridge.

Aaron came up behind me and wrapped his arms around me, preventing me from continuing my dervish around the kitchen.

"I don't want anything. Why don't you come with me? Even if you don't feel like sleeping, you need to lie down for just a little while."

He led me into my room and gently guided me down to the bed.

"Do you have something to change into? PJs or something?"

I pointed to the over-sized t-shirt thrown over the chair in the corner. He retrieved it and placed it on the bed next to me. Quietly and tenderly, Aaron removed my shirt. I unhooked my bra and let him slip the t-shirt over my head. His hand accidentally brushed against my exposed breast, and I felt instant heat. I slipped out of my jeans and left them in a pile on the floor.

He pulled back the covers, and I lay down while he tucked the covers around me. Before he could step away from the bed, I wrapped my arms around his neck and pulled him down close. He leaned over me with both his hands braced on the mattress.

"Don't go." I pulled him closer kissing him.

He returned the kiss, the need building with each brush of our lips; the passion sparking and creating a sultry heat in the air between us. I started to unbutton his shirt wanting desperately to feel his skin on mine, but he placed a hand over mine, stopping me.

"Hannah." Aaron lowered his head and tried to catch his breath. The staccato beat of his heart pulsed against my hand as it rested on his chest. "This isn't a good idea."

"Why not? I thought you wanted this, to be with me."

"No. I mean yes, I do want to be with you more than you can imagine. I wanted to be with you from the moment you turned around and looked at me at Albright's. But not like this. I want to make love to you, to have you come to me wanting to share your heart in the same way, not because you are scared. I understand what you are feeling, but having sex with me won't take away the fear. I won't take advantage of your pain. Not ever."

I covered my face with my hands, too embarrassed to look at him. Now, all I wanted was for him to leave. I felt stupid and rejected.

"But I will stay with you," he continued, as he got up from my side of the bed. I lowered my hands and watched him strip off his clothes down to his boxers and slip in between the sheets, stretching his body out next to mine. "You're not alone, Hannah. I'll be here tonight while you sleep, and I'll be here when you wake up."

I turned on to my side and spooned with him, my body fitting into the curve of his. He wrapped his arm around me and pulled me closer. I reached over and shut the light out and I lay there in the dark, comforted by the rhythm of his breathing and the strong steady beat of his heart.

Chapter Thirty

The next morning, Aaron was there when I woke up, like he said he would be. He slept soundly, his arm still lying protectively over my body. I lay there for a moment just looking at his face as he slept.

It felt so right to wake up with him next to me. I felt a strange mixture of joy and fear. Joy at what he had said to me last night. Fear that my da might not make a full recovery, despite what the doctor had said. Aaron's words echoed in my head and nestled in my heart, sweeter than any poem, more poignant than any masterpiece could be.

This newfound joy was tempered with my new understanding about life. Da's heart attack shattered any illusion or denial I may have had. He was getting older; he wasn't going to be in my life forever. Life was so fleeting, and every moment with the people I love should be cherished.

Yet, there was my mother. I didn't know if we'd ever be close. If the potential of losing the one man we both loved couldn't bring us together, I feared nothing would. How long would my mother make me pay for Noni not loving her?

As much as I wanted to, I couldn't lie in bed any longer. I had things to do. I needed to get my mother's things from the farm and go to the hospital. I shifted as slowly as I could, trying not to wake Aaron, but as soon as I moved, he opened his eyes.

"Good morning, you," Aaron said, his voice husky from sleep.

"Good morning." I kissed him lightly on the lips, a thrill running through me as I did.

"How did you sleep?"

"Surprisingly good, considering. Thank you for staying with me."

"Anytime." He pulled me close. "Are you going to the hospital right away?"

"Yes, but then I have to go to my parent's house to pick up a few things my mother wants, and then I'll probably spend the rest of the day with Da."

"Did you want company when you go to the farm?"

"I appreciate the offer, but I need to spend some time alone with my thoughts. I have some things I need to sort out."

"Are you having second thoughts about what happened between us last night?"

"No, that's the one thing I'm certain of. I want you to be a part of my life, and I'm just sorry it took me so long to figure that out."

He leaned in, kissed me, long and slow. The urge to stay in bed all day with him and pretend the world outside this room didn't exist was so tempting. Instead, I broke the kiss first and climbed out of bed.

"If you change your mind, just let me know. I'll keep my cell turned on. If you want me to come over later, call me."

Aaron offered to make coffee while I jumped in the shower. I was just pouring coffee into two travel mugs for us when Jas wandered into the kitchen. If she was surprised to find Aaron standing in the kitchen at seven in the morning, she didn't let it show.

She handed me the keys to her truck and told me to give her love to my da. Aaron walked me down to the truck, and with a sweet lingering kiss, sent me on my way.

My first stop was the hospital to check on Da. When I walked into his room, I thought he was sleeping. His eyes were closed, his hands by his side, the blanket tucked in neatly around him. My mother sat at his bedside, reading a magazine. She looked up when I stepped inside the room.

"How's he doing?" I asked in a hushed whisper, going to stand next to his bed.

Before my mother could reply, Da opened he eyes. "I'm doing just fine," he said, his voice sounding gravelly and tired.

I squeezed the hand he held out to me and kissed him on the cheek. "You gave us quite the scare." I tried not to cry.

"Scared myself, too. But don't worry; I'm not going to do it again. You'll see, a few days of lolling about here and being waited upon by your mother, and I'll be back to my old self."

"I'm going to hold you to that promise," I said.

I was just going to settle in next to him when my mother asked if I had been to the house yet.

"No, I was going to go right after I came to see how Da was doing."

"You'd better get moving, then. I've made a list of the things I need, and don't forget to get your father his books, his crib board, and his robe—not the ratty one hanging in the bathroom, but the grey flannel one hanging in the closet. Honestly, the things that pass as robes in this hospital are abominable, and they keep the rooms so cold. I mean really, how is someone supposed to recover from surgery when they are always chilled?"

She handed me her list. I took it, tucked it into the pocket of my jeans, and willed myself not to lose my temper. The last thing my da needed right now was to have to deal with the stress of us going at each other. If my mother couldn't see that, I would have to be the mature adult here.

I said goodbye to Da and promised to be back as quickly as I could. I drove out to the farm, venting out loud, trying to rid myself of the prickly, hot anger my mother always ignited in me. By the time I arrived at the farm, I had calmed down. Before I pulled onto the property, I drove to the Jensen's farm. I wanted to thank Mr. Jensen and update him on Da's condition.

He and his family were just sitting down to breakfast when I arrived. He invited me in and asked me to join them, but I declined, telling them I needed to get back to the hospital.

He wished my da a speedy recovery and said that we needn't worry about the farm. He and his family would take care of things for as long as need be. I thanked him, fighting off the urge to burst into tears at his kindness. Instead, I shook Mr. Jensen's calloused hand and headed over to my parents' place.

Putting the key in the front door felt strange and unnatural. This was the first time in my whole life that the door to my family's house was locked. When I stepped over the threshold, the only sound was the ticking of the clock in the kitchen echoing through the empty rooms. It was as if the house was holding its breath until the return of its rightful occupants. I couldn't help but imagine my da lying on the floor, his heart giving out, my mom frantically trying to save him, and I wasn't there to help. A chill rippled up my spine.

I popped my head into the kitchen and noticed clean dishes sitting on the drain board. Mrs. Jensen must have come and tidied up because my mother would never have left dishes to air-dry on the drain board. I put them away in the cupboards and went upstairs.

I opened my parent's bedroom door to collect the things on my mother's list. I stood there, with my hand on the doorknob, staring at the wall in disbelief. I slowly walked up to the painting hanging on the wall opposite their bed. I traced the smudge mark in the corner of the painting with my finger. I didn't know what to make of it. Da wouldn't have hung this painting, especially not in their bedroom, without my mother's permission. She simply wouldn't have allowed it.

I sat on the corner of the bed staring at the picture. I didn't know if I should be happy or angry. I finally stirred and set about going through my mother's dresser drawers, carefully pulling out and packing all the items t she had written down on the back of an old grocery list.

I pulled Da's new bathrobe out of the closet and put it on the bed. Next, I went into the bathroom. His old bathrobe hung on the back of the door. I took it off the hook and put it on. It smelled of him. Soap and Old Spice aftershave. Wrapped in the robe, I curled up on the bed and sobbed. The doctor said Da was out of danger, but I was still scared.

He's my da; he's supposed to live forever, not get old and have a heart attack. What would mom and I do without him?

I couldn't bear the thought of losing yet another person I loved.

I didn't know how much time had passed with me lying on my parent's bed, bundled in my da's robe, numb and tired. Eventually, I hauled myself off the bed to get a tissue to blow my nose. I took off Da's robe, folded it up, and put it in my mother's suitcase leaving the new one lying on the bed. I did a quick tour through their bathroom, collecting the toiletries my mother wanted. It felt weird going through their personal stuff. I did it as quickly as possible and left the house.

Back at the hospital, I sat on the corner of the bed talking to Da while mom unpacked his things. When she pulled out his robe I heard her sniff. She didn't say anything as she hung the robe in the small closet. When I left the room she followed me out, cornering me in the hall.

"Why did you pack that ratty old robe when I specifically asked you to bring his new one?" She hissed trying to keep her voice low.

"Because that's the one he likes. That's the one he wears all the time. It's his favorite, and I think it's more important that he be comfortable than stylish."

"That's not the point. I asked you—"

"Yes, it is *exactly* the point. Da's needs are the most important thing right now." I stomped down the hallway, leaving my mother to fume by herself.

Chapter Thirty-One

The doctor and the nurses had been right, Da recovered in no time. He was moved out of the ICU and into a semi-private room after three days. My mother spent the first three days sleeping in an uncomfortable chair by his bed. When it was clear that Da was completely out of danger, my mother stayed at Khandi's place so she didn't have to make the commute from the farm every day. I offered to have her stay with me, but she insisted Jas's place was too small for the three of us, and she didn't want to be a burden on Jas. She was going to stay in a hotel until Khandi's unrelenting persistence wore my mother down into accepting her offer.

I visited Da in the hospital every day after class. I would go see him at five when I knew my mother would be over at Khandi's having an early dinner. It was simply easier to visit with him when my mother wasn't around.

Aaron came with me to the hospital on most evenings. I still hadn't told my mother about him, and for some reason I had yet to understand, I didn't want her to know. Da said he was fine with not telling her either. And pleased to see Aaron, he greatly enjoyed beating him at a few rounds of crib.

Aaron and I hadn't spent another night together since Da's heart attack, but I sensed a tangible shift in our relationship. We shared a tenderness and closeness that hadn't been there before.

No, that wasn't quite right. It had been there all along, I just didn't want to acknowledge it, to set it out into the light and let it flourish. Watching my mom and da at the hospital, I realized I wanted that too. I wanted that kind of love—that all-consuming melding of hearts that once joined cannot exist without the other. Aaron and I hadn't taken the relationship to the next level yet, but I knew it would happen soon and in its own time. I wasn't going to rush it. I enjoyed every single moment of anticipation.

Today, I was making my last trip to the hospital. Da was going home. It was the weekend and Jas had generously offered to cover the phones at the salon while I was gone for a few hours. I wanted to be there just in case my mother needed help getting Da settled in for the drive home. She insisted that she drive him home alone, so I said goodbye to my parents in the hospital parking lot.

I drove Duckie back to the salon and headed in to work. For the first time in a long time All I needed to do for the rest of the day was focus on making appointments, answering the phone, and keeping the hair stations clean and the towels stocked. It was comforting to be in the midst of the commotion of the busy salon, the laughter, the constant buzz of conversation.

"Good afternoon, Blue Funk, Hannah speaking," I spoke into the phone.

"Hello, is this Hannah Morgan?"

"Yes it is. How may I help you?" I assumed it was one of our regulars calling. She sounded familiar, but I couldn't place a name to go with the voice.

"No, I'm calling to speak with you."

"Me?"

"Yes. My name is Pepper Dempsey. The college gave me your number. I called and the message on the answering machine said to try the salon if no one answered. I wouldn't normally bother you at work, but I really needed to talk to you because it's a time sensitive matter."

Pepper Dempsey. Pepper Dempsey. Her name sounded familiar. Where had I met her? Then I remembered. She was my client at the Serenity. Normally I wouldn't have remembered her except she had a unique name. Apart from making a mess of her waxing appointment, we'd had a wonderful conversation about art and museums.

"About what?" I asked, still completely at a loss as to why this woman would be calling me.

"About your work. I frequently visit the student gallery at the college to check out the emerging talent. I was impressed by your skill, so much so that I have a proposition for you. I love art, but sadly, I have no talent for creating it. But I know how difficult it is for an emerging artist to get exposure, and when I can help, I feel I've contributed to bringing art into the world.

"I'm hosting an open house to showcase new artists and put them in touch with the right people. This year, I actually had the time to plan it. It's scheduled for the end of August, and I had already chosen three up-and-coming Calgary artists before I saw your work. One of the artists had to pull out at the last minute. His loss is your gain. Are you interested?"

"Yes, I am." I couldn't believe how calm I sounded when my insides had just dropped to my toes.

"Great! We need to set up an appointment to go over your portfolio and select the pieces I want for the show. How does next Thursday sound, say at about five?"

I didn't even look at the calendar. "Yes, that would be great. I'll be there." I jotted down the date, time, and her address.

It took all my focus to ring up the next client's bill. I had to count the change back twice. When she left, I jumped up from the reception desk to find Jas. She was just sweeping up the hair around her chair getting ready for her next appointment. I didn't care that the shop was full of customers; I had to share this news.

"You're not going to believe what just happened." I grabbed her by the shoulders causing her to drop the broom with a clatter. "I just got the most amazing phone call. I'm going to be in an art show. A real art show!"

We jumped up and down squealing like little kids.

"This is unbelievable." She let out a hoot of excitement. "Do first year students usually get an opportunity like this?"

"I don't think so." I couldn't stop smiling.

"How do you feel?"

"Excited, scared." I met her eyes. "Unbelievably happy."

"Just remember us little people when you hit the big time." Jas gave me one of her spine-snapping hugs as both of us broke into fits of giggles.

The rest of the girls shouted their congratulations from their stations, Jamie gave me a loud smooch on the lips, and a few of the clients clapped. I thanked everyone and hurried back to the front desk to answer the phone. When there was a lull with the phones and with clients, I made a quick call to Aaron.

"This is great! I know Pepper; we've met a few times at art events. If you've got someone like her supporting your talent, you're on your way."

I had to end my call with Aaron because I had clients to tend to. He promised to come by after work and take me out to dinner to celebrate.

A few minutes before Aaron was due to pick me up, I called my parents to tell them my incredible news. My mother answered the phone.

"Hello?"

299

"Hi, it's me, I've got great—"

"Hold on, I'll go get your father." I heard the phone clunk down on the kitchen counter.

"What's up?" Da asked.

"I've got great news! I've just been invited to be a part of an open house highlighting new artists! It's not a real show at a gallery, but the lady hosting it knows everybody who's anybody in the art scene. I think this will be great exposure for me."

"That sounds wonderful! I'm so proud of you. Where and when is it going to happen?"

I gave him the details. "Do you think you could come?"

"Of course, not even another heart attack could keep me away."

"Please don't joke about your health like that."

"Sorry, you know your old Da is made of tougher stuff than that. I'll be kicking around for a long time. The heart attack was just a little blip in the road. Now don't you worry about me."

"Da...."

"Yes?"

"Do you think mother would come if I invited her?"

He waited just a beat too long in answering. "I'm sure she would be pleased as punch to come. Let me talk to her okay."

"Okay. I love you."

"Love you too. I'll talk to you later."

After I hung up, I sat staring at the phone.

"If she hates me so much, why did she hang that stupid painting in her bedroom?!" I screamed at the wall.

The Calgary Chronicle
Classified Section

Business For Sale: Highly profitable day spa located in the Devonshire Building just minutes from the affluent neighbourhood of Mount Royal. The 5,000 sq. ft. spa boasts in-house laundry facilities, and for increased revenue possibilities, two large conference spaces. Spa comes equipped with several pedicure and manicure stations, hydro tub, Vichy shower, and steam rooms. There is also an upscale hair salon on the premises. Building lease negotiable. Contact realtor for more details.

Chapter Thirty-Two

The bus rattled along the street, picking up the few passengers who had places to be at four o'clock on a weekday. It wasn't quite rush hour, so I shared the bus mostly with old ladies carrying shopping bags and loud, gregarious teenagers. I was on my way to Pepper's place in Mount Royal.

I smiled, as the bus passed by the Devonshire Building. A sandwich board sitting on the front steps announced the opening of a new day spa called Revive where the Serenity had once been. One of the girls I worked with at the spa had called last week to let me know that Revive was hiring, in case I wanted to submit my resume. Apparently, quite a few of the staff from the now defunct Serenity were putting in their applications. It felt marvelous to say thanks but no thanks; I didn't need to work as an esthetician anymore because I was following my new career path.

My smile soon faded when the bus rumbled past the imposing blue, glass high-rise of Thorpe Industries. I turned my head and looked out the other window. It was just my luck that Pepper's house was near the building owned by a jerk I once knew. I consoled myself with the thought that Calgary was a big city. The chances of bumping into Christian on the street were pretty minimal.

I stepped off the bus and onto the street filled with people desperately trying to soak up the last warm rays of summer. A soft breeze ruffled my hair and played with the hem of my skirt as I made my way down the sidewalk. Before I left class, I had changed out of my grubby painting gear and into a dark brown skirt, a pale blue sweater, and a matching blue cardigan. Dressed up and carrying my black leather portfolio, a birthday gift from Da, I felt like I fit in with all the other business people populating the streets.

I glanced at my watch. If I headed straight to Pepper's, I would be way too early for my appointment. That's the trouble with using the transit system—you are at the mercy of the bus schedules. When I sold enough paintings, I silently vowed, the first thing I was going to do was buy myself a car. Jas had offered to lend me Duckie, but I had said no. I relied on her generosity way too much, and I needed to start doing things on my own and in my own way.

To kill time, I headed into a coffee shop and ordered an iced coffee. I sat outside at one of the metal tables sipping the icy sweet drink and watching the people go by. I was enjoying the day and the anticipation of meeting with Pepper when I saw *him* strolling down the street. I couldn't believe it, but there was no mistaking that familiar, self-assured, sexy gait.

I looked away, focusing on the other people on the street. He hadn't seen me. I tipped my cup back to finish my drink and sucked an ice chip straight down my throat, where it stuck.

If I had hoped Christian would walk by not noticing me, I just dashed it by asphyxiating myself on a piece of frozen water. I started to cough uncontrollably; tears streaked my carefully applied makeup. I saw, through a blur of tears, the figure of Christian coming closer. I gasped for air and hoped the ice would melt before I passed out.

"Oh my God, are you okay?" Christian stood over me his voice full of concern.

I tried to wave him away while I sputtered and choked. He started pounding on my back. That didn't help; it just made me cough harder. I shook my head trying to get him to stop.

"Stay right there, I'll go get you some water." He dashed into the café. The ice finally melted and I could breathe again, but I now had a wicked chest freeze, and I couldn't stop coughing. I wiped the tears away with the back of my hand, and it came away streaked with mascara. I grabbed my portfolio, getting ready to run down the street, when he appeared carrying a cup of water.

"Here take a sip."

I grudgingly accepted it. He pulled out a chair and sat down across from me. I put down the water and tried nonchalantly to wipe the rest of my smeared mascara off my face.

"Thanks," I croaked.

"Are you okay?"

"Yes." I moved the plastic cup around the table leaving little water rings on the surface.

"Funny meeting you here today."

"Yeah, funny."

"I mean, you just popped into my head today, and then I meet you on the street."

"Really." Now that I regained some of my composure and had enough oxygen flowing into my brain, my first instinct was to throw the water in his face. How could he sit there making chitchat with me as if nothing had happened? "And why would you bother thinking about me?"

"We had a good time together, and I was just wondering what happened to you. After that night, you just disappeared. I called you once but you didn't pick up..." He looked at his watch and then down the street. He got up and pushed in his chair. "Well, like I said it was nice bumping into you. See you around."

Just like that, he was going to leave, as if using me was no big deal.

"How dare you!" I slowly stood up from the table, my hands clenched at my sides. "How dare you talk to me as if nothing happened. You should be ashamed of yourself!"

"Ashamed of what?" He turned around. "Buying you a few drinks, talking to you, having a good time."

"You hypocritical, pompous ass. I'm talking about your little two-timing behavior." The confused look on his face only infuriated me more.

"Ha, you didn't think I knew about her did you? Three days after I spent the night with you, I showed up at your place. I had just quit my job, and I was upset. I needed to be with you. Obviously, you didn't expect me to come over unannounced because your other girlfriend answered the door."

"Let me explain."

"I think it's a little late for explanations. You're a cheat and a liar. Do you want me to add pathetic to the list?"

"There's no need to be rude." His tone changed from confused to irritated. "We had a few laughs. What's the big deal? And don't pretend you didn't want to sleep with me, or then I should call you a liar too. You know, as enjoyable as this conversation has been, I really must be going."

"Hello, darling, here I was rushing to meet you because I was going to be late for our dinner date, and I find you not at the restaurant, either." A striking blonde addressed Christian. She wore a smart business suit and carried a leather attaché case. Her corn silk hair was scraped back from her face in a neat little bun. She leaned in, kissed him on the lips, and turned her cool, blue eyes on me. Christian stepped in closer and put his arm around her waist.

"Sorry, love, I was on my way to the restaurant when I happened to bump into an old friend of mine. We were just catching up with each other," Christian said, looking more uncomfortable by the minute.

"Hello." She sounded British, but I wasn't sure if that was just an affectation.

"Oh, yes," he said. "Hannah, I'd like you to meet Dianne Wilson. Dianne, this is Hannah."

She held out her hand, limp-wristed. Did she expect me to kiss it? I gave her hand a perfunctory shake.

"You'll have to forgive Christian for his lack of manners. He can be so beastly sometimes. Men, no wonder they need us to keep them civilized. Mind you, I've only had six months to work on him. I've told Christian he has to shape-up before the wedding." Dianne gave him a mock stern look.

Wedding? I looked down at her left hand. A huge diamond solitaire winked on her finger, almost blinding me. For a moment, I toyed with the idea of making things really uncomfortable for him, but Noni had taught me to be better than that. Who was I to judge? Maybe Christian had reformed his ways. Besides, I was feeling rather generous in spirit because my artwork was going to be seen by some important people, and I was currently dating a man with real character and who truly cared about me.

"So how do you know each other, from work?"

"No, I used to work at a spa near here. Christian held a function for his staff there once." I glanced at my watch. "Look at the time. I'm going to be late for an appointment." I picked up my portfolio. "It was nice meeting you."

Dianne noticed my portfolio. "Are you an artist?"

"Yes, I've an upcoming show."

Christian looked at me, surprise evident on his face.

"What gallery are you showing at?" Dianne asked.

"Actually, it's not at a gallery. This woman I know, Pepper Dempsey, is hosting an open house at her place just over in Mount Royal."

"I know Pepper. It's true about what they say, that it really is a small world. I seemed to recall her mentioning this little open house thing. Well, we shan't keep you, besides we're already late for our reservation. It was a pleasure to meet you."

"Yeah, you too."

"See you later, it was really great to see you again, and I'm happy to hear you're painting. I really am." He actually sounded sincere.

Dianne linked her arm through Christian's, and they headed down the street towards the restaurant. I stood there watching the two of them walk away. Christian held open the door for his fiancée. I stood on the street as traffic rushed by. I breathed in and out, as people walked past. I waited on the street, my hands sticky from the iced coffee, my throat raw from choking.

I waited for the wave of anger to overtake me, but it never came. I checked the secret corners of my heart, but the anguish just wasn't there. A bit of embarrassment but nothing more. How curious. I headed into the coffee shop and fixed my makeup. Ready, I went to meet with Pepper.

Chapter Thirty-Three

The day before Pepper's show, I sat in Jas's chair at the salon getting what she described as a haircut suitable for an artist. The cut was my idea—I wanted something daring. When I showed Jas the picture of the cut I wanted, she couldn't wait to do it.

While her scissors snipped and shaped my hair, I looked at the mirror in front of me. Tucked in the corner, was the invitation to tomorrow's showing. My showing. The invitation was printed on a thick, cream-coloured stock with a crisp, navy border. The date, time, and Pepper's address were on the top of the invitation, followed by the names of the three featured artists. There it was, second on the list, my name, like a real artist.

Pepper said I could have as many invites as I wanted. I gave one to all the girls and Jamie at the salon and one to Jas. I also gave invitations to Aaron and my parents. I tried to ask my mother if she was coming, but she simply ignored the question and got Da on the phone as soon as she could. We were still doing the same old familiar dance. She made me weary.

"What was that sad sound?"

I wasn't aware I'd sighed.

"If that's a comment on your new cut, need I remind you that this was your idea?"

I spoke to Jas's reflection in the mirror. "No, I love it. It's just what I wanted. I guess I'm just a little tired. With finishing the summer school term, gearing up for the fall, getting ready for my show, working, and seeing Aaron whenever I can, there hasn't been much time for anything else, including sleep."

"I'm done with your cut, so why don't you go on upstairs and crash for a few hours?"

"As much as I would love to, I have a couple more things I need to do. I should be back around six. Why don't I pick up some take-out and we can have a quiet relaxing night to get ready for tomorrow."

"If that's what you want to do, I'm game." She undid the collar on the cape draped over my shoulders and with a flourish whipped it off.

I shook my head smiling at my new pixie cut. "You're a genius."

"I know," Jas replied.

I went upstairs feeling lighter. I changed my shirt so the stray hairs that had gotten past the cutting cape wouldn't bug me. I said goodbye to Jas and the rest of the girls, left the shop, and strolled down to Seventeenth Avenue, enjoying the feel of the fresh air on my neck and the movement of my short hair when the breeze stirred. I headed into the shops on my list and quickly made my purchases. On the way back home, I picked up some fresh sushi at Zen Eight for dinner.

I came in through the back of the salon. It was dark, closed up for the night. I reset the alarm and climbed the stairs to the apartment, shifting the bags to get a hand free to open the door. I let out a gasp when I stepped inside and looked around the room. Taped to the living room wall was a foil banner that said "Congratulations!" A bottle of champagne sat in an ice bucket on the coffee table, along with a huge bouquet of white lilies.

"This is great, but you shouldn't have gone to all this trouble."

"You're worth it, Pudding." Jas got up from her chair and gave me a hug. "And just so you don't think I am too extravagant, those flowers aren't from me."

"Aaron!"

I rushed over to the bouquet. They smelled exquisite. I couldn't believe he spent that much on flowers and they were for me. I started to read the card aloud but stopped as a blush of embarrassment flushed my cheeks.

On our last date, he had suggested that after the opening we spend the night at his place. I had agreed, my stomach quivering with excitement. His card outlined some of the things I could look forward to, mostly involving his tongue and a jar of chocolate body paint.

"Oh my, my, my! Someone's going to be very, very naughty," Jas laughed uproariously.

"I hope so," I said, joining her laughter. "Now enough about my impending sexcapade, let's eat. I bought us sushi for dinner." I held up the bag of food.

"Fabulous. I'll open the champagne while you dish out the food."

I arranged the sushi and chopsticks on plates, placing a few slices of pickled ginger and a dollop of wasabi on each one. I carried them into the living room and put them down on the coffee table. We raised our glasses.

"To you," Jas said, "for taking that leap of faith, for listening to your secret heart, and sharing that gift with all of us. You're one of us now."

"Cheers." I sipped my champagne; the bubbles tickled my nose. I was light-headed from excitement.

We both sat on the floor nibbling at our meal and sipping champagne.

Jas put her chopsticks down, reached under the sofa, and pulled out a large gift-wrapped box. She handed it to me. "This is just a little something to complete your outfit for tomorrow."

She had already helped me pick out a simple black sheath dress with spaghetti straps for my big night. She wanted to lend me a pair of delicate silver chandelier earrings with sapphire drops, but I declined her offer, choosing instead to wear the jet earrings Noni had left to me.

I opened the box and pulled out a light blue pashmina wrap. It was soft as a cloud.

"This is too much." I threw the wrap over my shoulders, luxuriating in the pure heaven of the fabric.

"You need something for your grand entrance, and you know how cold it gets at night even if it is technically still summer for a few more weeks. You have to keep your shoulders warm if you're going to wear that little black number we picked out." I leaned over and kissed her on the cheek. "And here's a little something else to complete the outfit." She handed me a small wrapped box.

"This really is too much." I ripped open the paper.

"Trust me girl, this gift you definitely need."

I opened the box and held up a lacy purple thong.

"I've seen your underwear, and frankly, if you want to get a little someth'n, someth'n going on with Aaron, your current selection of underwear ain't going to cut it. In fact, if he sees you in your granny panties he might swear off sex for good."

"I think I'm touched at your thoughtfulness, but I'm not sure," I said, flinging the thong in Jas's direction.

"In the spirit of being grateful for my ever so thoughtful friend I have something for you too." I pulled out a small box from one of the bags I had brought in. "Thank you for everything, Jas: for being my friend, for being there for me when everything went to pot. For believing in me even when I didn't." My voice cracked with emotions as I handed her the box.

"Don't you start with the waterworks or we'll both start boohooing." She opened the box and stared for a moment at the contents before slowly raising her eyes to meet mine.

"I—I can't accept this." Although, she was the one who chastised me for getting emotional, tears brimmed in her eyes. "I know how much these cost. I can't—"

"Yes you can. You've been like a sister to me, and I want you to have something that lets you know what a special person you are."

Jas slowly and lovingly pulled the scissors out of their nest of cotton. She slipped off the protective leather cover and held them expertly in her hand. She lifted her hand in the air and cut an imaginary head of hair.

"They're perfectly balanced. I never thought I'd own a pair of Flex Heavens. They are possibly the most beautiful pair of shears I have ever owned." She slipped the sheath back over the blades of the scissors and carefully placed them back in the box.

"This calls for more champagne." I refilled our glasses.

After finishing off the bottle and the rest of the sushi, I retired to the bathroom to indulge in a long, hot, bubble bath. I soaked and daydreamed about what the next day would bring. I laid out my dress for tomorrow, next to my new pashmina and my sexy new underwear. I carefully placed the jet earrings on my nightstand and put my second purchase of the day next to it. The silver bracelet was as beautiful as I remembered it. The metal looked burnished in the lamplight. That night I had a peaceful, dreamless sleep.

Chapter Thirty-Four

"This is bloody brilliant."

"Pardon me?"

"This canvas, the use of texture, the shading, the luminescent quality of the light. Bloody amazing. Pepper was right, this is a talent to watch. Who is this Morgan person anyway? I have to meet her."

"I am, and you just did," I said to the man peering at the nameplate affixed to the wall next to my painting.

"What?" he straightened up to look at me. "How charming. I'm J.P. Carmichael, Art Critic for the *Calgary Chronicle*." He held out his hand. It was damp when I shook it.

"Nice to meet you."

"The pleasure is all mine," J.P. said, still holding my hand.

His eyes slowly roved over my body stopping just a fraction too long on my chest. I tried gently to pull my hand out of his, but he wouldn't let go.

"We'll have to get together, just the two of us. I'd like to get some background on you to write a fair and accurate critique of the show. Maybe drinks, perhaps at Mars?"

I wanted my hand back, but other than tackling this creep or gnawing my hand off at the wrist, I was stuck.

"Congratulations, Hannah, you must be so pleased at the turn out!" Aaron stepped expertly between J.P. and me, forcing J.P. to finally let go of my hand.

I discreetly wiped my damp hand on my dress.

"J.P., good to see you again," Aaron said, not moving from his position.

J.P., sensing his moment to seduce me had passed, hastily excused himself on the pretext of needing to refill his glass at the bar.

"Thank you," I mouthed silently.

He looked good, so good, in his dark dinner jacket. He was an odd mix of strikingly handsome and quirky artist with his formal suit, which he paired with a deep orange shirt with a mandarin collar, no tie, and matching orange Converse lace-ups, but he managed to look sophisticated and incredibly sexy at the same time.

"You're welcome." He sidled up next to me. "Did I mention how sexy you look right now?"

"You mentioned it when you came to pick me up, but I won't stop you from repeating yourself," I said as he kissed my newly exposed neck.

His lips on my skin sent electric shivers down my back. My thoughts turned to what we would be doing later, after the event, and my knees went weak. I was wearing my new purple thong and couldn't wait to model it for Aaron.

"Hey, great show."

God, this was getting ridiculous. "Thank you, Christian. I'm glad you could make it," I said, stepping slightly away from Aaron and his erotic touch. I introduced him to Aaron. "Where's Dianne? I thought she was coming too."

"She's here somewhere." He waved at the throng of guests. "She stopped to talk to a friend."

Aaron's posture relaxed when he heard Christian had brought a date. He excused himself to say hello to a friend and artist he hadn't seen in a while. He gave me a kiss before leaving. I wasn't sure if it was for my benefit or Christian's.

Christian flashed me one of his dazzling smiles. It had no effect on me anymore. "I love your new haircut. It makes you look very sexy."

I mumbled something noncommittal while I looked around for a reason to excuse myself. I spied Jas, but she was too far away and too interested in talking to one of the artists for me even to hope to catch her eye. She looked a bit like an abstract piece of art herself. She was a collision of eye-catching colour artfully arranged to display her long legs and tiny waist. I almost felt sorry for the hapless hunk. He didn't stand a chance against her charms.

Christian gestured to the painting behind us. "This is really quite amazing, I'm impressed."

"You sound surprised." *Arrogant jackass.*

"No, not surprised. Intrigued would be a better word. I didn't think you had the guts to go after what you wanted, to pursue your passion."

"Oh." And to think I actually thought he was interesting. "I guess you were wrong. That's the funny thing about fear. The fear of change was more of a challenge than doing the things that brought me to this place in my life."

"Darling, there you are. Why is it I can always find you in a crowded room by looking for the pretty little things? It's a good thing I'm not the jealous type."

"You have nothing to worry about, seeing as you outshine everyone here. I just wanted to congratulate Hannah on a successful opening."

Dianne squeezed in between Christian and me, not unlike the earlier maneuver Aaron had used on J.P. She slid a slender arm around Christian's waist and peered down at me, as if she had just discovered the caviar wasn't Russian. The gesture wasn't lost on me.

Dianne was dressed in a curve-hugging red dress that barely made it to her knees. She was by far the most stunning woman in the room. I fiddled with the glass of mineral water I was holding in my hand.

"Yes, it appears to be a success for all the artists involved, but that is hardly surprising. After all, this is Pepper's event, and she knows how to do things properly."

She was right about Pepper. Her home was a beautiful two-story built in the Arts and Crafts style. The main doors opened onto a large foyer where elegantly arranged platters of hors d'oeuvres sat on tables set along the walls. A bar had been set up at the far end of the foyer. The artwork was displayed in two large rooms leading off the foyer. The furniture was removed for the night, and low leather benches were placed in the middle of each room. Each piece of art was expertly hung and lit.

It wasn't just the elements of the evening that were executed with taste and panache, Pepper also knew how to work a room and make us, the artists, feel comfortable amidst the feathers and finery of Calgary's elite society. Pepper glided around expertly guiding the right people over to meet each artist. She made introductions, initiated the conversation, and then quietly excused herself to do the same to her other protégés. The results of her efforts were evident by the red dots on the paintings indicating they were sold.

From the moment the event started, there had been a steady stream of guests. At first, they were mostly friends and family with the exception of my da. He hadn't arrived yet, but he told me he'd probably be late. It wasn't long before the other guests started to trickle in. The buyers, the art critics, Pepper's wealthy friends.

Christian, Dianne, and I stood for a few more minutes commenting on the other artists and their work, trying to make small talk. I was uncomfortable and couldn't think up a good excuse to leave the two of them. Then Pepper came to my rescue.

"Hello, Christian. Dianne, darling, I'm glad you could make it." Pepper leaned over and air kissed with Dianne and shook Christian's hand. I felt like such an unsophisticated dolt. "I hate to be rude, but I must steal Hannah for a few minutes. There is an interested party that wants to meet her."

Pepper gently guided me by the elbow and steered me over to a woman dressed in a virulent green silk evening dress. The woman had probably laid down thousands of dollars for her designer gown, but no one in their right mind should wear a colour that looks like baby puke.

"I am so pleased with the interest your pieces are generating. When Mrs. Weatherbee said she wanted to meet you, I knew I had found my next big talent. She is probably going to buy two of your works. She is very influential in the art world. This would be such a coup for your career."

Pepper was still talking to me, but I'd stopped listening.

Mrs. Weatherbee? Please let it not be *that* Mrs. Weatherbee. It had been almost a year since our fateful encounter. Mrs. Weatherbee turned to face us when we approached.

"Mrs. Weatherbee, may I introduce Hannah Morgan."

Great, so much for my career.

What were the odds that the woman I had given an eyebrowectomy was an important art patron? I glanced around the expansive room, looking for the nearest exit in case I needed to escape quickly.

"Miss Morgan, I asked Pepper to go and fetch you because I wanted to meet the young woman who could create such moving images. Your pieces positively speak to me. I told Pepper I'm a bit miffed t she found you first. I pride myself on being able to sniff out new talent."

I smiled and nodded. She didn't recognize me. *Thank you, thank you, thank you.*

I took a surreptitious look at her eyebrows. Thankfully, the one I had removed had grown back. A little sparse, perhaps, but it was there. She had drawn a few strokes with a brow pencil to make it match its mate.

"I have the strangest feeling we've met before. Perhaps at the McNabb Opening last June?"

Crap, maybe I thanked my lucky stars too soon.

"I don't think so. I would definitely have remembered meeting you. Your reputation is widely known, and I would have remembered such an honor." *Please, please let her believe me.* Sweat started to trickle down my neck and it tickled. I wished I had left my wrap on.

I glanced around the room, frantic now to escape from Mrs. Weatherbee before she figured out exactly where we'd met and under what circumstances. To my great relief, Da walked into the gallery, followed by my mother. I couldn't believe it. She actually came. I excused myself, as quickly and as politely as possible, and headed over to my parents.

My mother held Da's arm, leading him across the floor as if at any moment he might falter and shatter into a million pieces.

Da gave me a warm hug. "I'm so proud of you. And I like your new hairdo, so grown-up. You are definitely the prettiest woman in the room." He held my hand and gently patted it.

My mother hung back not saying a word, high spots of colour rising on her cheeks.

"Hi, mom, thanks for coming."

"Of course I came. I couldn't let your father drive in his condition, and he insisted on being here tonight. It was very thoughtful of Ms. Dempsey to have reserved a parking spot out front for us so your father didn't a have to walk so far. I must make sure to thank her. Hannah, why did you cut off all of your hair? It was your best feature. Now you look like some homeless waif," she rambled on, not stopping to take a breath.

"Because I needed a change." I quickly changed the subject before we could get into an argument. "Why don't I introduce you to Pepper and show you my paintings."

Da moved slowly as we made our way over to my work, his arm linked in mine. He stood there admiring my paintings and squeezing my hand. "These are wonderful, Hannah, just wonderful."

His love washed over me like a wave, the warmth of it spreading through my heart. It was almost enough to take the sting out of my mother's words.

Pepper happened to walk by at that moment and, seeing my parents, stopped to introduce herself. When she excused herself to see to her other guests, I noticed Da was drooping a bit. The act of standing so long was draining him. I steered my parents over to one of the many leather benches lining the inside of the space. My parents took a seat.

When he settled in, my mother spoke up, "Go get your father a glass of water, and I would like a glass of wine."

"Actually, I wouldn't mind a glass of wine, too," Da said.

"No you don't. Remember what the doctor said. If you want something else to drink, you can have tea."

"Water would be fine."

I left to get their drinks. I came back from the bar and handed my mother her wine and Da his water glass.

He took a sip and his eyes widened with surprise. "Thank you, dear."

I returned his conspiratorial grin and stood with my parents as they watched the party around them.

Aaron was making his way towards us from across the room, and, for a fleeting moment, I tried to figure out a way not to introduce him to my mother. We had talked about him meeting my mother, and I had warned him that it might not go smoothly. He assured me that no matter what my mother did or said he wouldn't take it personally. I guess now I would find out if that were true.

"Mother, Da, I would like you to meet my boyfriend, Aaron." I tried not to feel the rush of nerves dancing in my belly as my mother's eyes widened in surprise or disapproval, I couldn't tell which.

"Mrs. Morgan, Mr. Morgan." He shook their hands. "It's a pleasure to meet you. You must be very proud of your daughter."

"Yes we are, although I would be proud of her no matter what she was doing," Da said, playing along with the pretense that he and Aaron had never met before.

My mother just sat there mute, sipping her wine. There was a moment of awkward silence where I couldn't seem to think of anything more to say when Aaron came to the rescue.

"Mrs. Morgan, I was wondering if you would grant me the pleasure of showing you around."

My mother surprised me by agreeing. She surprised me even more when she took the arm Aaron offered her.

I took a seat next to Da. "How are you feeling?"

"I'm fine. I'm getting stronger every day. Still get a little tired in the afternoon, but that's why naps were invented. You don't need to worry. Your mother is making sure that I follow all the doctor's orders to the letter. If I hear the phrase "doctor's orders" one more time, I think I'll have to move in with you and Jas."

"You're welcome to stay anytime."

"Thanks, dear. All joking aside, it's really not that bad. Your mother is just doing what's best for me. I love her dearly, and I know she's been quite frightened over the whole thing."

"So how is the sale of the farm going?"

"Good, better than expected. The Jensen's have agreed to continue leasing out the land they already use, and we already have a potential buyer for the house and parcel of land that's left. And the Jensen's have no problem boarding Geronimo." He took another sip of his 'water.'

I looked down at my hands and tried to swallow around the lump in my throat. The farm that had been in my family for three generations would be no more. Sold off piece by piece. There didn't seem to be any other alternative. Da, in his condition, couldn't possibly keep running the farm, and I had no desire or inclination to be a farmer. My horse would be the only reminder left of my childhood; my family's history would no longer be accessible to me. Worst of all, my physical connection to Noni, her room, our studio, would be severed from me forever. I looked down at my feet afraid that he would see the sadness in my eyes.

"I know this is hard on you too, but your mother is right. I am getting to old to manage on my own. It's time we move into the city."

"Don't feel bad for me. I understand and I want what is best for you. It's just strange knowing I won't be able to go home."

"You can stay with us in the city. The house we're looking at has a guest room. Being in town just means you can visit more often."

"It's time we left; your father needs his rest," my mother said when she and Aaron returned.

They'd only stayed an hour, but I didn't argue with her. Da looked tired. Even this small outing had sapped his strength. Aaron was the epitome of a gentleman, thanking my mother for the pleasure of her company. With his eyes, he silently asked me if I wanted him to come with me as I walked my parents out. I gave him the slight shake of my head. I escorted my parents out to the street and to their truck. I hugged Da, waited for him to get into the truck, and kissed him as I closed the passenger door. I stood next to my mother, becoming edgy in the silence. What was she waiting for?

"Thanks for coming," I said, hoping this would send her on her way.

"Well, yes, it couldn't be helped. Your father still can't drive, not in his condition. Sometimes in life you have to put other people's needs ahead of your own; we can't all be selfish."

Here we go again. She had to spoil it. She just couldn't leave it alone. I refused to be baited into another verbal sparring match in the middle of the street.

"Thanks for coming, anyway. It meant a lot to me to have you here." I leaned over and gave her a kiss.

Clearly startled by my gesture, my mother cleared her throat. "We must get going before it gets too dark. You should get inside before you catch a chill. You should have put a coat on before coming outside."

"Good night, mother." I turned to leave, feeling hurt again.

"Here take this." She pulled out a small box from her purse.

"Oh." I took the box from her.

"Now go inside before you catch a cold." With that, she got into the truck and pulled away from the curb. Da leaned forward and waved goodbye. I waved back.

I was alone on the street. My skin broke out in gooseflesh in the crisp night air. She was right; I should have grabbed my wrap.

The box was covered in dark blue velvet worn with age and rather shabby looking. I recognized the case. I'd seen it before. I slowly opened the lid and the hinges creaked. It was a silver butterfly pin, a very old one. Noni's pin. She had left it to my mother. I remembered Noni wearing it on special occasions. As a child, I had admired it. Noni told me that the pin was a gift from a very special friend she'd met when she was traveling in Europe. I wondered if it was her German boy, the one who had broken her heart.

Pale blue aquamarines encrusted the butterfly's wings. Its body was studded with tiny diamonds. I took it out of its resting place and turned it slowly in the light. Even in the orange light of the sodium streetlights the stones sparked to life.

I walked back up the front steps to go back in, holding the butterfly in my hand, but I changed my mind and took a seat on the stone steps. I needed a minute to ponder this unexpected gift. I touched the brooch, outlining its shape over and over with my finger. The pin blurred and doubled as the tears finally came. I held the butterfly to my chest and rocked back and forth as I sobbed.

I wept for all the right reasons this time. I grieved for the loss of Noni, the friend who would never see me succeed and who wasn't here to share in this night. I cried for a mother whom I would never understand, for not knowing how to cross the wide gulf to my mother's heart.

"Hey, are you okay?"

I nodded as Aaron approached. I started to laugh then. Hysterical bubbles of laughter erupted as tears continued to streak down my face. I couldn't stop.

"Hey, hey, what's up?" He lightly touched my arm. "You're freezing." He draped his suit jacket over my bare shoulders. The jacket was warm from his body and smelled faintly of him, a clean, soapy smell.

I held out the pin to him. He took it from my outstretched hand. I took a deep breath finally getting myself under control.

"May I?" He gestured to the steps next to me.

"Sure," I hiccupped, drying my eyes with the back of my hand.

"It's beautiful."

"Yes, it is. It was my grandmother's. A gift from her lover she met in Paris. When Noni passed away, it became my mother's. My mother just gave it to me."

Aaron handed me back my gift. "Is that why you were crying?"

"Yes. No. I don't know. I guess I'm just confused and a little unsettled. You saw how my mother was in there. She made it quite clear her presence here tonight was only to take care of my da, yet she gives me this." I gestured to the pin.

"Do you want to talk about it?"

"No, not right now."

"We should get back inside, then. It's chilly out here and seeing as you are a big part of the show, you are eventually going to be missed."

"I suppose you're right." I peered past him at the front doors. Indistinct shapes of people milled about on the other side of the stained glass panels in the door. "It looks like everyone's enjoying themselves in there."

"More than enjoying themselves, I'd say. I believe the consensus is that the show is a big hit. The other artists have done pretty well, but the name on everyone's lips is yours."

"You're just saying that to be nice."

"No, if I wanted to say something nice, I would tell you how stunning you look tonight. I would say how sexy your new haircut makes you look, how it shows off your graceful and highly kissable neck." And to prove he meant what he said, he nuzzled my neck, sending shivers down my back.

"Oh, well—" I breathed, forgetting for a moment what I had been crying about while he worked his way down my neck.

I turned my head towards him and we kissed long and slow. When it ended, Aaron leaned his forehead against mine, and we sat together for a moment catching our breath.

"We'd better head in before I forget myself and ravage you right here on the steps."

"Yes, I guess you're right," I absently caressed Noni's pin that I still held in my hand.

"Here, let me," He took it and slid it through the fabric of my dress.

His hands were warm on my skin. Long, graceful, artist's hands. I looked up at him, while he worked on getting the clasp closed. His eyes fixed on what he was doing, his lips a straight line of concentration. He was handsome, but not the typical beefcake, model handsome. I thought of Christian and tried not to wince. Aaron was strong, but he had more of a swimmer's body, long and lean. He was not the type that I normally would have found attractive, but I did. I couldn't wait to put my hands all over his body.

"There you go." His eyes met mine.

They were such a startling blue, the colour of ice and sapphires, almost a perfect match to the stones in the butterfly broach.

He gave me a crooked grin. "Shall we go in?" Aaron slipped the velvet box in his jacket pocket for safekeeping. "Here you might want to use this before we do." He plucked the silk pocket square from his jacket and held it out to me. "Your mascara wasn't water proof by the looks of things."

"God, how bad do I look?" I dabbed under my eyes.

"Pretty good, from where I'm sitting."

I smiled not sure I believed him. I held on to his now ruined silk square and stood up, smoothing down my dress. We headed in, Aaron sliding his arm around my waist.

He held the door open for me. I hesitated and looked into the house at the people, my artwork, and my life. I drank in its bright and dazzling texture, the hum of the excitement and flow of energy.

As I walked past him, he leaned down and whispered in my ear. "I love you. You make me feel like the luckiest guy on the planet."

I looked up into his eyes. "I love you too."

I laughed, suddenly filled with joy, and stepped through the door with Aaron following close behind.

Once inside, I handed Aaron his jacket, and he went to get us two glasses of champagne. I told him I was heading off to the cloakroom to snag my pashmina and then to the powder room to fix my face. End route to get my wrap, Jas intercepted me.

"Hey, are you okay?" She laid her hand on my forearm.

"Yes, I'm fine. I was just saying good night to my folks when my mother handed me this." I pointed to the brooch. "She hardly spoke two words to me all night and then, just when she was leaving, she gives me this incredible gift."

"Was it your grandmother's?"

"Yes."

"It's gorgeous." She lightly touched the surface of the stones. "But I wish I could say the same about your make-up."

"Yeah, yeah, and you were right. I should have at least brought some face powder for touch ups like you told me but there just wasn't room in this little thing you call an evening bag." I swung the tiny little purse from its delicate silver chain straps. "As it was, I barely had room from my cell phone and a roll of breath mints."

"Not to worry, you know I never leave home without my little touch-up case. I have some mascara and you might want to think about a little powder and perhaps some more lip-gloss. Hold on a sec, I'll go get it. It's in my jacket in the cloak room."

"No, don't bother, I'll get it. I have to go get my wrap anyway."

"It's the little pink case in the left hand pocket."

"You're a doll. Back in a sec."

I stepped into the front hall closet, which was bigger than my bedroom at the apartment. It had miles of coat rail, shoe racks, and two ceramic urns to hold umbrellas. I scanned the many coats and wraps looking for the distinctive white buckskin jacket replete with fringe and beading. I spied it hanging on the back wall. I was just pulling out the makeup bag when someone called my name. I spun around to see Christian standing in the doorway.

"Hey there, just the girl I was looking for." He stepped into the cloakroom and kicked the door shut as he stepped towards me. He staggered slightly and grabbed a handful of coats to stop his sideways motion.

"You always go looking for women in coat closets?" I grabbed my pashmina from a hanger and threw it over my shoulders.

"No, I came in here to get my cigarettes. I wanted to go out for a smoke, but seeing as I found you here, that's even better than a cigarette."

"Well, you've found me, and now I'll just be going," I said, moving past him to the door.

"Not so fast missy." He grabbed my arm, stopping me in my tracks. "I just want to say congradila, congrabulation on your success, and you blow me off. I thought you were nice, Hannah, but that's not very nice." He tightened his grip on my arm and maneuvered me up against a wall of coats.

"Christian, you're hurting me, and you've had too much to drink. Let me go," I said, sounding way calmer than I was.

"God, you sound just like Dianne. Nag, nag, nag. Is that all you bitches know how to do? Maybe I need to teach you a lesson on how to treat a man." He tightened his grip on my arm.

I pushed on his chest with my free hand, but it was like pushing on a slab of concrete. I opened my mouth to tell him to get lost when he grabbed a handful of my hair pulling my head back painfully. His mouth was on mine, bruising my lips, his disgusting tongue filling my mouth. He tasted of sour booze. I tried to push him off me, to turn my head away from his, but he only tightened his grip on my hair.

"You want to play rough? I can play that game," Christian whispered in my ear.

The reek of liquor and the cloying smell of his cologne was making the bile rise in my throat. My upper body was pushed back against the wall and shrouded in coats, my scalp hurt where he had bunched my hair in his hands, and I couldn't breathe. Panic started setting in.

"Oops, sorry. I didn't know anyone was in here." I heard Aaron's voice. Thank God.

"Hey, no problem." Christian straightened up to face the door.

I took the opportunity, now that Christian had let go of me, to push myself away from the wall and out of the shroud of coats.

"Aaron!"

"Hannah?" A look of disbelief on his face.

"I know what this looks like, but it's not what you think." I said, trying to explain as I pulled the spaghetti straps up on my shoulders.

"Hey what can I say? Hannah and I go way back. We were just taking a walk down memory lane for old time's sake. No harm, no foul, hey buddy?"

Aaron backed away from the door, his face completely drained of colour, a look of hurt replacing the disbelief.

"Wait!" I tried to step past Christian, but he stood firm, blocking my way. Aaron didn't wait. Instead, he turned and left.

"Now, where were we before we were so rudely interrupted?" Christian said, taking a step towards me.

I didn't say a word. I simply stepped towards him, and powered by anger, drove my knee hard and fast between his legs. He dropped to the floor like a stone. I stepped over his prone body, as he lay there writhing and moaning incoherently. I slammed the door shut and ran to catch up with Aaron.

I stood for a moment scanning the crowd, but I couldn't see Aaron anywhere. I had to fight my way through the crowd of people standing around talking or looking at the artwork, but Aaron was nowhere to be found. I couldn't believe he would just leave and not wait for me to explain what happened.

Instead of Aaron, I found Jas on the arm of the sculptor she had been talking to earlier in the evening. She immediately came over to me.

"What's wrong? You look like you've seen a ghost."

"I don't have time to explain. Have you seen Aaron? I've got to find him."

"He came over here just a few minutes ago. I told him you were either in the powder room or getting your wrap from the cloakroom. What's this all about? What's happened?"

"He walked in on me and Christian in the cloakroom."

"You and Christian?"

"It's not what you think. Christian thought he could take what I wasn't going to give. I was so scared. If he hadn't walked in on us, I don't know what Christian would have done."

"If he thinks just because he's got money he can treat a woman that way, he's got another think coming. Where is the bastard?" She snarled.

In a strange way, watching her get upset had a calming effect on me. "He's already been taken care of. I don't think he'll be doing the tango any time soon. Jas, I need you to focus. I have to find Aaron. He didn't wait around for me to explain what was really going on, and I can't find him."

She helped me do a quick tour through the house but no Aaron. We went outside and looked for his car. It was gone. I pulled out my phone and dialed his number, but it went straight to voicemail. I left a message, trying the best I could to explain what he saw, trying to keep the hurt out of my voice. I called his home phone, and my anguish increased when his voice mail kicked in.

"I've got to find him. Explain to him what happened. I can't lose him. We need to go now and find him." I grabbed Jas's hand and frantically tried to maneuver her towards her truck but she held firm.

"I know you're upset, but chasing after him when your career, what you've hoped to become, is happening right now, in this moment, isn't worth it. No man is worth giving up who you are, it never can be. I know this sounds heartless, but if he assumes the worst of you and takes off, then he really isn't worth the sacrifice. Hannah, the best thing you could do is to go back inside, be there for yourself, and maybe when Aaron has calmed down and can listen to reason, you can see if there is anything there for you."

I knew what Jas said made all the sense in the world, but I just wanted him to come back. I wanted to enjoy this moment with him by my side. I wanted to end the evening in his arms, lying in his bed. I wanted to wake up with him beside me. Now, because of Christian, that son-of-a-bitch, my dreams were destroyed. I just wanted to curl up in a tight little ball and cry.

If I could just talk to Aaron, I knew I could make this whole awful situation disappear. I dialed his cell phone again, and again, it went straight to his voice mail. I started to dial his home phone when Jas grabbed my phone out of my hands.

"What are you doing? Give me my phone back!" I tried to snatch it out of her hands, but she took a quick step back and out of my reach.

"Don't do this to yourself. There is nothing you can do to bring him back. There is nothing you should do, except go back in to the party and enjoy your moment in the spotlight. And if I have any influence as your friend, you are not going to ruin this special night because of a man. Not again, Hannah. Please don't do this to yourself again."

She was right; there was nothing I could do. Jas joined me in the powder room after retrieving her makeup bag from the floor of the coat closet where I dropped it. While she helped me touch up my makeup, she told me she had seen Christian and Dianne leave. At least I wouldn't have to deal with those two.

With my makeup freshly applied, I went back out to the party, a cold numbness in the pit of my stomach. Jas kept close to me for the rest of the evening. I'd just applied a fresh coat of lipgloss, perfect for my painted on smile. I tried so hard to pretend to enjoy the evening that when it was time to go home, my face hurt, and my stomach ached from too much champagne. The faces and names of the patrons I met were a blur. When we were on our way, Jas finally relented and handed me back my phone. I tried one last time to get a hold of Aaron and it proved as fruitless as before.

In my room, I took Noni's pin off and placed it carefully on my nightstand. Then I yanked off my dress and left it crumpled on the floor. I stripped off my lacy panties and kicked them under the bed. So much for sexy underwear. I put on my worn t-shirt and baggy sweats and climbed under the covers. I told myself I wasn't going to waste any more tears on a man ever again, but I broke my own vow moments later. Aaron wasn't just any guy. He wasn't Mason or Christian. He wasn't just my boyfriend; he had become my friend. I couldn't imagine my life without him now.

Chapter Thirty-Five

The morning after the exhibition was painful. I woke up hung over and broken hearted. I didn't talk to Jas about it. There was nothing to say. I thought I had finally met a great guy, took things slow, got to know him, made sure that I was myself, didn't rush into the physical thing, gave my heart fully this time, and still I was left alone and bewildered.

I holed up in my room until I heard Jas leave the apartment to head downstairs for work. I nursed my hangover with a couple of aspirin and chased it with several cups of hot coffee. I called Aaron four more times, leaving messages on both his cell and home phone. He obviously still didn't want to talk to me, so I gave up and ran a scalding hot bath.

When the tub was full, and thick tendrils of steam curled above the surface of the water, I stepped in without hesitating. I let the hot water stab its needle-sharp teeth into my exposed skin. I strangled a moan as I plunged my whole body below the surface and was instantly engulfed in waves of exquisite pain. I gave myself over to the sensation, holding back tears, waiting for the heat of the water to seep into my pores to sear itself deep through the layers of my skin and burn away my pain.

But it didn't. Instead, the heat drew what little energy I had out of my body. My legs felt heavy, my arms too weak to hold above water, and I felt dizzy. I let my arms sink below the water. Slowly I let go and let the rest of me slide quietly under. I lay at the bottom in the watery silence, the only sound my own heart pulsing its rhythm in my ears.

My life didn't make a great deal of sense to me anymore. I had found a way to begin my life as an artist, my mother was attempting some kind of truce or connection, my da was on the mend, yet for all the good that had entered into my life, I couldn't deny the fact that I was destined to be alone. How could I experience so many amazing things but still keep stumbling blindly over obstacles I didn't even know were there? Why had Aaron been so quick to believe the worst of me? Was I completely unlovable? I held my breath, feeling the pressure building in my lungs, resisting the urge to exhale.

The water had cooled enough that I could open my eyes. While I looked at the ceiling through the watery curtain of bath water, I thought about how nice it would be to just disappear for a little while. Not forever, just for a little while. I'd find a place that was quiet and peaceful, a place of enduring silence. The thought was sweetly enticing, no fear or disappointment or hurt, just freedom and silence.

My lungs began to burn from the pressure of holding my breath so long. I let a few bubbles escape, watched them float to the surface and disappear, but then saw something move out of the corner of my eye. I turned my head slightly, letting a few more bubbles escape. There, standing at the edge of the tub, was a young woman. She was dressed in jeans and a t-shirt, her hands on her hips, her eyes flashed with fierceness as she stared down at me. I recognized her short dark hair and the peculiar shade of violet of her eyes.

"Get up!" She shouted.

Her appearance was startling enough, but the force of her shout scared me and I gasped reflexively, inhaling a mouth full of water in the process. I shot out of the water, choking and sputtering, trying to catch my breath. I held on to the edge of the tub and hung my head over. I wretched uncontrollably, my stomach sore from the effort.

When I felt able, I slowly climbed out of the tub moving like an old woman. I managed to wrap a towel around myself before slumping to the floor while stars danced in front of my eyes. The woman who startled me so badly had disappeared as quickly as she materialized, if she hadn't even been there to begin with.

I knew who the woman was. As impossible as it sounded, I had seen myself standing next to the tub while I lay at the bottom. She was me, but different. There was a power that flowed from her, a strength, a confidence I had never felt.

I knew what I experienced must have been a hallucination brought on by emotional exhaustion, soaking in too hot bath water, and perhaps a touch of oxygen deprivation from holding my breath too long, but the incident left an indelible mark upon my psyche. It wasn't just the sight of myself standing there looking so self-assured, so commanding, that altered my perceptions; it was the feeling that shot from my spectral self, straight into my soul. It felt like coming home.

When I felt steady enough to stand up, I toweled myself off and got dressed. I went to the kitchen, poured myself a large glass of water, headed into my room, and closed the door. Pulling out my sketchpad and charcoals I started to draw. I sketched what I had seen while lying at the bottom of the tub, I drew images of Aaron, my mother, Mason, Christian, Noni, Jas, and my da. While I sketched, I started to see the connections in my life. The directions and turns my life had taken based on the choices I had made. I had spent most of my life making the kind of decisions that would get me approval and validation, looking to others to show me my worth, to prove that I mattered. I expected to find my happiness in other people. I made a promise to myself that from now on I would focus on myself and making myself matter to no one else but me.

I had no idea how long I sat there drawing and thinking before I heard a soft knock on my door.

"Come in!"

Jas stepped in the door carrying my overnight bag. She sat down on the edge of the bed, placing my bag down on the floor between us.

"A courier dropped this off at the salon this afternoon."

"I see." I looked down at the bag, and it wavered as tears obscured my vision. It hurt that Aaron wouldn't even return my bag himself; that he didn't even want to talk to me. His actions cut to the bone.

I hoped this would slowly fade, like a scar over a deep wound. However, I had a feeling the part of me I gave to Aaron would never feel the same, never be as sensitive to the lightest touch. I wondered, if I were ever to love again, would it be a deadened sensation, a numbness where the feeling refused to return.

"Is there something I can get for you? Is there anything you need?"

I leaned over and gave Jas a hug. "No thanks, I have everything I need, right here." I smiled as I realized I really meant it.

I got off the bed and started to unpack the overnight bag while she curled up on my bed and flipped through my sketchbook.

"Did you draw all of these today?"

"Mm mmm," I replied, tucking my empty bag in the bottom of my closet. "They're really just rough sketches; studies for what I'm going to paint later."

"You seem to be handling what Aaron did a lot better than I thought. A lot better than I think I would under the same circumstances. Do these sketches have something to do with why?"

"They're not the reason, but they're helping me understand the why. Let's just say I had an epiphany of sorts while soaking in the tub. I don't have it all figured out yet, but I just know I'm going to be okay. No, better than okay, I'm going to be amazing."

"Jeez, that was some bath. You're gonna have to share what kind of bubble bath you used; it sounds like it would come in handy."

"I will, but not just yet. In the meantime, you must be starving after working all day, and I'm actually feeling a little peckish myself. Why don't I go make us something for dinner?"

"Wait, I've a better idea. Why don't we order in and watch a chick flick. I'll even let you pick the movie."

"That sounds like a plan. God, it's been ages since we've had a Girls' Night In."

Jas went to order the pizza, and, before I joined her, I gathered up my sketchbook, put my charcoals back in their box, and placed everything neatly on my nightstand next to Noni's portrait.

"I think I'm finally figuring this out, Noni. I matter—I matter to me and that's enough." I blew her a kiss before turning off the light and joining Jas in the living room.

Chapter Thirty-Six

Three months had passed since my infamous coming out as an artist and being dumped by my boyfriend. I was back at school and single, yet again; my parents had moved into their condo in the city; and Pepper had called shortly after the artist showcase to tell me all of my paintings had sold. My life was coming together at last. At school, I was honing my craft, I had money in my bank account, and—miracle of miracles—my mother was even speaking to me again. Granted, her conversation was limited to a few words, but it was a start. My life was taking shape in a way that gave me more joy and satisfaction than I could ever have hoped for, but still I missed Aaron every day. Even though he only taught the summer session, I kept hoping he might come by the school, but he never did.

Eventually, I stopped looking for him in the hallways at school. I stopped racing to the phone every time it rang on the remote chance it was Aaron calling to say he was sorry and really wanted to see me. Only once, when I was running errands in his neighborhood, was I even tempted to go by his studio to see if he was in. It took all my self-control to turn around and walk the other way.

Even though I accepted that, for now, being single was the healthiest place I could be, I still missed him terribly. I tried to keep myself occupied during the day with school, painting, working at the salon after school, hanging out with Jas and her current boyfriend, Jason, a cabinetmaker. He was amazingly talented with his hands, according to Jas. I did all I could to focus on finding out who I really was and what mattered to me, but at night I struggled with not having Aaron in my life. Especially when Jas and Jason were out on a date and I was all alone in the apartment. I had to get Aaron out of my system for good, but I wasn't sure how to do that.

* * * *

"Let's go out for dinner tonight," Jas said one Saturday while we were closing up the salon. "We could go to The King and I. I've been craving Thai coconut prawns."

"Sure, I love their food. Will Jason be joining us?"

"No, he's working. He's got a custom order that needs to be delivered on Monday, so he'll probably have to work all weekend."

"He's a good man. I like seeing the two of you together."

"I think so too. And thanks for saying that. I know you still miss Aaron, and I've wondered sometimes if it makes you miss him even more when you're hanging out with Jason and me."

"Absolutely not. If anything, watching you two love birds gives me hope that one day I could have that in my life too."

"You will, sweetie, you will."

We shared a wonderful dinner of crispy Paw Pia Thawt, Coconut Prawns, and a large plate of Bangkok Noodles.

Over coffee and dessert, Jas asked, "Do you mind if we make a quick stop before going home? Ever since you gave my mom one of your paintings for Christmas, she's been wanting to collect more art pieces. I decided on fine art photography and picked out two, but I can't decide which one would be better. I'd really appreciate your opinion."

"Sure, I'd love to."

Even though Jas said the gallery wasn't far, we drove instead of walking. A Chinook wind had blown in the day before, making the temperature unseasonably warm and unsettled. Storm clouds had been gathering all evening and the sky threatened rain. When she parked the truck in front of the gallery, my heart stopped. She had pulled up in front of the Albright Gallery. The one and only time I had been in there was the first time I had met Aaron. Of course, she wouldn't have known this, and it should have dawned on me this was where we were heading. Bernie's gallery was one of the few in Calgary that specialized in fine art photography.

She was about to enter the gallery, her hand on the door when she turned to me. "Are you coming?"

I nodded but didn't move. I had the truck door open, my hand still on the handle, but I stayed sitting in the truck.

"You can do this. You can do this," I said to myself as I willed my butt off the passenger seat.

Just when I stepped onto the curb, the sky opened up and fat drops of rain started falling, darkening the pavement with huge wet splotches. To avoid getting drenched, I had no choice but to run for cover inside the gallery.

"Hello, ladies. Ms. Jasmine, so good to see you again." Bernie stepped out from behind his desk.

"Hi, Bernie. How are you this evening?"

"Marvelous, now that you have brightened my doorstep, my dear girl. What brings you out on such a foul night?" He asked taking Jas's hand in his.

She leaned forward and kissed him lightly on each cheek. "My girlfriend and I were in the neighborhood, and I thought I could show her the two pictures I was looking at the other day."

"Of course, my dear. And I believe I have had the pleasure of meeting you before, Hannah," Bernie said, directing his focus on me. "You came in almost a year ago, if memory serves me."

The fact that he remembered me after one short meeting was surprising. "Yeah you're right. It would've been around that time."

"Well then, I'll just step into the back and get those pieces for you," Bernie said, but he made no move to leave.

He seemed nervous, his eyes kept moving from us to the wall behind us. It was unnerving and I had to resist the urge to turn around and look myself. Moments ticked by while Bernie stood there.

"Uh, Bernie." Jas motioned with her head to the backroom.

"Right, right. Feel free to look around until I get back. You never know if there is another piece that may tickle your fancy," Bernie said, finally making his way to the storeroom to retrieve the pictures.

When Bernie was out of sight, I turned around to see what had distracted him. I couldn't believe what I was seeing. I was looking at six large pieces. They were thirty-six by thirty-six inch, framed black and white photos. The photographer's style was familiar to me, all too familiar, and to my astonishment, I also recognized the subject of all the pictures.

Every single photo was of me. I slowly walked past each one. They were beautiful, evocative. Some of the photos were taken during the photo shoot for Aaron's "Essence" show; others had been taken at school. One in particular showed me painting a large canvas. Aaron must have captured the image from the doorway of the studio. Another showed me sitting under the big oak tree in the Quad, and yet another was a close-up of me with my head thrown back laughing. I had no idea when and where that one was taken.

I read the title cards as I slowly walked past each picture. He had called the series "The Muse." This installation was created after Aaron and I broke up. I didn't get it. If he didn't want me in his life anymore, why the hell did he choose to have me as his next subject and refer to me as his muse?

"Jas," I said, not taking my eyes off the photos. "Is this why you brought me here, to see these?"

"Not exactly," Jas said from behind me.

"Hannah?"

I was so distracted by what I was looking at I hadn't heard the bell over the door jingle announcing that someone had walked in. I turned around. Aaron stood in the doorway, his hair plastered against his head.

"Jas, why did you do this?" I choked back the emotions tightening my throat.

"Because I love you. Do me a favor and just shut up and listen to what he has to say. Now, I think I'll just go into the backroom and see what is taking Bernie so long." She escaped before I could reach over and strangle her.

"Please don't be angry at her, she only did this because she cares, and because I asked her to." He stepped towards me.

The joy of seeing him again was quickly replaced by anger and hurt. I held up my hands as if this simple gesture could hold off the pain I was feeling. "Aaron?"

"Please, just listen."

"No. No, I can't do this." I pushed past him and escaped out into the street.

Aaron followed me, and as I tried to turn and run away, he grabbed my arm and held me there. We stood in front of the plate glass windows of the art gallery, the rain coming down in sheets, neither of us moving. I refused to look at him. I kept my head turned away and let the rain mingle with my tears. I tried to pull away, but he refused to let go of my arm.

"Won't you even give me a chance?"

"Like you gave me?" I shot back, finally wrenching my arm free of his grip. I glared at him, blinking furiously through the rain. "You wouldn't even return my phone calls; you didn't even let me explain what happened! You believed the worst of me, and then you left me! And now you think you can just walk back into my life like nothing's happened! And what do you expect, Aaron, that I will fall over backwards to invite you back in?"

"Everything you said is true. I let you down, and I know there is nothing I can say or do that will ever make up for the hurt I caused you. All I'm asking is that you hear me out, and then you can walk away and never see me again," he pleaded.

Why did he have to look at me like that? I was angry, and I wanted to stay that way, but when I looked into his crystal-blue eyes, my resolve crumbled. Why did he still have that kind of power over me? I didn't answer him. Instead, I took a step back and nodded my head for him to continue. I'd let him explain, but I wasn't going to make it easy for him.

"I let my past cloud my judgment and hurt the one person that means the most to me. I told you Sandy and I broke up, but that wasn't what happened. I walked in on her with another man in our bed. So, when I walked in on you and that guy in the closet, I overreacted. I was hurt and angry. I just couldn't face what I thought I was seeing and ran away. I took off and spent a few weeks with friends in Tofino. When I got back into town, I was determined to move on without you, but everywhere I looked, everything I did, reminded me of you. I realized you'd become so much a part of my life that not having you in it was making me miserable. I wanted to call you, but I was a coward. I was scared you would send me away, and I didn't know what to do. That's when Jas dropped by the studio and gave me an earful. She's some firecracker."

I smiled at the thought of Jas unleashing her fury on him.

"Anyway, after calling me every name in the book, she told me what Christian did to you, which made me feel like an even bigger jerk. She told me how devastated you were, and I realized I couldn't do this over the phone. I needed to talk to you face to face, so I asked her to help me set up this meeting. I guess what I'm trying to say is that I'm so sorry for what I did, and maybe if you could find it in your heart you could give me a chance to make it right."

"After you disappeared, I was heartbroken, but I picked myself up and went on. I went on without you. That was hard enough, but what's worse is you didn't trust me enough to tell me what happened to you."

Anger welled up inside me and I wanted to hurt him as much as he had hurt me. I raised my arms, my hands clenched tightly. I pummeled his chest with my fists my words coming out in ragged sobs. "You weren't just my boyfriend, I thought you were my best friend, and best friends don't just walk away when things get rough."

He stood there while I continued to hit him, my fists striking each time with less strength as I cried. Finally, I stopped my assault and put my head down on his chest. As quickly as my rage had come over me, it dissipated, leaving me drained. He put his arms around me and I just stood there feeling the security of his embrace.

"People make mistakes, Hannah," he whispered into my hair. "You can't make them out to be perfect because when they screw up they have a long way to fall. I can't promise to be perfect, but I can promise to never walk away again. I will tell you everything that is in my heart, if you just give me another chance."

Slowly I raised my head, furiously blinking raindrops out of my eyes. I looked at Aaron and for the first time really saw him. We were so alike, the two of us, more than I had realized. We had both let fear stop us from really living. Being on my own had also taught me I was more than good enough just as I was. As much as I wanted to share my life with Aaron, I knew now that my happiness didn't depend on him being there. I saw that what had happened between the two of us over the last few months was really an incredible gift.

"Yes, I will give you another chance, but only if you do the same for me." I wrapped my arms around his neck. Our lips met and it was the sweetest kiss I had ever experienced.

I could have stood there in the rain kissing him for eternity, if it weren't for the sound of pounding on the gallery window behind us followed by the muffled sound of cheering. I opened my eyes to see Jas holding Bernie in an exuberant embrace. I couldn't help but laugh at the sight of Bernie, his spectacles askew and his kind round face flushed a deep crimson.

Aaron joined in the laughter when Jas gave us a high five and Bernie followed suit with a fluttery wave.

"Let's go home," Aaron said, a smile spreading across his face, erasing all hints of his earlier pain.

"Yes, let's go home," I said, not knowing if he meant his apartment or mine. It didn't really matter because standing in the pouring rain with Aaron's arms around me, I knew I was already there.

About the Author

"As a small child I dreamed of growing up to be a chestnut mare. I was terribly disappointed when I found out people couldn't magically transform into animals but I got over it by immersing myself in the world of fairy tales and thus began my lifelong passion for reading and make-believe."

Lora Deeprose has a B.A. in Drama with a minor in History. She was born in the small town of Fort Saskatchewan, Alberta; the middle child of five girls. In 2006, she and her eldest sister moved to a hobby farm in the remote Kootenay area of British Columbia and for five years had several country adventures which included raising chickens and goats, encounters with wildlife and wrangling the neighbour's horses. Currently, she lives in BC's Eastern Fraser Valley.
Website: www.LoraDeeprose.com

About the Cover Artist

Ilsie creates beautiful book covers with passion and integrity and is an artist we find enjoyable to work with. To learn more about her visit her website at http://thewoodsyfawn.format.com/home

Find more to read from Marion Margaret Press
http://www.marionmargaretpress.com

Book reviews are welcome.

You can also post a few sentences of what you thought and rate the book at various places around the internet.
Amazon.com encourages comments when you buy through their site and the comments help us with our ratings.
Join Goodreads.com to post your comments and rate the book.
Make a library at http://books.google.com/ and leave comments on any books you add in.

Or feel free to drop us a note via snail mail to:
Marion Margaret Press
Business Office:
PO Box 245
Hebron, NE 68370

You can also find us on Facebook as Marion Margaret Press (page) and at Twitter as marionmbooks.

Printed in Great Britain
by Amazon